JOSÉ SARAMAGO was born in Portugal in 1922. His oeuvre embraces plays, poetry, memoirs and several novels which have been translated into more than 20 languages. It was the publication of *Baltasar & Blimunda* in 1988 that first brought him to the attention of an English-speaking readership. This novel won the Portuguese PEN Club Award, as did his next, *The Year of the Death of Ricardo Reis*, which also won the *Independent* Foreign Fiction Award. His fiction has established him as one of Europe's most influential living writers. José Saramago was awarded the Nobel Prize for Literature in 1998.

GIOVANNI PONTIERO, formerly Reader in Latin-American Literature in the University of Manchester, was, until his death in 1996, Saramago's regular English translator. His translation of *The Gospel according to Jesus Christ* was awarded the Teixeira-Gomes Prize for Portuguese translation. He was also the principal English translator of the works of Clarice Lispector.

José Saramago

BALTASAR
& BLIMUNDA

Translated from the Portuguese by
Giovanni Pontiero

THE HARVILL PRESS
LONDON

First published in Portuguese with the title
Memorial do convento by Editorial Caminho, Lisbon, 1982

First published in Great Britain in 1988 by Jonathan Cape

This paperback edition of the revised English translation first published in 2001 by
The Harvill Press, 2 Aztec Row, Berners Road, London N1 0PW

www.harvill.com

1 3 5 7 9 8 6 4 2

© José Saramago and Editorial Caminho SARL, Lisbon, 1982
English translation © Harcourt Brace Jovanovich, 1987 and 1998 and Professor Juan Sager, 1998

José Saramago asserts the moral right to be identified as the author of this work

A CIP catalogue record for this book is available from the British Library

ISBN 1 86046 901 9

Typeset in Monotype Bembo at Libanus Press, Marlborough, Wiltshire

Printed and bound in Great Britain by Mackays of Chatham

Half title illustration by Jeff Fisher

In memoriam Giovanni Pontiero

A man was on his way to the gallows when he met another, who asked him: Where are you going, my friend? And the condemned man replied: I'm not going anywhere. They're taking me by force.

PADRE MANUEL VELHO

Je sais que je tombe dans l'inexplicable, quand j'affirme que la réalité – cette notion si flottante – la connaissance la plus exacte possible des êtres est notre point de contact, et votre voie d'accès aux choses qui dépassent la réalité.

MARGUERITE YOURCENAR

DOM JOÃO, THE FIFTH monarch so named on the royal list, will pay a visit this night to the bedchamber of the Queen, Dona Maria Ana Josefa, who arrived more than two years ago from Austria to provide heirs for the Portuguese crown, and so far has shown no signs of becoming pregnant. Already there are rumours at court, both within and without the royal palace, that the Queen is barren, an insinuation that is carefully guarded from hostile ears and tongues and confided only to intimates. That anyone should blame the King is unthinkable, first because infertility is an evil that befalls not men but women, who for that very reason are often disowned and second, because there is material evidence, should such a thing be necessary, in the horde of bastards produced by the royal semen, who populate the kingdom and even at this moment are forming a procession in the square. Moreover, it is not the King but the Queen who spends all her time in prayer, beseeching a child from heaven, for two good reasons. The first reason is that a king, especially a king of Portugal, does not ask for something that he alone can provide, and the second reason is that a woman is essentially a vessel made to be filled, a natural supplicant, whether she pleads in novenas or in occasional prayers. But neither the perseverance of the King who, unless there is some canonical or physiological impediment, vigorously performs his royal duty twice weekly, nor the patience and humility of the Queen, who, besides praying, subjects herself to total immobility after her husband's withdrawal, so that their generative secretions may fertilise undisturbed, hers scant from a lack of incentive and time, and because of her deep moral scruples, the King's prodigious, as one might expect from a man who is not yet twenty-two years of age, neither the one factor nor the other has succeeded so far in causing Dona Maria Ana's womb to become swollen. Yet God is almighty.

Almost as mighty as God is the replica of the Basilica of St Peter in Rome that the King is building. It is a construction without a base or foundation, resting on a table-top, which does not need to be very solid to take the weight of a model in miniature of the original basilica, the pieces lying scattered, waiting to be inserted by the old method of tongue and groove, and they are handled with the utmost reverence by the four footmen on duty. The chest in which they are stored gives off an odour of incense, and the red velvet cloths in which they are separately wrapped, so that the faces of the statues do not scratch against the capitals of the columns, reflect the light cast by the huge candelabras. The building is almost ready. All the walls have been hinged together, and the columns have been firmly slotted into place under the cornice with the name and title of Paolo V Borghese inscribed in Latin which the King no longer reads, although it always gives him enormous pleasure to observe that the ordinal number after the Pope's name corresponds to the V that comes after his own. In a king, modesty would be a sign of weakness. He starts to place the effigies of prophets and saints into the appropriate grooves on top of the walls and the footman gives a low bow as he removes each statue from its precious velvet wrappings. One by one, he hands the King a statue of some prophet lying face down, or of some saint turned the wrong way around, but no one heeds this unintentional irreverence as the King proceeds to restore the order and solemnity that befits sacred objects and turning them upright, he inserts each vigilant statue into its rightful position. What the statues see from their lofty setting is not St Peter's Square but the King of Portugal and his retinue of footmen. They see the floor of the dais and the screens looking on to the Royal Chapel, and tomorrow at early Mass, unless they have already been wrapped up and put back in the chest, the statues will see the King devoutly attend the Holy Sacrifice of the Mass with his entourage, different nobles from those who are with him at present, for the week is ending and others are due to take their place. Beneath the dais where we are standing, there is a second dais, also hidden by screens, but there are no pieces here waiting to be assembled, it is an oratory or a chapel where the Queen attends Mass privately, yet not even this holy place has been conducive to pregnancy. Now all that remains to be set in position is the dome by Michelangelo, a copy of that remarkable achievement in stone which, becauses of its massive proportions, is kept in a separate chest and, as the final, and crowning piece, is treated with special care. The footmen make haste to assist the King and, with a resounding clatter, the tenons and mortises are fitted together and the job is finished. If the overwhelming noise that echoes throughout the chapel should penetrate the long corridors and spacious apartments of the palace into the chamber where the Queen is waiting, she will know that her husband is on his way.

Let her wait. The King is still preparing himself before retiring for the night. His footmen have helped him to undress and have garbed him in the appropriate ceremonial robes, each garment passing from hand to hand with as much reverence as if they were the relics of holy virgins, and this ceremony is enacted in the presence of other servants and pages, one opens the huge chest, another draws back the curtains, one raises the candle, while another trims the wick, two footmen stand to attention, and two more follow suit, while several others hover in the background with no apparent duties to fulfil. At long last, thanks to their combined labours, the King is ready, one of the nobles in attendance straightens a last fold, another adjusts the embroidered nightshirt, and any moment now, Dom João V will be heading for the Queen's bedchamber. The vessel is waiting to be filled.

Now Dom Nuno da Cunha, the bishop who heads the Inquisition makes his entrance accompanied by an elderly Franciscan friar. Before he approaches the King to deliver his news, there is an elaborate ritual to be observed with reverences and salutations, pauses and retreats, the established protocol when approaching the monarch, and these formalities we shall treat as having been duly observed, given the urgency of the bishop's visit and the nervous tremors of the elderly friar. Dom João V and the Inquisitor withdraw to one side, and the latter explains, The friar who stands before you is Friar Antony of St Joseph, to whom I have confided Your Majesty's distress at the Queen's inability to bear you children. I begged of him that he should intercede on Your Majesty's behalf, so that God may grant you succession, and he replied that Your Majesty will have children if he so wishes, and then I asked him what he meant by these obscure words, since it is well known that Your Majesty wishes to have children, and he replied in plain words that if Your Majesty promises to build a convent in the town of Mafra, God will grant you an heir, and after delivering this message, Dom Nuno fell silent and bade the friar approach.

The King inquired, Is what His Eminence the bishop has just told me true, that if I promise to build a convent in Mafra I shall have heirs to succeed me and the friar replied, It is true, Your Majesty, but only if the convent is entrusted to the Franciscan Order and the King asked him, How do you know these things and Friar Antony replied, I know, although I cannot explain how I came to know, for I am only the instrument through which the truth is spoken, Your Majesty need only respond with faith, Build the convent and you will soon have offspring, should you refuse, it will be up to God to decide. The King dismissed the friar with a gesture and then asked Dom Nuno da Cunha, Is this friar a man of virtue, whereupon the bishop replied, There is no man more virtuous in the Franciscan Order. Reassured that the pledge requested of him was worthy, Dom João, the fifth monarch by that name, raised his voice so that all present might hear him speak, and so that what he had to say would be reported throughout the city and the realm the following day, I promise, by my royal word, that I shall build a Franciscan convent in the town of Mafra if the Queen gives me an heir within a year from this day, and everyone present rejoined, May God heed Your Majesty, although no one knew who or what was to be put to the test, Almighty God Himself, the virtue of Friar Antony, the King's potency, or the Queen's questionable fertility.

Meanwhile, Dona Maria Ana is conversing with her Portuguese chief lady-in-waiting, the Marchioness de Unhão. They have already discussed the religious devotions of the day, their visit to the convent of the discalced Carmelites of the Immaculate Conception at Cardais, and the novena of St Francis Xavier, which is due to start tomorrow in the parish of St Roch, the conversation one might expect between a queen and a woman of noble birth, exclamatory and at the same time fearful, as they invoke the names of saints and martyrs, their tones becoming poignant whenever the conversation touches on the trials and sufferings of holy men and women, even if these simply consisted in mortifying the flesh by means of fasting and wearing hairshirts. The King's imminent arrival, however, has been announced, and he comes with burning zeal, eager and excited at the thought of this mystical union of his carnal duty and the pledge he has just made to Almighty God through the mediation and good offices of Friar Antony of St Joseph. The King enters the Queen's bedroom accompanied by two footmen, who start to remove his outer garments, the Marchioness, assisted by a lady-in-waiting of equal rank who came with the Queen from Austria, doing the same for the Queen, passing each garment to another noblewoman, the participants in this ritual make quite a gathering, their Royal Highnesses bow solemnly to each other, the formalities seem interminable, until finally the footmen depart through one door and the ladies-in-waiting through another where they will wait in separate anterooms until the act is over and they are summoned to escort the King back to his apartments which were occupied by the Dowager Queen when the King's late father was still alive, and the ladies-in-waiting come to settle Dona Maria Ana under the eiderdown that she also brought from Austria, for she cannot sleep without it, be it summer or winter. This eiderdown is so suffocating, even during the chilly nights of February, that Dom João V finds it impossible to spend the entire night with the Queen, although it was different during the first months of marriage, when the novelty outweighed the consid- erable discomfort of waking to find himself bathed in perspiration, his own as well as that of the Queen, who slept with the covers pulled over her head, her body accumulating odours and secretions. Accustomed to a northern climate, Dona Maria Ana cannot bear the torrid heat of Lisbon. She covers herself from head to foot with the huge, overstuffed eiderdown, and there she remains, curled up like a mole that has found a boulder in its path and is trying to decide on which side it should continue to burrow its tunnel.

The King and Queen are wearing long nightshirts that trail on the ground, the King's has an embroidered hem, while the Queen's has much more elaborate trimmings, so that not even the tip of her big toe can be seen, for of all the immodesties known to man, this is probably the most audacious. Dom João guides Dona Maria Ana by the hand to the bed, like a gentleman leading his partner on to the dance floor. Before ascending the steps, each kneels on his or her respective side of the bed and says the prescribed prayers, for fear of dying unconfessed during sexual intercourse, Dom João V determined that his efforts should bear fruit on this occasion, his hopes redoubled as he trusts in God's assistance and in his own virile strength, and protesting his faith, he begs the Almighty to give him an heir. As for Dona Maria Ana, one may assume that she is imploring the same divine favour, unless for some reason she enjoys special dispensations under the seal of the confessional.

The King and Queen are now settled in bed. This is the bed that was dispatched from Holland when the Queen arrived from Austria, specially ordered by the King, and it cost him seventy-five thousand cruzados, for in Portugal no craftsmen of such excellence are to be found and were they to be found, they would certainly earn less. An untrained eye would find it difficult to tell that this magnificent piece of furniture is made of wood, concealed as it is under ornate drapes woven with gold threads and lavishly embroidered with rosettes, not to mention the overhanging canopy, which resembles a papal baldachin. When the bed was newly installed, there were no bedbugs although once in use, the warmth of human bodies attracted an infestation, but whether these bedbugs were lurking in the palace apartments or came from the city, no one knows. The elaborate curtains and hangings in the Queen's bedroom made it impractical to smoke them out, so there was no other remedy but to make an offering of fifty réis to St Alexis every year, in the hope that he would rid the Queen and all of us from this plague and the insufferable itching. On nights when the King visits the Queen, the bedbugs come out at a much later hour because of the heaving of the mattress, for they are insects who enjoy peace and quiet and prefer to discover their victims asleep. In the King's bed, too, there are yet more bedbugs waiting for their share of blood, for His Majesty's blood tastes no better or worse than that of the other inhabitants of the city, whether blue or otherwise.

Dona Maria Ana extends a moist hand to the King, which, despite having been heated under the covers, soon grows cold in the chilly atmosphere of the bedchamber and the King, who has already done his duty, and is feeling quite hopeful after a most convincing and skilful performance, gives Dona Maria Ana a kiss as his Queen and as the future mother of his child, unless Friar Antony of St Joseph has been rash with his promises. It is Dona Maria Ana who tugs the bell-pull, whereupon the King's footmen enter from one side and the Queen's ladies-in-waiting from the other. Various odours hover in the air and one of them is unmistakable for without its presence the long-awaited miracle could not possibly take place, and besides, the much-quoted immaculate conception of the Virgin Mary occurred but once so that the world might know that Almighty God, when He so chooses, has no need of men, though He cannot dispense with women.

Notwithstanding constant reassurances from her confessor, on these occasions Dona Maria Ana is overcome by a sense of guilt. Once the King and his retinue have departed, and the ladies-in-waiting, who remain in attendance until she is ready to fall asleep, have withdrawn, the Queen always feels a moral obligation to fall to her knees and pray for forgiveness but at her doctors' insistence she must not stir, lest she disturb the incubation, so she resigns herself to muttering her prayers in bed, the rosary beads slipping ever more slowly through her fingers, until finally she falls asleep in the midst of a Hail Mary full of grace, that Mary for whom it was all so easy, blessed be the fruit of thy womb Jesus, while in her own anguished womb she hopes at least for a son, Dear Lord, at least one son. She has never confessed to this involuntary pride because remote and involuntary, so much so that were she to be called to judgment she would truthfully swear that she had always addressed her prayers to the Virgin and her holy womb. These are the meanderings of her subconscious mind like those other dreams no one can explain, that Dona Maria Ana always experiences when the King comes to her bed, in which she finds herself crossing the Palace Square alongside the slaughterhouses, lifting her skirts before her as she flounders in the slimy mud smelling of men when they relieve themselves, while the ghost of her brother-in-law, the Infante Dom Francisco, whose former apartments she now occupies, reappears and dances all around her, raised on stilts like a black stork. Neither has she discussed this dream with her confessor, besides, what explanation could he possibly give her in return, since no such case is mentioned in the Manual for a Perfect Confession. Let Dona Maria Ana slumber in peace, submerged under that mountain of draperies and plumes as the bedbugs begin to emerge from every crease and fold, dropping from the canopy above to hasten their journey.

Dom João V will also dream tonight. He will see the Tree of Jesse sprout from his penis, covered with leaves and populated by the ancestors of Christ, and even by Christ Himself, the Heir of All Kingdoms, then the tree will vanish and in its place will appear the tall columns, bell towers, domes, and belfries of a Franciscan convent, which is unmistakable because of the habit worn by Friar Antony of St Joseph, whom the King can see throwing open the church doors. Such dreams are not common amongst kings, but Portugal has been well served by imaginative monarchs.

OUR PEOPLE HAS BEEN equally well served by miracles. It is too early, however, to speak of the miracle that is now being prepared, which is not so much a miracle as a divine favour, a downward glance at once compassionate and propitious upon a barren womb, which will give birth to a child at the appropriate hour, but this is the moment to speak of genuine and proven miracles which, having come from the same burning bush, the zealous Franciscan order, augur well for the promise made by the King.

Consider the notorious episode of the death of Friar Michael of the Annunciation, the provincial-elect of the Third Order of St Francis whose election, let it be said in passing although not without relevance, took place amid violent opposition by the parishioners of St Mary Magdalen, because of some obscure resentment, which was so vehement that, when Friar Michael died, lawsuits were still being fought and no one knew when, if ever, they would finally be settled, what with admonitions and petitions, judgments and appeals, the constant wrangling ending only after the good friar's death. It is certain that Friar Michael died not of a broken heart but of a malignant fever that might have been typhus or typhoid or some other, unnamed plague, a common enough death in a city where there are so few drinking fountains and where country folk think nothing of filling their barrels from water troughs intended for horses. Friar Michael of the Annunciation, however, was such a good-natured fellow that even after death he repaid evil with good, and if during his lifetime he carried out charitable works, once dead he worked wonders, the first of these being to prove the doctors wrong when they feared that the body would soon rot and recommended burial without delay, because not only did the friar's mortal remains fail to rot, but for three whole days they filled the Church of Our Lady of Jesus, where his body was exposed, with the sweetest perfume, and instead of becoming rigid, the limbs of his body remained flexible, as if he were still alive.

These were wonders of a lesser order but of the highest esteem, yet the miracles themselves were so extraordinary, that people flocked from all over the city to witness this prodigy and to profit therefrom, for it has been attested that in the very same church, sight was restored to the blind and limbs to the maimed, and so many people had gathered on the church steps, that punches and knife wounds were exchanged in the struggle to gain entry, causing some to lose lives that would nevermore be regained, miracle or no miracle. But perhaps those lives would have been restored, had the friar's corpse not been spirited away and secretly buried after three days, on account of the general pandemonium. Deprived of any hope of being healed until some new saint should come among them, deaf-mutes and cripples, if the latter had a free hand, cuffed one another in despair and frustration, screaming abuse and invoking all the saints in heaven, until the priests came out to bless the crowd, which, thus reassured and for lack of anything better, finally dispersed.

To be honest, this is a nation of thieves, what the eye sees the hand filches, and because there is so much faith that goes unrewarded, the churches are looted with daring and irreverence, as happened last year in Guimarães, also in the Church of St Francis, who, having shunned all worldly goods during his lifetime, allows himself to be robbed of everything in eternity, but then the order is supported by the vigilant presence of St Antony, who takes it amiss if anyone despoils his altars and chapels, as happened in Guimarães and subsequently in Lisbon.

In that city, thieves intent upon plunder climbed up to a window and found the saint waiting to greet them, he gave them such a fright that the wretch at the top of the ladder fell to the ground without breaking any bones, it is true, but he was paralysed and could not move, and his accomplices anxiously tried to remove him from the scene of the crime, for even among thieves one often finds generous, merciful souls, but to no avail, an incident not without precedent, for it also happened in the case of Agnes, the sister of St Clare, when St Francis still travelled the world, exactly five hundred years ago, in the year twelve hundred and eleven, but it was not theft on that occasion or it might have been theft, because they wanted to abduct Agnes and steal her from Our Lord. The thief remained transfixed as if struck by the hand of God or the devil's claw from the depths of hell, and there he lay until the following morning, when the local inhabitants discovered him and carried him to the church altar, so that he might be healed by some singular miracle, and, strange to relate, the statue of St Antony could be seen sweating profusely and for such a long time that judges and notaries could be summoned to verify the miracle, which consisted of a perspiring wooden statue and the thief's recovery when they wiped his face with a towel dampened with the saint's sweat. No sooner done than the thief got to his feet, healed and repentant.

Not all crimes, however, are so easily resolved. In Lisbon, for example, where another miracle was widely known, no one has yet been able to confirm who was responsible for the theft, although suspicions could be aired about a certain party who might be pardoned because of the good intentions that motivated the crime. It happened that some thief or thieves broke into the Convent of St Francis of Xabregas, through the skylight of a chapel adjacent to that of St Antony, and he or they made straight for the high altar and took the three altar lamps, and vanished by the same route in less time than it takes to recite the Nicene Creed. That someone could remove the lamps from their hooks and carry them off in darkness for greater safety, and then stumble and cause a commotion without anyone rushing to the scene to investigate, would lead one to suspect complicity, were it not for the fact that at that very moment the friars were engaged in their customary practice, noisily summoning the community to midnight matins with rattles and handbells, enabling the thief to escape and had he caused an even greater commotion the friars would not have heard him, from which one may assume that the culprit was perfectly familiar with the convent schedule.

As the friars began to file into the church, they found it plunged into darkness. The lay brother in charge was already resigning himself to the punishment he was certain to incur for this omission, which defied explanation, because the friars observed and confirmed by touch and smell that it was not the oil that was missing, spilled as it was all over the floor, but the silver altar lamps. The sacrilege was all too recent, for the chains from which the missing lamps had been hanging were still swaying gently, whispering in the language of copper, We've had a narrow escape. We've had a narrow escape.

Some of the friars rushed out immediately into the nearby streets, divided up into several patrols, had they apprehended the thief, one cannot imagine what they might have done to him in their mercy, but they found no trace of him or of his accomplices, if there were any, which is not surprising, for it was already after midnight and the moon was waning. The friars puffed and panted as they chased through the neighbourhood at a sluggish pace, before finally returning to the convent empty-handed. Meantime, other friars, believing that the thief might have concealed himself in the church by some cunning ruse, searched the place thoroughly from choir to sacristy, everyone tread-ing on sandalled feet in this frantic search, tripping over the hems of habits, raising the lids of chests, moving cupboards, and shaking out vestments, an elderly friar known for his virtuous ways and staunch faith noticed that the altar of St Antony had not been violated by thiev-ing hands, despite its array of solid silver, which was prized for its value and craftsmanship. The holy friar found himself bemused, just as we should have been bemused had we been present, because it was quite obvious that the thief had entered from the skylight overhead and in order to remove the lamps from the high altar, must have passed right by the chapel of St Antony. Inflamed with holy zeal and indignation, the friar turned on St Antony and rebuked him, as if he were a servant caught neglecting his duties, Some saint you are, to protect only your own silver while watching the rest get stolen, well, in return you'll be left without anything, and with these harsh words, the friar entered the chapel and began to strip it of all its contents, removing not only the silver but the altar cloths and other furnishings as well, and once the chapel was bare, he started stripping the statue of St Antony, who saw his removable halo vanish along with his cross, and would soon have found himself without the Child Jesus in his arms if several friars had not come to the rescue, who feeling the punishment was excessive, persuaded the enraged old man to leave at least the Child Jesus for the consolation of the disgraced saint. The old friar considered their plea for a moment before replying, Very well, then, let the Child Jesus remain as his guarantor until the lamps are returned. Since it was now almost two o'clock and several hours had elapsed while the search and episode just narrated took place, the friars retired to their cells, some of them seriously worried that St Antony would come to avenge this insult.

Next day, about eleven o'clock, someone knocked at the convent door, a student who, it should be explained immediately, had been aspiring to join the order for some considerable time and who visited the friars at every possible opportunity, this information being provided, first, because it is true and the truth is always worthwhile, and, second, to assist those who enjoy deciphering criss-cross patterns of words and events, in short, the student knocked at the convent door and said he wished to speak to the Superior. Permission granted, the student was shown into his presence, he kissed the prior's ring, or the cord hanging from his habit, or it might have been the hem, for this detail has never been fully clarified, and informed His Reverence that he had overheard in the city that the lamps were to be found in the Monastery of Cotovia, which belonged to the Jesuits and was located some distance away, in the Bairro Alto of St Roch. At first the prior was inclined to mistrust this information, coming as it did from a student who could have been taken for a scoundrel had he not been an aspirant to holy orders, although one often finds the two roles coincide, and besides, it seemed unlikely that thieves would hand over to Cotovia what they had taken from Xabregas, locations so different and remote from each other, religious orders with so little in common, and almost a league apart as the crow flies. Therefore prudence demanded that the student's information should be investigated and a suitably cautious member of the community was dispatched, accompanied by the aforesaid student, from Xabregas to Cotovia, and they entered the city on foot through the Gate of the Holy Cross, and so that the reader may be apprised of all the facts, it is worth noting the itinerary they followed before finally reaching their destination.

Passing close by the Church of St Stephanie, they walked alongside the Church of St Michael, passed the Church of St Peter and entered the Gate known by the same name, heading down towards the river by the Outlook of the Conde de Linhares, before turning right and going through the Sea-Gate to the Old Pillary, names and landmarks no longer in existence, they avoided the Rua Nova dos Mercadores, a street which even to this day is the haunt of money-lenders, and after skirting the Rossio they arrived at the Outlook of St Roch and finally reached the Monastery of Cotovia, where they knocked and entered, and having been ushered before the rector, the friar explained, This student who accompanies me has brought news to Xabregas that the altar lamps stolen from our church last night are to be found here, That is so, from what I have been told, it would appear that about two o'clock there was a loud knocking at the door, and when the porter asked the caller what he wanted, a voice replied through the peephole that he should open the door immediately because the caller was anxious to return some goods, and when the porter came to give me this strange news, I ordered that the door be opened, and there we found the altar lamps, somewhat dented and with a few of the embellishments damaged, here they are, and if there is anything missing you have our assurance that we found them in this condition, Did anyone catch sight of the caller, No, we saw no one, some of the fathers went out into the street, but they found no one.

The altar lamps were duly returned to Xabregas, and the reader may believe what he likes. Could it have been the student after all who was the culprit, devising this cunning strategy in order to force his way into the convent and don the habit of St Francis, as he did in the end, and could he have stolen and then returned the altar lamps in the hope that the worthiness of his intentions would absolve him from this wicked sin on the Day of Final Judgment, or could it have been St Antony, responsible for so many different miracles in the past, who also worked this miracle, upon finding himself suddenly deprived of all his silver because of the holy wrath of a friar who knew full well what he was doing, just like the boatmen and sailors of the Tagus who punish the saint when he fails to fulfil their wishes or reward their pledges by plunging him headfirst into the waters of the river, not so much the discomfort, because the lungs of any saint worthy of that name are as capable of breathing the air we all share, as gills of breathing the water which is the sky of fishes, but the mortification of knowing that the humble soles of his feet are exposed, and the sorrow of finding himself without silver and almost without the Child Jesus, make St Antony the most miraculous of saints, especially when it comes to finding lost objects. In the end, the student would have been completely exonerated, had he not become involved in yet another dubious episode.

Given similar precedents, because the Franciscans are so well endowed with means to change, overturn, or hasten the natural order of things, even the recalcitrant womb of the Queen must respond to the solemn injunction of a miracle. All the more so since the Franciscan Order has been petitioning for a convent in Mafra since the year sixteen hundred and twenty-four, a time when the King of Portugal was a Felipe imported from Spain, who had little interest in the religious communities of Portugal and persisted in withholding his permission throughout the sixteen years of his reign. This did not deter initiatives on the part of the friars, and the prestige of noble patrons in the town was invoked, but the influence of the province of Arrábida petitioning for the convent appeared to have diminished and its resolve had weakened, for only recently, which one can say of something that happened six years ago, in seventeen hundred and five, the same thing occurred, the Royal Court of Appeal turned down the petition, and expressed itself strongly, if not altogether disrespectfully, about the material and spiritual interests of the Church, and had the audacity to declare the petition inopportune, the realm being already overburdened with mendicant orders and other inconveniences dictated by human wisdom. The judges of the Court of Appeal reserved the right to determine what those inconveniences dictated by human wisdom might be, but now they will have to hold their tongues and bury their dark thoughts, for Friar Antony of St Joseph has promised that once the friars have their convent there will be an heir to the throne. A pledge has been made, the Queen will give birth, and the Franciscan Order will gather the palm of victory, just as it has gathered so many palms of martyrdom. A hundred years of waiting is no great sacrifice for those who count on living for all eternity.

We saw how the student was finally exonerated of blame in the episode of the stolen altar lamps. But it would be folly to suggest that because of secrets divulged in the confessional the friars knew of the Queen's pregnancy even before the Queen herself knew and could confide in the King. Just as it would be wrong to suggest that Dona Maria Ana, because she was such a pious lady, agreed to remain silent until the appearance of God's chosen messenger, the virtuous Friar Antony. Nor can anyone say the King will be counting the moons from the night the pledge was given until the day the child is born, and find the cycle complete. There is nothing to add to what has already been said.

So let not Franciscans be impugned, unless they should become involved in other equally dubious intrigues.

IN THE COURSE OF the year some people die from having overindulged during their lifetime, which explains why apoplectic fits recur one after another, why sometimes only one is needed to dispatch a victim to his grave, and why even when spared death they remain paralysed down one side, their mouths all twisted, sometimes unable to speak, and without hope of an effective cure apart from continuous blood-lettings. But many more people die from malnutrition, unable to survive on a miserable diet of sardines and rice along with some lettuce, and a little meat when the nation celebrates the King's birthday. May God grant that our river yield an abundance of fish, and let us give praise to the Holy Trinity with this intention in mind. And may lettuce and other produce arrive from the surrounding countryside, transported in great baskets filled to the brim by the country swains and maidens who do not excel in these labours. And may there be no intolerable shortage of rice. For this city, more than any other, is a mouth that gorges itself on one side and starves on the other, and there is no happy medium between ruddy and pale complexions, between bulging and bony hips, between great paunches and shrivelled bellies. But Lent, like the rising sun, is for everyone.

The excesses of Shrovetide could be seen throughout the city, those who could afford it stuffed themselves with poultry and mutton, with doughnuts and fritters, outrages were committed on every street corner by those who never miss an opportunity to take liberties, derisive tails were pinned to fugitive backs, water was squirted on faces with syringes meant for other purposes, the unwary were spanked with strings of onions, and wine was imbibed, accompanied by the inevitable belching and vomiting, there was a clanging of pots and pans, bagpipes were played, and if more people did not end up rolling on the ground, in the side streets, squares, and alleyways, it is only because the city is filthy, its roads full of sewage and rubbish, crawling with mangy dogs and stray cats, and mud everywhere even when there is no rain. Now the time has come to pay for all these excesses, the time to mortify the soul so that the flesh may feign repentance, the depraved, rebellious flesh of this pathetic and obscene pigsty known as Lisbon.

The Lenten procession is about to commence. Let us mortify our flesh with fasting and abstinence, let us punish our bodies with flagellation. By eating frugally, we can purify our thoughts, through suffering we can purge our souls. The penitents, all of them male, head the procession, and they are followed by the friars who carry the banners bearing images of the Virgin and of Christ crucified. Behind them comes the bishop under an ornate canopy, and then the effigies of saints carried on litters, followed by an endless regiment of priests, confraternities, and guilds, all of whom are intent upon salvation, some convinced they are already damned, others tortured by uncertainty until they are summoned to Judgment, and there may even be some among them who are quietly thinking that the world has been mad since it was conceived. The procession wends its way through the crowds lining the streets, and as it passes, men and women prostrate themselves on the ground, claw their faces, tear their hair out, and inflict blows on themselves, while the bishop makes fleeting signs of the cross to right and left and the acolyte swings his thurible. Lisbon stinks, but the incense bestows meaning on this putrid stench of decay, a stench that comes from the wickedness of the flesh, for the soul is fragrant.

Women can be seen watching from the windows, as is the custom. The penitents walk slowly, with balls and chains twisted round their ankles, or with their arms holding massive iron bars across their shoulders as if they were suspended from a cross, or they scourge themselves with leather thongs ending in balls of solid wax spiked with glass splinters, and these flagellants are considered to be the highlight of the spectacle, as real blood flows down their backs and they give out loud cries, of pleasure as much as pain, which we should find a little strange if we did not know that some of the penitents have spotted their mistresses at the windows, and they are in the procession not so much for the salvation of their souls as for inciting carnal pleasures, those already experienced and those still to come.

The penitents wear small coloured ribbons, pinned to their hoods or to the thongs, every man has his own colours, so if the mistress of his desire, languishing at her window consumed with pity for her suffering swain, perhaps even with that pleasure later to become known as sadism, should fail to recognise his face or gait amid the bustle of penitents, banners, and spectators who cry out in terror and supplication, and the chanting of litanies as the canopies lurch menacingly and the effigies collide, she will at least be able to recognise, from the ribbons in pink, green, yellow, and lilac, and even red and sky-blue, he who is her slave and admirer, who dedicates his flagellation to her, and who, unable to speak, roars like a rutting bull, and when the other women on the street and the mistress herself feel that he is not flogging himself with enough force to inflict open wounds and draw blood for everyone to see, then the female choir erupts into a hideous wailing, as if possessed, inciting the men to greater violence, they want to hear the whips crack and see the blood flow as it flowed from the Divine Saviour, only then will their bodies throb under their petticoats, and their thighs open and contract to the rhythm and excitement of the flagellants' procession. As the penitent arrives beneath the window of his beloved, she throws him a haughty glance, she is probably chaperoned by her mother, cousin, or governess, or by some indulgent grandmother or sour old aunt, but they are all aware of what is happening, thanks to their own memories, recent or distant, that God has nothing to do with all this fornication, the ecstasies at the windows mirroring the ecstasies on the street below, the flagellant on his knees, whipping himself into a frenzy and calling out in pain, while the woman ogles the vanquished male and parts her lips to drink his blood and the rest. The procession has paused, allowing the ritual to be concluded, the bishop has bestowed his blessing and consecration, the woman experiences languorous sensations, and the man passes on, relieved that he can now stop scourging himself with quite so much vigour, for now it is the turn of others to satisfy the cravings of their mistresses.

Once they have started to mortify their flesh and observe the rules of fasting, it seems that they will have to tolerate these privations until Easter and they must suppress their natural inclinations until the shadows pass from the countenance of Holy Mother Church, now that the Passion and death of Christ are nigh. It could be the phosphoric richness of fish that stimulates carnal desire, or the unfortunate custom of allowing women to visit churches unaccompanied during Lent, whereas for the rest of the year they are kept safely indoors, unless they are prostitutes or belong to the lower classes, women of noble birth leaving their homes only to go to church, and only on three other occasions during their lifetime, for baptism, marriage, and burial, for the rest of the time they are confined within the sanctuary of their homes, and perhaps the aforementioned custom shows just how unbearable Lent can be, because the Lenten period is a time of antici-pated death and a warning for all to heed, and so while husbands take precautions, or feign to take precautions so that their wives will not do anything other than attend to their religious duties, the women look forward to Lent in order to enjoy some freedom, although they may not venture forth unaccompanied without risking scandal, their chap-erones sharing the same desires and the same need to satisfy them, and so between one church and the next, women can arrange clandestine meetings, while the chaperones converse and intrigue, and when the ladies and their chaperones meet again before some altar, both parties know that Lent does not exist and that the world has been blissfully mad ever since it was conceived. The streets of Lisbon are full of women all dressed alike, their heads covered with mantillas and shawls that have only the tiniest opening to allow the ladies to signal with their eyes or lips, a common means of secretly exchanging forbidden senti-ments and illicit desires, throughout the streets of this city, where there is a church on every corner and a convent in every quarter, spring is in the air and turning everyone's head, and when no breeze blows, there is always the sighing of those who unburden their souls in the confes-sionals, or in secluded places conducive to other forms of confession, as adulterous flesh wavers on the brink of pleasure and damnation, for the one is as inviting as the other during this period of abstinence, bare altars, solemn mourning, and omnipresent sin.

By day their ingenuous husbands will be enjoying, or at least pretending to enjoy, their siestas, by night, when streets and squares mysteriously fill with crowds smelling of onion and lavender, and the murmur of prayers can be heard through the open doors of churches, they feel at greater ease as they will not have long to wait now, someone is already knocking at the door, steps can be heard on the stair, mistress and maid arrive, conversing intimately, and the black slave, too, if she has been brought along and through the chinks the light of a candle or oil lamp can be seen, the husband pretends to wake, the wife pretends that she has awakened him, and if he asks any questions, we know what her reply will be, she has come back exhausted, footsore, and with stiff joints, but feeling spiritually consoled, and she utters the magic number, I have visited *seven* churches, she says, with such vehemence that she has been guilty either of excessive piety or of some monstrous sin.

Queens are denied these opportunities of unburdening their souls, especially if they have been made pregnant and by their legitimate husband, who for nine months will no longer come near them, a rule widely accepted but sometimes broken. Dona Maria Ana has every reason to exercise discretion, given the strict piety with which she had been brought up in Austria and her wholehearted compliance with the friar's strategy, thus showing, or at least giving the impression, that the child being conceived in her womb is as much a daughter for the King of Portugal as for God Himself, in exchange for a convent.

Dona Maria Ana retires to her bedchamber at an early hour and says her prayers in singsong harmony with her ladies-in-waiting before getting into bed, and then, once settled underneath her eiderdown, she resumes her prayers, and prays on and on, while the ladies-in-waiting start to nod but fight their drowsiness like wise women, if not wise virgins, and finally withdraw, all that remains to watch over her is the light from the lamp, and the lady-in-waiting on duty, who spends the night on a low couch by the Queen's bed, will soon be asleep, free to dream if she so chooses, but what is being dreamed behind those eyelids is of no great importance, what interests us is the frightening thought still troubling Dona Maria Ana as she is about to fall asleep, that on Maundy Thursday she will have to go to the Church of the Mother of God, where the nuns will unveil the Holy Shroud in her presence before showing it to the faithful, a shroud that bears the clear impression of the Body of Christ, the one true Holy Shroud that exists in the Christian world, ladies and gentlemen, just as all the others are the one true Holy Shroud, or they would not all be shown at the same hour in so many different churches throughout the world, but because this one happens to be in Portugal it is the truest Holy Shroud of all and altogether unique. When still conscious, Dona Maria Ana imagines herself bending over the sacred cloth, but it is difficult to say whether or not she is about to kiss it with reverence, because suddenly she falls asleep and finds herself in a carriage that is taking her back to the Palace at dead of night with an escort of halberdiers, when unexpectedly a man appears on horseback, returning from the chase, accompanied by four servants mounted on mules, with furred and feathered creatures inside nets dangling from their pommels, the mysterious horseman races toward the carriage, his shotgun at the ready, the horse's hooves cause sparks to ignite on the cobbles, and smoke erupts from its nostrils, and when he charges like a thunderbolt through the Queen's guard and reaches the carriage steps, where he brings his mount to a halt with some difficulty, the flames of the torches illumine his face, it is the Infante Dom Francisco, from what land of dreams could he have come, and why should he appear time and time again. The horse is startled, no doubt because of the clattering of the carriage on the cobblestones, but when the Queen compares these dreams she observes that the Infante comes a little closer each time, What can he want, and what does she want.

For some Lent is a dream, for others a vigil. The Easter festivities passed and wives returned to the gloom of their apartments and their cumbersome petticoats, at home there are a few more cuckolds, who can be quite violent when infidelities are practised out of season. And since we are now on the subject of birds, it is time to listen in church to the canaries singing rapturously of love from their cages decorated with ribbons and flowers, while the friars preaching in the pulpits presume to speak of holier things. It is Ascension Thursday, and the singing of the birds soars to the vaults of heaven regardless of whether our prayers follow, without their assistance, our prayers have little hope of reaching God, so perhaps we shall all remain silent.

THIS SCRUFFY-LOOKING FELLOW with his rattling sword and ill-assorted clothes, even though barefoot, has the air of a soldier, and his name is Baltasar Mateus, otherwise known as Sete-Sóis or Seven Suns. He was dismissed from the army where he was of no further use once his left hand was amputated at the wrist after being shattered by gunfire at Jerez de los Caballeros, in the ambitious campaign we fought last October with eleven thousand men, only to end with the loss of two hundred of our soldiers and the rout of the survivors, who were pursued by the Spanish cavalry dispatched from Badajoz. We withdrew to Olivença with the booty we had taken in Barcarrota, feeling much too down-hearted to enjoy it, gaining little by the ten leagues march there, and then making a rapid retreat over the same distance, only to leave behind on the battlefield so many casualties and the shattered hand of Baltasar Sete-Sóis. By great good fortune, or by the special grace of the scapular he was wearing around his neck, his wound did not become gangrenous, nor did they burst his veins with the force of the tourniquet applied to stop the bleeding, and thanks to the surgeon's skill, it was only a matter of disarticulating the man's tendons, without having to cut through the bone with a handsaw. The stump was treated with medicinal herbs, and Sete-Sóis had such healthy flesh that after two months the wound was completely healed.

Having saved little or nothing of his soldier's pay, Sete-Sóis begged for alms in Évora till he had enough money to pay the blacksmith and the saddler for an iron hook to replace his hand. This was how he spent the winter, putting aside half of the money he managed to collect, reserving half of the other half for the journey ahead, and spending the rest on food and wine. It was already spring by the time he had paid off the final instalment he owed the saddler and collected the iron hook, as well as a spike he had ordered, because Baltasar Sete-Sóis fancied the idea of having an alternative left hand. Crafted leather fittings were skilfully attached to the tempered irons, and there were two straps of different lengths to attach the implements to the elbow and shoulder for greater support. Sete-Sóis began his journey when it was rumoured that the garrison at Beira was to remain there instead of coming to the assistance of the troops in Alentejo, where there was an even greater shortage of food than in the other provinces. The army was in tatters, barefoot and reduced to rags, the soldiers pilfered from the farmers and refused to go on fighting, a considerable number went over to the enemy, while many others deserted, travelling off the beaten track, looting in order to eat, raping any women they encountered on the way, in short, taking their revenge on innocent people who owed them nothing and shared their despair. Sete-Sóis, maimed and bedraggled, travelled the main highway to Lisbon, deprived of his left hand, part of which had remained in Spain and part in Portugal, and all because of a strategic war to decide who was to occupy the Spanish throne, an Austrian Charles or a French Philip, but no one Portuguese, whether unimpaired or one-handed, intact or mutilated, unless to leave severed limbs or lost lives behind on the battlefield is not only the destiny of soldiers who have nothing but the ground to sit on. Sete-Sóis left Évora and passed through Montemor, accompanied by neither friar nor demon, for when it came to extending a begging hand, the one he possessed was sufficient.

Sete-Sóis went at his leisure. There was no one waiting to greet him in Lisbon, and in Mafra, which he had left many years ago to join His Majesty's Infantry, his father and mother, if they remember him, will think he is alive since no one has reported him dead or believe him to be dead because they have no proof he is still alive. All will be revealed in good time. The sun shines brightly and there has been no rain, the countryside is covered with flowers and the birds are singing. Sete-Sóis carries his irons in his knapsack, for there are moments, sometimes whole hours, when he imagines he can feel his hand, as if it were still there at the end of his arm, and it gives him enormous pleasure to imagine himself whole and entire just as Charles and Philip will sit whole and entire on their thrones, for thrones they will certainly have when the war is over. Sete-Sóis is content, so long as he does not look to find that his hand is missing, to feel an itching at the tip of his index finger and imagine that he is scratching the spot with his thumb. And when he starts to dream tonight, if he catches a glimpse of himself in his sleep he will see that he has no limbs missing, and will be able to rest his tired head on the palms of both hands.

Baltasar keeps the irons in his knapsack for another good reason. He very quickly discovered that whenever he wears them, especially the spike, people refuse him alms, or give him very little, although they always feel obliged to give him a few coins because of the sword he carries on his hip, despite the fact that everyone carries a sword, even the black slaves, but not with the gallant air of a professional soldier, who might wield it this very moment, if provoked. And unless the number of travellers outweighs the fear provoked by the presence of this brigand, who stands in the middle of the road, barring their passage and begging alms, alms for a poor soldier who has lost his hand and who but for a miracle might have lost his life, for the solitary traveller does not want this plea to turn to aggression, coins soon fall into the outstretched hand, and Baltasar is grateful that his right hand has been spared.

After passing through Pegões, at the edge of the vast pine forests, where the soil becomes arid, Baltasar, using his teeth, attached the spike to his stump, also useful as a dagger if necessary, for this was a time when deadly weapons such as daggers were forbidden, but Sete-Sóis enjoyed what might be termed immunity, so, doubly armed with spike and sword, he set off amid the shadows of the trees. A little farther on he would kill one of two men who tried to rob him, even though he told them that he was carrying no money, but after a war in which so many have lost their lives, this encounter need not concern us, except to note that Sete-Sóis then substituted the hook for the spike so he could drag the corpse off the path, making good use of both implements. The robber who escaped stalked him for another half-league through the pine groves, but finally gave up the chase, continuing to curse and insult him from a distance but with no real conviction this would have much effect.

When Sete-Sóis reached Aldegalega, it was already growing dark. He ate some fried sardines and drank a bowl of wine, and with barely enough money left for the next stage of his journey, let alone for lodgings at an inn, he sheltered in a barn, underneath some carts, and there he slept wrapped in his cloak, but with his left arm and the spike exposed. He spent the night peacefully. He dreamt of the battle at Jerez de los Caballeros and knew that this time the Portuguese would be victorious under the leadership of Baltasar Sete-Sóis, who carried his severed left hand in his right hand, a prodigious talisman against which the Spaniards could not defend themselves with either shield or exorcism. When he opened his eyes, the first light of dawn had still not appeared on the eastern horizon, he felt a sharp pain in his left arm, which was not surprising, since the spike was pressing on the stump. He untied the straps and, using his imagination, all the more vivid at night, and especially in the pitch-black darkness under the carts, Baltasar convinced himself he still had two hands even if he could not see them. Both of them. He tucked his knapsack under his left arm, curled up under his cloak, and went back to sleep. At least he had managed to survive the war. He might have a limb missing, but he was still alive.

As dawn broke, he got to his feet. The sky was clear and transparent, and even the palest stars could be seen in the distance. It was a fine day on which to be entering Lisbon, and with time to linger before continuing his journey, he postponed any decision. Burying his hand in the knapsack, he took out his shoddy boots, which he had not worn once during the journey from Alentejo and had he worn them, he would have been obliged to discard them after such a long march, and demanding new skills from his right hand and using his stump, as yet untrained, he managed to get his feet into them, otherwise he would have them covered in blisters and calluses, accustomed as he was to walking in bare feet during his time as a peasant, then as a soldier, when there was never enough money to buy food, let alone to mend one's boots. For there is no existence more miserable than a soldier's.

When he reached the docks, the sun was already high. The tide was in, and the ferryman alerted any remaining passengers embarking for Lisbon that he was about to cast off. Baltasar Sete-Sóis ran up the gangway, his irons jangling inside his knapsack, and when a witty fellow quipped that the one-handed man was obviously carrying horseshoes in his sack to protect them, Sete-Sóis looked at him askance and, putting his right hand into his knapsack, drew out the spike. If that was not congealed blood on the iron, it looked uncannily like the real thing. The witty fellow averted his eyes, recommended his soul to St Christopher, who is reputed to protect travellers from evil encounters and other misfortunes, and from that moment until they reached Lisbon he did not utter another word. A woman sat down beside Sete-Sóis, unpacked her provisions, and invited those around her, out of politeness rather than any willingness to share her food, but with the soldier it was different, and she insisted at such length that Baltasar finally accepted. Baltasar did not like to eat in the presence of others with that solitary hand of his which made for difficulties, the bread slipping between his fingers and the meat dropping on the floor, but the woman spread his food on a large slice of bread, and by manoeuvring with his fingers and the tip of the penknife he had drawn from his pocket, he managed to eat quite comfortably and with a certain finesse. The woman and her husband were old enough to be his parents, this was no flirtation over the waters of the Tagus, but friendship and compassion towards a man who had come back from the war, maimed for life.

The ferryman raised a small triangular sail, the wind assisted the tide, and both wind and tide assisted the ship. The oarsmen, restored by alcohol and a good night's rest, rowed steadily at an easy pace. When they rounded the coastline, the ship was buffeted by a strong current, it was like a journey to paradise, with the sunlight flickering on the surface of the water, and two shoals of porpoises, first one, then the other, were crossing in front of the ship, their skins dark and shiny, their movements arched as if they were striving to reach the sky. On the other side, towering above the water and in the far distance, Lisbon could be seen stretching beyond the city walls. The castle dominated the panorama, while church towers and spires rose above the rooftops of the houses below, a blurred conglomeration of gables. The ferryman began to tell a story, An amusing thing happened yesterday, if anyone is interested, and everyone was interested, because storytelling is a pleasant way to while away the time, and this was a long journey. The English fleet, which can be seen over there in front of the coast of Santos, anchored yesterday, and is carrying troops on their way to Catalonia, bringing reinforcements to the army awaiting them, and with the fleet arrived a ship carrying a number of criminals on their way to exile on the island of Barbados, and some fifty prostitutes who were also going there, to form a new colony, for in such places the honest and the dishonest amount to pretty much the same thing, but the ship's captain, old devil that he is, thought they could form a much better colony in Lisbon, so he decided to lighten his cargo and ordered that the women be put ashore, I've seen some of those slender English wenches for myself, and some of them are quite attractive. The ferry-man laughed in anticipation, as if he were drawing up his own plans for carnal navigation and calculating the profits to be made from those who would board his ship, while the oarsmen from the Algarve roared with laughter, Sete-Sóis stretched out like a cat basking in the heat of the sun, the woman with the provisions pretended not to be listening, her husband vacillated, wondering whether he should look amused or remain solemn, because he could not take such tales seriously, nor was it to be expected of one who came from the distant region of Pancas, where from the day a man is born until the day he dies, everyday life, real or imagined, is the same old drudge. Hitting on one idea, then another, and for some mysterious reason linking the two, he then asked the soldier, How old are you, sir, whereupon Baltasar replied, I am twenty-six years of age.

There stood Lisbon, presented on the palm of the earth, a façade of high walls and tall houses. The ship landed at Ribeira, the boat-swain manoeuvred the vessel alongside the quay, the sail having been lowered beforehand, and with one concerted movement the oars-men on the mooring side raised their oars, while those on the other side of the ship strained to keep the vessel steady, one final turn of the rudder, a rope was thrown over their heads, and it was as if the two banks of the river had suddenly been joined together. Because of the receding tide, the quay was rather high, and Baltasar assisted the woman with the basket and her husband, while the witty fellow got to his feet smartly and without a word took one leap and landed safely.

There was a confusion of fishing boats and caravels unloading cargo, the foremen hurled insults and bullied the black stevedores, who worked in pairs and were drenched by the water trickling from the baskets and bespattering their faces and arms with fish scales. It looked as if the entire population of Lisbon had congregated in the market place. Sete-Sóis could feel his mouth watering, it seemed as if all the hunger accumulated during the four years of war was now bursting the dykes of resignation and self-control. He felt his stomach contract in knots, and his eyes searched instinctively for the woman who had offered him food, where could she have gone with that passive husband of hers who was probably staring at the women in the crowd and trying to catch a glimpse of the English whores, for every man is entitled to his dreams.

With little money in his pocket except for a few copper coins that jingled far less than the irons in his knapsack, Baltasar had to decide where to go next, to Mafra, where he would find it difficult to wield a hoe with only one hand, or to the Royal Palace, where he might receive alms because of his disability. Someone had made this suggestion in Évora, while warning him that you had to beg with insistence and at great length and to be sure to flatter your benefactors, for even when you adopted these tactics, you could still become hoarse or drop dead without seeing so much as the colour of a coin. When all else failed, you could turn to the guilds, who dispensed charity, or the convents, where you were always certain of a bowl of soup and a slice of bread. Besides, a man who has lost his left hand does not have much to complain about, if he still has his right hand to extend to passers-by or a sharp spike with which to intimidate them.

Sete-Sóis strolled across the fish market. The fishwives hollered at potential buyers, vying for their attention with waving arms that jangled with gold bracelets, and screaming oaths, hands on hearts, bosoms heaving with necklaces, crosses, charms, and chains, all made from Brazilian gold, as were the large earrings they wore in every conceivable shape, valued possessions that enhance a woman's beauty. In the middle of this filthy rabble, the fishwives looked remarkably clean and tidy, as if untainted even by the smell of the fish they handled.

At the door of a tavern standing next to a jeweller's shop, Baltasar bought three grilled sardines on top of the indispensable slice of bread, and blowing and nibbling as he went, he headed for the Palace. He entered the slaughterhouse that looked on to the square, to feast his eyes on the gaping carcasses of pigs and oxen, on whole sides of beef and pork hanging from hooks. He promised himself a banquet of roast meats just as soon as he could afford it, little suspecting that one day soon he would come here to work, thanks to his godfather's good offices but also to the hook he carried in his knapsack, which was to prove useful for heaving carcasses, draining tripe, and tearing away layers of fat. Apart from the blood, the slaughterhouse was a clean establishment with white tiles on the walls, and unless the butcher cheated on the scales, there was no other danger of being cheated, for in terms of quality and protein there is nothing to compare with meat.

The building that looms in the distance is the Royal Palace. The Palace is there but not the King, for he has gone off to hunt at Azeitão with the Infante Dom Francisco and his other brothers, accompanied by the footmen of the royal household and two Jesuit fathers, the Reverend João Seco and the Reverend Luís Gonzaga, who certainly were not in the party simply to eat and to pray, perhaps the King wished to brush up his knowledge of mathematics or Latin and Greek, subjects the good fathers had taught him when he was a young prince. His Majesty also carried a new rifle made for him by João de Lara, master of arms in the royal arsenal, a work of art embellished with gold and silver, which were it to be lost en route, would soon be returned to its rightful owner, for along the barrel of the rifle, in bold lettering and written in Latin, as on the pediment of the Basilica of St Peter's in Rome, are inscribed the words, I BELONG TO THE MONARCH. MAY GOD PROTECT DOM JOÃO V, yet some people continue to insist that rifles can speak only through the mouth of the barrel and solely in the language of gunpowder and lead. That is certainly true of ordinary rifles, such as the one used by Baltasar Mateus, alias Sete-Sóis, who at this very minute is unarmed and standing quite still in the middle of the Palace Square as he watches the world go by, a constant procession of litters and friars, ruffians and merchants, and watching bales and chests being weighed, he feels a sudden nostalgia for the war, and if he did not know that he is not wanted any more, he would return to Alentejo without a moment's hesitation, even if it meant certain death.

Baltasar took the broad avenue leading to the Rossio, after attending Holy Mass in the Church of Our Lady of Oliveira, where he engaged in mild flirtation with an unaccompanied woman who obviously fancied him, a fairly common pastime, for since the women are on one side of the church and the men on the other, they soon start to exchange billets-doux, make signs with their hands and handkerchiefs, twitching their lips and giving knowing winks, but when the woman took a close look at Baltasar, who was worn out after his long journey and had no money to spend on trifles and silk ribbons, she decided not to pursue the flirtation, and leaving the church, she took the broad avenue in the direction of the Rossio. This seemed to be a day for women, he thought, as a dozen or so emerged from a narrow side street, surrounded by black street-urchins who jostled them with sticks, nearly all of the women fair, with eyes that were pale blue, green, or grey, Who are these women, Sete-Sóis inquired, and by the time a man standing nearby told him, Baltasar had already surmised that they were probably the English whores being taken back to the ship from which they had been disembarked by the wily captain, and there was no other solution but to send them to the island of Barbados, rather than allow them to wander this fair land of Portugal, so greatly favoured by foreign whores, for here is a profession that defies the confusion of Babel, and you can enter these workshops as silent as a deaf-mute, so long as your money has spoken first. Yet the ferryman had said that there were some fifty whores in all, but here there were no more than twelve, What happened to the others, and the man explained, Most have already been recaptured, but some found means of hiding, and no doubt have by now discovered the difference between English and Portuguese men. Baltasar continued on his way, promising St Benedict a heart fashioned from wax if he would grant him the favour of being able to sample, at least once in his lifetime, a fair English wench, preferably tall and slender with green eyes, for if on the Feast of St Benedict the faithful knock at the church doors and pray that they might never go without bread, and women who are anxious to find a good husband have Masses celebrated every Friday in the Saint's honour, why should a soldier not pray to St Benedict for the favours of an English whore, just once, before he meets his Maker, rather than die in ignorance.

Baltasar Sete-Sóis wandered around the city's quarters and squares all afternoon. He drank a bowl of soup at the gates of the Convent of St Francis of the City, asked which of the guilds were most generous in distributing alms and made a careful note of three of them for further investigation, the Guild of Our Lady of Oliveira, the patron saint of pastry-cooks, which he had already tried, the Guild of St Eloi, the patron saint of silversmiths, and the Guild of the Lost Child, which aptly described his own situation, although he could scarcely recall ever having been a child, lost yes, if they will ever find him.

Dusk fell, and Sete-Sóis went off to find a place to sleep. He had already struck up a friendship with another former soldier, older and more experienced, João Elvas who now made his living as a pimp, a profession he pursued by night, and now that the weather was warmer, he made good use of some abandoned sheds against the walls of the Convent of Hope, near the olive grove. Occasionally Baltasar visited João Elvas, with whom you could always be certain of meeting a new face or of finding someone to talk to but rather than take any risks, Baltasar, on the pretext that he wanted to give his right hand a rest after carrying his knapsack all day, attached the spike to his stump, anxious not to alarm João Elvas and the other rogues for it is a deadly weapon as we well know. There were six of them huddled under the shed, but no one tried to do him any harm and he had no intention of harming them.

To while away the hours before falling asleep, they reminisced about crimes that had been committed. Not their own, the crimes of their leaders, which nearly always went unpunished, even when the guilty parties could easily be identified, the powerful had no fear of being discovered and brought to justice. But the common thieves, bullies, or petty criminals, since there was no danger of anyone betraying the leaders, soon found themselves in Limoeiro prison, where they could be sure of a bowl of soup, not to mention the excrement and urine fouling the cells. Recently they released a hundred and fifty petty criminals from Limoeiro, who were joined by more than five hundred men, who had been recruited for India and then dismissed because they were no longer required, and there were so many of them, and so much hunger, that a plague broke out, threatening to kill all of us, so that the recruits were disbanded, and I was one of them. Another man said, This country is a hotbed of crime, more people are murdered in this city than are killed in war, as anyone who has ever fought will tell you, What do you say, Sete-Sóis, whereupon Baltasar replied, I can tell you how men die in war, but I don't know how men die in Lisbon, so I can't make any comparison, ask João Elvas, for he knows as much about military strongholds as he does about city slums, but João Elvas, merely shrugged his shoulders and said nothing.

The conversation turned back to the previous topic, and they listened to the story of the gilder who stabbed a widow whom he wanted to marry but she refused to satisfy his desire, so he murdered her and sought sanctuary in the Convent of the Holy Trinity, and then there was the tale of the unfortunate woman who rebuked her philandering husband, whereupon he slashed her from head to foot with his sword, and that of the clergyman who, because of some amorous intrigue, was rewarded with three magnificent scars, all these misadventures occurring during Lent, a season of hot blood and dark passions. But August is not much better, as we saw last year, when the dismembered body of a woman was discovered cut into fourteen or fifteen pieces, the precise number of pieces was never verified, but there was no doubt that she had been flogged with great violence about the vulnerable parts of her body, such as the buttocks and the calves, the flesh had been stripped from the bones and abandoned in Cotovia, one half of her limbs had been scattered near the fortifications of Conde de Tarouca and the rest down in Cardais, but scattered so blatantly that they were soon discovered, no attempt had been made to bury her remains or dump them at sea, so we can only conclude that they were deliberately left exposed to arouse public outrage.

Then João Elvas took up the story saying, It was a terrible slaughter, and the poor woman must have been dismembered while she was still alive, because no one could have treated a corpse so badly, the remains that were discovered came from some of the most sensitive parts of her body, and only a man whose soul was a thousand times cursed and damned could have committed such a crime, nothing like it has ever been seen in war, Sete-Sóis, although I can't vouch for what you may have seen on the battlefield, and the ruffian who had begun the story took advantage of this pause and picked up the thread of his narration, Not until much later were the woman's missing limbs discovered, why, only the other day her head and one of her hands were found in Junqueira, and then a foot at Boavista, and to judge from her hand, foot, and head, she was an attractive, well-bred woman, not much older than eighteen or twenty, and in the sack where her head was discovered, there were also her intestines and her breasts, which had been peeled like oranges, and the body of a child some three or four months old, which had been strangled with a silken cord, even in a city like Lisbon, where so many crimes have been committed, nothing quite like this has ever been witnessed.

João Elvas added some final details about the episode, The King ordered notices to be posted promising a thousand cruzados to anyone who finds the culprit, but almost a year has passed and the culprit, alas, has not been found, people soon realised that the search was hopeless, the murderer was no ordinary shoemaker or tailor, for they only cut holes in your pocket, and the lacerations on this woman's body had been made with expert knowledge, her flesh and bones were carved with professional skill, and the surgeons ordered to inspect the evidence agreed that the crime was the work of a man professionally trained in anatomy, without daring to confess that they themselves could not have done such a skilful job. From behind the convent wall, the nuns could be heard intoning their hymns, little do they know what they are spared, to conceive a child is something that has to be paid for at great cost, then Baltasar asked, Did anyone ever discover the identity of the murdered woman, No, neither that of the woman nor of her assassins, they hung her head from the door of the Alms house to see if anyone might recognise her, but to no avail and one of the ruffians there, whose beard was more white than black and who had said nothing so far, interrupted, They must have been strangers, for had they been from these parts, a missing wife would soon have caused people to gossip, it could have been a father who decided to kill his daughter because of some dishonour and who ordered the body to be cut into pieces and concealed in a mule pack or litter and then scattered throughout the city, and, no doubt, near his home he has buried the carcass of a pig so he can pretend that it is the murdered girl, and has informed his neighbours that his daughter died of smallpox or from some virulent disease, rather than have to open up the shroud, for some people are capable of anything.

The men fell silent, unable to conceal their indignation, from the nuns over the wall not even a whimper could be heard, and Sete-Sóis exclaimed, In war you find greater charity, War is still a child, João Elvas said suspiciously. And since there was nothing more to be said, they all settled down to sleep.

DONA MARIA ANA will not attend the auto-da-fé which is to be held today. She has gone into mourning upon receiving the news of the death of her brother Joseph, the Emperor of Austria who, stricken by virulent smallpox, died within days at the relatively young age of thirty-three, but this is not the Queen's only reason for remaining in her apartments, it will be a sad day for nations if a queen allows a family bereavement to interfere with her royal duties, when she has been brought up to face much greater misfortunes. Although now in her fifth month of pregnancy, she still suffers from morning sickness, but even this would scarcely excuse her from fulfilling her obligations and from participating in the solemn ceremonies with her faculties of sight, touch, and smell, besides the auto-da-fé is spiritually elevating and constitutes an act of faith, with its stately procession, the solemn declaration of the sentences, the dejected appearance of those who have been condemned, the plaintive voices, and the smell of charred flesh as their bodies are engulfed by the flames and whatever little fat remains after months of imprisonment starts to drip on to the embers. Dona Maria Ana will not attend the auto-da-fé because, despite her pregnancy, the physicians have bled her three times and left her feeling extremely weak, in addition to all the other humiliating symptoms of pregnancy that have troubled her for months. The physicians delayed the blood-lettings, just as they delayed giving her the news of her brother's death, because they were anxious to take every precaution at this early stage of pregnancy. To be frank, the atmosphere in the Palace is not at all healthy, the foul air has just provoked a resounding belch from the King, for which he has begged everyone's pardon, and this has been readily granted, because it always does the soul so much good, but he must have been imagining things for once they purged him he felt fine and had simply been suffering from constipation. The Palace seems even gloomier than usual now that the King has decreed court mourning and stipulated that it be observed by all the palace dignitaries and officials, after eight days of strict seclusion, there is to be a further six months of formal mourning, long black cloaks are to be worn for three months, followed by short black cloaks for the following three months, as a token of the King's deep sorrow upon receiving the news of the death of his brother-in-law, the Emperor.

Today, however, there is an air of general rejoicing, although that might not be the right expression, because the happiness stems from a much deeper source, perhaps from the soul itself, as the inhabitants of Lisbon emerge from their homes and pour into the city's streets and squares, crowds descend from the upper quarters of the city and gather in the Rossio to watch Jews and lapsed converts, heretics, and sorcerers being tortured, along with criminals who are less easily classified, such as those found guilty of sodomy, blasphemy, rape and prostitution, and various other misdeeds that warrant exile or the stake. One hundred and four condemned men and women are to be put to death today, most of them from Brazil, a land rich in diamonds and vices, fifty-one men and fifty-three women in all. Two of the women will be handed over naked to the civil authorities by the Inquisition after being found guilty of obdurate heresy, of having steadfastly refused to comply with the law, and of persistently upholding errors they accept as truths, although denounced in this time and place. And since almost two years have passed since anyone was burned at the stake in Lisbon, the Rossio is crowded with spectators, a double celebration, for today is Sunday and there is to be an auto-da-fé, and we shall never know what the inhabitants of Lisbon enjoyed more, autos-da-fé or bullfights, even though only the bullfights have survived. Women cram the windows looking on to the square, dressed in their Sunday best, their hair groomed in the German fashion as a compliment to the Queen, their faces and necks are rouged, and they pout their lips to make their mouths look dainty, so many different faces and expressions trained on the square below as each lady wonders if her make-up is all right, that beauty spot at the corner of her mouth, the powder concealing that pimple, while her eye observes the infatuated admirer below, while her confirmed or aspiring suitor paces up and down clutching a handkerchief and swirling his cape. The heat is unbearable and the spectators refresh themselves with the customary glass of lemonade, cup of water, or slice of water-melon, for there is no reason why they should suffer from exhaustion just because the condemned are about to die. And should they feel in need of something more substantial, there is a wide choice of nuts and seeds, cheeses and dates. The King, with his inseparable Infantes and Infantas, will dine at the Inquisitor's Palace as soon as the auto-da-fé has ended, and once free of the wretched business, he will join the Chief Inquisitor for a sumptuous feast at tables laden with bowls of chicken broth, partridges, breasts of veal, pâtés and meat savouries flavoured with cinnamon and sugar, a stew in the Castilian manner with all the appropriate ingredients and saffron rice, blancmanges, pastries, and fruits in season. But the King is so abstinent that he refuses to drink any wine, and since the best lesson of all is a good example, everyone accepts it, the example, that is, not the abstinence.

Another example, which no doubt will be of greater profit to the soul since the body is so grossly over-fed, is to be given here today. The procession has commenced, the Dominicans in the vanguard carrying the banner of St Dominic, followed by the Inquisitors walking in a long file until the condemned appear, one hundred and four of them, as we have already stated, all carrying candles and with attendants at their sides, their prayers and mutterings rending the air, by the different hoods and sanbenitos you can tell who is to die and who will be sent into exile, although there is another sign, which never lies, namely that crucifix held on high with its back turned on the women who are to be burned at the stake and the gentle, suffering face of Christ turned toward those who will be spared, symbolic means of revealing to the condemned the fate that awaits them, should they have failed to understand the significance of the robes they are wearing, for these, too, are an unmistakable sign, the yellow sanbenito with the red cross of St Andrew is worn by those whose crimes do not warrant death, the one with the flames pointing downward, known as the upturned fire, is worn by those who have confessed their sins and may therefore be spared, while the dismal grey cassock bearing the image of a sinner encircled by demons and flames has become synonymous with damnation, and is worn by the two women who are to be burned at the stake. The sermon has been preached by Friar John of the Martyrs, the Franciscan provincial, and certainly no one could be more deserving of the task, considering that it was also a Franciscan friar whose virtue God rewarded by granting that the Queen should become pregnant, so profit from this sermon for the salvation of souls, just as the Portuguese dynasty and the Franciscan Order will profit from the assured succession and the promised convent.

The rabble hurls furious insults at the condemned, the women scream abuse as they lean from their window-sills, and the friars prattle amongst themselves, the procession is an enormous snake that cannot be accommodated in the Rossio in a straight line and is therefore forced to coil round and round, as if determined to reach everywhere and offer an edifying spectacle to the entire city, that fellow over there is Simeão de Oliveira, a man without profession or benefice, who claimed to be registered as a secular priest with the Holy Office of the Inquisition and therefore entitled to celebrate Mass and hear confessions and preach, yet who at the same time declared himself to be a heretic and a Jew, rarely has there been such a muddle and to make matters worse, he sometimes called himself Padre Teodoro Pereira de Sousa or Friar Manuel of the Holy Conception, at other times Belchior Carneiro or Manuel Lencastre, and who knows what other names he might have assumed, because every man ought to have the right to choose his own name and be able to change it a hundred times daily, for there is nothing in a name, and that fellow over there is Domingo Afonso Lagareiro, a native and an inhabitant of Portel who claimed to have visions in order to be revered as a saint and practised miraculous cures with blessings, invocations, signs of the cross, and other superstitions, and you can imagine how many impostors there have been before him, and that is Padre António Teixeira de Sousa from the Island of St George, who has been found guilty of soliciting women, a canonical phrase meaning that he fondled and sexually assaulted them, almost certainly by seducing them with words in the confessional, only to end up having furtive intercourse in the sacristy until he was caught, he will be exiled to Angola for life, and this is me, Sebastiana Maria de Jesus, one-quarter converted Jewess, and I have visions and revelations that the Tribunal has dismissed as fraudulent, I hear heavenly voices, but the judges insist they are the devil's work, I believe that I might well be a saint just like all the other saints, or even better, for I can see no difference between them and me, but the judges rebuked me, accusing me of intolerable presumption, of monstrous pride, and of offending God, they told me that I am guilty of blasphemy, heresy, and evil pride, they have gagged me to silence my assertions, heresies, sacrileges, and they will punish me with a public flogging and eight years of exile in Angola, and having listened to the sentences they have passed on me and on others in the procession, I've heard no mention of my daughter, Blimunda, Where can she be, Where are you, Blimunda, if you were not arrested after me, you must have come here looking for your mother, and I shall see you if you are anywhere in the crowd, for only to see you do I want these eyes of mine, they have covered my mouth but not my eyes, ah, heart of mine, leap in my breast if Blimunda is out there, among that crowd that spits on me and throws melon skins and garbage, how they are deceived, I alone know that all may become saints if they so desire, but I am forbidden to cry out and tell them so, at last my heart has given me a sign, my heart has given a deep sigh, I am about to see Blimunda, I am about to see her, ah, there she is, Blimunda, Blimunda, Blimunda, my child, and she has seen me but cannot speak, she must pretend that she does not recognise me, or even pretend to despise me, a mother who is bewitched and excommunicated, although no more than a quarter Jewess and converted, she has seen me, and at her side is Padre Bartolomeu Lourenço, do not speak, Blimunda, just look at me with those eyes of yours, which have the power to see everything, but who can that tall stranger be who stands beside Blimunda and she does not know, alas, she does not know who he can be or where he comes from, whatever will become of them, why do my powers fail me, judging from his tattered clothes, that harrowed expression, that missing hand, he must be a soldier, farewell, Blimunda, for I shall see you no more, and

Blimunda said to the priest, There is my mother, then, turning to the tall man standing beside her, she asked, What is your name, and the man spontaneously told her, thus acknowledging that this woman had a right to question him, Baltasar Mateus, otherwise known as Sete-Sóis.

Sebastiana Maria de Jesus had already passed, along with all the others who were sentenced and the procession came full circle, they whipped those who had been sentenced to a public flogging, and burnt the two women, one having been garrotted first, after she declared that she wanted to die in the Christian faith, while the other was roasted alive for refusing to recant even at the hour of death, in front of the bonfires men and women began to dance, the King withdrew, he saw, ate, and left, accompanied by the Infantes, and returned to the Palace in his coach drawn by six horses and escorted by the royal guard, evening is closing rapidly, but the heat is still oppressive, the heat of the sun is fierce, and the great walls of the Carmelite Convent cast their shadows over the Rossio, the corpses of the two women have fallen among the embers, where their remains will finally disintegrate and at nightfall their ashes will be scattered, not even on the Day of Final Judgment will they be resuscitated, the crowds begin to disperse and return to their homes, having had their faith renewed, and carrying gummed to the soles of their shoes some of the ashes and charred flesh, perhaps even clots of blood, unless the blood evaporated over the embers. Sunday is the Lord's day, a trite observation since every day belongs to the Lord, and the days go on consuming us unless in the name of the same Lord the flames have consumed us more quickly, a double outrage, when with my own reason and will, I refused the aforesaid Lord my flesh and bones and the spirit that sustains my body, son of mine and of me, direct union with myself, the world descending over my hidden face, no different from my hooded face, therefore unknown. Yet we must die.

To anyone present, the words uttered by Blimunda must have sounded callous, There goes my mother, she said, without as much as a sigh, a tear, or any sign of pity, for people are still capable of expressing pity, despite all the hatred, mocking, and jeering, yet this woman who is a daughter and who was much loved, as could be seen from the way her mother gazed upon her, had nothing to say other than, There she is, before turning to a man she had never seen before and asking him, What is your name, as if that were more important than the flogging inflicted on her own mother after months of torture and imprisonment, for no name could save Sebastiana Maria de Jesus once she was sentenced to exile in Angola, where she would remain for the rest of her life, perhaps consoled in spirit and in body by Padre António Teixeira de Sousa, who had acquired a great deal of experience in such matters while still in Portugal, and just as well since the world is not such an unhappy place, even when one is condemned. Once she is back in her own home, however, tears flow from Blimunda's eyes as if they were two fountains, if she should ever see her mother again, it will be at the point of embarkation, but from a distance, much easier for an English captain to release prostitutes than for a condemned mother to kiss her own daughter, for a mother and daughter to bring their faces cheek to cheek, Blimunda's smooth complexion against her mother's furrowed skin, so close and yet so far, Where are we, Who are we, and Padre Bartolomeu Lourenço replies, We are as nothing when compared with the designs of the Lord, if He knows who we are, then resign yourself, Blimunda, let us leave the terrain of God to God, let us not trespass His frontiers, and let us adore Him from this side of eternity, and let us make our own terrain, the terrain of men, for once it has been made, God will surely wish to visit us, and only then will the world be created. Baltasar Mateus, alias Sete-Sóis, makes no attempt to speak but gazes upon Blimunda, each time she returns his gaze, he feels a knot in his stomach, because eyes such as hers have never been seen before, their colouring uncertain, grey, green, or blue, according to the outer light or the inner thought, sometimes they even turn as black as night or a brilliant white, like a splinter of anthracite. Baltasar had come to this house not because they told him he should come, but because Blimunda had asked him his name and he had replied and no further justification seemed necessary. Once the auto-da-fé was over, and the debris cleared away, Blimunda withdrew accompanied by the priest, and when she arrived home she left the door open so that Baltasar might enter. He came in behind them and sat down, the priest closed the door and lit the oil-lamp by the last rays of light coming through a chink in the wall, the reddish light of sunset, which reaches this altitude when the low-lying parts of the city are already enshrouded in darkness, soldiers can be heard shouting on the castle ramparts, in other circumstances Sete-Sóis would be reminiscing about the war, but for the moment he has eyes only for Blimunda, or, rather, for her body, which is tall and slender, like that of the English wench he visualised the very day he disembarked in Lisbon.

Blimunda got up from her stool and lit a fire in the hearth and put a pot of soup on the trivet, and when it began to boil she ladled the soup into two large bowls, which she then served to the two men in silence, for she had not spoken since asking Baltasar some hours before, What is your name, and although the priest was the first to finish eating, she waited until Baltasar had finished, so that she could use his spoon, it was as if in silence she were answering another question, Do your lips accept the spoon that has touched the lips of this man, thus making his what was yours, now making yours what was his, until the meaning of yours and mine was lost, and since Blimunda had answered yes before being asked, I therefore declare you man and wife. Padre Bartolomeu Lourenço waited until Blimunda had finished eating the rest of the soup from the pot, then extended his blessing over her person, over the food and the spoon, over the stool and the fire in the hearth, over the oil lamp and the mat on the floor, and over Baltasar's amputated wrist. Then he left.

Baltasar and Blimunda sat in silence for a whole hour. Baltasar got up only once, to put some wood on the dying fire, and Blimunda stirred once, to trim the wick in the oil lamp, which was consuming the flame, and now that there was light in the room, Baltasar felt able to ask, Why did you ask me my name, whereupon Blimunda replied, Because my mother wanted to know and she was anxious that I should know, How can you tell, when you were unable to speak to her, I can tell, even though I can't explain why I can tell, don't ask me questions I cannot answer, behave as you did before, when you followed me home without asking any questions, and if you've no place to go, why not remain here, I must go to Mafra, there I have my family, my parents, a sister, Stay here until you have to leave, there will always be time for you to return to Mafra, Why do you want me to remain here,

Because it is necessary, I'm not convinced, If you don't wish to remain, then go, I cannot force you to stay here, I cannot find the strength to go away from this place, you have bewitched me, I have bewitched no one, I have uttered no words, I have not touched you, You looked into my soul, I swear I will never look into your soul, You swear you will never do it, yet you have done so already, You don't know what you're saying, I've never once looked inside you, If I stay here, where do I sleep, You sleep with me.

They lay down together. Blimunda was a virgin. What age are you, Baltasar asked her and Blimunda replied, Nineteen, but even as she spoke, she became older. Some drops of blood trickled on to the mat. Dipping the tips of her middle and index fingers into the blood, Blimunda made the sign of the cross and marked a cross on Baltasar's chest, near his heart. They were both naked. From a nearby street they heard the angry shouts of a quarrel, the clashing of swords and scurrying of feet. Then silence. The bleeding had stopped.

When Baltasar woke next morning, he saw Blimunda lying at his side, eating bread, but with her eyes firmly closed. She only opened them when she had finished eating, at that moment they looked grey, and she told him, I shall never look into your soul.

To raise this bread to one's mouth requires little effort, an excellent thing to do when hunger demands it, eating bread nourishes the body and benefits the farmer, some farmers more than others, who from the moment the wheat is cut until the bread is eaten know how to turn their labours to profit, and that is the rule. In Portugal there is never enough wheat to satisfy the perpetual hunger of the Portuguese for bread, and they give the impression of being unable to eat anything else, and that explains why the foreigners who live here, in their anxiety to satisfy our needs, which germinate more abundantly than pumpkin seeds, have dispatched from their own and other lands fleets of a hundred ships laden with grain, like the fleets that have just sailed up the Tagus, firing their salute at the Torre de Belém and presenting the customary documents to the Governor and this time there are more than thirty thousand sacks of grain imported from Ireland, and such abundant supplies have transformed the shortage into a temporary surfeit, so that the granaries and private storehouses are so full of grain that the dealers are desperate to hire storage at any price, posting notices on doorways throughout the city for the attention of anyone with space to rent, the importers find themselves in serious difficulties and are obliged to lower prices because of the sudden glut, and to make matters worse, there is talk of the imminent arrival of a Dutch fleet carrying much the same cargo, but subsequently news arrives that the Dutch fleet has been attacked by a French squadron almost at the approach to the straits, causing the price that was about to be lowered to stay where it is and whenever it proves necessary, several granaries are burned to the ground and a shortage is immediately declared because of the grain lost in the blaze, although it is widely known that there is more than enough grain for everyone. These are the mysteries of commerce as taught by foreign merchants and learned by those who live here, though our own merchants are on the whole cretins and leave it to foreigners to arrange the import of merchandise from other lands and are quite content to buy the grain from foreigners who take advantage of our ingenuousness and get rich at our expense, by buying at prices we do not know and selling at prices we do know to be excessive, while we repay them with malicious tongues and eventually with our lives.

However, since laughter is so close to tears, reassurance so close to anxiety, relief so close to panic, and the lives of individuals and nations hover between these extremes, João Elvas describes for Baltasar Sete-Sóis the splendid martial display the navy of Lisbon marshalled from Belém to Xabregas for two days and two nights, while the infantry and cavalry took up defence positions on land, because a rumour had spread that a French fleet was about to invade, a hypothesis which would transform any nobleman or commoner into another Duarte Pacheco Pereira, and convert Lisbon into another Fortress of Diu, but the invading armada turned out to be a fishing fleet with a consignment of cod, obviously in short supply, judging from the greed with which it was devoured. The ministers received the news with a withered smile, soldiers, arms, and horses were disbanded with a jaundiced smile, and the guffaws of the populace were loud and strident when they found themselves avenged of so many vexations. In short, it would have been much more shameful to have expected a consignment of cod only to find a French invasion than to have expected a French invasion only to be confronted with crates of cod.

Sete-Sóis agrees, But put yourself in the shoes of any soldiers prepared for battle, you know how a man's heart beats furiously at such moments as he thinks to himself, What will become of me, will I come out of this alive, a soldier tenses up when he faces possible death, and imagine his disappointment when he is told they are simply unloading supplies of cod at Ribeira Nova, if the French were to discover our mistake, they would be even more amused at our stupidity. Baltasar is about to become nostalgic again for the war when suddenly he remembers Blimunda and longs to contemplate the colour of her eyes, a battle he wages with his own memory, which remembers one colour much like any other, his own eyes unable to distinguish the colour of her eyes even when he looks straight into them. These thoughts soon dispel any nostalgia he was about to indulge in, and he remarks to João Elvas, There should be some means of discovering who is arriving and what brings them here, the seagulls know these things when they perch on the ship's mast, while we, for whom it is much more important, know nothing, and the old soldier rejoined, The seagulls have wings, the angels, too, but the seagulls do not speak, and angels I have never seen.

Padre Bartolomeu Lourenço was crossing the Palace Square, coming from the Palace, where he had gone at the insistence of Sete-Sóis, who was anxious to find out whether he was entitled to a war pension, if the simple loss of a left hand warranted as much and when João Elvas, who did not know everything about Baltasar's life, saw the priest approach, he continued the conversation and informed Baltasar, That priest who is now approaching is Padre Bartolomeu Lourenço, whom they call the Flying Man, but his wings have not grown sufficiently, so we shall not be able to go and spy out the fleets hoping to enter port or to discover what merchandise they bring or why they have come here. Sete-Sóis was unable to offer any comment, because the priest, pausing at a distance, was beckoning him to approach, and João Elvas was much bemused that his friend should enjoy the protection of Church and State, and began to ask himself if there could be some advantage here for a vagrant soldier like himself. But, busying himself in the meantime, he stretched out his hand for alms, first to a fine gentleman, who readily obliged, then distractedly to a mendicant friar, who passed by bearing a sacred relic that he extended to the faithful so they might kiss it with reverence, with the result that João Elvas finished up by parting with the alms he had collected, Well I'll be damned, it may be a sin but there is nothing like a good curse for giving vent to one's feelings.

Padre Bartolomeu Lourenço assured Sete-Sóis, I've discussed these matters with the judges, they have promised to consider your petition, and when they have reached their decision they will inform me, and when are you likely to know, Father, Baltasar asked with the innocent curiosity of someone who has just arrived at court and is still unfamiliar with its ways, I cannot tell you, but should things delay, perhaps I shall have a word with His Majesty, who honours me with his esteem and protection, You can speak to the King, Baltasar asked in astonishment, while thinking to himself, He can speak to the King, yet he knew Blimunda's mother, who was condemned by the Inquisition, what kind of priest can he be, and this final question, which Sete-Sóis was careful not to voice aloud, left him feeling troubled. Padre Bartolomeu made no attempt to reply but looked him straight in the eye, and there they stood confronting each other, the priest somewhat shorter and more youthful in appearance even though they are both the same age, twenty-six years old, the age we have already established for Baltasar, yet their lives could scarcely be more different, that of Sete-Sóis destined to labour and war and although the war is now over the labour is about to commence, Bartolomeu Lourenço, on the other hand, was born in Brazil and arrived in Portugal for the first time as a young lad endowed with a good mind and an excellent memory, so that by the time he was fifteen his enormous potential was already being fulfilled, he could recite Virgil, Horace, Ovid, Quintus Curtius, Suetonius, Maecenas, and Seneca from beginning to end and back again, or from any passage you cared to quote, and he could also interpret all the fables that had ever been written and explain why they had been invented in the first place by the Greeks and Romans, identify the authors of all the books and verse, both ancient and modern, right back to the year twelve hundred, and if someone were to suggest a theme for a poem, he would improvise some ten verses then and there without a moment's hesitation, he could also expound and defend every philosophical system and discuss the most complicated details, elucidate all the discourses of Aristotle, unravel their intricacies, terms, and middle terms, and clear up all the controversial issues in the Holy Scriptures, whether from the Old or the New Testament, he could recite from memory, in their entirety or in snatches, all the Gospels of the four Evangelists in any order, likewise the Epistles of St Paul and St Jerome, he knew by heart the sequence and dates of every prophet and holy king, and could quote from any passage and in any order from the Book of Psalms, Song of Songs, Book of Exodus, and all the Books of

Kings, as well as from the somewhat less canonical Books of Esdras, which, confidentially speaking, do not give the impression of being all that orthodox, this sublime genius, this prodigious intellect and memory, was the product of a land from which the Portuguese have only exacted gold and diamonds, tobacco and sugar, the riches of the jungle, and everything else that may still be waiting to be discovered there, the land of another world, the land of tomorrow and for centuries to come, not to mention the evangelisation of the Tapuyan Indians, which in itself would gain us eternity.

My friend João Elvas has just told me that you are known as the Flying Man, tell me, Father, why have they given you such a nickname, Baltasar asked him. Bartolomeu Lourenço started to move away, but the soldier pursued him and, walking two paces apart, they proceeded alongside the Arsenal de Ribeira das Naus and past the Royal Palace, and further on, when they reached Remolares, where the square opens up towards the river, the priest rested on a boulder and invited Sete-Sóis to join him and finally answered his question as if it had just been asked, They call me the Flying Man because I have flown, Baltasar was puzzled and, begging pardon for his boldness, pointed out that only birds and angels can fly, and men when they are dreaming, although there is nothing very stable about dreams, You haven't been living in Lisbon very long, at least I don't recall ever having seen you before, No, I was away in the war for four years, and my home is in Mafra, Well, it was two years ago that I flew, the first time I constructed a balloon it went up in flames, then I made a second balloon which landed on the palace roof, and finally I made a third balloon, which went out through a window of the Casa da India, never to be seen again, But did you fly in person or was it only the balloons that flew, Only the balloons but it was just as if I myself had flown, Surely a balloon flying is not the same thing as a man flying, A man stumbles at first, then walks, then runs, and eventually flies, Bartolomeu Lourenço replied, but suddenly he fell to his knees, because the Blessed Sacrament was being taken to some invalid of rank and importance, the priest carrying the pyx containing the Host walked under a canopy supported by six acolytes, trumpets to the fore, and members of a confraternity behind, wearing red cloaks and bearing candles in one hand as well as the religious objects required for administering the Holy Sacrament, some soul was impatient for flight and only waiting to be released from its anchorage, to be set before the wind blowing in from the high seas, from the depth of the universe, or the ultimate confines of the horizon. Sete-Sóis also knelt, resting his iron hook on the ground as he made the sign of the cross with his right hand.

Padre Bartolomeu Lourenço was already on his feet and heading slowly towards the edge of the river, with Baltasar at his heels, and there on one side, a barge was unloading straw in great bales that youths balanced on their shoulders as they ran down the gangway, on the other side, two black slave women were coming to empty their masters' chamber pots, the urine and faeces of the day or week, amidst the natural odours of straw and excrement, the priest confided, I have been the laughing-stock of the court and its poets, one of them, Tomás Pinto Brandão, dubbed my invention a wind machine and declared it would soon perish, and had it not been for the King's support, I don't know what would have become of me, but the King, had faith in my invention and consented that I continue with my experiments on the estate of the Duke of Aveiro at São Sebastião da Pedreira, which finally silenced the gossips and scandalmongers who were maliciously hoping that I would break my legs when I took off from the castle ramparts, although I had never promised any such thing, and that my art had more to do with the jurisdiction of the Holy Office of the Inquisition than with the laws of geometry, Padre Bartolomeu Lourenço, this is something I don't understand, I started life as a simple peasant, and my career as a soldier was short-lived, I do not believe that anyone can fly unless he has grown wings, and those who claim otherwise know as much about flying as they do about olive presses, Nevertheless, you yourself did not invent that hook you are wearing, someone had to discover the need for such an implement and hit on the idea of combining iron and leather in order to make it practical, and the same is true for those ships on the river, at one time sails had not been invented, and before that there were no oars, and before that no helm, and just as man, who inhabits the earth, found it necessary to become a sailor, so he will find it necessary to become a flier,

Anyone who puts sails on a boat is in the water, and in the water he remains, to fly is to soar above the earth up into the sky, where there is no ground to support our feet, We must imitate the birds, who spend as much time in the sky as they do settled on land, So it was because you wanted to fly that you came to know Blimunda's mother, possessed as she was of hidden powers, I heard it rumoured that she had visions of people flying with cloth wings and there are many people who claim to have experienced visions, but what I learned about her sounded so convincing that I secretly went to visit her one day, and we became close friends, And did you discover what you wanted, No, I did not, I soon realised that her insights, if they were genuine, were of another order, and that I should have to go on struggling to overcome my own ignorance without help, and I hope I'm not deceiving myself, It strikes me that those who claim that flying has more to do with the Holy Office of the Inquisition than with the laws of geometry are right and if I were in your shoes I would be twice as cautious, don't forget that prison, exile, and the stake are often the price to be paid for such excesses, but a priest ought to know more about these matters than a common soldier, I'm cautious and I'm not without friends who can protect me, the day will come.

They retraced their steps and passed through Remolares once more. SeteSóis made as if to speak, then held back, and the priest, sensing his hesitation, asked, Is there something worrying you, I'm anxious to know, Padre Bartolomeu Lourenço, why Blimunda always eats bread before opening her eyes in the morning, So you have been sleeping with her, We live under the same roof, Take heed that you're committing adultery and you'd do better to marry her, She doesn't want to marry me, and I'm not certain that I want to marry her and if I go back to my native Mafra one day and she prefers to remain in Lisbon, there's little point in our marrying, but to come back to my question, Why does Blimunda eat bread before opening her eyes in the morning, Yes, if you ever do find out, it will be from her, not me, So you know the answer, That's right, But you won't tell me, All I will tell you is that it's something of a mystery, flying is simple when compared with Blimunda.

Walking and chatting together, they arrived at the stables of a horse trader at the Gate of Corpo Santo. The priest hired a mule and climbed on to the saddle, I'm on my way to São Sebastião da Pedreira to inspect my machine, if you would like to come with me, the mule can carry both of us, Yes I'll come, but on foot, for that's the route followed by the infantry, You're just an ordinary man without either the hooves of a mule or the wings of the Passarola, Is that what you call your flying machine, Baltasar asked, and the priest replied, That's what others have called it to show their contempt.

They climbed up to the Church of St Roch and then, skirting the hills around Taipas, descended through the Praça da Alegria as far as Valverde. Sete-Sóis kept abreast of the mule without any difficulty, and only when they were on flat ground did he fall behind a little, to catch up again on the next slope, whether going up or coming down. Although not a single drop of rain had fallen since April, and that was four months ago, all the fields were green and luxuriant above Valverde, because of the large number of perennial springs, whose waters were exploited for the cultivation of the vegetables that grew in abundance on the outskirts of the city. Having passed the Convent of St Martha and, farther along, that of Princess Joan the Saint, they came upon vast stretches of olive groves, here, too, vegetables were culti- vated, but, in the absence of any natural springs to irrigate the land, the problem was solved by the well sweeps which drew water in buckets tied to a long pole and by donkeys turning water wheels, with their eyes blinkered so that they might imagine themselves to be moving in a straight line like their masters ignoring the fact that if they were really going in a straight line, they would eventually finish up in the same place. For the world itself is like a water wheel, and it is men who by treading it pull it and make it go, and even though Sebastiana Maria de Jesus is no longer here to assist us with her revelations, it is easy to see that if there are no men, the world comes to a standstill.

When they arrived at the gates of the estate, there was no sign of the Duke of Aveiro or of his footmen, for his property was confiscated by the crown, and lawsuits are still in progress to have the estate restored to the House of Aveiro, such lawsuits being painfully slow, and only when the dispute has been resolved will the Duke return from Spain, where he now lives and where he is known as the Duke of Baños, when they arrived, as we were saying, the priest dismounted, took a key from his pocket, and opened the gates as if he were entering his own property. He led the mule into the shade, where he tethered it and slipped a basket of hay and broad beans over its muzzle, and there he left it, relieved of its burden and shaking off with its bushy tail the gnats and horseflies buzzing around the provisions newly arrived from the city.

All the doors and windows of the villa were shuttered, and the estate was abandoned and uncultivated. On one side of the spacious square was a granary, stable, or wine-cellar and now that it was empty it was difficult to say which it had been, for there was no sign of any storage bins, there were no metal rings on the walls, not a single barrel in sight. There was one door with a padlock that could be opened with an ornate key fashioned in the shape of Arabic script. The priest removed the crossbar and pushed the door open, the main building was not empty after all, inside there were canvas cloths, joists, coils of copper wire, iron plates, bundles of willow, all laid out neatly according to the type of material, and in the clear space in the middle stood what looked like an enormous shell, with wires sticking out all over, like a half-finished basket with its structural frame exposed.

Filled with curiosity, Baltasar followed the priest inside, and he could scarcely believe his own eyes, perhaps he had been expecting a balloon, giant sparrow wings, or a sack of feathers, but he never expected anything as strange as this, So, this is your invention, and Padre Bartolomeu Lourenço replied, This is it, and opening a chest, he took out a parchment, which he unrolled, it turned out to be a drawing of a large bird, it had to be the Passarola, this much Baltasar could perceive, and because the design was clearly that of a bird, he was prepared to believe that once all those materials had been assembled the machine would be capable of flying. More for his own reassurance than for that of Sete-Sóis, who saw nothing other than a bird in the design, which was good enough for him, the priest began to explain the details, at first calmly, and then in tones of great excitement, What you see here are the sails, which cleave the wind and move as required, this is the rudder, which steers the machine, not at random but under the skilled control of the pilot, this is the main body of the machine, which assumes the shape of a seashell from prow to stern, with bellows attached just in case the wind should drop, as frequently occurs at sea, and these are the wings, which are essential for balancing the machine in flight, I shall say nothing about these globes, for they are my secret, I need only tell you that without their contents the machine would not be capable of flying, but this is a detail that still causes me some uncertainty, and from the wires forming the roof we shall suspend amber balls, because amber reacts favourably to the heat of the sun's rays, and this should achieve the desired effect, and here is the compass, without which you cannot travel anywhere, and here are the pulleys, used to raise and lower the sails, just as on ships at sea. He fell silent for several minutes, then continued, When everything is assembled and in good working order, I shall be ready to fly. Baltasar found the design most impressive and felt no need for explanations, for since no one can see what is inside a bird, no one really knows what makes it fly, yet it flies nonetheless, a bird is shaped like a bird, and nothing could be simpler, When will you fly, Baltasar inquired, I don't know yet, the priest replied, I need someone to help me, I can't do everything on my own, and there are certain jobs for which I have not enough strength. He fell silent once more, and then asked, Would you like to come and help me. Baltasar drew back, feeling somewhat bewildered, I don't know anything about flying, I'm a simple peasant, apart from tilling the soil, all they ever taught me was how to kill, and as you can see, I've only one hand, With that hand and that hook you can manage anything, and there are certain jobs that a hook can do better than a human hand, a hook feels no pain when it grips a piece of wire or metal, it doesn't get cut or burned, I assure you that Almighty God himself is one-handed, yet He made the world.

Baltasar recoiled in alarm, he made a rapid sign of the cross, in order not to give the devil time to commit any mischief, What are you saying, Padre Bartolomeu Lourenço, where is it written that God is one-handed, No one ever said so, nor has it ever been written, only I say that God's left hand is missing, because it is on His right, at His right hand, that the chosen sit, nor do you find any reference to God's left hand either in the Holy Scriptures or in the writings of the holy doctors of the Church, no one sits at God's left hand, for it is a void, a nothingness, an absence, therefore God is one-handed. The priest gave a deep sigh and concluded, He has no left hand.

Sete-Sóis had been listening attentively. He looked at the design and the materials spread out on the floor, the shell still waiting to take shape, he smiled and, raising his arms slightly, said, If God has only one hand and He made the universe, then this man with only one hand is capable of fastening a sail and tightening the wires to make the machine fly.

THERE IS A time for everything. Padre Bartolomeu Lourenço finds that he does not have enough money to buy the magnets that he believes are essential to make his machine fly and, besides, the magnets have to be imported from abroad, and so, for the present, Sete-Sóis is employed, through the priest's good offices, in the slaughterhouse on the Palace Square where he fetches and carries on his back great carcasses of meat of every kind, rumps of beef, suckling pigs by the dozen, lambs strung together in pairs, passed from hook to hook, causing the sacking with which they are covered to ooze blood. It is a filthy job, although recompensed now and then with leftovers, a pig's foot or a piece of tripe and, when God is willing and the butcher is in the right mood, even with the odd flank of mutton or a slice of rump, wrapped in a crisp cabbage leaf, so that Baltasar and Blimunda are able to eat somewhat better than usual, by dividing and sharing out, and although Baltasar has no say in the sharing, the trade offers some advantages.

Dona Maria Ana's pregnancy is almost over. Her stomach simply could not bear to grow any larger, however much her skin might stretch, her belly is enormous, a cargo-laden ship from India or a fleet from Brazil, from time to time the King inquires how the navigation of the Infante is progressing, if it can be sighted from a distance, if it is being borne by fair winds or has suffered any assaults, such as those inflicted recently on our squadrons off the islands, when the French captured six of our cargo ships and one man-of-war, for all this and worse one might expect from our leaders and the inadequate convoys we provide, and now it seems that the same French are preparing to ambush the rest of our fleet at the entrance to Pernambuco and Bahia, if they are not already lying in wait for our ships, which must have set sail already from Rio de Janeiro. We Portuguese made so many discoveries when there were still discoveries to be made, and now other nations treat us like tame bulls who are incapable of charging, unless by accident. Dona Maria Ana, too, has been informed of these worrying reports about events that had taken place some months earlier, when the Infante in her womb was a mere jelly, a little tadpole, a thingumajig with a large head, extraordinary how a man or a woman are formed, regardless, there inside the ovary, and protected from the outside world, even though it is this very same world that they will have to confront, as king or soldier, as friar or assassin, as an English whore in Barbados or a condemned woman in the Rossio, always as something, never as everything, and never as nothing. For, after all, we can escape from everything, but not from ourselves.

The Portuguese navigations, however, are not always so disastrous. Several days ago a long-awaited ship from Macao finally arrived, having set sail some twenty months earlier, just as Sete-Sóis was leaving to fight in the war, and the ship had made a good voyage despite the time it took, for Macao is situated well beyond Goa, in China, that much-favoured land that excels all other nations in riches and treasures, and merchandise as cheap as one could wish for, besides having the most agreeable and healthy of climates, infirmities and diseases are virtually unknown, which eliminates any need for doctors or surgeons, and the Chinese die only from old age or when they find themselves abandoned by nature, which cannot be expected to protect us forever. The ship took on a load of precious cargo in China, then sailed to Brazil to do some trading and to fill the hold with sugar and tobacco and an abundant supply of gold, activities which detained it for two and a half months in Rio and Bahia, and the return journey from Brazil to Portugal took another fifty-six days, and it was nothing short of miraculous that not a single man fell ill or died during this long and hazardous voyage, the Mass celebrated here every day in honour of Our Lady of Compassion for the Wounded clearly secured the ship's safe return, and helped it to stay on course, notwithstanding allegations that the pilot did not know the route, if such a thing is possible, hence the popular saying that there is nothing so profitable as trade with China. Since things are never quite perfect, however, news soon arrived that civil war had broken out between the settlers in Pernambuco and those in Recife, clashes break out in the region daily, some of them extremely violent, and there have been reports that certain factions are threatening to set fire to plantations and destroy crops of sugar and tobacco, which mean heavy losses for the Portuguese crown.

Whenever it seems opportune, these and other items of news are given to Dona Maria Ana, but she is already floating, indifferent to all around her in the torpor of pregnancy, so it makes little difference whether they give her those reports or decide to suppress them, even that initial moment of glory when she discovered she was pregnant has become a faded memory, the tiniest breeze in the wake of the tornado of pride that gripped her during the first weeks of pregnancy, when she felt like one of those figureheads erected on the ship's prow, though incapable of seeing into the distant horizon, therefore there has to be a telescope and lookout for they can see further. A pregnant woman, no matter whether queen or commoner, enjoys a moment in life when she feels herself to be the oracle of all wisdom, even of that which cannot be translated into words, then, as she watches her stomach swell out of all proportion and begins to experience the other discomforts that accompany pregnancy, her thoughts, not all of them happy, turn to the day when she will finally give birth, and the Queen's mind is constantly beset by disturbing omens, but here the Franciscan Order will come to her assistance, rather than lose the convent they have been promised. All the Franciscan communities of the province take up the challenge by celebrating Masses, making novenas, and encouraging prayers for intentions at once general and particular, both explicit and implicit, so that the Infante may be delivered safely and at a propitious hour, without any defects either visible or invisible, and that the child be male, which would compensate for any minor blemishes unless they were to be regarded as an auspicious sign ordained by divine providence. Most important, a male heir would give the King enormous satisfaction.

Dom João V, alas, will have to be satisfied with a little girl. One cannot have everything, and often when you ask for one thing you receive another, this is the mysterious thing about prayer, we address them to heaven with some private intention, but they choose their own path, sometimes they delay, allowing other prayers to overtake them, frequently they overlap and become hybrid prayers of dubious origin, which quarrel and argue among themselves. This explains why a little girl is born when everyone had prayed for a boy, but, judging from her screams, she is a healthy child with a fine pair of lungs. The entire kingdom is blissfully happy not simply because there is an heir to the throne or on account of the three days of festive illuminations that have been decreed, but also because of the secondary effect achieved by prayers concerning natural forces, for no sooner had the prayers ended than the serious drought that had lasted for eight months was over, and there was rain at long last, only prayers could have brought about this change, the birth of the Infanta has been marked by favourable omens auguring prosperity for the nation, and now there is so much rain that it could only come from God, who is relieving Himself of the vexations we cause Him. The peasants are busy working the land, tilling their fields even when it is raining, the seed springs from the humid earth, just as children spring from wherever they originate, incapable of screaming like a child, the seed murmurs as it is raked by iron tools, and falls over on its side, glistening and offering itself to the rain, which continues to trickle very slowly, an almost intangible dust, the furrow undisturbed, the soil turned over to shelter the seedlings. This birth is very simple but it cannot come about without the things essential for any form of birth, namely, energy and seed. All men are kings, all women are queens, and the labours of all are princes.

We should not, however, lose sight of the numerous distinctions that exist. The Princess is taken to be baptized on the feast of Our Lady of O, a day that is contradictory *par excellence,* for the Queen has already shed her plumpness, and it is easy to see that not all princes are equal after all, the differences clearly demonstrated by the pomp and ceremony with which the name and sacrament are bestowed on this infante or on that infanta, with the entire Palace and Royal Chapel bedecked with draperies and gold, and the court dressed up with so much finery that faces and shapes can scarcely be distinguished beneath all the frills and furbelows. The members of the Queen's household have left the chapel, passing through the Hall of the Tedeschi, and behind comes the Duke of Cadaval, with his train trailing behind him. He walks under a baldachin, the shafts supported by privileged nobles of the highest rank and the counsellors of state, and in his arms he carries none other than the newborn Infanta, swathed in fine linen robes that are gathered with bows and ribbons, and behind the baldachin comes the appointed governess, the dowager Condesa de Santa Cruz, and all the Queen's ladies-in-waiting, some pretty and some not so pretty, and finally a half-dozen marquises and the Duke's son, who carry the symbolic towel, the salt cellar, the holy oils, and all the other para-phernalia associated with the sacrament of baptism, so there is something for everyone to carry.

Seven bishops, who look like seven planets in gold and silver as they officiate on the steps of the high altar, baptise the Infanta Maria Xavier Francisca Leonor Bárbara, already referred to as Dona, even though she is only a tiny babe in arms and is given to drooling and who can tell what she will be doing when she grows up. The Infanta wears a cross set with precious gems, valued at five thousand cruzados, a gift from her godfather and uncle, the Infante Dom Francisco, and the same Dom Francisco presented her mother, the Queen, with a decorative aigrette, no doubt out of gallantry, and a pair of exquisite diamond earrings valued at twenty-five thousand cruzados, truly magnificent but made in France.

For this special occasion, the King has momentarily laid aside his royal prerogatives and attends the ceremony in public instead of from behind a screen and in order to show his respect for the mother of his child, he joins the Queen on her dais, so the happy mother is seated beside the happy father, although on a lower chair, and in the evening there are fireworks. Sete-Sóis has come down with Blimunda from the castle above the city to see the lights and decorations, the palace festooned with banners, and the festive arches specially erected by the guilds. Sete-Sóis is feeling more weary than usual, probably as a result of having carried so much meat for the banquets being held to celebrate the birth and baptism of the Infanta. His left arm is hurting after so much pulling, dragging, and heaving. His hook rests inside the knapsack that he carries over one shoulder. Blimunda is holding his right hand.

Some months previously, Friar Antony of St Joseph died a holy death. Unless he should appear to the King in his dreams, he will no longer be able to remind him of his promise, but there is no cause for alarm, Neither lend to the poor, nor borrow from the rich, and make no promises to a friar, but Dom João V is a king who keeps his word. We shall have our convent.

BALTASAR HAS SLEPT on the right-hand side of the pallet ever since they spent their first night together, because his right arm and hand are intact and when he turns towards Blimunda he can hold her against him, run his fingers from the nape of her neck down to her waist, and even lower still if their sexual appetites have been roused in the heat of sleep, in the fantasy of some dream, or because they were already craving sex when they went to bed. Their union is illicit out of choice, and their marriage is unsanctified by Holy Mother Church, for they disregard the social conventions and proprieties, and if he feels like having sex, she will oblige, and if she craves it, he will gratify her. Perhaps some deeper and more mysterious sacrament sustains this union, the sign of the cross imprinted with the blood of breached virginity when, by the yellow light of the oil lamp, they lie on their backs resting, and their first breach of custom is to lie there as naked as the day they were born, Blimunda has wiped from between her legs a discharge of deep-red blood, and this was their communion, if it is not heresy to say so and even greater heresy to have done so. Many months have passed since that first night together, and we have already entered into a new year, the rain can be heard pattering down on the roof, there are strong currents of wind blowing across the river and the straits, and although dawn is approaching the sky is still in darkness. Anyone else might be deceived, but not Baltasar, who always awakens at the same hour, long before the sun rises, a habit he acquired during his restless days and nights as a soldier, and he remains alert as he lies watching the shadows recede to uncover objects and humans, his chest heaving with that enormous sense of relief as day breaks and the first, indistinct rays of greyish light filter through the chinks in the wall until Blimunda is awakened by a faint sound, and this provokes another, more persistent sound, which is unmistakable, the sound of Blimunda eating bread, and once she has finished she opens her eyes, turns toward Baltasar, and rests her head on his shoulder while placing her left hand where his is missing, arm touches arm, wrist touches wrist, life is amending death as best it can. But today things will be different. On several occasions Baltasar has asked Blimunda why she eats bread every morning before opening her eyes and has begged of Padre Bartolomeu Lourenço to explain all this secrecy she once told him that she had fallen into this habit as a child, the priest, however, confided that it was a great mystery, so great that flying was a mere trifle by comparison. Today we shall know.

When Blimunda awakens, she stretches out her hand to retrieve the little sack in which she keeps her bread, only to find that it is not in its usual place by her pillow. She runs her hand over the floor and the pallet and fumbles under the pillow and then she hears Baltasar say, Don't bother searching, for you will not find it and Blimunda, covering her eyes with clenched fists, implores him, Give me my bread, Baltasar, for pity's sake, give me my bread, First you must tell me what all this means, I cannot, she cried out, as she made a sudden effort to get up, but Sete-Sóis restrained her with his right hand and gripped her firmly by the waist, she put up a fierce struggle but he held her down with his right leg, and with his free hand he tried to pull her fists from her eyes, terrified, she started to cry out once more, Let me go, she screamed, making such a din that Baltasar released her, startled by her vehemence, he felt almost ashamed of having treated her so roughly, I didn't mean to hurt you, I only wanted to clear up this mystery, Give me my bread and I shall tell you everything, On your oath, What use are oaths if a simple yes or no is not enough, There's your bread, eat, said Baltasar removing the small bag from the knapsack he was using as a pillow.

Shielding her face with her forearm, Blimunda finally ate the bread. She munched it slowly. When she had finished she gave a deep sigh and opened her eyes. The grey light pervading the room was tinged with blue on the far side, a thought that might have occurred to

Baltasar had he learned to think in such poetic terms, but, rather than indulge in refinements better suited to the antechambers at court or the convent parlour, he was absorbed by the heat of his own blood as Blimunda turned to face him, her eyes growing dark with sudden flashes of green light, what did secrets matter now, much better to go back to learning what he already knew, Blimunda's body, her secret could be solved some other time, because once this woman has made a promise, she is certain to keep it,. Do you remember the first time we slept together, she asks him, when you said I had looked inside you, I remember, You did not know what you were saying, nor did you know what you were hearing when I told you that I would never look inside you. Baltasar had no time to reply and he was still trying to comprehend the meaning of those words and of other incredible words heard in that room when she told him, I can look inside people.

Sete-Sóis raised himself on the pallet, feeling suspicious and uneasy, You're making fun of me, no one can look inside people, I can, I don't believe you, First you insisted on knowing and said you would not rest until you knew, now you know, and you say you don't believe me, perhaps it's just as well, but in future don't take away my bread, I will only believe you if you can tell me what I am feeling this very minute, I can't see anything unless I'm fasting, besides, I promised that I would never look inside you, I'm sure you're trying to make fun of me, And I'm telling you it's the truth, How can I trust you, Tomorrow I shan't eat anything when I awake, we'll go out together and then I will tell you what I can see, but I won't look at you, and you will avoid my eyes, Is that agreed, Agreed, Baltasar replied, but explain this mystery, how did you come by these powers, if you're not deceiving me, Tomorrow you will see that I am telling the truth, But aren't you afraid of the Inquisition, others have paid dearly for much less, My powers have nothing to do with heresy or witchcraft, my eyes are quite normal, Yet your mother was flogged and sentenced to exile for having spoken of visions and revelations, did you learn these things from her, It's not the same thing, I only see what is in the world, I cannot see what lies beyond it, whether it be heaven or hell, I practise neither enchantments nor hypnosis, I simply see things, Yet you signed yourself with your own blood, then made the sign of the cross on my chest with the same blood, surely that is witchcraft, The blood of virginity is the water of baptism, that much I discovered when you possessed me and as I felt you ejaculate inside me, I divined your gestures, What powers are these you possess, I see what exists inside bodies, and sometimes what lurks beneath the earth, I can see what lies below the skin, and sometimes even what is underneath people's clothing, but I only see these things when I am fasting, I lose my gift when the quarter of the moon changes, but it is soon restored, and I only wish that I did not possess it, Why, Because what the skin conceals ought never to be seen, The soul as well, have you seen into someone's soul, No, never, Perhaps the soul does not reside in the body after all, I cannot tell you, for I have never seen a soul, Perhaps because the soul cannot be seen, Perhaps, but now let me go, take your leg away, I want to get up.

For the rest of that day, Baltasar wondered if he had really held such a conversation or if he had dreamed it or if he had simply been in Blimunda's dream. He looked at the enormous carcasses suspended from the iron hooks waiting to be quartered, he strained his eyes, yet all he could see was animal flesh, opaque, flayed, and livid, and as he looked at the lumps and slices of raw meat scattered over the wooden benches and being thrown on to the scales, he realised that Blimunda's powers were more of a curse than a benefit, the entrails of these animals were not exactly a pleasant sight, which was no doubt equally true of the entrails of people, who are also made of flesh and blood. Besides, he had learned on the battlefield what he was now confirming, namely, that to discover what is inside human beings, you always have to use a cleaver, a cannon ball, a hatchet, the blade of a sword, a knife, or a bullet, only in this way can you pierce the virginity of fragile skin, then the bones and entrails are exposed, and it is not worth blessing yourself with this blood because it is no longer the blood of life, but of death. Although Baltasar's mind is confused, these are the things he would say if he could order his thoughts and rid them of everything superfluous, it is not even worth asking him, What are you thinking about, Sete-Sóis, for he would only reply, believing himself to be telling the truth, I'm not thinking about anything, and yet he had thought of all these things and much more upon recalling the sight of his own bones, a deathly white in that torn flesh, when they carried him behind the lines, and that severed hand, which he saw being kicked aside by the surgeon's foot, Bring in the next casualty, and the next to be carried in, wretched fellow, were he to have escaped with his life, would have been left without both legs. One would like to probe these mysteries, but to what purpose, when it ought to be enough for any man to wake up in the morning and feel lying beside him, asleep or awake, the woman who has appeared with time, the same time that will take her tomorrow, perhaps to some other bed, some humble pallet like the one here on the ground, or some luxurious four-poster with marquetry and gilded festoons, because fortunes change and it is madness or a tempta- tion sent by Satan to ask her, Why are you eating your bread with your eyes closed, if you're blind when you don't eat, then don't eat it, Blimunda, and you won't see so much, for to see as much as you do is the greatest of sorrows, some sixth sense we humans cannot yet with- stand, And you, Baltasar, what do you think about, Nothing, I think about nothing, nor can I say if I have ever thought about anything, Hey, Sete-Sóis, fetch that lump of salt pork over there.

He has not slept and she has not slept. Dawn has broken and they have stayed in bed, Baltasar got up only to eat some cold crackling and to drink a mug of wine, then went back, Blimunda remained still, her eyes firmly closed, prolonging her fast so that her powers of vision might be intensified, her eyes sharp and penetrating when they should finally confront the light of day because this is a day for seeing, not just for looking, which may be all right for all those who possess eyes yet suffer from another form of blindness. The morning passed and it was time for dinner, the name given to the midday meal, let us not forget. Blimunda finally gets up, her eyelids barely open, and Baltasar has his second meal, Blimunda, in order to see, eats nothing, Baltasar, even fasting would still see nothing, and then they leave the house together. The day is so tranquil that it seems at variance with these events, Blimunda walks ahead, Baltasar close behind, so that though she does not see him, he will be able to listen when she tells him what she is seeing.

And she tells him, That woman who is seated on the doorstep is carrying a male infant in her womb, but the child has two strands of cord around its neck, so it could either live or die, I cannot be sure what will happen and this ground we are treading has a top surface of red clay and a layer of white sand underneath, below the sand is gravel, and farther down is granite, right at the bottom is a huge cavity full of water, with the skeleton of a fish bigger than me, that old man who is passing also has an empty stomach, and he's losing his sight, and the young man staring at me has his penis wasted away by venereal disease and it oozes pus like a tap dripping water, yet despite his infirmity he's always smiling, his male vanity makes him go on staring and smiling at women in the street, I hope that you suffer from no such vanity, Baltasar, and that you will avoid catching any disease, and there goes a friar who has a solitary worm in his bowels, which he has to nourish by eating enough for two, but he would gorge himself even if he had no such worm, and now observe those men and women kneeling before the Shrine of St Crispin, you see them make the sign of the cross, and strike their breasts and one another as an act of penance, but what I see there are sackfuls of excrement and worms and a tumour that will end up strangling the man, he doesn't know yet, but tomorrow he will know, and then, as now, it will be much too late, for the tumour is incurable, But how can I believe these things to be true, when I cannot see them with my own eyes, Baltasar asked her, where-upon Blimunda told him, Make a hole over there in the ground with your spike and you will unearth a silver coin, Baltasar obeyed, he made a hole in the ground and extracted a coin, You were wrong, Blimunda, the coin is made of gold, All the better for you, I should not have ventured to make any guesses, because I always confuse silver with gold, nevertheless, I did foretell that you would find a coin and that it would be precious, what more can you ask, when you have been told the truth and found something of value, and if the Queen passed by this very minute, I could tell you that she is pregnant again, but it is still too early to verify whether it will be a boy or a girl, my mother always used to say that the worst thing about the female womb is that, when it has swollen once, it has a tendency to go on swelling over and over again, I can also tell you that the quarter of the moon has started to change, because I can feel my eyes burning and there are yellow shadows passing before them like vermin crawling and extending their claws, gnawing at my eyes, for the love of God, Baltasar, I beg of you to take me home and give me something to eat, and then lie down beside me, walking ahead of you, I cannot see you, and I have no wish to see inside you, I only want to look at you, at that swarthy, bearded face, those tired eyes, and that sad expression even when you lie at my side and make love to me, take me home, I shall walk behind you with my eyes lowered, for I have sworn never to look inside you, I shall keep that oath and deserve to be punished if I ever break my promise.

Let us now raise our eyes, for it is time to watch the Infante Dom Francisco firing shots from the window of his palace on the banks of the Tagus at the sailors perched on the yards of their ships to prove what a good shot he is, and when he hits, they fall on to the deck, all of them bleeding profusely, several of them dead and when he misses, they are left with broken limbs, the Infante claps his hands with irrepressible glee, while his footmen reload his gun, one of the footmen might even be the brother of that wounded sailor, but from this distance not even the voice of blood and kinship can be heard, there goes another blast, another shout, and another casualty, and the quartermaster does not dare to order the sailors to get down, for fear that he should annoy His Royal Highness, besides, no matter how many casualties, the manoeuvres have to be carried out, and the interpretation that the quartermaster does not dare annoy His Royal Highness is the ingenuous opinion of someone viewing events from afar and it is much more likely that no such humane considerations even enter his head, There goes that son of a bitch taking potshots at my sailors who are preparing to sail across the ocean to make fresh discoveries in India or Brazil and all he can do is order them to scrub the decks instead, and there we shall leave the matter rather than bore the reader with tiresome repetition, after all, if the sailors are ultimately fated to die beyond the straits from bullets fired by some French pirate, it is preferable that they be shot here, for, dead or wounded, at least they are in their own country, and speaking of French pirates, our gaze travels as far as Rio de Janeiro, where a French armada has invaded without firing a single shot, for the Portuguese officials, whether responsible for governing on land or sea, were having their siesta, the French were free to anchor at their convenience and disembarked without being challenged, they behaved as if they were on their own territory, and the Governor acceded to their demands by giving formal instructions that no one was to attempt to remove or conceal their possessions, he must have had his own good reasons, at least those induced by fear, and the French exploited the situation by looting and plundering everything they could find, anything they were unable to remove and transport back to their ships, they sold and auctioned in the public squares, and there was no lack of customers to purchase what the French had stolen from them within the last hour and they could scarcely have shown more contempt for the Portuguese authorities as they set fire to the Treasury Buildings, and some of the invaders marauded in the surrounding countryside, at the instigation of Jewish informers who put them on the trail of caches of gold and treasure belonging to certain high-ranking officials, outrages committed by some two or three thousand Frenchmen against our force of ten thousand, the Governor was clearly in collusion with the enemy, so no more need be said, there were also many traitors among the Portuguese forces, although appearances can be deceptive, for example, the soldiers from the regiments of Beira who, as we mentioned, went over to the enemy were not deserters, they simply went where they could be sure of finding something to eat and others returned to their homes, which is only to be expected and scarcely an act of disloyalty, any nation that wants soldiers so that it may lead them to their death should at least try to feed and clothe them while they are still alive, and not leave them to rove barefoot and in tatters without any discipline or military manoeuvres, for these same men would derive greater satisfaction from putting their own captain in the line of fire than from wounding a Spaniard on the opposing side, and what could be more amusing than the sight of those thirty ships from France we mentioned earlier. Some claimed to have seen them from Peniche, others in the nearby Algarve, and as a precaution the watch-towers on the Tagus were garrisoned and the entire marine force put on the alert as far as Santa Apolónia, it is unlikely that the ships could have made their way downriver from Santarém or Tancos, but the French are capable of anything, and because the Portuguese had few ships at their disposal, they sought the assistance of some English and Dutch convoys that were at hand, combined forces were then positioned to confront the enemy, which was believed to be approaching in that imaginary zone and just as on the famous occasion when a fishing fleet landing cod was mistaken for an invading fleet, this time the supposed enemy turned out to be a consignment of wine from Porto, the ships assumed to be French men-of-war were in fact English trading vessels, and their crews had a jolly good laugh at our expense, foreigners find us an easy target for jokes, although it should be said that we are also quite good at making them about ourselves, We might as well be frank, our stupidity is clear for all to see, without recourse to Blimunda's visionary powers, and then there was the episode of the clergyman, who frequented prostitutes who did everything to please their client, and, better still, allowed their client to do everything he pleased, thus satisfying the appetites of the stomach while indulging those of the flesh, and this clergyman dutifully said his Masses but whenever he saw his chance would make off with any valuables in sight, until one day he was denounced by a prostitute from whom he had taken a great deal more than he had given, the bailiffs arrived to arrest him by order of the district magistrate at a house where he had moved in with other innocent women, they forced an entry but were so haphazard in carrying out their search that they failed to find him, the clergyman was hiding in one bed while they searched another, thus allowing him enough time to make his escape, stark naked, he scampered down the stairs, clearing his way with kicks and punches, the bailiffs' men took quite a beating and, muttering to themselves, chased after this lecherous clergyman, who knew how to use his fists, they pursued him down the Rua dos Espingardeiros at eight o'clock in the morning, just as people were getting out of bed, a fine start to the day, with howls of laughter coming from every door and window in the street as the naked clergyman ran like a hare, the bailiffs' men in hot pursuit, his mighty penis erect, and may God bless him, for a man so well endowed should not be servicing altars but women in bed, the sight of his penis gave quite a shock to the female residents, poor souls, taken unawares, just as the innocent women who were praying in the Church of Conceição Velha were taken unawares when they saw the clergyman rush down the aisle panting for breath, as naked as Adam but covered with sins, sounding bell clappers and rattles, he appeared at the stroke of one, hid at the stroke of two, and had disappeared forever at the stroke of three and the providential intervention of the clergy played some part in this vanishing trick and after covering his nakedness, they helped him escape over the rooftops, an incident which need cause no great surprise for the Franciscan friars of Xabregas are notorious for hoisting women up into their cells and enjoying their favours, and at least this clergyman climbed on foot to the brothels, where the women longed to receive the sacrament, as usual, everything oscillates between sin and penance, for it is not only during the Holy Week processions that excited flagellants come out on the streets, how many wicked thoughts the women who live in the centre of Lisbon must have to confess, and those sanctimonious old maids of Conceição Velha, once they have feasted their eyes on that lustful clergyman with the bailiffs' men after him, Catch him, catch him, and how they wished they could catch him for something else I could mention, ten paternosters, ten salve reginas, and an offering of ten réis to our patron, St Antony, and to lie down for a whole hour, with arms crossed, on one's stomach, as prostration demands, or on one's back, which is a position of the most heavenly pleasure, but always lifting up one's thoughts and not one's skirts, for that is being reserved for the next sin.

Every man uses his eyes to see what he can or what his eyes will permit, or some little part of what he would like to see, unless it happens to be a coincidence, as in the case of Baltasar who, since he worked in the slaughterhouse, went with the youngest of the porters and apprentice butchers to the square to watch the arrival of Cardinal Nuno da Cunha, who is about to receive the red hat from the hands of the King, accompanied by the Papal Legate in a litter upholstered in crimson velvet and trimmed with gold braiding, the panels, too, are sumptuously decorated in gilt, with the Cardinal's coat of arms on either side. The Cardinal's procession includes a carriage that travels empty as a mark of personal esteem, and another carriage for the steward and private secretary, and the chaplain who carries the Cardinal's train when there is a train to be carried, two open carriages of Spanish origin carry the chaplains and pages, and in front of the litter are twelve footmen, who, together with all the coachmen and litter-bearers, add up to an impressive entourage, and we must not forget the liveried servant who heads the procession with the silver mace, it is indeed a happy populace that rejoices in such feasts and gathers in the streets to watch the nobility pass in procession as they accompany the Cardinal to the Royal Palace where Baltasar cannot enter to watch the ceremony, but, knowing the powers of Blimunda, let us imagine that she is there, we shall see the Cardinal moving forward between the guard of honour, and as he enters the last of the audience chambers, the King comes out to greet him and he gives him the holy water, and in the next chamber the King kneels on a velvet cushion and the Cardinal on another and farther back, in front of an ornate altar suitably decorated for the occasion, one of the palace chaplains celebrates High Mass with all due pomp and ceremony, and once the Mass is ended, the Papal Legate takes the papal brief of nomination and hands it to the King, who formally receives it before handing it back so that the Papal Legate may read it aloud, this, it should be said, to conform with protocol, not because the King is incapable of reading Latin, and once the reading is over, the King receives the Cardinal's biretta from the Papal Legate and places it on the Cardinal's head who is naturally overcome with Christian humility, for these are onerous responsibilities for a poor man finding himself chosen to become one of God's intimates, but the courtesies and reverences are not quite finished, first the Cardinal goes off to change his vestments and when he reappears he is dressed all in red, as befits his rank and is summoned once more into the presence of the King, who stands beneath the ceremonial canopy, twice the Cardinal puts on and then removes his biretta, and the King goes through the same ritual with his hat, and then, repeating it a third time, he steps forward four paces to embrace the Cardinal, finally they both cover their heads and, seated, the one higher than the other, they say a few words, and their speeches made, it is time for them to take their leave, hats are raised and replaced, the Cardinal, however, still has to pay his respects to the Queen in her apartments, where he goes through the same ritual once more, step by step, until finally the Cardinal descends to the Royal Chapel, where a Te Deum is about to be sung, Praise be to God, who has to endure such ceremonies.

Upon arriving home, Baltasar tells Blimunda what he has seen, and since fireworks have been announced, they go down into the Rossio after supper and either there are few torches on this occasion, or the wind has blown them all out, but what matters is that the Cardinal has his biretta, it will hang at the top of his bed while he sleeps, and should he get up in the middle of the night to admire it unobserved, let us not censure this prince of the Church, for we are all susceptible to vanity, and unless a cardinal's biretta specially commissioned and sent from Rome is some mischievous plot designed to test the modesty of these great men, then their humility deserves our wholehearted confidence, they are truly humble if they are prepared to wash the feet of the poor, as this Cardinal has done and will do again, as the King and Queen have done and will do again, the soles of Baltasar's boots are now worn through and his feet are dirty, thus complying with the first condition whereby the Cardinal or King should kneel before him one day, with fine linen towels, silver basins, and rose-water, the second condition Baltasar is certain to satisfy, since he is poorer than ever, and the third condition is that he be chosen for being a virtuous man who cultivates virtue. There is still no sign of the pension he petitioned, and the entreaties of his patron, Padre Bartolomeu Lourenço, have been to no avail, he will soon lose his job at the slaughterhouse on some flimsy pretext, but there are still bowls of soup to be had at the convent gates and alms from the confraternities, it is difficult to die of hunger in Lisbon, and the Portuguese have learned to eke out a meagre existence. Meantime, the Infante Dom Pedro has been born, though as the second child, he only warranted four bishops at his baptism, he did gain some advantage, however, by having the Cardinal at the ceremony, who had still not been elected when his sister was baptized, and meantime, news arrived that in the siege of Campo Maior large numbers of the enemy had been killed and that few men died on our side, although by tomorrow they may be saying that large numbers of our men have died and few on the enemy side, or tit for tat, which is how things are likely to turn out when the world finally comes to an end and the dead are counted on all sides. Baltasar tells Blimunda of his experiences in the war, as she grips the hook protruding from his left arm as if she were holding a human hand and he can remember the feel of his own skin as it touches Blimunda's hand.

The King has gone to Mafra to choose the site where the convent is to be built. It will stand on the hill known as the Alto da Vela from where one can look out to sea, and where there is no lack of fresh water for irrigating the convent's future orchards and kitchen gardens, the Franciscans have no intention of being outdone by the Cistercians at Alcabaça when it comes to cultivating the land, and although St Francis of Assisi was content with a wilderness, he was a saint and is now dead. Let us pray.

THERE IS NOW another piece of iron in the knapsack of Sete-Sóis, the key to the Duke of Aveiro's estate. Having obtained the aforesaid magnets but not the secret substances, Padre Bartolomeu Lourenço was able to start assembling his flying machine and carry out the contract which named Baltasar as his right-hand man, since his left hand was unnecessary, just as God Himself has no left hand, according to the priest, and he has studied these highly sensitive matters and so should know. And since Costa do Castelo is some distance from Sebastião da Pedreira, and much too far to travel to and fro every day, Blimunda decided that she would abandon her home and follow Sete-Sóis wherever he might be. It was no great loss, the roof of the house and three of its walls were unsafe, the fourth wall on the other hand, could not have been safer, for it formed part of the castle wall, which had been standing there for many centuries, just so long as no one passes by and thinks to himself, Look, an empty house, and without further ado moves in, the house will crumble within the next twelve months, nothing but a few cracked bricks and rubble remaining of the house where Sebastiana Maria de Jesus lived and where Blimunda first opened her eyes to perceive the world, for she was born fasting.

One trip proved sufficient to transport their modest possessions, Blimunda carrying a bundle on her head and Baltasar another on his back, and that was all. They rested at intervals during the long journey, silent as they went, for they had nothing to say to each other, even a simple word becomes superfluous when our lives are changing, and even more so when we are changing, too. As for baggage, it should always be light when a man and a woman take their possessions with them, or those of the one to the other, so that they do not have to retrace their footsteps, for that is a great waste of precious time.

In a corner of the coach-house they unrolled their pallet and mat, and at the foot of the pallet they placed a bench in front of a chest, as if tracing an imaginary line to mark the boundaries of new territory, they then improvised partitions with cloths suspended from wires, to give the impression of a real house where they could be alone if they so desired. When, for example, Padre Bartolomeu Lourenço comes, Blimunda, if she has no washing to keep her at the wash-tub or cooking to keep her at the stove, or if she is not helping Baltasar by passing the hammer and pincers, the wire and cane, will be able to withdraw into her own little domain, which even the most adventurous of women long for at times, even though the adventure may not be as exciting as the one about to unfold. Drawn curtains also serve for the confessional, the father confessor seated on the outside, the penitents, one after the other, kneeling on the inside, which is precisely where both constantly commit sins of lust, besides being cohabitants, if that word is not more grievous than the sin itself, a sin readily absolved, however, by Padre Bartolomeu Lourenço, who has before his eyes an even greater sin, namely that of ambition and pride, for he plans to ascend into the heavens one day, where so far only Christ and the Virgin have made their ascent, along with a few chosen saints, these various parts scattered around which Baltasar is painstakingly assembling while Blimunda says from the other side of the partition, in a voice loud enough for Sete-Sóis to hear, I have no sins to confess.

To fulfil the obligation of attending Holy Mass, there is no lack of churches in the vicinity, such as that of the discalced Augustinians, which is closest of all, but if, as often happens, Padre Bartolomeu Lourenço is occupied with his priestly duties or commitments at court which take up more time than usual even though he does not have to come here every day, if the good padre does not turn up to kindle the flame of Christian zeal that Baltasar and Blimunda undoubtedly possess, he with his irons, she with her fire and water, and both with the passion that drives them on to that pallet on the floor, then they often forget their obligation to attend the divine sacrifice and fail to confess their omission which leads us to question whether their presumed souls are all that Christian after all. Whether they remain in the coach house or go out to bask in the sunshine, they are surrounded by extensive lands in a state of neglect, fruit trees are returning to their natural wildness, brambles cover the pathways, and where there was once a kitchen garden, weeds and ivy have taken over, but Baltasar has already cleared the worst of the overgrowth with a scythe, and Blimunda has used a hoe to cut the roots and lay them out to dry in the sun and in the fullness of time, this land will produce something to compensate for their labours. But they also enjoy moments of leisure, and when Baltasar begins to feel his head itching, he rests it on Blimunda's lap and she picks off the lice, we should not be too surprised by the behaviour of these lovers and inventors of airships, if such a term existed in those days, just as one now talks about armistice instead of peace. Blimunda, alas, has no one to remove the lice from her head. Baltasar does his best, but though he has enough hands and fingers to catch lice, he has neither the fingers nor the hand to secure Blimunda's dark, honey-coloured hair, for no sooner does he succeed in separating the strands than they fall back into place, thus concealing the prey. Life provides for everyone.

Nor are things always easy at work. It is a mistake to believe that no one misses his left hand. If God can manage without it, that is because He is God but a man needs both hands, the one hand washes the other and they both wash the face, how often has Blimunda had to wash away the grime on the back of Baltasar's hand, something he found impossible to do, such are the misfortunes of war, and insignificant ones at that, for many a soldier has lost both arms or both legs or even his private parts, nor do they have a Blimunda to assist them, or, perhaps have lost her because of their wounds. The hook is perfect for gripping a sheet of metal or weaving cane, the spike is ideal for boring eyeholes in the canvas, but material objects are loath to obey without the contact of human flesh, they are afraid that if human beings, to whom they have become accustomed, should disappear, then the world will degenerate into chaos. That is why Blimunda always comes to Baltasar's assistance, for when she arrives the rebellion ends, Just as well you've come, Baltasar says to her, or could it be the objects responding.

Sometimes Blimunda rises early, and before eating her bread, she moves quietly along the wall, taking great care not to look at Baltasar, she draws back the curtain and examines the work that has been already completed, to see if there are any flaws in the canework or any air bubbles in the metal, then, having finished her inspection, she finally starts to munch her daily ration of bread, and as she eats she gradually becomes just as blind as all those people who see only what is before their eyes. When she carried out this inspection for the first time, Baltasar commented to Padre Bartolomeu Lourenço, This iron is no good, because it's fractured inside, How do you know, It was Blimunda who saw it, whereupon the priest turned to Blimunda, smiled, then looked from the one to the other, and said, You are Sete-Sóis or Seven-Suns, because you can see in the light of day, and you are Sete-Luas or Seven-Moons, because you can see in the darkness of night, and so Blimunda, who until that moment had only been called Blimunda de Jesus after her mother, became known as Sete-Luas and she was well baptised, for that name had been bestowed on her by a priest, and was not just a nickname given by a nodding acquaintance. That night the suns and moons slept together in each other's embraces while the stars circled slowly in the heavens, Moon, where are you, Sun, where are you going.

Whenever possible, Padre Bartolomeu Lourenço comes to the estate to rehearse the sermons he has written, the walls here have an excellent echo, sufficient to make the words ring, yet without any of those loud reverberations that convey the sound but end up obliterating meaning. This is how the words of the prophets must have sounded in the desert or the public square, locations without walls, or at least without walls in the immediate vicinity, and therefore unaffected by the laws of acoustics, the eloquence of words depends on the instrument rather than on the ears that listen or the walls that cause them to reverberate. These holy sermons require the ambience of a graceful oratory with chubby angels and saints in ecstasy, with much swirling of robes, shapely arms, curvaceous thighs, ample bosoms, and much rolling of eyes, which proves that all roads lead not to Rome but to the gratification of the flesh. The priest takes enormous pains with his diction, especially since there is someone here to listen, but, either because of the inhibiting presence of the flying machine or because of the indifference of his audience, the phrases fail to soar or resound and the priest's words become muddled and one can scarcely believe that this is the same Padre Bartolomeu Lourenço whose fame as an orator has provoked comparisons with that of Padre António Vieira, whom may God watch over as he was once watched over by the Inquisition. Padre Bartolomeu Lourenço was here to rehearse the sermon he was about to deliver at Salvaterra de Magos, where the King and his court were in residence, a sermon for the feast of the Nuptials of St Joseph, which he had been invited to deliver by the Dominican friars, therefore it is clearly no great disadvantage to be known as the Flying Man and to be regarded as being somewhat eccentric, if even the followers of St Dominic solicit your services, not to mention the King himself, who is still young and amuses himself playing with toys, this explains why the King protects Padre Bartolomeu Lourenço and why he has such an enjoyable time with the nuns in their convents as he gets them pregnant one after another, or several at a time, and when the King's story is finally told, historians will be able to list the scores of children he fathered in this way, pity the poor Queen, what would have become of her had it not been for her father confessor, Padre António Stieff of the Society of Jesus, who counselled resignation, and those dreams in which the Infante Dom Francisco appeared with the corpses of sailors dangling from the pommels of his mules, and what would have become of Padre Bartolomeu Lourenço if the Dominicans who commissioned the sermon had arrived unexpectedly and discovered his flying machine, the maimed Baltasar, the clairvoyant Blimunda, and the preacher in full spate, chiselling fine phrases and perhaps concealing thoughts that Blimunda would not perceive even if she were to fast for a whole year.

Padre Bartolomeu Lourenço finishes his sermon but he is not interested in knowing whether he has edified his audience, and is content to inquire somewhat distractedly, Well, then, did you enjoy that, whereupon the others hasten to assure him, We most certainly did, however, they reply much too forcefully, and their hearts betray no signs of having understood what they have heard, and if their hearts have not understood, the words that come to their lips are an expression of bewilderment rather than of cunning. Baltasar went back to hammering his irons while Blimunda swept up the discarded fragments of cane in the yard, the diligence with which they worked giving the impression that their tasks were urgent, but the priest suddenly declared, like someone unable to suppress his anxiety any longer, At this rate I shall never fly my machine, his voice sounded tired, and he made a gesture of such profound despair that Baltasar suddenly realising the futility of his labours, laid down his hammer, but anxious to avoid giving any impression of giving up, he suggested, We must build a forge here and temper the irons, otherwise even the weight of the Passarola will cause them to bend, and the priest replied, I don't mind if they bend, the important thing is that my machine should fly, and it simply can't be done until we have obtained ether, What is ether, Blimunda asked, That's what keeps the stars in the sky, And how can it be brought down here, asked Baltasar, By means of alchemy, about which I know nothing, but you must not mention these things to anyone, whatever happens, Then what shall we do, I shall leave shortly for Holland, which is a nation of learned men, and there I shall study the art of extracting ether from the atmosphere in order to filter it into the globes, because without ether the machine will never be able to fly, What's the good of this ether, asked Blimunda, It's part of the general principle that attracts human beings and even inanimate objects to the sun once they're released from their earthly weight, Put that into simple words, Father, Well before the machine can rise into the air, it's essential that the sun should attract the amber that is attached to the wires on top, which in turn will attract the ether we'll have filtered into the globes, the ether will then attract the magnets below, which in turn will attract the metal plates that form the body of the ship. Only then can we rise into the air assisted by the wind, or by air fanned by the bellows should the wind drop, but, as I said before, without any ether, the other materials serve no purpose. Blimunda interrupted him, If the sun attracts the amber, and the amber attracts the ether, and the ether attracts the magnets, and the magnets attract the metal, the machine will be drawn toward the sun without being able to stop. She paused and thought aloud, I wonder what the sun is like inside. The priest explained, We won't have to go near the sun, to avoid any such collision there will be sails on top, which we can open and close as required, so that we can stop at the altitude we choose. He also paused before concluding, As for knowing what the sun is like inside, let's get the machine airborne first and the rest will follow, so long as we're determined to succeed and God doesn't thwart our efforts.

Yet these are difficult times. The nuns of St Monica are about to rebel, in open defiance of the King's edict that they consort in the convent parlour only with their parents, children, brothers, sisters, and relatives to the second degree, a measure with which the King is resolved to put an end to the scandals provoked by noble and not-so-noble philanderers who have a penchant for the brides of Christ and make them pregnant in less time than it takes to recite the Ave Maria, if Dom João V, does it, it is to his credit, but not when it is any old João or José. The provincial superior at Graça was asked to inter-vene in order to calm the nuns down and try to persuade them to obey the King's orders under threat of excommunication, but to no avail, incensed and outraged, three hundred nuns overcome by sacred wrath at the idea of being cut off from secular life rebelled and defied the edict time and time again and, as if to prove how dainty feminine hands can force doors open, they took to the streets, dragging the prioress with them by force, holding the crucifix aloft, they marched in procession, until they were confronted by the friars from Graça, who begged of them in the name of Christ's five sacred wounds to end their mutiny, a holy colloquium ensuing then and there between friars and nuns, each side arguing their case, the crisis resulted in the magistrate's running to the King to ask whether or not he should suspend the Order, and between the comings and goings to discuss the matter, the morning soon passed for, anxious to make an early start, the rebel-lious nuns had been on their feet since dawn, and while they waited for the magistrate to come back and report there was much toing and froing and, after hours of standing the older nuns sat on the ground, while the excited novices remained on the alert, all of them rejoicing in the warmth of that summer day, which is always so spiritually uplift-ing, bemused at the sight of those who passed or stopped to stare, for these were pleasures nuns could not enjoy every day, and they chatted freely with whomsoever they pleased, using this opportunity to renew their association with the forbidden visitors who now rushed to the scene and between secret pacts, knowing gestures, quiet rendezvous, and coded signals with hands and handkerchiefs, the hours passed until noon, when the nuns began to get hungry and started to eat the sweetmeats they had brought in their knapsacks, for those who go to war must carry their own provisions, and the demonstration ended with a countermand from the Palace, whereby things became as lax as before, the nuns of St Monica were overjoyed when they received the news and sang hymns of praise and there was one further consolation, when the provincial sent them a formal pardon by messenger rather than come in person, just in case he might be the victim of a stray bullet, for revolts staged by nuns are the most dangerous of hostilities. These women are often condemned against their will to perpetual seclusion in some convent in order to protect the family fortunes in favour of the male heir, where they are trapped for life so that even the simple pleasure of holding hands through the grilles, or having some amorous encounter or sweet embrace is bliss, even if it should lead to hell and damnation. For, after all, if the sun attracts the amber and the world attracts the flesh, someone must gain something, even if it is only to take advantage of what has been left behind by those who were born to possess everything.

Another predictable vexation is the auto-da-fé, not for the Church, which regards it as a means of strengthening the faith, along with its other advantages, and not for the King, who, having hauled a number of Brazilian plantation owners before the Inquisition, wastes no time in expropriating their lands, but for those who are flogged in public, sent into exile, or burned at the stake and just as well that there was only one woman sentenced to death for immorality on this occasion, for it will not take long to paint her portrait and hang it in the Church of St Dominic, alongside all those other portraits of women whose depraved bodies have been roasted alive and whose ashes have been dispersed, yet, surprisingly enough, the torture and agony of so many does not appear to deter others, so one can only assume that human beings like to suffer or have greater esteem for their spiritual convictions than for the preservation of their bodies, God clearly did not know what He was doing when He created Adam and Eve. What is one to make of cases such as that of the professed nun who turned out to be Jewish and was sentenced to life imprisonment and solitary confinement, or the recent case of the woman from Angola who arrived here from Rio de Janeiro and was accused of being Jewish, or that merchant from the Algarve who asserted that every man is saved according to the faith he upholds, for all faiths are equal, and Christ is worth as much as Mohammed, the Gospel as much as the Cabala, the sweet as much as the bitter, sin as much as virtue, or that strapping mulatto of dubious origin from Caparica whose name is Manuel Mateus, no relation to Sete-Sóis, but is known to his friends as Saramago and whose notoriety as a sorcerer led to his being tortured and condemned with three young women who were found guilty of similar offences, what is one to make of these heretics and the other one hundred and thirty who have been brought before the Inquisition, many of whom will soon be keeping Blimunda's mother company if she is still alive.

Sete-Sóis and Sete-Luas, two such lovely names that it seems a pity not to use them, did not come from São Sebastião da Pedreira to the Rossio to watch the auto-da-fé, but nearly everyone else flocked to watch the spectacle, and from eye-witness accounts and the official records that always survive despite the numerous earthquakes and fires, we know what and whom they saw being sentenced to torture, to the stake or exile, the black woman from Angola, the mulatto from Caparica, the Jewish nun, those impostors masquerading as priests who said Mass, confessed, and preached without any authority to do so, the judge from Arraiolos who had Jewish blood on both his father's and his mother's side of the family, some one hundred and thirty-seven miscreants altogether, for the Holy Office of the Inquisition tries to cast its nets as widely as possible, in order to ensure that they will be full, thus obeying Christ's mandate when He told Saint Peter that He wanted him to be a fisher of men.

The great sorrow shared by Baltasar and Blimunda is that they do not possess a net capable of dragging down those stars along with the ether which keeps them suspended in mid-air, according to Padre Bartolomeu Lourenço, who is about to leave them and cannot say when he will return. The Passarola, which had started out looking like a castle under construction, is now like a tower in ruins, a Babel rudely interrupted without warning, and cords, canvas, wires, and irons are all in disarray and they no longer even have the consolation of opening the chest and studying the design, for the priest is carrying it in his luggage, he departs tomorrow, is travelling by sea, and with no greater risk than one might expect from the hazards of a sea journey, for peace with France has finally been declared, the signing of the peace treaty warranting a solemn procession of judges, magistrates, and bailiffs on horseback, followed by the trumpeters and buglers, then the palace footmen bearing silver maces on their shoulders, and behind them seven kings-at-arms wearing sumptuous robes, and the last of them carrying in one hand the parchment that formally declared peace, the treaty was read first of all in the Palace Square below the King's apartments, from where the royal family could look down on the crowds who filled the courtyard, the palace guards standing in formation and after the treaty was read out in the King's presence, it was read out once more in the Praça de Sé, and a third time in the hospital grounds adjoining the Rossio and now that a peace treaty has been signed with France, treaties with other nations will follow, But who will give me back the hand I've lost, Baltasar muses sadly, Don't worry, between us we have three hands, Blimunda reassures him.

Padre Bartolomeu Lourenço gave his blessing to the soldier and the clairvoyant and they kissed his hand, but at the last moment all three embraced, for friendship was stronger than reverence, and the priest said, Farewell, Blimunda, farewell, Baltasar, Look after each other and take care of the Passarola, for I shall return one day with the secret substance I mean to obtain, it will be neither gold nor diamonds, but the very air God Himself breathes, guard the key I gave you safely, and when you leave for Mafra, remember to pass by here from time to time to inspect my machine, you may enter and leave without permission, for the King has entrusted me with the estate and he knows what is stored here, and with these words the priest mounted his mule and departed.

Padre Bartolomeu Lourenço must already be on the open sea, so how should we amuse ourselves now, until we can fly, let's go to a bullfight, they can be very entertaining, In Mafra there are no bullfights, Baltasar explains, and since we don't have enough money to attend the entire four-day event, because the Palace has demanded an exorbitant fee for leasing the Palace Square this year, let's go on the last day for the grand finale, with tiered stands erected all around the square, even on the side where the river is, which makes it difficult to see anything except the upper decks of the ships anchored beyond, Sete-Sóis and Blimunda have found themselves good seats, not because they arrived earlier than anyone else but simply because an iron hook stuck to the end of an arm clears one's path just as quickly as the cannon that came from India and is preserved in the Tower of St Julian, someone feels a tap on the shoulder and turns around to find he might just as well be looking into the mouth of a cannon. The square is surrounded by masts that have tiny flags on top and are covered with streamers trailing all the way down to the ground and fluttering in the breeze, at the entrance to the arena is a wooden portico painted in simulated marble, and the columns are painted to look like stone from Arrábida with gilded cornices and friezes. The main pillar is supported by four enormous figures painted in a variety of colours and with a lavish display of gold leaf, the flag, made of tin plate, depicts on both sides the glorious St Antony standing on fields of silver, and the fittings are also gilt, the enormous crest of multicoloured plumes is so skilfully painted that the plumes look real, they give a nice finishing touch to the flagpole. The stands and terraces are swarming with people, spectators of rank and influence are seated in specially reserved seats, while the Royal Family watches from the palace windows, stewards are still watering the square, some eighty men dressed in the Moorish style with the arms of the Senate of Lisbon embroidered on their capes, the crowd is growing impatient as it eagerly waits for the bulls to appear, the preparations are now over, and the stewards withdraw from the arena, the square is as clean as a pin, and a fresh smell comes from the moistened ground, it is as if the world had been created anew, the spectators eagerly await the onslaught, soon that same ground will be covered with the blood, excrement, and urine of the bulls, or the droppings of the horses, and if some spectator should wet himself with excitement, let us hope that his breeches will protect him from the shame of making a fool of himself in the presence of all the inhabitants of Lisbon and of His Majesty Dom João V.

The first bull entered the arena, then the second, and then the third, then the eighteen bullfighters on foot whom the Senate had contracted in Castela at vast expense, then the picadors cantered into the arena and stabbed with their pikes, while those on foot embedded darts festooned with coloured papers in the necks of the bulls, one of the picadors showed his anger at a bull that had pulled his cape to the ground by charging at the animal and wounding it with his lance, which is one way of avenging tarnished honour. The fourth bull charges in, then the fifth, and the sixth, and on and on up to ten, twelve, fifteen, twenty bulls, until the square is like a blood-bath, the women laugh, screech with joy, and clap their hands, the palace windows look like branches in full blossom, while down below the bulls expire one after another, their corpses being removed on low wagons drawn by six horses, the same number as are used for members of the Royal Family and the titled aristocracy, and if the six horses are not a sign of the majesty and dignity attributed to the bulls, they do show how much the bulls weigh, just ask those horses groomed and resplendent, their embroidered trappings in crimson velvet and their saddles and caparisons trimmed with silvered fringes while the poor bulls are riddled with darts and pierced with lance wounds and their entrails dragging along the ground, in their frenzy, the men grope the frenzied women, who brazenly snuggle up against them, including Blimunda, who clings to Baltasar, and why not, he can feel all that blood being shed in the arena rush to his head, those rivulets on the flanks of the bulls pour out the blood of living death and make his head spin, but the image that imprints itself on his mind and brings tears to his eyes is the bull's drooping head, its gaping mouth, its great tongue hanging out, a tongue that will never again taste pastures, except those mythical pastures in the other world of bulls, whether it be paradise or hell.

If there is any justice, it will be paradise, for there could scarcely be a greater hell than what they have already experienced, for instance, those mantles of fire, which consist of various types of fireworks tied to the bulls and lit from both ends, and as the mantle of fire starts to burn, the fireworks go on exploding for a considerable time, lighting up the entire arena, it is as if the bull were being roasted alive, maddened and enraged, the wretched creature races to and fro across the arena, rearing and bellowing, while Dom João V and his subjects applaud its miserable death, and the bull is given no opportunity to defend itself or to kill while being slaughtered. The place smells of burned flesh, but this odour gives no offence to nostrils accustomed to the great barbecue of the auto-da-fé, besides, the bull ends up on somebody's plate and is put to good use in the end, whereas all that remains of a Jew burned at the stake is whatever property he may have left behind.

The stewards now carry in some gaudily painted figures in terracotta, larger than life-size, with arms raised to heaven, and put them in the centre of the arena, What kind of show is this, ask those who have never seen it before, perhaps the spectators are giving their eyes a rest after so much carnage, for if the figures are made of terracotta, the worst that one is likely to see is a pile of rubble which can easily be swept up, The feast has been ruined, the sceptical and violent will protest, Bring on another mantle of fire so we can laugh with the King, there are not all that many occasions when we can enjoy a good laugh together, and now two bulls emerge from their pen and are startled to find the arena deserted except for those terracotta figures with raised arms and no legs, with bulging paunches and sinister pockmarks. The bulls decide to avenge all the wrongs they have suffered and they charge, shattering the figures with a dull explosion that sends dozens upon dozens of rabbits scampering frantically in all directions, only to be pursued and clubbed to death by the bullfighters and spectators who dart into the arena, one eye on the rabbit they are pursuing, the other on the bull that might start to pursue them, the crowds hoot with laughter, hysterical mob that they are, and suddenly the uproar assumes another pitch, from two of the exploding terracotta figures emerge flocks of pigeons flapping their wings, disoriented by the shock and dazzled by the harsh light, some of them losing all control fail to gain altitude and end up crashing into the upper stands, where they are seized by avid hands, not so much interested in having a tasty meal of stuffed pigeon, as in reading the quatrains written on the pieces of paper attached to the birds' necks, like the following, Freed from captivity, I should welcome falling into certain hands, In fear and trembling, I await my fate for those who soar highest suffer the greatest fall,

Tranquil in the face of death, I watch my assassins die in my pursuit for when bulls charge, pigeons also try to run, but not all of them, for some circle skywards thus escaping the vortex of hands and cries, and soaring ever higher, they capture the sunlight and shimmering like birds of gold, they disappear over the rooftops.

Early next morning, before sunrise, Baltasar and Blimunda, taking no more luggage than a bundle of clothes and some food in their knapsack, left Lisbon and headed for Mafra.

THE PRODIGAL SON has returned and brought his wife, and if he does not come empty-handed, it is because he left one of them on the battlefield and the other is clasped in Blimunda's hand, whether he comes richer or poorer is a question one does not ask, for every man knows what he possesses without knowing what it is worth. When Baltasar pushed the door open and appeared before his mother, Marta Maria, she embraced him with a vehemence that seemed almost virile, such was the strength of her emotion. Baltasar was wearing his hook, and it was painful and moving to see a crooked iron resting on the old woman's shoulder instead of that human cradle of fingers which follows protectingly the contours of the person it embraces. His father was not at home, for he was labouring in the fields and Baltasar's only sister is married and already has two children, her husband is named Álvaro Pedreiro, a name chosen to match his trade as a bricklayer, a fairly common practice in those days, and there must have been some good reason for calling certain people Sete-Sóis, even if it was only a nickname. Blimunda stayed at the door waiting for her turn, and the old woman could not see her because she was hidden behind the much taller Baltasar and besides, it was dark inside the house. Baltasar stepped aside to introduce Blimunda, that was his intention, at least, but Marta Maria was distracted by something she had not noticed at first, perhaps forewarned by the sense of something cold and empty resting on her shoulder, an iron hook instead of a human hand, nevertheless, she could now perceive a face in the doorway, poor woman, her emotions torn between sorrow at the sight of her son's maimed limb and disquiet at the sudden appearance of this other woman while Blimunda stood aside, allowing things to take their course, and from the entrance she could hear the old woman's tears and questions, My dear son, how did it happen, who did this to you, and it was already growing dark when Baltasar finally came to the door and called to Blimunda, Enter, an oil lamp had been lit, Marta Maria was still sobbing quietly, Mother, this is my wife, and her name is Blimunda of Jesus.

It ought to be sufficient to state what someone is called and then wait for the rest of your life to find out who he or she is, if you can ever know, but the custom is otherwise, Who were your parents, where were you born, what is your trade, and once you know these facts, you think you have learnt everything about the person. As dark began to fall, Baltasar's father arrived home, he was named João Francisco, the son of Manuel and Jacinta, and was born here in Mafra, where he had always lived in this same house, in the shadow of the Church of St Andrew and the Viscounts' Palace, and to fill in a few more details, João Francisco is as tall as his son, although now somewhat bent by age as well as by the weight of the bundle of wood he has carried home. Baltasar helped him to unload the bundle, and the old man looked at him and exclaimed, Ah, my son, noticing at once that Baltasar's left hand was missing but simply saying, We must resign ourselves, after all, you've been fighting a war, then he saw Blimunda and, aware that she was his son's wife, allowed her to kiss his hand, mother-in-law and daughter-in-law were soon preparing supper, while Baltasar spoke of the battle in which he had lost his hand and of the years spent away from home, but said nothing of the two years he had passed in Lisbon without sending them any news of his whereabouts, when the first and only word they had received from him had been some weeks previously, a letter written by Padre Bartolomeu Lourenço at the request of Sete-Sóis, informing his parents that he was alive and well and about to return home, ah, how cruel children can be when they are alive and well and transform their silence into death. He had still not told them whether he had married Blimunda while he was in the army or after the war had ended, or explained what kind of marriage he had contracted or in what circumstances, but either the old couple did not remember to ask him or they preferred not to know, for they were perplexed by the girl's strange appearance, that sand-coloured hair of hers, a somewhat unkind description, for it was honey-coloured, and those pale eyes that could have been green, grey, or blue when she looked into the light, only to become suddenly very dark, the colour of earth, of murky waters, even black as coals, if so much as tinged by shadows, so they all sat there in silence when it would have been opportune for them to speak, I never knew my father, I think he was already dead when I was born, my mother has been exiled to Angola for eight years, only two of those years have passed and I don't know if she is still alive, for there has been no news, Blimunda and I intend to stay here in Mafra, Baltasar declared, and I hope to find a house, There's no need to look for a house, this one is big enough for four people, and it has sheltered many more in the past, his father said, then asked, Why was Blimunda's mother sent into exile, Because, Father, they denounced her to the Holy Office of the Inquisition, Blimunda is neither Jewish nor converted, and this trouble with the Holy Office of the Inquisition and her sentence to imprisonment and exile came about because of certain visions and revelations, Blimunda's mother claimed to have had, and voices she had heard, There isn't a woman alive who hasn't had visions and revelations, or who doesn't hear voices, we women hear mysterious voices all day long, and one doesn't have to be a sorceress to hear them, My mother was no more a sorceress than I am, Do you have visions, too, Only those visions that all women experience, Mother, You will be as a daughter to me, Yes, Mother, Swear, then, that you are neither Jewish nor converted, Baltasar's father intervened, I swear it, Father, Welcome, then, to the home of Sete-Sóis, Blimunda is also known as Sete-Luas, Who gave you that name, The priest who married us, Any priest with so much imagination is scarcely a product of the sacristy, and at these words they all laughed heartily, some knowingly, the others less so. Blimunda and Baltasar exchanged glances and perceived the same thoughts in each other's eyes, the Passarola lying in pieces on the floor, Padre Bartolomeu Lourenço mounted on his mule as he disappeared through the gates of the estate on the start of his journey to Holland. Hovering in the air was the falsehood that Blimunda had no trace of Jewish blood, if it can be called a falsehood, for we know that this couple tended to disregard such matters, in order to safeguard greater truths, one often resorts to deception.

Baltasar's father informed him, I sold the plot we had on the Alto da Vela, I sold it for the reasonable sum of thirty-five hundred réis, but we shall miss that land, Then why did you sell it, Because the King wanted it, my land as well as everybody else's, And why should the King want to buy those lands. He's going to build a convent for the Franciscan friars, haven't you heard it discussed in Lisbon, No, Father, I've heard nothing, The local parish priest explained that the convent had been promised to the Franciscans by the King if an heir to the throne should be born, the person who is likely to earn good money now is your brother-in-law, for there will be plenty of work for stone-masons. They had supped on cabbage and beans, the women on their feet and keeping out of the way, and João Francisco Sete-Sóis went to the salting-box and took out a lump of pork, which he cut into four pieces, he then put each piece on a slice of bread and parcelled them out. He watched Blimunda attentively as she took her portion and tranquilly began to eat, She's no Jewess, her father-in-law thought to himself. Marta Maria had also been watching the girl anxiously, and she gave her husband a severe look, as if to rebuke him for his mistrust. Blimunda finished eating and smiled, and it did not occur to João Francisco that even if she were Jewish she would have eaten the salt pork, for Blimunda has another truth to safeguard.

Baltasar said, I must look for work, and Blimunda, too, must find employment, we must earn a living somehow, For Blimunda there's no hurry, I want to keep her at home with me for a while, so that I can become better acquainted with my new daughter, That's fine, Mother, but I must look for a job without delay, With only one hand, what job are you likely to find, I have my hook, Father, which is a great help once you get used to it, That's all very well, but you cannot dig, you cannot wield a scythe, and you cannot chop firewood, I could look after animals, Yes, I suppose you could, I could also be a drover, the hook is good enough to hold the rope, and my right hand will manage the rest, I'm pleased you've come back home, my son, I should have returned sooner, Father.

That night Baltasar dreamt that he went out to plough the entire Alto da Vela with a yoke of oxen, Blimunda walking behind and sticking bird feathers into the ground and these began to flutter as if they were about to become airborne and take the soil with them, then Padre Bartolomeu Lourenço appeared from nowhere, carrying his design and pointing out the mistake they had made, We must start again, he said when suddenly the land waiting to be ploughed reappeared, and Blimunda, who was sitting on the ground, beckoned to Baltasar, Come and lie down beside me, for I have finished eating my bread. It was still the dead of night when he woke up and drew Blimunda's sleeping body close to him, with its moist, enigmatic warmth, she murmured his name and he whispered hers, as they lay there on the kitchen floor on an improvised bed of folded blankets and, taking great care not to make any noise in case they roused his parents, they made love.

Next day Baltasar's sister, Inês Antónia, and her husband, Álvaro Diogo, came to welcome Baltasar home and make the acquaintance of their new sister-in-law. They brought their two children, one four years old, the other two, only the older will survive, for the younger child will be stricken by smallpox and die within the next three months. But God, or whoever in heaven determines the span of human lives, is very scrupulous when it comes to maintaining some balance between rich and poor, whenever it proves necessary, He will even cast His eye on those of noble birth to find some counterweight to put on the scales, and to balance the death of the child of Inês Antónia and Álvaro Diogo, the Infante Dom Pedro will die at the same age, for when God so wills, death may be caused by the most unlikely causes, the heir to the Portuguese throne, for example, will die once he is denied his mother's milk, and only a child as delicate as a royal infante could perish in such circumstances, for Inês Antónia's child was already eating bread and all the rest when it fell ill and died. Once He has levelled the score, God shows no interest in their funerals, and so, when that little angel was buried in Mafra, as so often happens, the event went unnoticed, but the Infante's burial in Lisbon was quite another matter, mourning was observed with all due solemnity, the corpse was borne from the royal apartments in a tiny casket by the counsellors of state, who were escorted by all the nobility, the King himself presiding with his brother, and if the King grieved as a father, he grieved most of all at the loss of his first son and natural heir to the throne, and in accordance with court protocol, the funeral cortège went down into the chapel courtyard, all the men wearing their hats, but when the coffin was placed on the bier that was to carry the corpse to its final resting place, the King and father of the dead Infante removed and replaced his hat twice before returning to the Palace, such are the inhumanities of official protocol. The Infante made his lonely journey to São Vicente de Fora, with a magnificent entourage but without father or mother, the Cardinal headed the procession, followed by the mace-bearers on horseback, then the officials and dignitaries of the royal household, behind them came the clergy and altar boys attached to the Royal Chapel, with the exception of the canons who had gone to await the arrival of the corpse at São Vicente, this last contingent carried lighted torches, and behind them came the palace guards, led by lieutenants, in double file, and finally the funeral bier itself, bearing the coffin, which was covered with a magnificent red drape like that which covers the royal coach, and behind the bier came the elderly Duke of Cadaval, in his capacity as the veteran major-domo of the Queen's household, and the Queen, if she has a mother's heart, must surely be mourning the death of her child, also present is the Marquis of Minas, the Queen's chief steward, whose devotion can be judged from his tears rather than from his titles, as is the ancient custom, the aforesaid drapes, along with the harnesses and trappings of the mules, will be given to the friars of São Vicente, and the hostlers of the mules, which also belong to the friars, will receive twelve thousand réis, a form of hiring like any other, and we should not be surprised, for human beings are not mules, yet they, too, are frequently hired, and thus united, they form the solemn procession wending its way through the streets, with soldiers and friars among the crowds lining the pavements, there are friars from all the religious orders as well as the mendicant friars who are the trustees of the sanctuary that will receive the Infante, who died after being deprived of his mother's milk, a privilege the friars richly deserve, just as they deserve the convent that will soon be built in the town of Mafra, where within the last year a little boy has been buried whose identity has never been established but who also had a funeral cortège, which included his parents, his grandparents, his uncles and aunts, and other relatives, and when the Infante Dom Pedro arrives in heaven and learns of this discrimination, he will be most upset.

Eventually, since the Queen was so well disposed towards maternity, the King gave her another child who would certainly become king and give rise to more celebrations and upheavals, and lest anyone should be curious to know how God will balance this royal birth with that of a commoner, He will balance it, all right, but not by means of anonymous men and women, Inês Antónia will show no desire to see any more of her children die, and as for Blimunda, she suspects that she has mysterious powers at her disposal to avoid giving birth to any children. Let us, therefore, concentrate on the adults, on the endless stories Sete-Sóis will tell of his military exploits, of the modest contribution he made to the nation's history, of how he came to be wounded and how they amputated his hand, showing them his iron implements as they listen once more to the same old lamentations, These are the misfortunes that befall the poor, he tells them, but not so, for generals and captains also died in the war or have been left crippled for life, and God provides in the same measure as He takes away, but after an hour everyone has got used to this novelty except for the children who sit there staring in utter fascination and tremble with fear when their uncle playfully lifts them off the ground with his hook, he is doing what he can to keep them amused, the younger child shows the greatest interest of all in this singular game, let the poor child enjoy himself, let him enjoy himself while there is still time, for he has only three months left in which to play.

During those first days back in Mafra, Baltasar helps his father on the land he has rented from a neighbour, he has to learn everything anew, he has not forgotten any of his farming skills, but they are now difficult to apply. As proof that there is no substance in dreams, he now realises that, although he was capable of ploughing the Alto da Vela in his dream, without his left hand he can do little with a plough in the light of day. There is no more blissful occupation than that of a drover, but since one cannot be a drover without a cart and a yoke of oxen, Baltasar will have to borrow his father's in the meantime,

Now it's my turn, now it's yours, One day you will have your own, And if I die soon, perhaps you will be able to save some of the money you inherit to buy the cart and oxen, Father, don't even mention such things. Baltasar also finds some work on the site where his brother-in-law is employed, a new wall is being built around the estates of the Viscounts of Vila Nova da Cerveira. Baltasar will find it difficult to lay a single stone on the wall, it would almost have been preferable to have lost a leg, after all, a man can support himself just as firmly on a stilt as on a leg, it is the first time Baltasar has given this any thought, but then he thinks how awkward it would be when lying down beside Blimunda and on top of her, and decides, No, thank you, much better to have lost a hand, and what a stroke of good fortune that it should have been his left hand at that. Álvaro Diogo comes down from the scaffold and, taking refuge behind a hedge, eats the midday meal brought to him by Inês Antónia, whom he assures there will be no lack of work for stone-masons once they start to build the convent, and it will no longer be necessary to leave one's own town in order to find work in surrounding districts, which means spending week after week away from home, for no matter how restless a fellow might be, his own home, if he has a wife he respects and children he loves, has the same satisfying taste as bread, a man's home is not for all hours, but he soon begins to miss it if he does not go back there every day.

Baltasar strolled all the way up to the Alto da Vela, from which one can see the entire town of Mafra nestling in the hollow of the valley. This is where he used to play when he was the same age as his eldest nephew, and for several more years before he had to start labouring in the fields. The sea lies at some considerable distance yet appears to be close, it shimmers like the blade of a sword catching the light of the sun, which the sun will gradually sheathe once it starts to go down and disappear beyond the horizon. These are similes invented by someone who is writing on behalf of a soldier who fought in the war, Baltasar did not invent them, but, for some reason best known to himself, he suddenly remembers the sword he hid safely away in his parents' house, which he has never again unsheathed, probably covered with rust by now, but one of these days he will oil it, for one never knows when the need might arise.

Formerly these were cultivated lands, but now they are abandoned. Though the boundaries are barely visible, the hedgerows, ditches, and fences no longer divide the land. All these fields now belong to the same landowner, His Majesty the King, who has not yet paid for it but will no doubt pay, for, to do him justice, his credit is good. João Francisco Sete-Sóis is awaiting compensation for his part of the land, what a pity the entire sum does not come to him, otherwise he would be a very rich man indeed, so far the deeds of sale amount to three hundred and fifty-eight thousand, five hundred réis, and with the passage of time that sum will go on increasing until it exceeds fifteen million réis, an inconceivable amount of money for the minds of weak mortals, so to make things easier we shall convert it into fifteen contos and almost one hundred thousand réis, a tidy sum. Whether it is a good or a bad deal depends, for money does not always keep its value, unlike mankind, whose value is always the same, everything and nothing. And will the convent be a large affair, Baltasar inquired of his brother-in-law, to which he replied, To begin with, a community of thirteen friars was mentioned, then the figure went up to forty, now the Franciscans in charge of the hospice and the Chapel of the Blessed Sacrament are saying that there will be as many as eighty, It will be the most powerful place on earth, said Baltasar. This was their topic of conversation when Inês Antónia withdrew, leaving Álvaro Diogo free to speak with Baltasar man to man. The friars come here to fornicate with women, and the Franciscans are the worst of all, if I catch any of them taking liberties with my wife, I'll give him such a thrashing that I'll break every bone in his body, and, as he spoke, the stone-mason struck the boulder where Inês Antónia had been sitting with his hammer and smashed it into smithereens. The sun has now set and down in the valley Mafra is as dark as the interior of a well. Baltasar starts to descend the slope, he looks at the boundaries traced out with stones, which divide off the land on the far side, the whitest of stone as yet untouched by the first frosts, stone that has never known excessive heat, stone still astonished by the light of day. These stones are the initial foundations of the convent, the King has ordered that they be cut from Portuguese stones fashioned by Portuguese hands, for the Garvos, the family contracted to supervise the final stages of the building, have not yet arrived from Milan to take charge of the bricklayers and stonemasons. When Baltasar enters the house he hears whispers and murmurings coming from the kitchen, he recognises his mother's voice, then that of Blimunda, as they converse in turn, they scarcely know each other yet have so many things to confide, it is the prolonged and interminable conversation of women, men think such conversations frivolous without perceiving that they keep the world in orbit, if women did not converse with one another, men would long ago have lost all sense of home and of the world at large, Give me your blessing, dear Mother, May God bless you, my son, Blimunda remained silent, and Baltasar did not greet her, they simply looked at each other, finding refuge in each other's eyes.

There are various ways of bringing a man and a woman together, but since this is neither a guide nor a handbook for the marriage-broker, only two ways will be recorded here, the first of which is when he and she are standing close to each other, two complete strangers watching an auto-da-fé, from the sidelines, of course, as the penitents go past, and the woman suddenly turns to the man and asks him, What is your name, prompted neither by divine inspiration nor by her own free will, it was a mandate instilled by her own mother, that mother who walked in the procession, and who had experienced visions and revelations, and if, as the Holy Office of the Inquisition insists, she had shammed, she was not shamming then, not at all, for she truly saw the maimed soldier, the man destined to wed her daughter, and by these means she brought them together. Another way is for the man and the woman to be distant from each other and oblivious of each other's existence, both installed in their own court, his in Lisbon, hers in Vienna, he nineteen years of age, she twenty-five years of age, married by proxy negotiated by their respective ambassadors, and the betrothed had their first glimpse of each other from portraits that were suitably flattering, he cutting a fine figure with his dark good looks, she plump and fair, as befitted an Austrian princess, and whatever their private inclinations, they were persuaded they were perfect for each other and that their marriage had been sealed in heaven, he will succeed in recouping his losses, she, poor thing, being an honest woman and incapable of raising her eyes so much as to look at another man, will resign herself to her fate, what happens in her dreams does not count.

In the war of Dom João, Baltasar lost his hand, in the War of the Holy Inquisition, Blimunda lost her mother, João gained nothing, for once peace had been declared things reverted to normal, the Inquisition gained nothing, because with every sorceress burned at the stake another ten appeared, not to mention the sorcerers of whom there were also many. Each man has his own system of accounts, his own ledger and day-book, the names of the dead are entered on one side of the page, the living on the other, there are also different ways of paying and imposing taxes, with the money of blood and with the blood of money, but there are those who favour prayers, such as the Queen, a natural and dedicated mother who came into the world solely to bear children, she will give birth to six children altogether, but her prayers should be calculated in millions, she is constantly making pilgrimages to the Jesuit Novitiate or the Parish Church of St Paul, or making a novena at the Shrine of St Francis Xavier, then she visits the shrine of Our Lady, Consoler of the Afflicted, then she goes to the Monastery of St Benedict run by the friars of St John the Evangelist, then she visits the Parish Church of the Incarnation, then the Convent of the Holy Conception at Marvila, then the Convent of St Benedict the Healer, then the Shrine of Our Lady of Light, then the Church of Corpus Christi, then the Church of Our Lady of All Graces, then she goes to the Church of St Rock, then to the Sanctuary of the Holy Trinity, then to the Royal Convent of the Mother of God, then she visits the Shrine of Our Lady of Remembrance, then the Churches of St Peter of Alcântara and Our Lady of Loreto, and the Convent of Good Counsel, and the moment she is about to leave the Palace to fulfil her religious devotions, there is a drum roll and the shrill sound of flutes, not emanating from her, good heavens, as if a queen would play a drum or a flute, and the halberdiers line up, and since the roads are perpetually filthy, despite numerous warnings and edicts demanding that they be cleaned up, porters run ahead of the Queen carrying wooden planks on their shoulders, when she steps from her carriage, the planks are set on the ground, there is quite a stir, no sooner does the Queen step over the planks than the porters move them forward, so that while she remains clean they are forever walking in the mire, our mistress, the Queen, is like our Lord Jesus Christ when He walked over the waters, and in this miraculous fashion she proceeds to the Convents of the Trinitarians, of the Cistercian Nuns, of the Sacred Heart and of St Albert, the Church of Our Lady of Mercy, whose mercy we implore, to the Church of St Catherine, to the Convent of the Sisters of St Paul, and that of the Holy Hour, which is looked after by the discalced Augustinians, and to that of Our Lady of Mount Carmel, to the Church of Our Lady of Martyrs, for we are all martyrs in our own way, to the Convent of Princess Joan the Saint, to the Convent of Christ the Saviour, to the Convent of the Sisters of St Monica, to the Royal Convent of Holy Redress, and to that of the Beneficiaries, but we know where she dare not go, to the Convent of Odivelas, and we can all guess why, a sad and deceived queen who is undeceived only by praying every hour of each day, sometimes for a good cause, at other times for no apparent reason, sometimes for her wayward husband, for her family so far away, for this country which is not hers and the children who are only partly hers, and perhaps not even that, as the Infante Dom Pedro swears in heaven, for the Portuguese Empire, for deliverance from imminent plague, for the war that has just finished and that which is about to break out, for the Infantas and Infantes, for her royal in-laws, and for Dom Francisco, too, and to Jesus, Mary, and Joseph for the trials of the flesh, for the delights glimpsed or visualised between a man's legs, for arduous salvation, for the hell that covets her soul, for the torture of being a queen, for the sorrow of being a woman, and for those two inseparable woes, transient life and approaching death.

Dona Maria Ana will now have other, more urgent motives for praying. The King is far from well these days and is subject to sudden bouts of flatulence, a debility from which he has long suffered but is rapidly worsening, the fainting fits now last much longer than usual, and it teaches one humility to see such a mighty king reduced to a state of unconsciousness, what good does it do him to be Lord of India, Africa, and Brazil when we are nothing in this world and must leave all our possessions behind. Custom and caution dictate that the last rites should be administered without delay, His Majesty must not die unconfessed like any common soldier on the battlefield where chaplains are not to be seen and have no desire to be seen, yet from time to time certain problems arise, such as when the King is in Setúbal watching a bullfight from the windows of his apartments and suddenly, without any warning, goes into a deep swoon, a doctor is hastily summoned, who checks the King's pulse and summons a blood-letter, the father confessor comes with the holy oils, but no one can tell what sins Dom João V may have committed since he made his last confession, and that was only yesterday, how many evil thoughts could he have had, how many wicked acts could he have committed within the past twenty-four hours, and on top of everything, this awkward situation whereby bulls are dying in the arena while the King, his eyes staring upwards, may or may not be close to death, and if he should die it will not be from some wound, like those being inflicted on the animals below, who nevertheless succeed now and then in taking their revenge on the enemy, which is precisely what happened a moment ago to Dom Henrique de Almeida, he was tossed into the air with his horse and is being carried away on a stretcher with two fractured ribs. The King has finally opened his eyes, and he has escaped death after all, but his legs are still wobbly, his hands tremble, and his face is deathly pale, he no longer resembles that gallant gentleman who conquers nuns at a glance and for nuns substitute another word, as recently as last year, a French girl gave birth to a child he had fathered, and if those women of his, whether locked up or on the loose, were to see him now, they would not recognise this shrivelled, pathetic little man as the royal and indefatigable seducer they once knew. Dom João V makes the journey to Azeitão to see if a cure and good country air will rid him of this illness, which the doctors have diagnosed as melancholy, in all probability, His Royal Highness is suffering from a disturbance of the humours, which often results in bouts of flatulence and bilious attacks, infirmities that stem from black melancholy, for that is the King's real problem, so let us hope that he is not suffering from any diseases in his private parts, despite his amorous excesses and those traces of gallic acid, which are treated with extracts of comfrey, an excellent remedy for mouth ulcers and any infection of the testicles and upper appendages.

Dona Maria Ana has remained in Lisbon to pray and then gone on to continue her prayers at Belém. It is rumoured that she is peeved because Dom João V refuses to entrust her with governing the kingdom and it really is wrong for a husband to be so mistrustful of his wife's capacity to govern, he will soon relent, and eventually the Queen will be appointed regent while the King pursues his cure amidst the rural delights of Azeitão, where he is nursed by the Franciscan friars from Arrábida and the lapping of the waves, the colour of the sea, the tang in the air remain unchanged, the magic spell is the same, and nature exudes the same intoxicating odours as before while the Infante Dom Francisco remains alone in Lisbon, wooing the Queen, and the plot starts to thicken and events to unfold, calculating the death of his brother and his own life, If no remedy should be found for the melancholy that cruelly torments His Royal Highness, and if God were to decide to end his mortal life prematurely so that he might embark upon eternal life all the sooner, then it would be possible for me as next in line, as a close member of the Royal Family, as Your Majesty's brother-in-law, and a deeply devoted admirer of your beauty and virtue, to presume to suggest that I might succeed to the throne and to your bed on the way, by wedding you in holy matrimony, and when it comes to manly attributes I can assure you that I am not inferior to my brother, Good heavens, such an unseemly conversation between a brother- and sister-in-law, the King is still alive, and should God hear my prayers, His Majesty's life will be saved for the greater glory of the kingdom and, most of all, for the sake of those six children I am destined to bear him, for there are three more still to come, Yet I know that Your Majesty dreams about me nearly every night, I cannot deny that I have such dreams, these are weaknesses of womanhood, which I conceal in my heart and do not even discuss with my father confessor, although others may clearly surmise our dreams by looking into our eyes, Well, then, when my brother dies let us wed, If such a union were to bring prosperity to the realm, give no offence to God, and safeguard my honour, then I should consent, How I wish my brother would die, for I want to be king and to sleep with Your Majesty, I'm tired of being simply the Infante, And I'm tired of being queen, but I cannot aspire to anything else, so I resign myself and pray that my husband will live, lest I find myself saddled with an even worse fate, Is Your Majesty suggesting, then, that I would be worse than my brother, All men are evil in their own way, and on this astute and cynical note their conversation in the Palace ends, the first of many such conversations with Dom Francisco, who would importune the Queen on every possible occasion, in Belém, where she is in residence at present, in Belas, where she will journey at her leisure, and in Lisbon when she finally becomes regent, at court and in the country, until Dona Maria Ana's dreams are no longer as enjoyable as before, so uplifting for the spirit if distressing for the body, for now the Infante only appears in her dreams to tell her that he wants to become king, and much good may it do him, he is wasting his time, say I who am queen. The King became so gravely ill that Dona Maria Ana's dream vanished, but the King will eventually recover his health while the Queen's dreams will never be revived.

B ESIDES THE CONVERSATION of women, it is dreams that keep the world in orbit. But dreams also form a diadem of moons, therefore the sky is that splendour inside a man's head, if his head is not, in fact, his own unique sky. Padre Bartolomeu Lourenço has returned from Holland, whether he succeeded or failed to solve the mystery of ether we shall know later, it is even possible that the secret cannot be resolved with the alchemy of ancient times, perhaps a mere word will suffice to fill the globes of the flying machine, Almighty God, after all, did nothing more than speak and yet He succeeded in creating everything with such little effort, that is what the priest had been taught in the Seminary of Belém in Bahia, and it was further confirmed by learned debates and advanced studies in the Faculty of Theology at Coimbra, long before he ever launched his first balloon into the air, and now that he has come back from the Netherlands, he intends to return to Coimbra, a man might be a great flier, but he would be well advised to study for his master's degree and doctorate, and then, even if he should never fly, he will be deemed worthy of respect.

Padre Bartolomeu Lourenço went to the estate at São Sebastião da Pedreira, three whole years had passed since he had been there, he found the coach house abandoned, the materials were lying scattered around the floor, which nobody had seen fit to tidy up, since nobody knew what was going on there. Inside the large building sparrows flitted to and fro having found their way in through a hole in the roof where two tiles had cracked, the sparrows were unremarkable creatures, and it was unlikely that they would ever soar higher than the tallest of the ash trees on the estate, the sparrow belongs to the soil and the loam, the dungheap and the cornfield, to observe a dead sparrow is to realise that it was never intended to scale great heights, its wings are so fragile, its bones so minute, in comparison, my Passarola will soar as high as the eye can reach, just look at the solid frame of this shell that will carry me through the air, with time, the irons have rusted, a bad sign, suggesting that Baltasar has not been looking after things as I asked, but surely these footprints made with bare feet must be his, yet he does not appear to have brought Blimunda with him, perhaps something has befallen her, Baltasar has obviously slept on the pallet, for the blanket is drawn back as if he just got out of bed, I shall lie down on this same pallet and cover myself with this same blanket, I, Padre Bartolomeu Lourenço, newly returned from Holland, where I went to confirm whether people in other parts of Europe know how to fly with wings, and whether they are more advanced in the science of flying than I am, coming as I do from a land of mariners, and in Zwolle, Ede, and Nijkerk, I studied with highly respected alchemists and scientists, learned men who are capable of creating suns in retorts, and yet they die from mysterious causes, withering up until they become as hollow as a sheaf of broken straw and burn just as easily, for this is what all of them ask at the hour of death, that they leave nothing but ashes as they set themselves alight, and here, awaiting my return, was this flying machine, which still cannot fly, and these are the globes I must fill with celestial ether, for people should know what they are saying when they look up at the sky and exclaim, Celestial ether, of course I know what it is, it's as straightforward as God's saying, Let there be light, it's a manner of speaking, meanwhile, night has fallen, I am lighting this oil lamp Blimunda left behind, I extinguish this tiny sun, and it depends on me whether it is to be lit up or extinguished, I refer to the oil lamp, not to Blimunda, no human being can achieve all he or she desires in this life except in dreams, so good night all.

After some weeks, Padre Bartolomeu Lourenço, armed with all the necessary contracts, licences, and other legal documents, leaves for Coimbra, a city so renowned as a seat of learning that, had there been any alchemists there, the journey to Zwolle would have been quite superfluous, the Flying Man sets off on this stage of his journey riding a tranquil mule he has hired, a suitable mount for a priest of modest means who has little experience of riding, upon reaching his destination, he will share a horse with another gentleman, who has probably already completed his doctorate, although for anyone of doctoral status a sedan chair intended for long distances would be much more fitting, it is like tossing on the ocean waves, if only the fellow riding in front were not quite so incontinent when it comes to letting off wind. The journey as far as Mafra passes without incident, there is nothing to relate about the trip, only about the people who inhabit these regions, we clearly cannot stop en route and ask, Who are you, what are you doing, where is the pain, and if Padre Bartolomeu Lourenço made several stops, they were but brief, and lasted no longer than it took to give his blessing to those who requested it, although many of them were ready to digress at length in order to insinuate themselves into our story, they see a simple encounter with a priest as a sign, for travelling to Coimbra, he would not have passed this way unless he had to stop off at Mafra in order to locate Baltasar Sete-Sóis and Blimunda Sete-Luas. It is not true that tomorrow belongs only to God, that men must wait to see what each day brings, that death alone is certain but not the hour when it will strike, these are the maxims of those who are incapable of understanding the signs pointing to our future, such as the sudden appearance of this priest on the road from Lisbon, who has given his blessing upon request, and who proceeds in the direction of Mafra, and this means that the person blessed must also go to Mafra and help to build the Royal Convent, and there he will meet his death by falling from a scaffold, or be struck down by plague or a stab wound, or be crushed beneath the statue of St Bruno.

It is still a little early for such mishaps. When Padre Bartolomeu Lourenço rounded the final bend on the road and began to descend into the valley, he came across a multitude of people, multitude is perhaps an exaggeration, for they were no more than several hundred, and at first he could not see what was happening, because the crowd was running to one side, a trumpet sounded, some festivity perhaps, or even war, then suddenly came an explosion of gunfire, and rubble and gravel were hurled through the air, there were twenty shots in all before the trumpet sounded once more, but this time on a different note, labourers advanced toward the scene of the blasting with hand-carts and spades, filling in here on the hill, and clearing yonder on the slope facing Mafra, others, with their hoes slung over their shoulders, disappeared down into the excavations, while still others lowered baskets and then hauled them up filled with soil, which they then emptied out some distance away, where another group of workers were shovelling earth into carts, to be scattered over the embankment, there is no difference whatsoever between a hundred men and a hundred ants, the soil is transported from here to there because a man has not enough strength to do any more, then another man carries the load to the next ant, until, as usual, everything finishes up in the hole, for ants a place of life, for men a place of death, so, as you can see, there is no difference whatsoever.

Prodding with his heels, Padre Bartolomeu Lourenço spurred his mule forward, it was a seasoned animal, inured to the sound of gunfire, that is the advantage of not being a thoroughbred, hybrid creatures have been through so much, and as a result of their crossbreeding they are not easily alarmed, which is the best way for beasts and men to survive in this world. Along the road bogged down in mud, a sign that the springs in the earth were lost in that disturbance and were welling up to no advantage, or dividing into many little veins until the atoms of water completely separated and the hill remained dry, along this road, gently spurring on his mule, Padre Bartolomeu descended into the town, where he called on the parish priest to inquire about the family of Sete-Sóis. This particular parish priest had made a handsome profit from the sale of some land he had owned on the Alto da Vela, either because the land was considered to be worth a great deal or the owner himself was, it was valued at one hundred and forty thousand réis, a much higher sum than the thirteen thousand five hundred réis paid to João Francisco. The parish priest feels very pleased at the thought of the impressive convent that is about to enhance his parish with its community of eighty friars, such a convent here on his very doorstep will undoubtedly increase the number of baptisms, marriages, and deaths in the town, each sacrament will bestow material and spiritual benefits by reinforcing the church's coffers and the hope of salvation in direct ratio to the various functions and stipends, Truly, Padre Bartolomeu Lourenço, it is a great honour to receive you here in my house, the Sete-Sóises live nearby, they owned some land adjacent to mine on the Alto da Vela, a smaller holding than mine, needless to say, now the old man and his family earn their living by farming rented land, their son, Baltasar, returned home four years ago, he came from the war maimed for life and turned up here with his wife, I don't believe that they're married in the eyes of Holy Mother Church, and the woman has a name that's certainly not Christian, Is she called Blimunda, interrupted Padre Bartolomeu Lourenço, Then you know her, I married them, Ah, so they are married, I married them myself in Lisbon, whereupon the Flying Man, although not known in these parts by that name, expressed his gratitude to the parish priest, whose effusive welcome could be attributed to certain recommendations from the Palace, he then went off to call on the Sete-Sóis household, secretly pleased at having lied before God in the safe knowledge that God could not care less, for a man must know for himself when lies can be forgiven even as they are being told.

It was Blimunda who opened the door. Dusk was already falling, but she recognised the priest the moment he dismounted, after all, four years is not such a long time, she kissed his hand and were it not for the presence of some inquisitive neighbours, the greeting might have been quite different, for these two, or three when Baltasar is present, are governed by their emotions, all three have shared the same dream, all will see the flying machine beat its wings, the sun explode into even greater splendour, the amber attract the ether, the ether attract the magnet, the magnet attract the iron, all things attract each other, the real problem being to know how to arrange them in the right sequence, Padre Bartolomeu, this is my mother-in-law, Marta Maria had approached, puzzled that she could hear no one speaking, yet convinced that she heard Blimunda go to open the door although no one had knocked, and now there was an unknown priest standing there and inquiring about Baltasar, this is not the manner in which visits were conducted in those days, but there were exceptions, just as there are exceptions in every age, so here was a priest who came from Lisbon to Mafra to speak to a crippled soldier and a clairvoyant of the worst possible kind, because she can see what exists, as Marta Maria has already discovered for herself, because when she confided her fears that she might have a tumour in her stomach, Blimunda dismissed the idea, but it was true and they both knew it, Eat your bread, Blimunda, eat your bread.

Padre Bartolomeo Lourenço was sitting by the fire, for the night was already becoming chilly, when Baltasar and his father finally arrived. They saw the mule tethered in front of the house under the olive tree and noticed that it was still harnessed, Whose could this be, João Francisco asked and Baltasar made no reply but suspected that it might be a priest, the mules used by the clergy betray a certain evangelical submissiveness, which is quite unlike the spirited rebelliousness you find among the horses ridden by laymen, if, as Baltasar imagined, the mule belonged to a priest and had travelled for some distance, and no one was expecting a papal legate or nuncio, then it must be Padre Bartolomeu Lourenço, as indeed turned out to be the case. Anyone who expresses surprise that Baltasar Sete-Sóis should have observed all those details when it was already growing dark should know that the splendour of the saints is no vain illusion reflected by the anguished souls of mystics, or religious hocus-pocus propagated by effigies and oil paintings, for, after sharing Blimunda's bed for so long and enjoying sexual intercourse night after night, Baltasar was beginning to experience a spiritual light that bestowed dual vision, and though it did not provide for any deep probings, it did enable him to make such observations. João Francisco undid the mule's harness and came back into the house just as the priest was telling Baltasar and Blimunda that he had accepted an invitation to supper from the parish priest and accommodation for the night, first because there was not enough room in the Sete-Sóis household, and, second, because it would cause people in Mafra to gossip if a priest who had travelled a considerable distance should decide to lodge in a house that was little better than the stable at Bethlehem rather than avail himself of the comforts at the parochial residence or at the Viscounts' Palace, where hospitality would not be denied to a future doctor of canon law, Marta Maria told him, Had we known Your Reverence was coming, we would at least have killed a cockerel, for we've nothing in the larder worth offering an important guest, I should be happy to accept whatever you have to offer me, but it will cause everyone less inconvenience if I do not stay here for supper, as for the cockerel, Senhora Marta Maria, let it crow as much as it likes now that it has been saved from the pot, hearing it crowing is certain to give much greater pleasure, besides, it wouldn't be fair to the hens. João Francisco laughed heartily at this witty little speech, but Marta Maria could not even muster a smile as she tried to suppress a sharp twinge of pain in her stomach, Baltasar and Blimunda smiled politely, feeling that no more was expected of them, for they knew only too well that the priest's sayings always deviated from the words one expected and this was simply further proof, Tomorrow, one hour before sunrise, bring the mule already harnessed to the presbytery, both of you come, because we must have a chat together before I leave for Coimbra, and now, Senhor João Francisco and Senhora Marta Maria, receive my blessing, should it serve any purpose in the eyes of God, for it is a great presumption to imagine that we priests can judge the effectiveness of our own blessings, don't forget, one hour before sunrise, and with these words he departed, Baltasar accompanied him, carrying an oil lamp that gave scarcely any light, it was as if the lamp were saying to the night, I am a light and during the short walk, they did not exchange a single word, Baltasar made his way back in pitch darkness, his feet knew where they were treading, and when he entered the kitchen Blimunda asked, Well, then, did Padre Bartolomeu say what he wanted, He said nothing, tomorrow we shall find out, and João Francisco, remembering the priest's words, burst out laughing, That was a good story about the cock. As for Marta Maria, she was pondering some enigma, Now let's have supper, the two men sat at the table while the women ate apart, as was the custom.

They all slept as best they could, each with his own secret dreams, for dreams are like human beings, bearing some resemblance to one another but never quite identical, it would be as inaccurate to say, I saw a man, as to say, Today I dreamt about flowing water, for this is not enough to tell us who the man was or which water was flowing, the water that flowed in the dream belongs only to the dreamer, we shall never know what the flowing water signifies if we know nothing about the dreamer, and so we move to and fro, from the dreamer to the dreamt and from the dreamt to the dreamer, in search of an answer, Future generations will take pity on us, Padre Francisco Gonçalves, because they will know us so little and so badly, these were Padre Bartolomeu's words before retiring to his room, and Padre Francisco Gonçalves dutifully replied, All knowledge resides in God, That is true, the Flying Man replied, but God's knowledge is like a river coursing towards the sea, God is the source and men are the ocean, it would scarcely have been worth His while to have created so much universe if things should have turned out otherwise, and it seems incredible to us that anyone should be able to sleep after having said or heard such things.

At dawn, Baltasar and Blimunda arrived, leading the mule by its halter, but Padre Bartolomeu Lourenço did not need to be called, he opened the door the moment he heard the sound of the mule's hoofs striking the cobblestones and came out at once, he had already taken his leave of the parish priest of Mafra and left him with something to ponder, if God were the source and men the ocean, then how much did he still have to discover, for the parish priest of Mafra had forgotten almost everything he had ever learned, except, thanks to continuous practice, the Latin of the Mass and the sacraments, and the road that led between the legs of his housekeeper, who had slept in a cupboard under the stairs last night because there was a guest in the house. Baltasar held the mule by the reins while Blimunda stood a few paces away, her eyes lowered and her hood pulled forward, Good morning, they greeted him, Good morning, the priest replied before asking Blimunda if she had broken her fast, and from the shadows cast by her hood, she replied, I have not yet eaten, Tell Blimunda not to eat, Padre Bartolomeu had said to Baltasar, and those words were passed on to her, whispered into her ear as she and Baltasar lay together, so that the old couple would not hear, and their secret should remain safe.

Through the dark street they made their way up to the Alto da Vela, not the road to the village of Paz, which the priest should have taken if he was heading north, however, they seemed to feel obliged to avoid inhabited places, though there might be men sleeping or waking up in the huts they were passing, ramshackle buildings where you would find no one apart from roadworkers, men of brute strength and few graces, and should we chance to pass along these roads in a few months, or, better still, within the next few years, then we shall see a large city built from wood, bigger than Mafra, those who survive will see this and more, for the present, these primitive dwellings provide a refuge where men who are worn out from hours of digging and shovelling soil may rest their weary bones, soon there will even be a military fanfare, for the regiment has also arrived, but not to die in battle this time, now their only task is to keep a watchful eye over the hordes of workers and to lend a hand from time to time without disgracing the uniform, and frankly, one can scarcely distinguish the guards from those whom they are guarding, for if the latter are in tatters, the former are in rags. The sky has turned a pearly grey towards the sea, while over the hills a patch of colour like diluted blood gradually becomes more and more vivid, dawn will break soon, a medley of blue and gold, for the weather is perfect at this time of the year. Blimunda, however, sees nothing, her eyes are lowered, in her pocket nestles a piece of bread, which she must not eat just yet, What are they about to ask of me.

It is the priest who wants something, not Baltasar, who is as much in the dark as Blimunda. Below you can scarcely make out the outlines of the excavations, black forms against shadows, that must be the basilica down there. Labourers begin to crowd the site, they start to light bonfires and heat up some food, yesterday's leftovers, before the day's work begins, soon they will be enjoying broth from their porringers, which they soak up with chunks of rough-grained bread. Blimunda will have to bide her time. Padre Bartolomeu Lourenço says, In this world I have you, Blimunda, and you, Baltasar, my parents are in Brazil, my brothers in Portugal, so I have both parents and brothers, but for this enterprise I need neither parents nor brothers but friends, so listen carefully, I discovered everything there is to know about ether in Holland, it is not what most people believe and teach, and it cannot be obtained by means of alchemy, in order to go up into the sky and fetch it, we would have to be able to fly, and that is something we are still unable to do, but, mark my words, before it rises into the atmosphere to keep the stars aloft and become the air that God breathes, ether is to be found inside men and women, Then it must be the soul, Baltasar concluded, No, it is not the soul, at first I, too, thought that it might be the soul, I also thought that the ether might be formed by souls when death releases them from bodies and before they are finally judged, but ether is not constituted from the souls of the dead, it is constituted, note carefully, from the wills of living souls.

Down below, the men were starting to descend into the excavations, which were still enshrouded in darkness. The priest said, Inside us there is a will and a soul, the soul departs with death and goes where souls await judgment, no one knows for certain, but the will either detaches itself from man while he is still alive, or it is separated from the soul at death, and that will is ether, therefore it is the human will that sustains the stars, it is the human will that God breathes, And what must I do, Blimunda asked, but she guessed the reply, You will see the will inside people, I have never seen their will, just as I have never seen their soul, You do not see their soul because the soul cannot be seen, you have not seen their will because you were not looking for it, What does will look like, It's like a dark cloud, What does a dark cloud look like, You will recognise it when you see it, try it out with Baltasar, for that is why we have come here, I cannot, for I have promised that I'd never look inside him, Then try it with me.

Blimunda lifted her head, looked at the priest, and saw what she had always seen, that people are more alike inside than outside, and only differ when they are ailing, she took another look and insisted, I cannot see anything. The priest smiled, Perhaps I no longer have any will, but take a closer look, Yes, now I can see, I can see a dark cloud over the cavity of your stomach. The priest made the sign of the cross, Thanks be to God, now I shall fly. He took from his knapsack a glass phial with a flat piece of yellow amber stuck inside the bottom, This amber, which is also known as electron, attracts the ether, carry it with you wherever you are likely to meet people, for example, in processions, at autos-da-fé, or here on the site where the convent is being built, and the moment you perceive that a cloud is about to emerge from anyone, which invariably happens, hold out the open phial and allow the will to filter inside, And when the phial is full, It needs only a single will to make the phial full, but this is the impenetrable mystery of wills, where one can be stored, millions can be stored, one is equal to an infinite number, And what shall we do in the meantime, I'm off to Coimbra, from there, at the right moment, I shall send a message, then you will both travel to Lisbon, you will build the machine, and you, Blimunda, will collect wills, we three shall meet when the day finally comes for us to fly, I embrace you, Blimunda, and beg of you not to look at me so closely, I embrace you, Baltasar, and bid you farewell until we meet again. He mounted his mule and began to descend the slope. The sun had appeared over the crest of the hills. Eat your bread, Baltasar said, and Blimunda replied, Not yet, first I must go and see the wills of those men.

THEY HAVE RETURNED from Holy Mass and are seated under the roof of the oven. A light shower of rain falls gently amid the sunshine, Autumn is early this year, therefore Inês Antónia scolds her little boy, Come away from there or you'll get wet, but the child pretends not to hear, even in those days it was what one expected of children, although their acts of disobedience were less radical than they are today, and having warned him once, Inês Antónia does not insist, barely three months have passed since she buried his little brother, so why bother nagging this child, let him play in the rain if it makes him happy, splashing around barefoot in the puddles in the yard, May the Virgin Mother protect him from the smallpox that carried off his brother. Álvaro Diogo tells her, I've been promised work on the site of the Royal Convent, this was what they appeared to be talking about, but the mother is thinking about the child she has buried, their thoughts are divided, and just as well, for certain obsessions can become unbearable, just like this pain that troubles Marta Maria, a persistent stabbing that pierces her womb like the daggers piercing the heart of the Mother of God, why her heart, when it is in the womb that children are born, it is in the womb that the furnace of life is to be found, and how should one nourish life unless by labour, which explains why Álvaro Diogo is feeling so happy, the building of such a convent will take many, many years to complete, any stonemason who knows his trade will earn a good living, three hundred réis for a day's work, five hundred réis when they can work longer hours, And what about you, Baltasar, have you decided to go back to Lisbon, you're making a big mistake, for there will be plenty of work here,

They won't want disabled men with so many labourers around, With that hook of yours you can do almost as much as any able-bodied man, That's true, unless you are only trying to spare my feelings, but we must go back to Lisbon, is that not so, Blimunda, and Blimunda, who has remained silent, nods her head in agreement. Lost in thought, the elderly João Francisco is braiding a leather thong, he hears them converse but pays little attention to what they are saying, he knows that his son will leave home during the next few weeks, but he is displeased with him, to leave home once more after all those years of enforced separation because of the war, you would only have yourself to blame if you were to come back without your right hand next time, such is love that people harbour these thoughts. Blimunda rose to her feet, crossed the yard, and went out into the countryside, she walked under the olive trees skirting the road all the way up to the boundaries of the building site, her heavy clogs sinking into the soil, which had been softened by the rain, but even if she had been walking barefoot and stepping over rough stones she would have felt nothing, how could she feel so little pain, when her whole being is filled with horror at her rash behaviour that very morning, when she took communion while still fasting, she had pretended to eat her bread in bed, out of habit and obligation, but she had not eaten it, with lowered eyes and pretending to be contrite and submissive, she went into church, attended Holy Mass as if she were in the presence of Almighty God and listened to the sermon without raising her head, overwhelmed, or so it appeared, by all the threats of hell and damnation that rained from the pulpit, then she finally went up to the altar to receive the Sacred Host, and she saw. During all these years since she had first become aware of the gift she possessed, she had always taken communion in a state of sin, with food in her stomach, but today, without mentioning anything to Baltasar, she had decided that she would take communion while fasting, not to receive God but to see Him, if He truly existed.

She sat on the protruding root of an olive tree, from where she could watch the sea merging with the horizon, it was almost certainly raining heavily out at sea, Blimunda's eyes filled with tears, her shoulders shaking as she began to sob, and Baltasar stroked her hair, she had not heard him approach, What did you see in the Sacred Host, so she had not deceived him after all, how could she possibly have deceived him, when they spend night after night in each other's embrace, well, perhaps not every night, but certainly for the last six years they have been living together as husband and wife, I saw a dark cloud, she replied. Baltasar sat on the ground, the plough had not reached this patch of land, and it was overgrown and dried up, though moistened recently by the rain, these countryfolk are used to roughing it and sit or lie down wherever they happen to be, better still if a man can rest his head on a woman's lap, I'll wager that this was man's last gesture before the great flood swamped the earth. Blimunda told him, I was hoping to see Christ crucified or resurrected in glory, but all I could see was a dark cloud, Forget what you saw, Forget it, how can I forget it, if what is inside the Sacred Host is what is inside men, which, after all, is religion, the person we need here is Padre Bartolomeu Lourenço, perhaps he might be able to clear up the mystery, Perhaps, perhaps not, it's just possible that certain things cannot be explained, who knows, and no sooner were these words spoken than the rain began to fall with greater force, either as a sign of affirmation or denial, the sky is now overcast while a man and woman shelter beneath a tree, bereft of any children, after all, there is no guarantee that situations recur, locations differ as well as the times, and even the tree itself is different, but as for the rain, it has the same comforting touch on one's skin and on the soil, a life so excessive that it can kill, but this is something to which man has become accustomed since the beginning of creation, when the wind is gentle it mills the grain, when it is strong it tears the windmill's sails, Between life and death, said Blimunda, hovers a dark cloud.

Padre Bartolomeu Lourenço had written soon after settling in Coimbra, stating simply that he had reached his destination safely, but now a second letter arrived, asking them to proceed to Lisbon without delay, as soon as there was some respite from his studies, he would join them, besides, he had certain ecclesiastical duties to perform at court, and this would provide an opportunity to plan the next stage of their joint enterprise, And now tell me, how are your wills progressing, a seemingly innocent question, which gave the impression that he was inquiring about their wills rather than about the wills of others and about those who had lost them, but he raised the question without expecting any answer, just as in battle, when the captain gives orders or allows the bugle to give them on his behalf, Forward march, and the captain does not stand there waiting until the soldiers have consulted one another and reply, We'll go, we won't go, we're not going, either they start marching at once or find themselves up before a court-martial, We'll leave next week, Baltasar decided, but another two months were to pass, because in the meantime it was rumoured in Mafra, and confirmed by the parish priest in his sermon, that the King was coming to lay the foundation stone of the future convent with his own royal hands. First it was announced that the inauguration cere-mony would be on a date in October, but that would not have allowed enough time to dig the foundations to the right depth, despite the six hundred workers on the site and the constant blasting that rent the air morning, noon, and night, then it was to be in the middle of November, but further postponed because winter had arrived and the King would be in mud up to his garters. May His Majesty come soon, so that Mafra's age of glory may commence, so that the town's inhab-itants may raise their hands to heaven and witness with their mortal eyes the achievements of this mighty king, thanks to whom we can enjoy a foretaste of heaven before entering those celestial gates, and better to enjoy such bliss while still alive than after death, We'll watch the festivities then leave for Lisbon, Baltasar decided.

Álvaro Diogo has already been contracted as a stonemason and for the time being he is cutting stone brought from Pêro Pinheiro, massive blocks transported on wagons drawn by ten or twenty yokes of oxen while other labourers are engaged in breaking up inferior stone for the foundations, which are to be almost six metres deep, metre being the modern term, although in those days everything was measured in spans, which are still the standard used by those who measure men both great and small, for example, Baltasar Sete-Sóis, who has never been king, is taller than Dom João V, and Álvaro Diogo, who is no weak-ling, is accustomed to tackling large-scale constructions, there he is hammering the stone and hacking away at its surface, but he will go on to do other jobs. Having helped to set one block on top of another, he will subsequently become a stone-cutter and carver, for it is a truly royal task to erect a straight wall with a plumb line, and it is quite unlike all that business with battens and nails which occupies the carpenters who are building the wooden church where the solemn act of benediction and inauguration will be held when the King finally arrives. Strong poles are laid out to mark the perimeter where the improvised church will eventually be replaced by the basilica itself, but for the moment the roof is made from sailcloth lined with durable cotton, and the form of a cross is observed to add a note of dignity to this provisional wooden construction, which will one day be rebuilt in stone, and in order to watch these preparations, the inhabitants of Mafra start to neglect their workshops and fields, they have become idle at the sight of this enormous project being erected on the Alto da Vela, although still in its initial stages. Some might be excused, such as Baltasar and Blimunda, who bring their nephew to see his father, and since it is already midday Inês Antónia also comes with a pot of cooked cabbage and a lump of cured pork, the entire family is here except for the grandparents, and if we did not know that this construction is the fulfilment of a sacred vow because an heir was born to the King, we might mistake the crowd for some mass pilgrimage, each and all honouring their pledges to Almighty God, But no one is going to give me back my son, Inês Antónia thinks to herself, and she almost feels hatred for this other son who goes off to play among the rocks.

A few days earlier a miracle had taken place in Mafra when a raging gale had swept in from the sea and dashed the wooden church to the ground, poles, planks, beams, and joists collapsed in a tangle with the sails and canvas, just like the prodigious puffing of the mythical giant Adamastor when he puffed his way around the cape of his and our labours, and lest anyone be scandalised that an act of destruction should be described as a miracle, what other word could be used when the King, upon being informed of the incident, no sooner arrived in Mafra, then he began distributing gold coins with the same ease as we are telling this story, for the overseers had managed to rebuild the church within two days, and the coins were multiplied to reward their diligence, much better than simply multiplying loaves. The King is a prudent monarch who always carries coffers of gold wherever he travels, to cope with these and any other eventualities.

The day of the inauguration finally arrived, Dom João V had slept at the Viscounts' Palace, where the gates were guarded by the sergeant in command at Mafra with a contingent of auxiliary soldiers and Baltasar was anxious not to miss this opportunity to speak to the troops, but it was useless, because no one knew him or what he wanted, they were puzzled that anyone should want to discuss war at a time of peace, Look here, old fellow, these gates must be kept clear, for the King is expected to leave shortly, so a disheartened Baltasar, accompanied by Blimunda, went up to the Alto da Vela, where they were fortunate to find a place inside the improvised church, though many were turned away, and the interior presented an extraordinary sight, for the ceiling of the church was lined in taffeta in a subtle variety of contrasting reds and yellows, and the walls of the church were covered with opulent satin hangings that substituted for doors and windows, everything matched to perfection, and the red damask draperies were adorned with gold braiding and fringes. When the King arrives, the first thing he will confront will be three large imitation doors on the façade, with a painting overhead depicting St Peter and St John healing the beggar at the doors of the Temple in Jerusalem, an encouraging preliminary to all the other miracles that will be witnessed here, although none of them will be as resounding as the one already narrated about the gold coins, and above the aforesaid painting is another, depicting St Antony, to whom the basilica is to be dedicated because of a special pledge made by the King, if this has not already been mentioned, for so many things have happened within the last six years that something is bound to have been forgotten. Inside the church, as we started to narrate, there is the most magnificent spectacle, and it is difficult to believe that this is a wooden construction due for demolition. On the gospel side, that is, to the left of anyone facing the altar, which is not the main altar because it is the only one, and these observations are not meant to be offensive, what does he think we are, a bunch of ignoramuses, these details are given because after faith and its knowledge comes an age without faith and with other forms of knowledge, and who will read to us then, on the gospel side, there is a stool raised on a dais reached by six steps and adorned with precious white linen, with a hanging above and in front, and on the epistle side there is another stool on a dais with only three steps, instead of the six steps to which the other rises, an observation worth repeating so as to emphasise the difference, and here there is no canopy overhead, because it is clearly to be used by someone of less exalted rank. Here the vestments are laid out that will be worn by the Patriarch, Dom Tomás de Almeida, and there are silver artefacts for the divine service, a display worthy of this supreme monarch who is about to make his entrance. No detail has been overlooked, to the left of the crucifix an enclosure has been erected for the musicians, draped with crimson damask, and complete with an organ that will be played at the appropriate moments, and there the canons of the diocese will also sit in specially reserved benches, and Dom João V will proceed, upon arrival, to the dais on the right, from where he will preside over the ceremony, with the nobility and other important personages seated on the benches below. The floor of the church has been covered with rushes and reeds, and green cloths have been spread over them, this penchant for green and red among the Portuguese dating from centuries ago, and these will subsequently become the national colours on the creation of a republic.

The cross was blessed on the first day, an enormous piece of wood some five metres high, comparable in size with Adamastor or any similar giant, and with the natural dimensions of God Himself, and the entire congregation prostrated itself before the cross, especially the King, who shed many devout tears, and when the veneration of the cross was over, four priests lifted the cross, one at each extremity, and erected it by inserting the stem into a hole in a boulder which had been prepared for this purpose, although not by Álvaro Diogo, for however divine a symbol, the cross cannot stand up unless supported, unlike men, who even without legs can manage to stand erect, it is clearly a question of will power. The organ was playing merrily, the musicians were blowing on their instruments, and the voices of the choir intoned hymns of praise, and out here, the people who had flocked from the town and surrounding districts only to find there was no more room inside the church consoled themselves with the echoes of the psalms and hymns, and so the first day of the official ceremonies ended.

The following day, a second gust of wind blowing in from the sea threatened to blow down the entire contraption once more, but it subsided without incident, the celebrations were revived and the solemnities continued with even greater pomp in the town square to mark the seventeenth of November of this year of grace, one thousand seven hundred and seventeen, and by seven in the morning, in the biting cold, the parish priests were assembled from all the surrounding districts, with their assistant chaplains and parishioners, hence the firm belief that the expression biting cold dates from this historical occasion, to be used for centuries thereafter. The King arrived at half past eight after drinking his morning cup of chocolate, which the Viscount himself served, the royal procession then set out, headed by sixty-four Franciscan friars followed by all the clergy of the region, then came the patriarchal cross, six attendants dressed in red capes, the musicians, the chaplains in their surplices, and representatives from every conceivable order, then there was a gap to prepare the crowd for what followed, the canons of the chapter wearing their cloaks, some in white linen, others embroidered, and each canon with his personal attendant, chosen from the nobility walking before him, and his train-bearer behind, then came the Patriarch, wearing sumptuous vestments and a priceless mitre encrusted with precious stones from Brazil, then the King with his court, the Attorney General with his counsellors, and a great following of more than three thousand people, unless they were counted wrongly, and this extraordinary gathering had been assembled simply to lay a foundation stone, all the powers of the land were united here, with bugles and drums resounding through the air, above and below, there were cavalry and infantry troops as well as a German contingent of guards, and crowds upon crowds of spectators, the likes of which Mafra had never seen, but since it was impossible for all these people to fit into the church, entry was restricted to adults and the odd child who was smuggled in or managed to slip past the guards, earlier the soldiers had given the military salute and presented arms, it was still morning, and the strong wind had dropped at last, there was only the lightest breeze coming in from the sea, causing the flags to flutter and lifting the skirts of the women, a fresh little breeze in keeping with the season, but hearts burned with ardent faith, the souls of the faithful were exalted, and if some wills were flagging and anxious to take leave of their bodies, Blimunda arrived on the scene, and they were neither lost nor allowed to ascend to the stars.

The foundation stone was blessed, and then a second stone and a jasper urn, for all three were to be buried in the foundations, they were then carried in solemn procession in a litter, and inside the urn were placed coins of the day minted in gold, silver, and copper, some medals cast from gold, silver, and copper, and the parchment on which the solemn vow had been inscribed, the procession circled the entire square to give the crowd a good view, and people genuflected as the procession passed, only to find themselves constantly genuflecting for one reason or another, first the cross, then the Patriarch, then the King, and finally the friars and canons, so that many of them did not even bother to get up and remained on their knees. Finally the King, the Patriarch, and some acolytes proceeded to the chosen spot, where the foundation stone was to be laid, descending into the excavations by means of a broad wooden stairway two metres wide and comprising thirty steps, perhaps to commemorate the thirty pieces of silver given to Judas. The Patriarch carried the principal stone, assisted by the canons, while other canons followed carrying the second stone and the jasper urn, behind came the King and the Father General of the Sacred Order of St Bernard, who was almoner-in-chief and in that capacity he carried the money.

And so the King descended the thirty steps into the bowels of the earth, it looks as if he is departing this world, and that would mean a descent into hell were he not so well protected by blessings, scapulars, and novenas, and if these high walls inside the excavations should collapse, Your Royal Highness need have no fear, for we have propped them up with hardwood from Brazil to ensure greater strength, in the centre of the cavity stands a bench covered with crimson velvet, a colour frequently used in formal ceremonies of state, and the time will come when we shall see the same colour used for furnishing the interiors of theatres, on the bench is a silver bucket filled with holy water, and two small brushes made of green heather, their handles adorned with cords of silk and silver, and I as master of works pour a hod of lime and, Your Majesty, with this silver trowel will spread the lime, which has already been moistened with holy water sprinkled by the tiny brush, now lend a hand, we can lay the stone in position just as long as Your Majesty is the last to touch it, ready now, one tap more for everyone to hear, Your Majesty can climb up now, be careful not to slip, we shall look after the rest and lay the other stones in position, each stone carefully slotted into its own groove, and let the nobles bring twelve more stones, a lucky number ever since the time of the apostles, and hods of lime inside silver baskets for the greater protection of the foundation stone, the local Viscount wishes to imitate the mason's apprentices by carrying a hod of lime on his head, thus showing greater devotion, since he did not make it in time to help Christ carry His cross, he pours out the lime that will dispose of him one day, and this would make a fine conceit, dear Sir, except that this lime is not quick but slaked, Just like the wills of human beings, as Blimunda would observe.

The following day, after the King had gone back to Lisbon, the church was dismantled without the assistance of the wind for there was nothing but the rain sent down by God, the planks and poles were set aside for less regal necessities, such as scaffolding, bunks, berths, tables, or clogs, the taffeta and damask silks, the sailcloths and canvas were folded and stored away, the silverware went to the treasury, the nobility and aristocracy back to their mansions, the organ to play other notes, the choir to sing other melodies, and the soldiers to parade elsewhere, only the friars remained, to keep a watchful eye, and those five metres of crucified wood, the cross, erected over the excavations. Men started to go back down into the waterlogged cavities, because the required depth had not been reached everywhere, His Majesty had not seen everything and only said, as he got into the carriage that would take him back to court, Let them get on with the job, it's more than six years since I made my pledge, and I don't want these Franciscans on my tail for much longer, let no expense be spared, as long as the work is completed soon. Back in Lisbon, the keeper of the privy purse informed the King, Your Royal Highness should be warned that the princely sum of two hundred thousand cruzados has been spent on the inauguration of the convent at Mafra and the King replied, Put it on the account, for the work is still in its initial stages, one day we shall need to total up our expenses, and we shall never know how much we have spent on the project unless we keep invoices, statements, receipts, and bulletins registering imports, we need not mention any deaths or fatalities for they come cheap.

When the weather cleared up, after a week, Baltasar Sete-Sóis and Blimunda left for Lisbon, in this life everyone has something to build, the labourers remain here to build walls so that once everything is assembled and ready we shall take off, for men are angels born without wings, nothing could be nicer than to be born without wings and to make them grow, this much we have achieved with our minds, and if we have succeeded in making our minds grow, we shall grow wings, too, So farewell, dear Father, farewell, dear Mother. They simply said farewell, nothing more, for Baltasar and Blimunda did not know how to compose pretty speeches, nor were the old couple capable of understanding them, but with the passage of time you will always find yourself imagining that you might have said this or that, even believing that you actually said those words, so that what one narrates often becomes more real than the actual events narrated, however difficult it may be to put real events into words, such as when Marta Maria says, Farewell, I shall never see you again, and she never spoke truer words, for the walls of the basilica will not have risen one metre above the ground before Marta Maria is laid to rest in her grave. With her death, João Francisco will suddenly become twice as old, and take to sitting under the roof of the oven, his eyes devoid of expression, just as they are at this moment, as his son, Baltasar, and his daughter Blimunda, for daughter-in-law is a cheerless word, make their departure, however, he still has Marta Maria here beside him, even though she is alienated from life and has one foot in the grave already, her hands clasped over her womb, which begot life and is now begetting death. Her children emerged from the mine of her body, some to perish, though two survived, this one will not be born, for it is her own death, We cannot see them any more, let's go inside, says João Francisco.

It is December, and the days are short, heavy clouds hasten the encroaching darkness, so Baltasar and Blimunda decide to take refuge for the night in a hayloft at Morelena, they have explained they are travelling from Mafra to Lisbon, the farmer can see they are decent folk and loans them a blanket to cover themselves, such is his confidence. We already know how much these two love each other with their bodies, their souls, and their wills as they lie in each other's arms, their wills and souls witness their enraptured bodies, and possibly cling to them even more closely, in order to share their pleasure, difficult to know which part resides where, if the soul is losing or gaining when Blimunda lifts her skirts and Baltasar undoes his breeches, whether the soul is gaining or losing as they lie there sighing and moaning, or if the body conquers or is vanquished when Baltasar reposes inside Blimunda and she gives him repose, their bodies at rest. There is no more satisfying smell than that of turned hay, of bodies under a blanket, of oxen feeding at the trough, the scent of cold air filtering through the chinks in the hayloft, and perhaps the scent of the moon, for everyone knows that the night assumes a different smell when there is moonlight, and even a blind man, who is incapable of distinguishing night from day, will say, The moon is shining, St Lucy is believed to have worked this miracle, so it is really only a question of inhaling, Yes, my friends, what a splendid moon this evening.

In the morning, before sunrise, they got up, Blimunda had already eaten her bread. She folded the blanket, simply a woman respecting an ancient gesture, opening and closing her arms, securing the folded blanket under her chin, then lowering her hands to the centre of her own body, where she makes one final fold, no one looking at her would ever suspect that Blimunda has strange visionary powers, that if she could step outside her body this night, she would see herself lying underneath Baltasar, and it can truly be said of Blimunda that she can see her own eyes seeing. When the farmer comes to the hayloft he will find that the blanket has been folded as a sign of gratitude, and, being a mischievous fellow, he will cross-examine the oxen, Tell me, was Mass celebrated here last night, they will turn their heads with serene indifference, men always have something to say, and sometimes hit the nail on the head, for there was no difference whatsoever between the ritual of those lovers and the sacrifice of Holy Mass, and if there were, the Mass would surely lose out.

Blimunda and Baltasar are already on their way to Lisbon, skirting the hills, where windmills suddenly loom up from nowhere, the sky is overcast, the sun momentarily appears, only to vanish from sight once more, a southerly wind brings the threat of heavy rain, and Baltasar thinks, If it begins to rain we shall have nowhere to shelter, He then looks up at the cloud-ridden sky, one great sombre plaque, the colour of slate, he tells her, If wills are dark clouds, perhaps they're trapped in these thick, black clouds shutting out the sun, and Blimunda replies, If only you could see the dark cloud inside you, Or inside you, Or inside me, but if only you could see it, then you would realise that a cloud in the sky is nothing compared with the cloud inside man, But you've never seen my cloud or yours, No one can see his own will, and I swore that I would never look inside you, my mother was not mistaken, Baltasar Sete-Sóis, for when you give me your hand, when you embrace me, I do not need to see inside you, If I should die before you, I beg of you to look inside me, When you die, your will takes leave of your body, Who knows.

There was no rain throughout the journey, just that grey, dark roof extending southwards and hovering over Lisbon, level with the hills on the horizon, and this gave the impression that by raising one hand you might touch its surface, at times nature is a perfect companion, a man is journeying, a woman is journeying, and the clouds say among themselves, Let's wait until they are safely home, then we can turn to rain. Baltasar and Blimunda arrived at the estate and entered the coachhouse, and at last the rain began to fall, and because some of the tiles were cracked, the water trickled in discreetly, whispering softly, I'm here, now that you've arrived safely. And when Baltasar went up to the shell of the flying machine and touched it, the metal frame and wires creaked, but it is more difficult to know what they were trying to say.

THE WIRES AND irons have started to rust, the cloths have become covered in mildew, the dried out canes have started to untwine, a half-finished job does not need to grow old in order to disintegrate. Baltasar walked around the flying machine twice and was much put out by what he saw, with the hook on his left arm he tugged violently at the metallic skeleton, rubbing iron against iron to test its resistance, which he found to be poor, It strikes me that it would be better to dismantle the entire machine and start again, Dismantle it, by all means, but is it worth starting to rebuild it before Padre Bartolomeu Lourenço arrives, We could have remained in Mafra a little longer, If Padre Bartolomeu Lourenço said that we should come at once, then he is likely to arrive soon, who knows, perhaps he has already been here while we were waiting for the inauguration, there are no signs that he has been here, I hope you're right, So do I.

Within a week the machine was no longer a machine and bore no resemblance to its former self, what remained might have been mistaken for a thousand different things, men do not make use of all that many materials, and much depends on the way they are produced, arranged, and combined, just think of the hoe and the plane, a little metal and a little wood, and what the one implement does the other does not. Blimunda suggested, While we're waiting for Padre Bartolomeu Lourenço to arrive, let's build the forge, But how can we make the bellows, You must go to a blacksmith and see how it's done, if it doesn't work at first, try a second time, and if that doesn't work, try a third time, that's as much as anyone can expect of us, There's no need to take so much trouble, for Padre Bartolomeu Lourenço has left us enough money to buy the bellows, But someone is bound to ask why Baltasar Sete-Sóis needs bellows when he is neither a blacksmith nor an ironsmith, better to make them yourself, even if it means trying a hundred times.

Baltasar did not go alone. Though this expedition did not call for dual vision, Blimunda possessed the greater powers of observation, a more precise eye for linear detail, and a much keener perception of relative proportions when assessing a job. Dipping a finger into the murky oil of the lamp, she drew the various parts on the wall, the length of hide they required, the spout through which the air would be released, the fixed base, which would be made from wood, and the other section, which would be jointed, so that all they required now was a treadle for the bellows. In the far corner they built four walls with regular-shaped stones to the height of a man's waist, bracing them with wires inside and all around on the outside, then filling it in with soil and rubble. This operation robbed the Duke of Aveiro's estate of some of its walls, but although the estate does not strictly belong to the King like the convent at Mafra, it does have a royal licence, which has probably been long since ignored or forgotten, otherwise Dom João V might have sent someone to inquire whether Padre Bartolomeu Lourenço still hoped to fly one day or if this was simply a ruse to allow three people to live out their dreams when they could be more usefully employed, the priest in spreading the word of God, Blimunda in divining sources of water, and Baltasar in begging alms so that the gates of paradise might be opened to his benefactors, for when it comes to flying, it has been clearly shown that only the angels or the devil can fly, everyone knows that angels fly, and some have even attested to this phenomenon, and as for the devil, it is confirmed by Holy Scripture that he can fly, for there it is written that the devil took Jesus to the pinnacle of the Temple, and he must have carried Him through the air, because they did not climb up a ladder, and he taunted Jesus, saying, Cast thyself down, and Jesus refused, because He had no desire to be the first man to fly, One day the sons of men will fly, Padre Bartolomeu Lourenço said when he arrived to find the forge ready and also the trough for tempering the metal, All they needed now were the bellows, the wind will blow at the right moment, just as some mysterious spirit has blown through this place.

How many wills did you collect today, Blimunda, the priest asked during supper that same evening, No fewer than thirty, she replied, So few, have you collected more from men or from women, he went on to ask, Mostly from men, the wills of women seem less inclined to be separated from their bodies, for some strange reason. The priest did not react, but Baltasar said, Sometimes when my dark cloud covers your dark cloud they almost merge, Then you must have less will power than me, Blimunda replied, it is just as well that Padre Bartolomeu Lourenço is not offended by these frank exchanges, perhaps he, too, has had some experience of enfeebled wills during his travels through Holland or even here in Portugal, without its being brought to the attention of the Inquisition, or perhaps the Inquisition chooses to ignore the matter since this frailty is accompanied by much more grievous sins.

Let's turn to more serious matters now, said Padre Bartolomeu Lourenço, I shall come here as often as possible, but the work can only make progress if you are both involved, you did well to build the forge, and I shall find some means of obtaining bellows, you mustn't tire yourselves out with this labour, but we must make certain that the bellows are large enough for the machine, I'll leave you a drawing, so that in the absence of any wind, the bellows will do the job, and we'll fly, and you, Blimunda, mustn't forget that we need at least two thousand wills desiring to be free of their unworthy bodies or souls, the thirty wills you have gathered there could not lift Pegasus off the ground, even though he was a horse with wings, just think how big the earth is that we tread, it pulls bodies downwards, and although the sun is even greater, it still cannot pull the earth towards it, now, if we are to succeed in flying through the air, we shall need the combined forces of sun, amber, magnets, and wills, but the wills are the most important of all, without them, the earth will not allow us to ascend, and if you want to collect wills, Blimunda, mingle with the crowds at the Corpus Christi procession, amidst such a large gathering of people, there are bound to be plenty of wills ready for collecting, for you ought to know that processions encourage bodies and souls to weaken to such an extent that they are no longer even capable of safeguarding their wills, this doesn't occur at bullfights or at autos-da-fé, where there is so much excitement that the darkest clouds grow even darker than souls, it's like being in war, universal darkness pervading the hearts of men.

Baltasar asked, How shall I set about rebuilding the flying machine. Just as before, the same large bird you see in my sketch, and these are the various sections of the construction, I'm also leaving you this other drawing, with the measurements of the different parts, you must build the machine from the base upwards, just as if you were building a ship, you will entwine the cane and wire as if you were attaching feathers to bones, as I said before, I shall come whenever possible, to purchase the iron you should go to this place, the willows growing in the region will provide you with all the cane you need, and you can obtain hides from the slaughterhouse for the bellows, and I'll show you how to cure and cut them, Blimunda's sketches are all right for bellows to be used in a forge, but not for bellows capable of helping a machine to fly, and here is some money to buy a donkey, otherwise you'll find it impossible to transport all the necessary materials, you should also buy some large baskets, and stock up on grass and straw so that you can conceal what you carry in them, don't forget that this whole operation must be carried out in absolute secrecy, You should say nothing either to friends or relatives, there must be no other friends apart from our three selves, if anyone should come around snooping, you will say that you're looking after the estate by order of the King, to whom I, Padre Bartolomeu Lourenço de Gusmão, am responsible. De what, Blimunda and Baltasar asked with one voice, De Gusmão, the surname I assumed to show my indebtedness to the priest who tutored me in Brazil, Bartolomeu Lourenço was name enough, Blimunda blurted out, for I shall never get used to adding on de Gusmão, That won't be necessary, for you and Baltasar I shall always be the same Bartolomeu Lourenço, but the court and the academies will be expected to address me as Bartolomeu Lourenço de Gusmão because anyone who, like me, has a doctorate in canon law must have a name that accords with his status, Adam had no other name, Baltasar observed, And God has no name at all, the priest rejoined, for God cannot be named, and in paradise there was no other man from whom Adam had to be distinguished, And Eve was known only as Eve, Blimunda intervened, And Eve continues to be no one other than Eve, for I'm of the firm opinion that woman is but one in this world and multiple only in appearance, so she can dispense with any other name, and you are Blimunda, tell me, are you in need of Jesus, I am a Christian, Who denies it, Padre Bartolomeu reassured her before continuing, You understand my meaning, but anyone who claims to belong to Jesus, in conviction or name, is nothing but a hypocrite, so be yourself, Blimunda, and give no other reply when someone asks you your name.

The priest has returned to his studies in Coimbra, already in possession of bachelor's and master's degrees and soon he will also possess a doctorate, meanwhile, Baltasar takes the iron to the forge and tempers it in the well, and Blimunda scrapes the hides brought from the slaughterhouse, together they cut the willow cane and work at the anvil, she holding the sheet metal with pincers while he beats it with a hammer, both of them working to the same rhythm to ensure a steady pace, she holds out the smelted iron and he deals a cautious blow as they labour in perfect harmony without any need for words. And so the winter passed, and the spring, sometimes the priest came to Lisbon, and the moment he arrived, he would store in a chest the globes of yellow amber that he had brought with him, saying nothing of how he had obtained them, he would ask about the wills and inspect the machine from every angle which was rapidly taking shape and already much larger than when Baltasar had dismantled it, he then advised them how to proceed and returned to Coimbra to his decrees and those who issue them, Padre Bartolomeu was no longer a student and already giving lectures, *Iuris ecclesiastici universi libri tre, Colectanea doctorum tam veteram quam recentiorum in ius pontificum universum, Reportorium iuris civilis et canonici, et coetera*, without coming across any passage where there was written, You will fly.

June arrives. The sad news rapidly spreads throughout Lisbon that this year the Corpus Christi procession will not parade the ancient effigies of the giants, or the hissing serpent, or the fiery dragon, and there will be no mock bullfights, no traditional dances typical of Lisbon, no marimbas or bagpipes, nor will King David appear dancing in front of the canopy. The people ask themselves what sort of a procession this will turn out to be if there are no jesters from Arruda to deafen the streets with their tambourines, and the women from Frielas are forbidden to dance their version of the chaconne, and if the sword-dance is not to be performed, nor are there to be any floats, bagpipes, or drums, no frolicking of satyrs and nymphs to cover up frolics of another kind, the dance of the bishop's crozier will be banned, and the ship of St Peter will not sail forth on sturdy male shoulders, so what kind of procession is this meant to be, what pleasure will it give the people, for even if they should decide to allow the float organised by the kitchen gardeners, we shall no longer hear the hissing serpent, dear cousin, which used to give me the shivers, when it went swishing past, I cannot tell you how it used to terrify me.

The people flock to the Palace Square to see the preparations for the feast, and it all looks very promising, yes, sir, with a colonnade of sixty-one columns and fourteen pillars at least eight metres high, and the entire arrangement is more than six hundred metres in length, there are no fewer than four façades with innumerable statues, medallions, pyramids, and other decorations. The crowds begin to admire this latest pageant, and there is much more to see if you look ahead at the streets covered in bunting, where the masts supporting the marquees are decorated with silver and gold, and the medallions suspended from each marquee are overlaid with gold, on one side they depict the Blessed Sacrament surrounded by rays of light, and on the other, the Patriarch's coat of arms, while both sides carry the coat of arms of the Senate Chamber, And what about the windows, just look at those windows, as someone rightly exclaimed, for eyes are bewitched by the magnificent spectacle of draperies and valances in crimson damask fringed and tasselled with gold, We've never seen anything like it, the populace is almost ready to voice its approval, they have been robbed of one feast only to gain another, and it is difficult to decide which is the better of the two, the one is probably as good as the other, for some reason or other, the goldsmiths have announced that they intend to pay for illuminations in all the streets, and perhaps for the same reason the hundred and forty-nine columns of the archways in the Rua Nova have been adorned with silk and damask, no doubt, shopkeepers are anxious to exploit this opportunity to do good business. The crowds stroll by, reach the end of the road, and turn back, without so much as stretching out their fingers to touch those magnificent draperies, they are content to feast their eyes on these, as well as on the other silks and satins that enhance the display of merchandise under the archways, we appear to be living in the kingdom of trust, every shop, however, has its own black slave in the doorway, a club in one hand and a rapier in the other, any would-be pilferer is likely to receive a blow on the back, and the bailiffs are on hand to deal with more serious crimes, they carry neither helmet nor shield, but if the magistrate orders, Off with him to the Limoeiro, what is to be done except obey and miss the procession, and this might explain why there are so few thefts from the Body of Christ.

Nor will there be any stealing of wills. It is time for the new moon, for the moment, Blimunda's eyes are no different from those of other people, no matter whether she eats or fasts, and this makes her tranquil, content to allow wills to do as they please, to remain in the body or depart, hoping this will bring some rest, but suddenly she is troubled by a fleeting thought, What other dark cloud shall I perceive in the Body of Christ, in His carnal body, she whispered to Baltasar, and he replied in the same hushed tones, It must be that and that alone which would get the Passarola off the ground and into the skies, and Blimunda added, Who knows, perhaps all we really see is nothing but the dark cloud of God.

These are the words exchanged by a disabled man and a clairvoyant, one must forgive them their eccentricities and this conversation about transcendental things, while night has already fallen as they stroll through the streets between the Rossio and the Palace Square, amid the crowds who will not sleep this night and who, like them, tread the blood-red sand and the grass brought in by peasants to carpet the pavements, the city has never looked cleaner, this city that on most days has no equal in filth and squalor. Behind the windows the ladies are putting the finishing touches to their coiffures in elaborate rituals of pomp and artifice, soon they will be exhibiting themselves at their windows, none of these ladies wishes to be the first to appear, for while she is certain to attract the immediate attention of passers-by, no sooner does she start to enjoy this success than all is lost as the window opposite opens and another woman, her neighbour and rival, appears to divert the gaze of the admiring spectators, jealousy tortures me, especially when the other woman is so offensively ugly while I am divinely beautiful, her mouth is enormous, mine but a rosebud, and before my rival has time to speak, I call out, Away with you, flatterer. In these tournaments among the ladies, those who live on the lower floors enjoy certain advantages, without further ado the gallants beat out the metre and the rhyme of some conceit in their empty heads, while from the upper floors of the building descends another conceit, declaimed for all to hear, the first poet responds by reciting his lines while the others eye him coldly, betraying their rage and contempt that he should win the lady's favours, thus confirming their suspicions that this coupling of epigraph and gloss hints at coupling of another order. These suspicions remain unspoken, because they are all equally at fault.

The night is warm. People stroll to and fro, playing and singing, street urchins chase one another, this is a plague without remedy that has been with us since the world began, the little wretches hide behind the women's skirts and receive a kick in the pants or cuff on the ear from the men accompanying the women, which merely sends them scampering off to make a nuisance of themselves elsewhere. They improvise mock bullfights with a simple little bull made out of two ram's horns, perhaps ill-matched, and the branch of an aloe tree fixed to a wooden board with a handle in front, held against the body like a shield, the urchin who plays the bull attacks with great panache and receives the wooden banderillas embedded in his shield with cries of feigned torment, but if the banderillero misses his aim and is butted by the bull, all nobility of caste is lost and another chase ensues, which soon gets out of hand, the tumult unsettles the poets, who ask to have the conceit repeated, calling up, What did you say, and grinning, the ladies reply, A thousand little birds bring me tokens of love, and so, with these intrigues, frolics, and scamperings, the crowd whiles away the night on the streets, and indoors there is revelry and cups of chocolate, as dawn breaks, the troops who will flank the procession start to assemble once more in ceremonial dress in honour of the Blessed Sacrament.

In Lisbon, no one has slept. The frolickings are over, the women have withdrawn from their windows to renew their smudged or faded cosmetics, they will be back at their windows shortly, once more resplendent with rouge and powder. The crowd of whites, blacks, and mulattos of every hue, these, those, and all the others line the streets in the hazy morning light, only the Palace Square, open to the river and the sky, reveals a blue patch amid the shadows, which unexpectedly turns to red in the direction of the Palace and patriarchal church as the sun breaks over the terrain beyond and dispels the mist with a luminous puff. The procession is about to begin. It is led by the Masters of the House of the Twenty-Four Guilds, first come the carpenters, carrying the banner of their patron, St Joseph, then come the other insignia, huge banners depicting the patron saint of each guild, made from damask brocade and trimmed with gold, are so enormous that it takes four men to support them, who alternate with four others so that they may rest in turn, fortunately, there is no wind, and as they proceed the silk cords and gilt tassels hanging from the tips of the poles sway to the rhythm of their gait. Next comes the statue of St George with all due solemnity, drummers on foot, buglers mounted, the former drumming, the latter blowing, rataplan tarara ta tara, Baltasar is not among the spectators in the Palace Square, but he hears the bugles in the distance, he breaks out in goose-pimples as if he were back on the battlefield, watching the enemy prepare to attack before our forces retaliate, and suddenly he feels a sharp pain in his stump, he has not felt such pain in a long time, perhaps it is because he has not attached his hook or spike, for the body registers these things, as well as other memories and illusions, Blimunda, were it not for you, whom would I have at my right-hand side to embrace with this arm, it is you I hold tight by the shoulder or waist with my good hand, something people find strange, unaccustomed as they are to seeing a man and a woman being so demonstrative in public. The flags have disappeared, the sounds of the bugles and drums fade into the distance, and now comes the standard-bearer of St George, the king-at-arms, the armoured knight, clad from head to foot in armour, with plumed helmet and lowered visor, the saint's adjutant in battle, who carries his flag and lance and precedes him to ascertain whether the dragon is roused or asleep, an unnecessary precaution now, because the dragon is unlikely to appear or to be caught napping when he has been eliminated, alas, from the Corpus Christi procession, this is no way to treat dragons, serpents, and giants, and it is a sad world that allows itself to be deprived of such attractions, in the end, some will be preserved or will prove to be so attractive that those responsible for transforming the procession will be reluctant to retain them, in case people speak of nothing else, for horses either have to be kept in their stables or left like miserable lepers to pasture as best they can in the open fields, and here come forty-six black and grey horses with opulent saddle-cloths, so help me God if these animals are not better dressed than the spectators who watch them go past, this being the feast of Corpus Christi, everyone dresses up in his Sunday best, in clothes worthy to witness the Lord, who, having made us naked, only admits us to His presence when we are dressed, what is one to make of such a God, or the religion that represents Him, it is true that not many of us are beautiful to behold when we are naked, as you can tell from certain faces without cosmetics, let us imagine what St George, who is now looming into sight, would look like if we were to remove his silver armour and plumed helmet, a puppet on hinges, without a wisp of hair where men are hirsute, a man should be able to be a saint and still have what other men possess, and there should be no conceivable sanctity that has not experienced a man's strength plus the weakness that is often inherent in that strength, how can one explain these things to St George, who comes mounted on a white horse, if such an animal can be called a horse, for it lives in the royal stables with its own groom to brush and exercise it, a horse kept solely for the saint to ride, never mounted by the devil or by man, a sad beast that will die without ever having lived, may God grant that once it is dead and flayed, its skin will be used for a drum and that whosoever plays that drum will rouse its savage heart, now aged and spent, everything in this world, however, is ultimately balanced and recompensed, as was seen with the death of the child in Mafra and that of the Infante Dom Pedro, and today that conviction is reaffirmed, St George's page is a young squire riding a black steed, with raised lance and plumed helmet, and how many mothers lining those streets, watching the procession over the shoulders of the soldiers, will dream this night that it is their own son who rides that horse, St George's page on earth and perhaps even in heaven, for such an honour it would be worth bearing a child, and once more St George approaches, this time depicted on a huge banner carried by the Confraternity of the Royal Church of the Royal Hospital, and to conclude this opening highlight come timpanists and trumpeters dressed in velvet with white plumes in their caps, and now there is the briefest pause as the confraternities exit from the Royal Chapel, thousands of men and women according to rank and sex, here Adams do not mingle with Eves, look, there goes António Maria, and Simão Nunes, and Manuel Caetano, and José Bernardo, and Ana da Conceiçao, and António de Beja, and the somewhat less important José dos Santos, and Brás Francisco, and Pedro Caim, and Maria Caldas, names as varied as the colours of their cloaks of red, blue, white, dark crimson, green, and black, just as some of the passing brethren are black, but sadly, this confraternity, even while participating in the procession, is unlikely to arrive at the steps of the altar of Our Lord Jesus Christ, unless one day God disguises Himself as a black man and proclaims in every church throughout the land that a white man is worth half a black one, so it is up to you if you want to enter the gates of paradise, which explains why the beaches of this garden, planted, as it so happens, on the seashore, will one day become crowded with aspirants trying to darken their skin, an idea that would cause amusement, some do not even frequent the beaches, but stay at home and use various oils to darken their complexions, so that when they go out they are no longer recognised even by their neighbours, who comment, What's this fellow doing here, and this is the great difficulty faced by the coloured confraternities, meanwhile the following appear, more or less in this order, the confraternity of Our Lady of Holy Doctrine, that of Jesus and Mary, of the Holy Rosary, of St Benedict, a portly figure despite much abstinence, of Our Lady of All Graces, of St Crispin, of the Mother of God from São Sebastião of Pedreira, where Baltasar and Blimunda live, of the Via Sacra of St Peter and St Paul, another confraternity of the Via Sacra but this time from Alecrim, of Our Lady of Succour, of Jesus, of Our Lady of Remembrance, and of Our Lady of Good Health, for without her how will Rosa Maria keep her virginity, and what virtue can Severa hope to preserve, then comes the Confraternity of Our Lady da Oliveira, under whose shade Baltasar once ate, that of St Antony of the Franciscan Nuns of St Martha, of Our Lady of Repose of the Flemish Nuns from Alcântara, of the Holy Rosary, of Holy Christ, of St Antony, of Our Lady of the Penitentiary, and of St Mary the Egyptian, and if Baltasar were a soldier in the royal guard, he would be entitled to belong to this particular confraternity, and it is a great pity that there is no confraternity for the disabled, next comes the Brotherhood of Charity, which might be a suitable confraternity for Baltasar, and yet another Confraternity of Our Lady of the Penitentiary, but this time from the Carmelite Convent, for the previous one was that of the Tertiaries of St Francis, the procession appears to have run out of invocations, so the participants start repeating them, the Confraternity of Holy Christ reappears, this time from the Holy Trinity, whereas the previous one came from the Convent of St Paul, then the Brotherhood of Eternal Rest, then that of St Lucy, of Our Lady of a Good Death, if there is such a thing as a good death, and of Jesus of the Forgotten, then the Confraternity of the Souls of the Church of the Immaculate Conception, come rain or shine, that of Our Lady of the City, of the Souls of Our Lady of Perpetual Succour, of Our Lady of Mercy, of St Joseph, Patron Saint of Carpenters, of Holy Succour, of Compassion, of St Catherine, of the Lost Child, some lost, others forgotten, neither found nor remembered, for not even remembrance does them any good, that of Our Lady of the Purification, another Confraternity of St Catherine, the previous one was for booksellers, this one is for road pavers, the Confraternity of St Anne, that of St Eloi, the rich little patron saint of the goldsmiths, that of St Michael and the Holy Souls, of St Martial, of Our Lady of the Holy Rosary, of St Justa, of St Rufina, of the Souls of the Martyrs, of Wounds, of the Mother of God and St Francis of the City, that of Our Lady of Sorrows, as if we did not already have enough sorrows, and finally of the Holy Remedies, for remedies always come afterwards and nearly always when it is much too late, so any remaining hopes are placed in the Blessed Sacrament, which is now arriving, the image is depicted on a banner and preceded by the precursor St John the Baptist, who appears as a child, dressed in skins and accompanied by four angels who scatter flowers as they advance, and it is difficult to believe that there could be another land where more angels roam the streets, you need only stretch out a finger to perceive at once that they are real, it is true they do not fly, but that goes to show that to be able to fly is not sufficient proof of the angelic state, if Padre Bartolomeu de Gusmão, or simply Lourenço, should start to fly one day, he will not suddenly find himself transformed into an angel, other qualities are essential, but it is much too soon to pursue these inquiries, for we still need to collect many more wills and we are only halfway through the procession, the heat becomes more intense as the morning advances on the eighth of June in the year seventeen hundred and nineteen, what comes next, the religious communities, but the crowd pays little attention, friars pass and are ignored, and no one seems interested in identifying the different orders, Blimunda was looking up at the sky and Baltasar was looking at Blimunda, she doubting whether there would be a new moon until she saw some sign above the Carmelite Convent, that first tapered crescent, a curved blade, a pointed scimitar capable of prising open all those bodies before her very eyes, just at that moment the first religious order passed, which one, I didn't notice, they were friars, tertiaries of St Francis of Jesus, Capuchins, monks from the Convent of St John of God, Franciscans, Carmelites, Dominicans, Cistercians, Jesuits from St Rock and St Antony, with so many colours and names that heads begin to spin and memories to wander, and now it is time to eat the food one has either provided or bought, and as we eat, we comment on the habits of the religious orders who have just passed, the gold crosses, the mutton sleeves, the white kerchiefs, the long cloaks, the high stockings, the buckled shoes, the puffs and gatherings, the full skirts, the colourful mantles, the lace collars and long jackets, only the lilies of the field do not know how to thread or weave and are therefore naked, and if God had wanted us to go around naked, He would have made men lilylike, fortunately, women do look like lilies, but with clothes on, Blimunda looks like one, with or without clothes, what thoughts are these, Baltasar, what sinful memories to be having when the cross from the Patriarchal Basilica is arriving, immediately behind the communities of the Congregation of Missions and the Oratory, and innumerable members of the clergy from the parishes, ah, dear friends, so many people anxious to save our souls, which still have to be found, do not imagine, Baltasar, because you are a soldier, even though disabled, that you belong to the confraternity now passing, one hundred and eighty-four men from the Military Order of St James of the Sword, one hundred and fifty from the Order of Aviz, and about the same number from the Order of Christ, the last of these is formed by monks who decide for themselves who can join their confraternity, although God has no wish to see defective animals on His altars, especially if they are of the lower orders, so let Baltasar stay where he is, watching the procession go by, the pages, the choristers, the chamberlains, two lieutenants of the royal guard, one, two, in full dress uniform, which nowadays we would probably refer to as ceremonial dress, then the patriarchal cross, with blood-red whips hanging from one side, the chaplains carrying staffs crested with posies of carnations, ah, the sad destiny of flowers, for one day they will be attached to the barrels of rifles, then the choirboys of the Basilica of St Mary Major, which is both umbrella and basilica, with alternate sections in red and white, and in two or three hundred years people will start referring to umbrellas as basilicas, and you will hear them say, My basilica has a broken rib, I've left my basilica on the bus, I've had a new handle made for my basilica, When will my basilica at Mafra be ready, the King muses as he walks behind, holding one of the poles supporting the canopy, but first comes the cathedral chapter, the deacons in their white dalmatics, then the priests wearing chasubles of the same colour, and finally the church dignitaries with amice, cope, and silver plaque, what are the masses likely to know about these names, when it comes to the mitre, they are familiar with both the word and the form, for mitre is the pope's nose you find in the chicken's arse and the hat stuck on the canon's head, each canon in the procession is assisted by three members of his household, one with a lighted torch, another carrying the canon's hat, and both in court dress, while his train-bearer is dressed in coat of mail, now the Patriarch's entourage appears, first come six relatives of noble birth carrying lighted torches, then his beneficed assistant with the crozier, accompanied by another chaplain with the incense boat, followed by the acolytes swinging thuribles in wrought silver, two masters of ceremonies, and twelve pages who also carry torches, ah, you sinners, you men and women who spend your ephemeral lives courting perdition by fornicating and eating and drinking in excess, neglecting the sacraments, omitting to pay tithes, and speaking of hell with contempt and bravado, you men who at the slightest opportunity fondle women's buttocks in church, you shameless women who do everything in church short of fondling men's private parts, look at what is passing, the canopy supported by eight poles and I, the Patriarch beneath it, holding up the sacred monstrance, kneel, kneel, you sinners, you should castrate yourselves at once and fornicate no more, you should gag your mouths at once rather than contaminate your souls with so much food and drink, you should empty your pockets at once, because you will have no use for escudos in paradise or in hell, and in purgatory debts are honoured with prayers, your escudos are needed here on earth to purchase gold for another monstrance, to keep all these church dignitaries in silver, the two canons who raise the corners of my cape and carry the mitres, the two subdeacons who raise the hem of my vestments in front, and the train-bearers behind, which explains why they grovel so, this intimate friend who has the rank of count and carries the train of my cape, the two esquires with the flabella, and the mace-bearers with their silver staffs, the first subdeacon carries the veil of the golden mitre, for it must not be touched by hand. Christ was foolish never to have worn a mitre on His head, He may have been the Son of God, but He was somewhat gauche, for it is common knowledge that no religion can prosper without the wearing of a mitre, tiara, or bowler hat, had Christ worn any one of these three, He would have been made a high priest and been appointed governor instead of Pontius Pilate, just think what I should have escaped, and what a better world this might have been, had it turned out otherwise and they had not made me Patriarch, render unto Caesar what belongs to God, and render unto God what belongs to Caesar, then we shall settle accounts and share the money, one piece of silver for me and one for you, truly I say unto you, as say I must, Behold how I, your sovereign King of Portugal, the Algarves and all the rest, walk devoutly in the procession holding one of these gilded poles, and how a sovereign strives to protect his homeland and people both temporally and spiritually, I could have just ordered a footman to take my place, or have appointed a duke or marquis to take my place, but here I am in person and accompanied by the Infantes, my relatives and your masters, kneel, kneel, for the sacred monstrance is about to pass and I am passing, and Christ the King is inside the monstrance, and inside me is the grace of being king on earth, the king made of flesh, in order to feel, for you well know how nuns are regarded as the spouses of Christ, and that is the holy truth, for they receive me in their beds as they receive the Lord, and it is because I am their Lord that they sigh in ecstasy, clutching their rosary in one hand, mystical flesh, mingled and united, while the saints in the oratory strain their ears to hear the words of passion whispered under the canopy, a canopy stretched over heaven, for this is heaven and there is none better, and Christ crucified droops His head to one side, wretched fellow, perhaps overwhelmed by suffering, perhaps to get a better look at Paula as she removes her clothes, perhaps consumed with jealousy that He should be robbed of this spouse, a flower of the cloister perfumed by incense, adorable flesh, but that's that, I then depart, leaving her behind, and if she ends up pregnant the child is mine, no need to announce it a second time, there come the choristers behind, singing motets and hymns, and this gives me an idea, for kings are a veritable mine of ideas, how could they govern otherwise, so let the nuns of Odivelas come to sing the Benedictus in Paula's chamber as we lie in each other's arms, before, during, and after intercourse, amen.

Salvos rang out and rockets were fired from the ships, there was also a salute from the nearby fortress in the Palace Square, its echoes resounding far and wide, cannons were fired from garrisons and towers, the royal regiments from Peniche and Setúbal presented arms, and formed ranks in the square. The Body of Christ is carried through the city of Lisbon, the sacrificial lamb, the Lord of all armies, unfathomable contradiction, golden sun, crystal, and monstrance that causes heads to bow, divinity devoured and digested until it becomes faeces, who will be astonished to see you hand in glove with these inhabitants, slaughtered sheep, devourers of their own devoured selves, which is why men and women drag themselves through the streets, strike themselves and others in the face, beat loudly on their breasts and thighs, stretch out their hands to touch the hems that pass, the brocades and lace, the velvets and ribbons, the embroidery and jewels, *Pater noster qui non estis in coelis.*

It is getting late. In the sky there is the faintest light, almost invisible, the first sign of the moon. Tomorrow Blimunda will have her eyes, today is a day for blindness.

P ADRE BARTOLOMEU LOURENÇO has now returned from Coimbra with his doctorate in canon law, and de Gusmão has been officially added to his surname and signature, and who are we to accuse him of the sin of pride, better to forgive him his lack of humility for the reasons he himself gave, so that we might be forgiven our own sins, that of pride and all the others, for it would be much worse to change one's face or word than to change one's name. His face and word do not appear to have changed, nor has his name for Baltasar and Blimunda, and if the King has made him a chaplain of the royal household and an academician of the Royal Academy, these are faces and words that can be assumed and dropped, and together with his adopted name, they remain outside the gates of the Duke of Aveiro's estate and do not enter although one can imagine how these three would react if they were to confront the machine, the aristocrat would see them as mechanical inventions, the chaplain would exorcise the diabolical work there on display, and, because this was something destined for the future, the academician would withdraw and only return when it finally belonged to the past. However, this is today.

The priest lives in one of the houses overlooking the Palace Square, in apartments rented out by a woman who has been widowed for many years, and whose husband was a mace-bearer at the Palace until he was stabbed in a brawl during the reign of Dom Pedro II, an incident long since forgotten and only raised here because the woman happens to live in the same house as the priest and it would look bad not to give those few facts at least, even while withholding her name, which tells us nothing, as I have already explained. The priest lives close to the

Palace, and just as well, because he goes there frequently, not so much because of his duties as a chaplain appointed to the royal household, for that title is honorary in the main, but because the King is fond of him and has not given up hope of seeing his enterprise completed, and since eleven years have already elapsed, the King inquires tactfully, Shall I see your machine fly one day, a question Padre Bartolomeu Lourenço cannot honestly answer except to say, Your Majesty may rest assured that my machine will fly one day, But will I be here to see it fly, May Your Majesty live almost as long as the ancient patriarchs of the Old Testament, and may you not only see the machine fly but fly it yourself. This answer borders on insolence, but the King does not appear to notice, or if he does, he chooses to be indulgent, or perhaps he is distracted as he remembers having promised to attend the harpsichord lesson about to be given to his daughter, the Infanta Dona Maria Bárbara, that must surely be the reason, he invites the priest to join his entourage, and not everyone can boast of such an honour.

The Infanta is seated at the harpsichord, and although she is barely nine years of age, heavy responsibilities already weigh on that little head, learning to place her stubby fingers on the right keys, to be aware, if she is aware, that a convent is being built in Mafra, for there is much truth in the saying that trivial events can spark off the most prodigious consequences, the birth of a child in Lisbon results in a convent being built, a gigantic edifice in stone, and Domenico Scarlatti being contracted to come all the way from London. Their Royal Majesties preside at the lesson with little ostentation, some thirty people are present, if that, counting the footmen of the week attending upon the King and the Queen, the governesses, several ladies-in-waiting, as well as Padre Bartolomeu de Gusmão in the background along with several other clerics. The maestro corrects her fingering, fa la do, fa la do, the royal Infanta pouts and bites her lip, in this she is no different from any other child her age, whether born in a palace or anywhere else, her mother suppresses a certain impatience, her father is regal and severe, only women, with their tender hearts, allow themselves to be lulled by music and by a little girl, even when she plays so badly, and we need not be surprised to find Dona Maria Ana expecting miracles, even though the Infanta is still a beginner and

Signor Scarlatti has been in Lisbon only a few months, and why must these foreigners complicate their names, when it takes so little to discover that his real name is Scarlet, and very suitable, too, for he is a fine figure of a man, with a long face, a broad, firm mouth, and eyes set wide apart, I do not know what it is about the Italians, especially this one, who comes from Naples and is thirty-five years old. It's the force of life, my dear.

Once the lesson was over, the gathering dispersed, the King went in one direction, the Queen in another, the Infanta went who knows where, everyone observing precedence and protocol, and making endless courtesies, the governesses with their rustling skirts and the footmen with their beribboned breeches withdrew last of all, and in the music room there remained only Domenico Scarlatti and Padre Bartolomeu de Gusmão. The Italian fingered the keyboard of the harpsichord, first at random, then as if searching for a motif or attempting to modify certain reverberations, and suddenly he appeared to be totally absorbed in the music he was playing, his hands running over the keyboard like a barge flowing on the current, arrested here and there by branches overhanging the riverbanks, then away at rapid speed before vacillating over the distended waters of a deep lake, the luminous bay of Naples, the mysterious and echoing canals of Venice, over the bright, shimmering light of the Tagus, there goes the King, the Queen has already retired to her apartments, the Infanta is bent over her embroidery frame, for an Infanta learns these things from childhood, and music is a profane rosary of sounds, Our Mother who art on earth. Signor Scarlatti, the priest said when the maestro had stopped improvising on the keyboard and all the reverberations ceased, Signor Scarlatti, I cannot claim to know anything about the art of music, but I'll wager that even an Indian peasant from my native Brazil who knows still less about music than I do would feel enraptured by these celestial harmonies, Perhaps not, the musician replied, for it is a well-known fact that the ear has to be educated if one wishes to appreciate musical sounds, just as the eyes must learn to distinguish the value of words and the way in which they are combined when one is reading a text, and the hearing must be trained for one to comprehend speech, These weighty words moderate my frivolous remarks, for it is a common failing among men to say what they believe others wish to hear them say, without sticking to the truth, however, for men to be able to stick to the truth, they must first acknowledge their errors, And commit them, That is a question I couldn't answer with a simple yes or no, but I do believe in the necessity of error.

Padre Bartolomeu de Gusmão rested his elbow on the lid of the harpsichord, watched Scarlatti at some length, and while they remain silent, let us say that this fluent conversation between a Portuguese priest and an Italian musician is probably not pure invention but an admissible transposition of phrases and compliments they undoubtedly exchanged during those years, both inside and outside the Palace, as we shall have occasion to see in subsequent chapters. And lest anyone should express surprise that Scarlatti was able to speak Portuguese within a few months, let us not forget that he was a musician, and that during the previous seven years he had grown familiar with the language in Rome, where he had been in the service of the Portuguese Ambassador, not to mention his missions throughout the world to royal and episcopal courts, and whatever he learned he never forgot. As for the erudite nature of his dialogue, and the pertinence and eloquence of his words, he must have had help from someone.

You're right, the priest said, but this means that man is not free to believe that he is embracing truth only to find himself clinging to error, Just as he is not free to assume he is clinging to error, only to find himself embracing truth, the musician replied, and then the priest said, Don't forget that when Pilate asked Jesus what the truth was, he expected no answer, nor did the Saviour give him one, Perhaps they both knew that there is no answer to such a question, Therefore Pilate becomes like Jesus, In the final analysis, yes, If music is such an excellent mistress of debate, I would rather be a musician than a preacher, Thank you for the compliment, Padre Bartolomeu de Gusmão, I dearly hope that one day my music will achieve the same pattern of exposition, counterpoint, and conclusion you find in sermons and orations, Yet, if one carefully considers what is said and how it is said, Signor Scarlatti, when something is expounded and counterpoised, it is nearly always nebulous and obscure and finishes up in a meaningless void. The musician offered no comment, and the priest concluded,

Every honest preacher is aware of this as he descends from the pulpit. Shrugging his shoulders, the Italian said, There is silence after listening to music or a sermon, what does it matter if a sermon is praised or music applauded, perhaps only silence truly exists.

Scarlatti and Bartolomeu de Gusmão went down to the Palace Square, where they parted to go their separate ways, the musician to create music for the city until it was time to start rehearsing in the Royal Chapel, the priest to his veranda, from where he could view the Tagus and, across the river, the lowlands of Barreiro, the hills of Almada and Pragal, and, way beyond, the Cabeça Seca do Bugio, which was barely visible, what a glorious day, when God went forth to create the world, He did not simply say, Fiat, because one word and no more would have resulted in the creation of a world of total uniformity, God went forth and made things as He went, He made the sea and sailed thereon, then He made the earth in order to go ashore, in some places He tarried, others He passed through without pausing to look, and here He rested and, because there was no human being around to watch, bathed in the river, and to commemorate this event, great flocks of seagulls continue to gather near the river-bank, waiting for God to bathe once more in the waters of the Tagus, although these are no longer the same waters, hoping to see Him just once in recompense for having been born seagulls. They are also anxious to know if God has aged much. The mace-bearer's widow came to tell the priest that the meal was served, below a detachment of halberdiers passed, escorting a carriage. Adrift from her sisters, a seagull hovered over the eaves of the roof, sustained there by the wind that swept inland, and the priest murmured, May God bless you, bird, and deep down he felt that he himself was made of the same flesh and blood, he shuddered as if he had suddenly discovered feathers growing on his back, and when the seagull vanished he found himself lost in a wilderness, This would make Pilate the same as Jesus, he suddenly thought as he returned to this world, numbed by the feeling that he was naked, as if he had shed his skin inside his mother's womb, and then he said in a loud voice, God is one.

All that day, Padre Bartolomeu Lourenço remained closeted in his room, groaning and sighing, and it was already night when the mace-bearer's widow knocked on his door and announced that supper was ready, but the priest ate nothing, as if he were beginning a long fast and sharpening his powers of perception, although he could not imagine what more there was to perceive once he had proclaimed the unity of God to the seagulls of the Tagus, an act of great daring, for that God should be one in essence is something not even the heresiarchs deny, and although Padre Bartolomeu Lourenço had been taught that God, although one in essence, is triune in person, today the seagulls made him feel less certain about this. It is now darkest night, the city is asleep, or, if not asleep, silent as the tomb, all that can be heard are the cries of the sentries from time to time, intent upon dissuading any French pirates from attempting to land, and Domenico Scarlatti, after closing all the doors and windows, seats himself at the harpsichord, and the most subtle music wafts out into the Lisbon night through openings and chimneys, the Portuguese and German guards hear the music, the latter listening as appreciatively as the former, the sailors hear it in their dreams as they sleep on deck in the open air and on awakening they can recognise that music, the vagrants and tramps hear it as they take shelter at Ribeira, underneath the grounded boats, the friars and nuns of a thousand convents hear it and say, They are the angels of the Lord, for this is a land most fertile in miracles, hooded assassins hear it as they stalk the streets ready to kill, and when their victims hear that music they no longer plead to be confessed and die absolved, a prisoner of the Holy Office of the Inquisition who hears it from the depths of his dungeon grabs a guard by the throat and strangles him, but for this crime there will be no worse death, Baltasar and Blimunda hear it from a distance as they lie together, and they ask themselves, What music can this be, Padre Bartolomeu Lourenço was the first to hear it, because he lived so close to the Palace, and, getting out of bed, he lit his oil lamp and opened the window to listen more attentively. Several mosquitoes also entered and settled immediately on the ceiling, where they remained, at first hesitant on their long legs, then immobile, as if that faint light were incapable of attracting them, or perhaps hypnotised by the grating sound of Padre Bartolomeu Lourenço's quill as he began to write, *Et ego in illo*, And I am in him, and as dawn broke, he was still writing his sermon about the Body of Christ, and the mosquitoes did not feast that night on the priest's body.

Several days later, when Bartolomeu de Gusmão was in the Royal Chapel, the Italian musician came to see him. Having exchanged the usual pleasantries, they left by one of the doors beneath the King and Queen's dais which led into the passageway that connected with the Palace, they strolled at a leisurely pace, pausing here and there to inspect the tapestries hanging from the walls, the *Life of Alexander the Great,* the *Triumph of Faith,* and the *Exaltation of the Blessed Sacrament* after drawings by Rubens, the *Story of Tobias* after drawings by Raphael, and the *Conquest of Tunis,* and if these tapestries were to catch fire one day, not a single thread of silk will be salvaged. In a tone of voice that clearly conveyed that this was not the important matter they were about to discuss, Domenico Scarlatti said to the priest, the King keeps on his dais a miniature replica of the Basilica of Saint Peter in Rome, which he did me the honour of showing me yesterday, He has never conceded me any such favour, but I do not say this out of envy, for I am delighted to see Italy honoured through one of her sons, They tell me that the King is himself a great builder, and perhaps this explains his passion for building with his own hands this architectural monument of the Holy Church, even though on a reduced scale, How very different from the basilica being built at Mafra, which will be so enormous that it will become the wonder of ages, Just as the works men achieve with their hands manifest themselves in many different ways, mine are made from sound, Are you speaking about hands, No, I'm speaking about works, no sooner are they born than they perish, Are you speaking about works, No, I'm speaking about hands for what would become of them if they had no memory and I had no paper on which to write them, So you're speaking about hands, No, I'm speaking about works.

This appears to be nothing more than a witty play on words and their meanings, as was common in those times, without attaching too much importance to the sense, and sometimes even going so far as to obscure the meaning deliberately. It is like the preacher who assails the statue of St Antony in church with loud accusations of, Blackamoor, thief, drunkard, and after having scandalised the congregation with this barrage of insults, goes on to explain the point he is really trying to make, that he used the word *blackamoor* because of the Saint's dark skin, he called him a thief because he had robbed the divine child from the arms of the Virgin Mary, and a drunkard because St Antony was inebriated by divine grace, but I must warn you, Take heed, oh preacher, when you invert those conceits, for you are unwittingly betraying your secret leanings towards heresy that cause you to toss and turn in your sleep as you repeat, Cursed be the Father, cursed be the Son, cursed be the Holy Ghost, before adding, May the demons roar in hell, and in this way you think you will escape damnation, but He who sees everything, not this blind Tobias, but that other for whom there are no shadows or blindness, knows that you have uttered two profound truths, and He will choose one of the two, His own, for neither you nor I know which is God's truth, and even less whether God Himself is true.

This all appears to be a game of words, the works, the hands, the sound, the flight, But they told me, Padre Bartolomeu de Gusmão, that those very same hands raised a machine from the ground and it flew through the air, They spoke the truth about what they were witnessing at that moment, but were blind to the truth that the first truth concealed, Tell me more, This happened twelve years ago, since then the truth has changed considerably, Do tell me more, Can't you see it's a secret, But I thought only music is aerial, Well, then, tomorrow we shall go and witness a secret. They have come to a standstill before the final tapestry of the series depicting the life of Tobias, and this is the famous episode where the bitter gall taken from the fish restores the blind man's sight, Bitterness is the gaze of clairvoyants, Signor Domenico Scarlatti, One day this will be transposed into music, Padre Bartolomeu de Gusmão.

Next day they mounted their mules and rode to São Sebastião da Pedreira. The patio separating the palace on one side and the granary and coach-house on the other appeared to have been recently swept. Water ran along a funnel, and a chain pump could be heard working. The nearby flower beds had been tended, and the fruit trees had been tidied and pruned, here there were no remaining signs of the wilderness Baltasar and Blimunda had encountered when they first arrived some ten years earlier. Farther ahead, however, the estate was still uncultivated, it would remain like this as long as there were only three hands to work the land, and these were occupied most of the time in doing jobs that had nothing to do with the land. Through the open door of the coach-house came sounds of activity. Padre Bartolomeu Lourenço asked the priest to wait while he went inside. He found Baltasar alone, trimming a long joist with an adze. The priest said, Good afternoon, Baltasar, I've brought a visitor with me to see the machine, Who is it, Someone from the Palace, Surely not the King, No, not on this occasion, but one day soon, for only a few days ago he drew me aside to ask me when he could hope to see the machine flying, no, it is someone else who has come, But surely he'll discover our secret and that was not what we agreed, otherwise we'd not have kept it to ourselves all these years, Since the Passarola is my invention, I'll decide these matters, But we're doing the work and we are under no obligation to stay here, Baltasar, I don't know how to explain, but I'm confident that the person I've brought here is someone we can trust, someone for whom I'd be prepared to put my hand in the fire or pledge my soul, Is it a woman, It's a man, an Italian who has been at court only a few months, a musician who gives the Infanta lessons on the harpsichord and is also music-master of the Royal Chapel, and his name is Domenico Scarlatti, Did you say, Scarlet, Not quite, but there is so little difference that you might as well call him that as so many others do because they cannot pronounce his name. The priest made for the door, but paused to inquire, Where is Blimunda, She's somewhere in the kitchen garden, replied Baltasar.

The Italian had taken shelter in the cool shade of a sprawling plane tree. He did not seem to be curious about his surroundings, but looked impassively at the shuttered windows of the palace, at the coping where weeds were sprouting, the gutters where swallows flitted in search of insects. Padre Bartolomeu Lourenço approached, carrying a cloth in one hand, You must approach the secret blindfolded, he said playfully, and the musician replied in much the same tone, Yet how often one comes away from a secret still blindfolded, I hope this won't be the case, Signor Scarlatti, mind the doorstep and the large stone, now, before you remove the cloth I should tell you a couple lives here, a man named Baltasar Sete-Sóis and a woman named Blimunda, whom I have nicknamed Sete-Luas because she lives with Sete-Sóis, they are building the invention I am about to show you, I tell them what they have to do and they carry out my instructions, now you may remove your blindfold, Signor Scarlatti. Without haste, as if still calmly watching those swallows chasing insects, the Italian slowly untied the blindfold.

He was confronted by an enormous bird with outspread wings, a fan-shaped tail, an elongated neck, the head still unfinished, which made it difficult to tell whether it would eventually turn out to be a falcon or a swallow, Is this your secret, he asked, Yes, this is our secret, which until this moment has been shared by only three people, now we are four, this is Baltasar Sete-Sóis, and Blimunda should be back shortly from the kitchen garden. The Italian gave a slight nod in the direction of Baltasar, who gave a much deeper if somewhat clumsy nod in acknowledgment, after all, he was just a poor mechanic who looked very scruffy and was covered with grime from the forge, and the only thing about him that shone brightly was the hook, polished by constant labour. Domenico Scarlatti went up to the machine, which was balanced on supports at each side, placed his hand on one of the wings as if it were a keyboard, and to his astonishment the entire structure vibrated, despite the enormous weight of the wooden frame, metal plates, and entwined canes, and if there were forces capable of lifting this machine off the ground, then nothing was impossible for man, Are these wings fixed, That's right, But no bird can fly without flapping its wings, Baltasar would tell you that it's sufficient to have the form of a bird to be able to fly, but I can assure you that the secret of flying has nothing to do with wings, Won't you let me into the secret, All I can do is to show you what is here, And for that much I am grateful, but if this bird is to fly, how is it going to get through the door.

Baltasar and Padre Bartolomeu looked at each other in bewilderment, and then looked towards the open door. Blimunda was standing there with a basket filled with cherries, and she replied, There is a time for building and a time for destroying, certain hands tiled this roof, others will demolish it, and all the walls if necessary. This is Blimunda, said the priest, Sete-Luas, the musician added. She had cherries dangling from her ears and had come to show Baltasar and going up to him, she smiled and held out her basket, Venus and Vulcan, the musician reflected, and let us forgive him this rather obvious allusion to classical mythology, for how can he know what Blimunda's body is like underneath the rough garments she is wearing, or that Baltasar is not so scruffy or grimy as he looks at this moment, nor lame like Vulcan, one-handed perhaps, certainly, then, so is God. Not to mention that all the cockerels in the world would sing to Venus if the goddess had Blimunda's eyes, for then Venus would have the power to look into loving hearts, but simple mortals must have some advantages over divinities. Even Baltasar scores a point over Vulcan, for though the god lost his goddess, Baltasar will not lose his Blimunda.

They all sat down to eat, helping themselves from the basket without standing on ceremony, but took care not to reach out all at once, first Baltasar's stump, rough as the bark of an olive tree, then the soft ecclesiastic hand of Padre Bartolomeu Lourenço, then the fastidious hand of Scarlatti, and finally that of Blimunda, cautious and bruised and with the dirty nails of someone who has just come from the kitchen garden, where she had been weeding the soil before gathering cherries. They all throw the stones on the ground, and if the King were here he would do the same, and it is little things like these that make us realise that all men are equal. The cherries are big and juicy, some have already been pecked at by the birds, and what cherry orchard may there be in the sky where this other bird might feed when the time comes, it is still without a head, but whether it turns out to be that of a swallow or a falcon, the angels and saints feel reassured that they will eat their cherries intact, for, as everyone knows, these birds do not feed on plants.

Padre Bartolomeu Lourenço said, I shall not reveal the ultimate secret about flying, but, as I stated in my petition and memorandum, the whole machine will move by means of a force of attraction opposed to the laws of gravity, if I throw this cherry stone, it falls to the ground, now, the problem is to discover what will make it go up, Has anyone succeeded, I myself discovered the secret but the business of finding, collecting, and assembling the necessary materials has been the work of all three, It is an earthly trinity, the father, the son, and the holy ghost.

Baltasar and I are the same age, we are both thirty-five years old, so we could not possibly be father and son according to nature, more likely brothers and that would make us twins, but he was born in Mafra and I in Brazil, and we bear no resemblance to each other, And what about the holy ghost, That would be Blimunda, perhaps she is closest to being part of a trinity that is not terrestrial, I am also thirty-five years old, but I was born in Naples, so we couldn't form a trinity of twins, and how old is Blimunda, I'm twenty-eight, and I have neither brothers nor sisters, and as she spoke, Blimunda raised her eyes, which turned almost white in the semi-darkness of the coach-house, and Domenico Scarlatti heard the deepest chord of a harp resounding within his soul. Ostensively, Baltasar lifted the almost empty basket and said, We've eaten, let's get back to work.

Padre Bartolomeu Lourenço rested a ladder against the Passarola, Signor Scarlatti, perhaps you'd like to have a look inside the flying machine. They both climbed up, the priest carrying his design, and, once inside, as they walked over what resembled a ship's deck, he explained the location and function of the different components, the wires with the amber, the globes, the metal plates, while emphasising that everything would work by a process of mutual attraction, but he made no reference to the sun or to the mysterious substance the globes would contain, the musician, however, inquired, What will attract the amber, whereupon the priest replied, Perhaps God Himself, in whom all force resides, But what will the amber attract, The substance inside the globes, Is that the secret, Yes, that's the secret, Is it animal, vegetable, or mineral, It is neither vegetable, nor mineral nor animal, Everything is animal, vegetable, or mineral, Not everything, take music, for example, Padre Bartolomeu de Gusmão, surely you're not trying to tell me that these globes are going to contain music, No, but it's just possible that music could also lift the machine off the ground, I must give this some thought, after all, I myself am almost transported into the air when I hear the harpsichord being played, Is that meant to be a joke, Much less of a joke than you imagine, Signor Scarlatti.

It was getting late when the Italian finally departed. Padre Bartolomeu Lourenço had decided to spend the night there, and take advantage of his visit to prepare his sermon, since the Feast of Corpus

Christi would take place within the next few days. As he bade the musician farewell, the priest reminded him, Don't forget, Signor Scarlatti, whenever you get bored at the Palace, you can always come here, I'll certainly bear it in mind, and unless it would disturb Baltasar and Blimunda when they're working, I'd like to bring my harpsichord along and play for them and for the Passarola, perhaps my music will succeed in harmonising with that mysterious substance inside the globes, Signor Scarlet, said Baltasar, hastily interrupting, come whenever you like, if Padre Bartolomeu Lourenço gives his permission, but, Why but, Because instead of a left hand I have this hook, or instead of a hook I have this spike, and over my heart a cross in blood, My blood, Blimunda added, I'm the brother of all men, said Scarlatti, if they will accept me. Baltasar escorted the musician to the gates and helped him to mount his mule, If you need any help to transport your harpsichord here, Signor Scarlet, I'm at your service.

That night Padre Bartolomeu Lourenço shared a meal with Sete-Sóis and Sete-Luas of salted sardines, an omelette, a jug of water, and some hard, coarse bread. The coach-house was poorly lit by two oil lamps. In the corners the darkness appeared to spiral, advancing and retreating in unison with the vacillations of those tiny, pallid lights. The shadow of the Passarola flickered over the white wall. The night was warm. Through the open door, above the roof of the distant Palace, stars shone in the concave sky. The priest went out on to the patio and breathed in the night air, then contemplated the Milky Way, which stretched across the celestial dome from one end to the other, the road to Santiago, unless those stars were the eyes of pilgrims who gazed so intently into the sky that they left their light there, God is one in essence and in person, Bartolomeu de Lourenço suddenly exclaimed. Blimunda and Baltasar came to the door to hear what he was saying, they were no longer surprised at the priest's declamations, but this was the first time they had heard him making wild speeches out in the open air. There was a lull, during which the crickets went on screeching, and then the priest's voice cried out once more, God is one in essence and triune in person. His speech had fallen on stony ground the first time, and nothing happened now. Bartolomeu Lourenço returned to the coach-house and said to the others, who had followed him, I have made two contradictory statements, Tell me which you believe to be true, I really don't know, Baltasar said, Nor do I, said Blimunda. And the priest repeated, God is one in essence and in person, God is one in essence and triune in person, which is true, and which is false, We simply don't know, Blimunda replied, and we cannot grasp your meaning, But you do believe in the Holy Trinity, in the Father, the Son, and the Holy Ghost, I'm referring to the teachings of Holy Mother Church, not to what the Italian said, Yes, I do believe in the Holy Trinity, So God for you is triune in person, I suppose so, And if I were now to tell you that God is only one person and that He was alone when He created the world and mankind, would you believe me, If you say so, I believe you, I'm telling you to believe in things that I myself do not know, so don't repeat my words to anyone, and you, Baltasar, what's your opinion, Ever since I started building the machine, I have stopped thinking about these things, perhaps God is one, perhaps He is three, He might even be four, and one doesn't notice the difference, God is probably the only surviving soldier out of an army of a hundred thousand men, that's why He is at one and the same time soldier, captain, and general, and also one-handed, as you once explained to me and I've come to believe, Pilate asked Jesus what the truth was and Jesus did not reply, Perhaps it is still too soon to know, Blimunda suggested, and she went to sit beside Baltasar on a boulder near the door, that same boulder on which they often sat to delouse each other's hair, and now she was untying the straps that secured his hook and resting his stump on her bosom, to ease that great and incurable pain.

Et ego in illo, said Padre Bartolomeu Lourenço inside the coach-house, thus announcing the theme of his sermon, but today he was not striving for vocal effects, for the tremulous vibrato that would stir his audience, the urgent note in his exhortations, the persuasive pauses. He spoke the words that he had written, and others that suddenly came to mind, the latter negating the former, calling them into doubt, or putting some new slant on their meaning, *Et ego in illo,* yes, and I am in him, I, God, in him, man, in me, who am man, are you, who is God, God resides in man, but how can God reside in man if God is immense and man such a tiny part of God's creation, the answer is that God resides in man through the sacrament, that is clear and could not be clearer, but because He resides in man through the sacrament, it is essential that man should receive the sacrament, God, therefore, does not reside in man whensoever He wishes, but only when man wishes to receive Him, therefore one could say that to some extent the Creator has made Himself the creature of man, so a great injustice was done to Adam when God did not reside in him, for there was still no sacrament, and Adam might well argue that because of a single transgression God denied him the tree of life forevermore and the gates of paradise were closed to him for all eternity, whereas his descendants, who have committed many more sins and of a much more serious nature, have God inside them, and are allowed to eat freely from the tree of life, if Adam was punished for wishing to resemble God, how do men come to have God inside them without being punished, and even when they do not wish to receive Him they go unpunished, for to have and not to wish to have God inside oneself amounts to the same absurdity, and the same impossible situation, yet the words *Et ego in illo* imply that God is inside me or God is not inside me, how did I come to find myself in this labyrinth of yes and no, of no that means yes, of yes that means no, opposed affinities, allied contradictions, how shall I pass safely over the edge of the razor, well, summing up, before Christ became man, God was outside man and could not reside in him, then, through the Blessed Sacrament, He came to be inside man, so man is virtually God, or will ultimately become God, yes, of course, if God resides in me, I am God, I am God not in triune or quadruple, but one, one with God, He is I, I am He, *Durus est hic sermo, et quis potest eum audire.*

The night grew chilly. Blimunda had fallen asleep, her head resting on Baltasar's shoulder. Later he accompanied her indoors and they went to sleep. The priest went out on to the patio, and remained standing there all night, watching the sky and murmuring in temptation.

SEVERAL MONTHS LATER, a friar consulted by the Holy Office of the Inquisition wrote, in his critical assessment of the sermon, that the author of such a text was more worthy of applause than dismay, more deserving of admiration than scepticism. The friar in question, Friar Manuel Guilherme, must have felt some sense of foreboding even while recommending admiration and applause, some imperceptible trace of heresy must have passed to his pituitary gland as he struggled to silence the fears and doubts that must have assailed the compassionate censor as he listened to that sermon being delivered. And when it is the turn of another venerable scholar, Dom António Caetano de Sousa, to read and censure, he confirms that the text he has just examined contains nothing contrary to holy faith and Christian morals, he does not dwell on the doubts and fears that appear to have provoked some disquiet in the first instance, and urging in his closing comments that Dr Bartolomeu Lourenço de Gusmão be held in the same high esteem as that shown him by the Court, thus using the influence of the Palace to whiten doctrinal obscurities that probably warrant closer investigation. However, the final statement will be made by Padre Boaventura of St Julian, the royal censor, who concludes his eulogies and effusions by declaring that only silence could adequately express his sentiments of wonder and reverence. Those of us who are closer to the truth felt obliged to ask ourselves what other thundering voices or more terrible silences would respond to the words the stars heard on the Duke of Aveiro's estate while an exhausted Baltasar and Blimunda slept soundly, and the Passarola in the darkness of the coach-house strained its metallic frame in order to catch what its inventor out on the open patio was declaiming to the skies.

Padre Bartolomeu Lourenço has three, if not four, separate existences, and only when he is asleep, for even when dreaming differently, once awake, he cannot tell whether in his dream he was the priest who ascends the altar to celebrate Mass canonically, the scholar who is so highly esteemed that the King goes incognito to the Royal Chapel and listens to his sermons from behind a curtain, the inventor of the flying machine and the various mechanisms for draining ships that have sprung a leak, and this other, composite man, riddled with fears and doubts, who is a preacher in church, scholar in the academy, courtier in the Palace, and visionary and comrade of ordinary working-class people in São Sebastião da Pedreira, and he turns anxiously to his dream in an attempt to reconstruct the fragile and precarious unity that is shattered the moment he opens his eyes, nor does he need to fast like Blimunda. He has abandoned the familiar readings of the doctors of the Church, of scholars versed in canon law, of the various scholastic theories about essence and being, as if his soul had grown weary of words, but since man is the only animal who can be taught to speak and write long before achieving any social or intellectual standing, Padre Bartolomeu Lourenço makes a detailed study of the Old Testament, especially the first five books, the so-called Pentateuch, which is known as the Torah among the Jews, and as the Koran among the followers of Mohammed. Inside any of our bodies, Blimunda would have the power to see our organs and our wills, but she cannot read our thoughts, nor would she understand them, to see a man thinking as in a single thought, such opposed and conflicting truths, yet without losing one's mind, she were she to see it, he for having such thoughts.

Music is something else. Domenico Scarlatti brought a harpsichord to the coach-house, he did not carry it himself, but hired two porters who, with poles, ropes, and a pad filled with horsehair, and much perspiration on their brows, brought it all the way from the Rua Nova dos Mercadores, where it was purchased, to São Sebastião da Pedreira, where it would be played, Baltasar accompanied them to show the way, but they required no other assistance from him, for this method of transportation depends on skill and experience, on knowing how to distribute the weight and combine forces like the pyramid in the traditional dance known as the Bica, knowing how to use the ropes and poles in order to set up a steady pace, these, after all, are the secrets of the porter's trade and are as valid as any other, for a tradesman worthy of the name tries to acquire as many secret skills as he can. The Galician porters put the harpsichord down outside the gate, for no one wanted them to discover the existence of the flying machine, so Baltasar and Blimunda had to carry it into the coach-house themselves, a hazardous job, not so much because of its weight as because they did not know how to go about it, not to mention that the vibration of the chords were like anguished cries tugging at their heart-strings, which were also seized by alarm and dismay in the face of such extreme fragility. That same afternoon Domenico Scarlatti arrived, sat himself down and began to tune the harpsichord, while Baltasar wove willow canes and Blimunda sewed the sails, jobs they could carry out in silence without disturbing the music. Once he had finished tuning the instrument, adjusting the jacks, which had been disturbed in transit, and checking the duck quills one by one, Scarlatti began to play, starting off by letting his fingers glide over the keys, as if he were releasing notes that had been imprisoned, then organising the sounds in tiny sections, as if choosing between the right and the wrong notes, between harmony and discord, between phrasing and pauses, in short, as if giving new expression to what had previously seemed fragmentary and dissonant. Baltasar and Blimunda knew very little about music apart from the plain-chant sung by the friars, on rare occasions the operatic swell of the Te Deum, popular airs from the city and countryside, some familiar to Blimunda, others to Baltasar, but nothing that could even remotely be compared to the sounds the Italian drew from the harpsichord, which seemed as much a childish game as some fulminating oath, as much a divertissement for angels as the wrath of God.

After an hour, Scarlatti got up from the harpsichord, covered it with a canvas cloth, and then said to Baltasar and Blimunda, who had interrupted their work, If Padre Bartolomeu's Passarola were ever to fly, I should dearly love to travel in it and play my harpsichord up in the sky, and Blimunda rejoined, Once the machine starts to fly, the heavens will be filled with music, and Baltasar, remembering the war, interjected, Unless the heavens turn out to be hell. This couple can neither write nor read, yet they can say things that seem most unlikely at such a time and in such a place, but since everything has an explanation, we must look for one, and if nothing comes to mind just at present, we shall find it one day. Scarlatti returned many times to the estate of the Duke of Aveiro, he did not always play the harpsichord, but when he did, he sometimes urged them not to interrupt their labours, the forge roaring in the background, the hammer clanging on the anvil, the water boiling in the vat, so that the harpsichord could scarcely be heard above the terrible din in the coach-house, and meanwhile, the musician tranquilly composed his music as if he were surrounded by the vast silence of the space where he hoped to play one day.

Every man follows his own path in search of grace, whatever that grace may be, a simple landscape with the sky overhead, a certain hour of the day or night, two trees, three if they are painted by Rembrandt, a sigh, without our knowing whether this closes or finally opens the path or where the path may lead us, whether to some other landscape, hour, tree, or sigh, behold this priest who is about to cast out one God and replace him with another, without knowing whether this new allegiance will do him any good in the end, behold this musician who would find it impossible to compose any other kind of music and who will no longer be alive a hundred years from now to hear that first symphony, which is mistakenly referred to as the Ninth, behold this one-handed soldier who has ironically become a manufacturer of wings, although he has never risen to being more than a common foot soldier, man rarely knows what to expect from life, and this man least of all, behold this woman with those extraordinary eyes, who was born to perceive wills, her revelations about a tumour, a strangled foetus, and a silver coin were mere child's play when compared with the wonders she is destined to achieve when Padre Bartolomeu Lourenço returns to the estate of São Sebastião da Pedreira and tells her, Blimunda, Lisbon is stricken by a horrendous plague, people are dying everywhere, and it has just occurred to me that this is an excellent opportunity to collect wills from the dying, if they still have any, but I must warn you that you will be taking a great risk, don't go unless you really want to, for I shall not put you under any obligation, even if it were within my power to do so, What is this plague, It is rumoured that the plague was carried here by passengers aboard a ship from Brazil and that it first broke out in Ericeira. That's close to my home, said Baltasar, whereupon the priest reassured him, No deaths have been reported in Mafra, judging from the symptoms, the disease is believed to be the black plague or yellow fever, the name scarcely matters, the fact is that people are dying like flies, you must decide, Blimunda. She got up from her stool, raised the lid of the chest, and brought out a glass phial, How many wills were in there, she wondered, about a hundred, perhaps, but certainly nothing like the number they needed, and even this amount had required a lengthy and arduous search and a great deal of fasting, often to find oneself lost as in a labyrinth, Where is that will, for all I can see are entrails and bones, an agonising maze of nerves, a sea of blood, viscous food lodged in the stomach before finally turning to excrement, Will you go, the priest asked her, I'll go, she replied, But not on your own, Baltasar added.

Early the next day there were signs of rain when Blimunda and Baltasar left the estate, she still fasting, he carrying their provisions in his knapsack until such time as sheer physical exhaustion or the desire to linger a while would permit or force Blimunda to eat some food. For many hours that day Baltasar was not to see Blimunda's face, because she always walked in front, warning him to look away whenever she turned her head, this game of theirs is a strange business, the one has no wish to see, the other has no wish to be seen, it looks easy to play, but only they know how difficult it is to avoid looking at each other. As the day draws to a close, Blimunda, who has eaten, finds that her eyes have been restored to normal, and Baltasar begins to emerge from his state of torpor, exhausted not so much by the journey as by not being looked at.

Blimunda has lost no time in visiting the dying. Wherever she goes she is greeted with acclaim and gratitude, no one inquires whether she is a relative or a friend, whether she lives on that very street or in some other district, and because this country is so accustomed to works of mercy, sometimes her presence goes unnoticed, the patient's bedroom is crammed with visitors, the corridor is blocked, the staircase swarms with people coming up and going down, the traffic is endless, the priest who has administered or is about to administer the last rites, the doctor if they thought it was worth summoning him and had the money to pay him, and the blood-letter who travels from house to house sharpening his knives, no one pays any attention when a woman intent upon theft enters and leaves concealing a glass phial with yellow amber inside, to which the stolen wills stick like birds to lime. Between São Sebastião da Pedreira and Ribeira, Blimunda entered some thirty-two houses and collected twenty-four dark clouds, six of the patients no longer had a will, which might well have been lost many years previously, and in the remaining two patients they were so firmly stuck to their bodies that only death was likely to remove them. In five other houses she visited, she found neither wills nor souls, only corpses, a few tears, and much lamentation.

Everywhere rosemary was being burned to ward off the epidemic, in the streets, in the doorways of houses, and above all in the bedrooms of the sick, there were traces of a bluish haze giving off an unmistakable fragrance, and the city bore no resemblance to that fetid pigsty of healthier times. There was much searching for tongues from St Paul, pebbles in the shape of a bird's tongue, which are to be found on the beaches that stretch all the way from São Paulo to Santos, whether because of the sanctity of these places or because of the sanctification bestowed by the names, it is well known that such pebbles, and several others that are round in shape and the size of chick-peas, are extremely effective in curing malignant fevers, made of the finest dust, these pebbles can mitigate excessive heat, alleviate gallstones, and sometimes cause perspiration. When ground to a powder, the pebbles are a decisive antidote to poison, whatever it may be and however it may have been administered, especially in the case of a poisonous bite inflicted by some animal or insect, you need only place the tongue from St Paul or the chick-pea over the wound and the poison is sucked out immediately. That explains why these pebbles are also known as snake eyes.

It seems inconceivable that so many people should still have been dying when there were so many remedies and precautions, Lisbon must have committed some irreparable crime in the eyes of God for four thousand people to die from the epidemic within three months, which means that more than forty corpses had to be buried daily. The beaches were stripped of pebbles and the tongues of the diseased were silenced, thus preventing them from complaining that such a cure had proved futile. To deny it would have betrayed their lack of repentance, for no one should be surprised that pebbles ground to a fine powder and dissolved in some beverage or broth can cure malignant fevers, when it is widely known what happened to Mother Teresa of the Annunciation when making sweetmeats and running out of sugar, she sent a messenger to borrow some from a nun in another convent who replied that she could not oblige because her own sugar was of an inferior quality, which greatly distressed Mother Teresa, who thought to herself, What am I going to do with my life, I know, I'll make some toffee, although it's a much less refined confection, let us be clear, she did not make toffee with her own life, but with the inferior sugar, but when it reached the setting point, it had become so greatly reduced and yellow that it looked more like resin than an appetising delicacy, ah, how upsetting and with no one else to turn to, Mother Teresa protested to the Lord, reminding Him of His responsibilities, an invariably effective strategy, as we saw in the case of St Antony and the silver lamps, You know perfectly well that I have no more sugar and have no means of finding any, these labours are Yours rather than mine, tell me how I am supposed to serve You, for it is You who provides the wherewithal, not I, and just in case this admonition might not be enough, she cut a tiny piece off the cord that the Lord wears around His waist and put it into the saucepan, and, lo and behold, the mixture began to gain volume and become much lighter in colour, and there was toffee the likes of which had never been tasted since monasteries and convents started producing such delicacies. If no such miracles are worked today in monastic kitchens, it is because the cord Our Lord once wore around His waist no longer exists, having been cut up in tiny pieces and distributed among all the congregations where nuns devoted themselves to making sweetmeats, such times are gone forever.

Exhausted after all that walking and going up and down stairs, Blimunda and Baltasar returned to the estate, seven pale suns and seven waning moons, Blimunda suffering from the most unbearable nausea, as if she were returning from a battlefield after witnessing a thousand bodies being blown to pieces by artillery, and if Baltasar wanted to divine what Blimunda was witnessing, all he had to do was merge into a single recollection his experiences of war and those in the slaughter-house. They lay together without any desire to make love, not so much because of their fatigue, which, as we know, can often be a wise counsellor of the senses, but because of their acute awareness of their internal organs, as if these were protruding through their skin, perhaps a difficult thing to explain, but it is by means of the skin that bodies come to recognise, know, and accept one another, and if certain deep penetrations, certain intimate contacts occur between the mucus and the skin, the difference is barely perceptible, it is as if one had sought and found a more remote skin. They are both asleep covered by an old blanket and still wearing their clothes, and it is cause for wonder to see such a mighty enterprise entrusted to two vagabonds, who look worse now that the bloom of youth has vanished, like foundation stones soiled by the earth they reinforce and perhaps, like them, over-whelmed by the weight they will have to bear. The moon was slow in appearing that night, they slept and did not see it, but the moonlight filtered through the chinks and slowly pervaded the entire coach-house, the flying machine and, in passing, lit up the glass phial and clearly exposed the dark clouds inside, perhaps because no one was watching or because moonlight is capable of revealing the invisible.

Padre Bartolomeu Lourenço was satisfied with the day's collection, it was only the first day, and they had been out at random into the heart of a city afflicted by disease and mourning, there were twenty-four wills to be added to the list. After a month, they calculated that they had stored a thousand wills in the phial, a force of elevation that the priest considered sufficient for one globe, so Blimunda was given a second phial. In Lisbon, rumours were rife about this strange couple who roved the city from one end to another, without fear of succumbing to the epidemic, he walking behind, she in front, never breaking their silence as they passed through the streets and entered houses, where they did not tarry, and she lowered her eyes when she had to pass him, and if this daily ritual did not provoke greater suspicion and wonder, it was because of the rumour that they were both doing penance, a ruse invented by Padre Bartolomeu Lourenço when people started to gossip. Had he been a little more imaginative, he would have passed off the mysterious couple as two envoys sent from heaven to assist the dying and to reinforce the effects of extreme unction, which might have weakened from overuse. It takes little or nothing to undo reputations, the merest trifle makes and remakes them, it is simply a question of finding the best means of engaging the confidence or interest of those who are to become one's unsuspecting echoes or accomplices.

When the epidemic finally began to pass and deaths from the plague became much rarer than deaths from other causes, two thousand wills all told had been collected in the phials. Then Blimunda was taken ill. There was no pain or fever, but she was desperately thin and a deep pallor made her skin look transparent. She lay on the pallet, her eyes closed day and night, yet she did not appear to be sleeping or resting, with those tensed eyelids and that agonised expression on her face. Baltasar never left her side except to prepare some food or to relieve himself, for it did not seem right to do it there. Looking sombre, Padre Bartolomeu Lourenço sat on the stool, remaining there for hours. At times he seemed to be praying, but no one could make out those mutterings or to whom they were addressed. The priest no longer heard their confessions, Baltasar raised the subject twice, since he felt obliged to mention that when sins are accumulated they are easily forgotten, whereupon the priest replied that God sees into the hearts of men and needs no one to give absolution in His name, and if a man's sins were so serious that they should not go unpunished, God would see to it that he was judged and dealt with in the proper place on the Day of Judgment, unless in the meantime his good deeds compensated for his evil ones, although it may also come to pass that everything will end with a general amnesty or universal punishment, all that remains to be known is who will pardon or punish God. But, watching Blimunda waste away and withdraw from this world, the priest bit his nails and felt remorse that he had exposed her so relentlessly to encroaching death, so that her own life was now in danger, for one could see that she was facing that other temptation of leaving life painlessly, like someone who has stopped holding on to the margins of this world and allows herself to go under.

Each night, returning to the city by obscure paths and narrow byways that descended towards Santa Maria and Valverde, the priest began to wish in his semi-delirium that he would be ambushed by bandits, perhaps even by Baltasar himself with his rusty sword and deadly spike, to avenge Blimunda and so end his torment. But Sete-Sóis was already in bed at this hour, he covered Sete-Luas with his good arm and murmured, Blimunda, and that name traversed a vast, dark wilderness full of shadows, took a long time to reach its destination, and just as long to return, the shadows slowly dispersing, her lips moving with difficulty, Baltasar, and outside, there was the sound of rustling trees, from time to time the cry of some nocturnal bird, blessed be the night, which conceals and protects things fair and foul with the same indifferent mantle, come, time-honoured and unchanging night. The rhythm of Blimunda's breathing altered, a sign that she had fallen asleep, and Baltasar, prostrate with anxiety, could sleep at last and there rediscover Blimunda's smile, and what would become of us if we were not to dream.

During her illness, if it was an illness and not merely a protracted regression of her own will into the inaccessible confines of her body, Domenico Scarlatti called frequently, first he came to visit Blimunda and find out if there was any improvement, then he would linger to converse with Sete-Sóis, and one day he removed the canvas cloth from the harpsichord, sat down, and began to play with such sweetness and delicacy that it was as if the music could scarcely bring itself to part from those gentle chords, subtle vibrations as of a winged insect hovering in mid-air, before suddenly moving from one to another, up and down, and all of this independent of the movements of his fingers over the keyboard, as if the vibrations were choosing the notes, music does not come from the movements of the fingers, how could it, when the keyboard has a first and last key, whereas music has no beginning or end, it comes from yonder to my left, and goes to that other remote point, on my right, but at least music has two hands, unlike certain gods. Perhaps this was the medicine that Blimunda was awaiting, or that thing inside her which was still awaiting something, for each of us consciously expects only what we know or find familiar or what we have been told is useful in each case, blood-letting, were the body not so weak, a tongue from St Paul if the epidemic had not left the beaches bare, some berries from the alkegengi plant, some foxglove leaves, a root of creeping thistle, the Frenchman's elixir, unless this is just a harmless mixture whose only merit is that of not causing any further harm. Blimunda could not have known that upon hearing that music her breast would swell in this way, and give out a deep sigh like that of someone about to die or be born, Baltasar leaned over her, fearful that she might expire just as she was reviving. That night Domenico Scarlatti remained on the estate, playing for hours on end, until daybreak, Blimunda's eyes were now open, and the tears streamed slowly down her face, had there been a doctor present, he would have diagnosed that she was expelling the humours of a damaged optic nerve, perhaps he would be right, perhaps tears are nothing other than the assuagement of some wound.

Every day for a whole week, braving the wind and the rain along the flooded roads to São Sebastião da Pedreira, the musician went to play for two or three hours, until Blimunda found the strength to get up, she sat at the foot of the harpsichord, still looking pale, engulfed by the music as if she were plunged into a deep sea, which we can confidently say she never sailed, for her shipwreck was figurative only. Her health now began to improve rapidly, if it had ever really deteriorated. And when the musician returned no more, either out of discretion or because he was too busy with his duties as music-master of the Royal Chapel, which he had probably neglected, or giving lessons to the Infanta, who was certainly not complaining about his frequent absences, Baltasar and Blimunda realised that Padre Bartolomeu Lourenço had not been back for some time, and they began to worry. One morning when the weather began to brighten up, they went down to the city, this time side by side, and as they walked and chatted, Blimunda could look at Baltasar and see nothing but him, to their mutual relief. The people they encountered on the way were like sealed chests or locked coffers, and if their expression was forbidding and unfriendly, no matter, for those looking did not need to know any more about the persons they were looking at than those being looked at needed to know about them. That was why Lisbon seemed so quiet, despite the cries of the street vendors, the hubbub of the women, the various bells that rang out, the prayers being said aloud at sanctuaries along the route, the blare of a distant trumpet, a drum roll, the gun salutes of ships leaving or arriving in the Tagus, the litanies and the altar bells of the mendicant friars. Let those who possess a will cherish and use it, let those who have no will resign themselves to their loss, Blimunda wishes to hear no more about counting wills, back there on the estate she has her own account, and only she knows how much it has cost her.

Padre Bartolomeu Lourenço was not at home, perhaps he has gone to the Palace, the mace-bearer's widow suggested, or to the academy, Would you care to leave a message, but Baltasar said no, they would call again later or wait for him in the courtyard. Finally, around noon, the priest turned up, he had lost weight, whether from illness or visions, and to their surprise looked quite dishevelled, as if he had slept in his clothes. When he spotted them sitting on a bench near the entrance to his home, he covered his face with his hands, then quickly removed them, and it appeared to them that he had just escaped some great danger, but not the one he confided with his opening words, I've been expecting Baltasar to come and murder me, we might be tempted to think that he feared for his life, but we would be wrong. No greater punishment could have been inflicted upon me, Blimunda, if you had died, But Signor Scarlet knew that I had got over my illness, I have been avoiding him, and when he tried to visit me I made excuses to put him off, and awaited my destiny, One's destiny always arrives, said Baltasar, the fact that Blimunda did not die was my, our, good fortune, and what shall we do now that the plague is almost at an end, the wills have been collected, and the machine is ready, if there are no more irons to be beaten, no more sails to sew and tar, no more willow canes to be woven, if we have enough yellow amber to make as many globes as there are crossed wires on the roof, and the bird's head is finished, it's not a seagull after all, even if it looks like one, so, if the work is finished, what is to become of it and of us, Padre Bartolomeu Lourenço. The priest turned even paler, looked all around him as if afraid that someone might be listening, then replied, I shall need to inform the King that the machine is ready, but we must try it out beforehand, I have no desire to be ridiculed at court, as happened fifteen years ago, go back to the estate now and I shall join you shortly.

They withdrew several paces, then Blimunda paused, Padre Bartolomeu Lourenço you're ill, you're as white as a ghost, your eyes are discoloured, and you weren't even pleased to hear our news, I was pleased, Blimunda, truly I was, but news of one's destiny is never the whole truth, what happens tomorrow is what really counts, today means little or nothing, Give us your blessing, Father, I cannot, for I no longer know in which God's name I should bless you, be content to bless each other, that is all the blessing you need, and how I wish that all blessings were so.

P EOPLE SAY THAT the kingdom is badly governed, that there is no justice, unaware that this is how she has to be, with a blindfold over her eyes, her scales and sword, what more would we wish for, surely not to be the weavers of the bandage, the inspectors of the weights, and the armourers of the sword, constantly patching the holes, making up losses, and sharpening the blade of the sword, and then asking the defendant if he is satisfied with the sentence passed on him once he has won or lost his case. We are not referring here to sentences passed by the Holy Office of the Inquisition, which is very astute and prefers an olive branch to scales and a keen blade to one that is jagged and blunt. Some mistake the olive branch for a gesture of peace when it is all too clear that it is kindling wood for the funeral pyre, either I stab you or I burn you, therefore, in the absence of any law, it is preferable to stab a woman suspected of infidelity than to honour the faithful who have passed on, it is a question of having protectors who are likely to forgive homicide, and a thousand cruzados to put on the scales, which is why Justice holds it in her hand. Let blacks and hoodlums be punished so that good example may be upheld, but let people of rank and wealth be honoured, without demanding that they pay their debts, renounce their vengeance or mitigate their hatred, and while the lawsuits are being fought, since certain little irregularities cannot be totally avoided, let there be chicanery, swindling, appeals, formalities, and evasions, so that those likely to gain a just decision will not gain it too readily, and those likely to lose their appeal will not lose it too soon. In the meantime, teats are milked for that delicious milk, money, those rich curds, prime cheese, and a tasty morsel for the bailiff and the solicitor, for the witness and the judge, and if there is anyone missing from the list, Padre António Vieira is to blame, because he has forgotten.

These are the visible forms of justice. As for the invisible forms, they are at best blind and disastrous, as was clearly shown when the King's brothers, the Infante Dom Francisco and the Infante Dom Miguel, were shipwrecked as they crossed to the other side of the river Tagus on a hunting expedition, for without any warning their boat capsized in a gust of wind, and Dom Miguel drowned while Dom Francisco was rescued, when any honourable justice would have decreed that it be the other way around, for the wicked ways of the surviving Infante are common knowledge now that he has tried to lead the Queen astray and usurp the King's throne, and takes potshots at innocent sailors, whereas no misdeeds have ever been attributed to the dead Infante, or if they have, they have not been of a serious nature. We must not, however, be rash in passing judgment, it is possible that Dom Francisco has already repented, and Dom Miguel may have lost his life for having cuckolded the ship's master or for having deceived his daughter, for the annals of these royal dynasties are full of similar scandals.

What happened in the end was that the King or, rather, the crown lost the lawsuit he had been contesting against the Duke of Aveiro since the year sixteen hundred and forty, because the House of Aveiro and the crown had been in litigation for some eighty years. It was no laughing matter, not merely a question of territorial rights on land and sea. Two hundred thousand cruzados in rents were at stake, just imagine, three times the amount of taxes the King charges for the black slaves who are shipped off to the Brazilian mines. Ultimately there is always justice in this world, and because of that justice the King is now obliged to restore to the Duke of Aveiro all his possessions, which do not greatly concern us, including the estate of São Sebastião da Pedreira, the keys, the well, the orchard, and the palace, none of which greatly concerns Padre Bartolomeu Lourenço, except the loss of the coach-house. But every cloud has a silver lining, the court's verdict has arrived at an opportune moment, for the flying machine is ready at last, the King can now be informed, after waiting for so many years without losing his royal patience, ever affable and solicitous in manner, although the priest now finds himself in that familiar situation of the inventor who cannot bear to be parted from his invention, of the dreamer who is about to lose his dream, Once the machine is flying, what is there left for me to do, he certainly has plenty of ideas for new inventions, such as coal made from mud and wattle, and a new system for grinding sugar cane, but the Passarola is his supreme invention, there will never be wings like them, except those that are never put to the test of flying, for they are the most powerful wings of all.

In São Sebastião da Pedreira, Baltasar and Blimunda are anxious to know what the future holds for them, the retainers of the Duke of Aveiro have wasted no time in taking charge of the estate, Perhaps we should go back to Mafra. But the priest disagrees, he promises to speak to the King within the next few days, the flying machine will be launched soon, and if all goes according to plan, the three of them will reap glory and profit, news of the Portuguese achievement will spread throughout the universe, and fame will bring them wealth, Any profits I may accrue will be shared by the three of us, for without your eyes, Blimunda, and without your right hand and patience, Baltasar, there would be no Passarola. Yet the priest feels uneasy, one might almost say that he has little confidence in what he is saying, or that what he is saying has so little value that it cannot quell his other anxieties, therefore Blimunda asks in a low voice, It is night, the forge has been extinguished, the machine is still there yet seems absent, Padre Bartolomeu Lourenço, what are you afraid of, and this direct question causes him to tremble, he rises nervously to his feet, goes to the door, and peers outside before replying in a whisper, Of the Holy Office of the Inquisition. Baltasar and Blimunda look at each other and Baltasar says, Surely it is not a sin or heresy to want to fly, fifteen years ago a balloon flew over the Palace and no evil came of it, a balloon is harmless, the priest tells him, If the machine were to fly now, the Holy Office might decide that there is some Satanic power behind this flight, and if they were to investigate which parts of the invention cause the machine to fly, I should find it impossible to reveal that there are human wills inside the globes, in the eyes of the Inquisition there are no wills, only souls, they will accuse us of imprisoning Christian souls and of preventing them from going up to paradise, you are well aware that if the Holy Office of the Inquisition so decrees, all good reasons become bad ones, and all bad ones become good, and in the absence of both good and bad reasons they use the torments of stake, rack, and pulley to invent reasons at their own discretion, But since the King is our ally, surely the Inquisition will not act contrary to the wishes and desires of His Majesty, Confronted with such a dilemma, the King will only do what the Holy Office of the Inquisition tells him to do.

Blimunda questioned him further, What do you fear most, Padre Bartolomeu Lourenço, what will happen, or what is happening, What are you trying to say, That the Inquisition might be already hounding us, just as it hounded my mother, I know the signs all too well, it's like an aura that encircles those who attract the attention of the Inquisitors, they have no idea what accusations are about to be made, yet they already behave as if they were guilty, I know what I shall be accused of when my hour comes, they will say that I have been converted from Judaism, and it's true, they will say that I devote myself to sorcery, and that's also true, if this Passarola is sorcery and all those other arts I am forever studying, and with these confidences I put myself in your hands, and I shall be lost if you denounce me. Baltasar says, May I lose my other hand were I to do such a thing. Blimunda says, Were I to do such a thing, may I never again be able to close my eyes, and may they always see as if I were constantly fasting.

Confined to the estate, Baltasar and Blimunda watch the days go by. August is over, September is well under way, the spiders are already weaving their webs over the Passarola, raising their own sails, adding wings, Signor Scarlet's harpsichord stands in silence with no one to play it, and there can be no sadder place in the wide world than São Sebastião da Pedreira. The weather has become much cooler, the sun hides for hours on end, How can the machine possibly be tried out with the sky so overcast, perhaps Padre Bartolomeu Lourenço has forgotten that without sunshine the machine will not rise from the ground, and if he should turn up with the King, it will be so embarrassing that I shall turn crimson with shame. But the King did not come, nor did the priest appear, the sky cleared again, the sun shone, and Blimunda and Baltasar returned to the same anxious waiting. Then the priest arrived. They heard the mule's hoofs stamping impatiently outside the gate, a strange event, since the mule is an animal that rarely loses its temper, there must be news, perhaps the King is coming after all to witness the maiden flight of the Passarola, but incognito, without any warning or advance party of footmen from the Palace to inspect the place, set up tents, and ensure that His Majesty will be comfortable, no, this must be something else. It was something else. Padre Bartolomeu Lourenço came rushing into the coach-house looking pale, livid, ashen, like someone resuscitated from the grave whose body was already rotting away, We must escape, the Holy Office of the Inquisition has issued a warrant for my arrest, they want to imprison me, where are the phials. Blimunda opened the chest and removed some cloths, They are in here, and Baltasar asked, What shall we do. The priest was shaking from head to foot and could scarcely stand up, Blimunda went to his assistance, What shall we do, Baltasar insisted, and the priest cried out, Let's escape in the machine, then suddenly, as if gripped by some new terror, he murmured almost inaudibly, pointing at the Passarola, Let's escape, But where, I don't know, but we must get away from here. Baltasar and Blimunda looked at each other, It was ordained, he said, Let's go, she said.

It is two o'clock in the afternoon and there is much work to be done and not a minute to be lost, the tiles have to be removed, the battens and joists, which cannot be pulled down by hand, have to be sawn, but first of all the amber balls have to be suspended where the wires cross, and the larger sails have to be opened so that the sun does not shine on the machine, two thousand wills have to be transferred into the globes, one thousand on this side and one thousand on the other, so that there is an even pull on both sides and no danger of the machine's capsizing in mid-air, and if such an accident should occur, let it be due to unforeseen circumstances. There is still so much work and so little time. Baltasar is already on the roof, removing the tiles, which he throws to the ground, and all round the coach-house there is the sound of shattering tiles, and Padre Bartolomeu Lourenço has recovered sufficiently to give them a little help by dismantling the thinner battens, but the joints require more strength than he can muster, so they must wait, while Blimunda behaves as if she had been flying all her life, with the utmost calm she examines the sails to make certain that the pitch is spread evenly and reinforces some of the hemming.

And now, Guardian Angel, what will you do, your presence has never been so necessary since you were first entrusted with this role, here you have three people who will shortly go up into the sky, where man has never ventured, and they need your protection, they have done as much as they can on their own, they have collected the necessary materials and wills, they have combined the solid with the evanescent, they have linked everything to their own audaciousness, and they are ready, all that remains to be done now is to demolish the rest of the roof, close the sails and expose the machine to the sun, and farewell, we're off, but if you, Guardian Angel, don't give us at least a little help, you are neither an angel nor anything else, there are of course lots of saints whom one can invoke, but none is as numerate as you, you know the thirteen words, can count from one to thirteen without making a mistake, and since this is a task requiring a sound grasp of all the geometries and mathematics ever devised, you can begin with the first word, which is the House of Jerusalem, where Jesus Christ died for all of us we are told, and now the two words, which are the Tables of Moses, where, we are told, Jesus Christ placed His feet, and now the three words, which are the three persons of the Holy Trinity, we are told, and now the four words, which are the four evangelists, Matthew, Mark, Luke, and John, we are told, and now the five words, which are the five wounds of Jesus Christ, we are told, and now the six words, which are the six blessed candles Jesus Christ received at birth, we are told, and now the seven words which are the seven sacraments, we are told, and now the eight words, which are the eight Beatitudes, we are told, and now the nine words, which are the nine months when the Virgin Mary carried her beloved Son in her most pure womb, we are told, and now the ten words, which are the Ten Commandments of God's Holy Law, we are told, and now the eleven words, which are the eleven thousand virgins, we are told, and now the twelve words, which are the twelve apostles, we are told, and now the thirteen words, which are the thirteen rays of the moon, and this most certainly does not need to be told, because at least we have

Sete-Luas here with us, that woman who is holding the glass phial, protect her, Guardian Angel, for if the phial should break, there will be no journey, and that priest, who is behaving so strangely, will not be able to make his escape, also protect the man working on the roof, his left hand is missing, and you are to blame, for you were inattentive out there on the battlefield when he was wounded, perhaps you still had not mastered your multiplication table.

It is four o'clock in the afternoon, only the walls of the coach-house are left standing, the place looks enormous with the flying machine in the middle, the tiny forge dissected by a band of shadows, and in the far corner the pallet where Baltasar and Blimunda have slept together for the past six years. The chest is no longer there, they have loaded it into the Passarola, what else do we need, the knapsacks, some food, and the harpsichord, what is to be done to the harpsichord, let it stay here, these are selfish thoughts, which one must try to comprehend and forgive, such is their anxiety that all three of them fail to reflect that if the harpsichord is left behind, the ecclesiastical and secular authorities are likely to become even more suspicious, why and for what purpose is a harpsichord in a coach-house, and if it was a hurricane that demolished the roof and scattered the tiles and beams, how did the harpsichord escape destruction, an instrument so delicate that even being transported on the shoulders of porters was enough to put the keys out of tune, Will Signor Scarlet not be playing for us in the sky, Blimunda asked.

Now they are ready to leave. Padre Bartolomeu Lourenço contemplates the clear blue expanse above, cloudless and with a sun as brilliant as a glittering monstrance, then he looks at Baltasar, who is holding the rope with which they will close the sails, and then at Blimunda, and he dearly wishes that she could divine what the future holds for them, Let us commend ourselves to God, if there is a God, he murmured to himself, and then in strangled tones he said, Pull, Baltasar, but Baltasar did not react at once, for his hand was trembling, besides, this was like saying *Fiat*, no sooner said than done, one pull and we end up who knows where. Blimunda drew near and placed her two hands over that of Baltasar and, with a concerted gesture, as if this were the only way it could be done, both of them pulled the rope. The sail veered to one side, allowing the sun to shine directly on the amber balls, and now what will happen to us. The machine shuddered, then swayed as if trying to regain its balance, there was a loud creaking from the metal plates and the entwined canes, and suddenly, as if it were being sucked in by a luminous vortex, it went up making two complete turns, and no sooner had it risen above the walls of the coach-house than it recovered its balance, raised its head like a seagull, and soared like an arrow straight up into the sky. Shaken by those rapid spins, Baltasar and Blimunda found themselves lying on the wooden deck of the machine, but Padre Bartolomeu Lourenço had grabbed one of the plummets that supported the sails, which allowed him to see the earth shrink at the most incredible speed, the estate was now barely visible, then lost amid the hills, and what's that yonder in the distance, Lisbon, of course, and the river, ah, the sea, that sea which I, Bartolomeu Lourenço de Gusmão, sailed twice from Brazil, that sea which I sailed to Holland, to how many more continents on land and in the air will you transport me, Passarola, the wind roars in my ears, and no bird ever soared so high, if only the King could see me now, if only that Tomas Pinto Brandão who mocked me in verse could see me now, if only the Holy Office of the Inquisition could see me now, they would all recognise that I am the chosen son of God, yes, I, Padre Bartolomeu Lourenço, who am soaring through the skies aided by my genius, aided, too, by Blimunda's eyes, if there are such eyes in heaven, and also assisted by Baltasar's right hand, Here I bring you God, one who also has a left hand missing, Blimunda, Baltasar, come and look, get up from there, don't be afraid.

They were not afraid, they were simply astounded at their own daring. The priest laughed and shouted. He had already abandoned the safety of the handrail and was running back and forth across the deck of the machine in order to catch a glimpse of the land below, north, south, east, and west, the earth looked so vast, now that they were so far away from it, Baltasar and Blimunda finally scrambled to their feet, nervously holding on to the cords, then to the handrail, dazed by the light and the wind, suddenly no longer frightened, Ah, and Baltasar shouted, We've done it, he embraced Blimunda and burst into tears, he was like a lost child, this soldier who had been to war, who had killed a man in Pegões with his spike, and was now weeping for joy as he clung to Blimunda, who kissed his dirty face. The priest came up to them and joined in their embrace, suddenly perturbed by the analogy the Italian had drawn when he had suggested that the priest himself was God, Baltasar his son, and Blimunda the holy ghost, and now all three of them were up there in the skies together, There is only one God, he shouted, but the wind snatched the words from his mouth. Then Blimunda said, Unless we open the sail, we shall go on climbing, and we might even collide with the sun.

We never ask ourselves whether there might not be some wisdom in madness, even while recognising that we are all a little mad. These are ways of keeping firmly on this side of madness, and just imagine, what would happen if madmen demanded to be treated as if they were equals with the sane, who are only a little mad, on the pretext that they themselves still possess a little wisdom, so as to safeguard, for example, their own existence like Padre Bartolomeu Lourenço, If we were to open the sail abruptly, we should fall to the ground like a stone, and it is he who is manoeuvring the rope and adjusting the slack so that the sail opens gradually, casting its shadow on the balls of amber and causing the machine to slow down, who would ever have thought that it would be so easy to fly, now we can go in search of new Indies. The machine has stopped climbing and hovers in the sky, its wings extended, its beak pointing northward, and it has every appearance of being motionless. The priest opens the sail a little more, three-quarters of the amber balls are already covered in shadow, and the machine starts to descend gently, it is like sailing across a tranquil lake in a small boat, a tiny adjustment to the rudder, a stroke with one oar, those little touches that only mankind is capable of inventing. Slowly, land begins to appear, Lisbon looms into sight, the uneven rectangle of the Palace Square, the labyrinth of streets and alleyways, the frieze of the veranda where the priest lives and where even now the officers of the Holy Office of the Inquisition are forcing an entry to arrest him, they have come too late, officers who are so scrupulous in the affairs of heaven, yet who forget to look up at the blue sky, where they would see the machine, a tiny dot in the remote distance, but how could they raise their eyes when they are confronted, to their horror, with a Bible whose pages have been torn out at the Pentateuch, when they are confronted by the Koran reduced to indecipherable fragments, they leave at once and head for the Rossio and the headquarters of the Holy Office of the Inquisition to report that the priest they had gone to arrest has already escaped, and it never occurs to them that he has taken refuge in the great celestial dome, which they will never know, because it is quite true that God has a weakness for madmen, the disabled, and eccentrics, but most certainly not for officers of the Holy Office of the Inquisition. The Passarola descends a little further, until the estate of the Duke of Aveiro comes into sight, and these three fliers are clearly beginners, they lack the experience that would enable them to distinguish important landmarks at a glance, rivers and streams, lakes, villages sprinkled like stars on earth, dense forests, they can see the four walls of the coach-house, the airport from which they launched their flight, Padre Bartolomeu Lourenço suddenly remembers that he has a spyglass in the chest, he fetches it at once and trains it downwards, ah, how wonderful to be able to live and invent things, he can now distinguish the pallet in the corner, and the forge, but the harpsichord has disappeared, what has become of the harpsichord, we know, and are able to reveal, that Domenico Scarlatti called at the estate just in time to see the machine rising into the sky with a great shuddering of wings, and just think what would happen if those wings could flap, and once inside the coach-house, the musician found the debris of their departure, broken tiles scattered all over the floor, battens and joists sawn off or broken away, there is nothing sadder than an empty space, the machine is already on its way and gaining altitude, only to leave behind the most acute melancholy, and this sends Domenico Scarlatti to the harpsichord where he starts to play a bagatelle, barely skimming his fingers over the keys, as if stroking someone on the face when all words have been spoken or when words fail, he knows full well that it is dangerous to leave the harpsichord there, so he drags it outside, over the rough ground, awkwardly bumping it as he goes, it emits jarring chords, and this time the jacks really will be dislodged beyond repair, Scarlatti eases the harpsichord to the mouth of the well, which fortunately is set low, and, heaving it off the ground with one mighty push, he drops it down, the frame knocks against the inside walls twice and it emits woeful chords as it finally sinks into the water, who can tell what destiny awaits it, a harpsichord that played so beautifully and now sinks like a drowning man gurgling ominously until it settles in the mud. The musician has disappeared from sight, he is already beating a hasty retreat along narrow lanes away from the main road, perhaps if he were to raise his eyes he would see the Passarola once more, he waves with his hat, just once, better to dissemble and pretend that he knows nothing, this explains why they did not spot him from the airship, and who knows if they will ever meet him again.

There is a southerly wind, a breeze that scarcely ruffles Blimunda's hair, with this wind they will not be going anywhere, it would be like trying to swim across the ocean, so Baltasar asks, Shall I use the bellows, every coin has two sides, first the priest proclaimed, There is only one God, now Baltasar wants to know, Shall I use the bellows, from the sublime to the ridiculous, when God refuses to blow, man has to make an effort. But Padre Bartolomeu Lourenço seems to have been struck dumb, he neither speaks nor moves, simply stares at the vast circumference of the earth, part river and sea, part mountain and plain, if that is not spray he perceives in the distance, it could be the white sails of a ship, unless it is a trail of mist, it could be smoke from some chimney, yet one cannot help feeling that the world has come to an end, and mankind as well, the silence is distressing, the wind has fallen, not a single hair on Blimunda's head is disturbed, Use the bellows, Baltasar, the priest commands.

It is like the pedals of an organ with treadles for inserting one's feet, they come up to a man's chest and are fixed to the frame of the machine, there is also a rail on which to rest one's arms, this time it is not another of Padre Bartolomeu Lourenço's inventions, but a design he copied from the organ in the cathedral, the main difference being that no music comes from the bellows but only the throbbing of the Passarola's wings and tail as it starts to move slowly, so slowly that one feels exhausted just watching, and the machine has scarcely flown the distance of an arrow shot from a crossbow, now it is Baltasar who is feeling tired, and at this rate we shall go nowhere. Looking cross, the priest appraises the efforts of Sete-Sóis, realising that his great invention has one serious flaw, travelling through the skies is not like sailing on waters, where one can have recourse to rowing when there is no wind, Stop, he orders Baltasar, Don't use the bellows anymore, and a weary Baltasar flops down on the deck.

The alarm and subsequent rejoicing have passed, all that remains is despondency, for they now know that by going up in the air and coming down again they are no different from the man who can get up or lie down but not walk. The sun is setting on the distant horizon, and shadows are already extending over the earth. Padre Bartolomeu Lourenço feels apprehensive for no apparent reason, but he is suddenly distracted by clouds of smoke coming from some forest fire in the distance and gradually moving northwards, and this would suggest that the wind is blowing lower down. He manoeuvres the sail, stretches it a little more so that the shade might cover another row of amber balls, and the machine descends abruptly, but not enough to catch the wind. One more row is sheltered from the sunlight, they descend so quickly that their hearts miss a beat, and now the wind seizes the machine with a powerful and invisible hand and hurls it forward with such force that Lisbon is suddenly far behind them, its outline blurred by the haze on the horizon, it is as if they had finally abandoned the port and its moorings in order to go off in pursuit of secret routes, who knows what dangers await them, what Adamastors they will encounter, what St Elmo's fires they will see rise from the sea, what columns of water will suck in the air only to expel it once it has been salted. Then Blimunda asks, Where are we going, and the priest replies, Where the arm of the Inquisition cannot reach us, if such a place exists.

This nation, which expects so much from heaven, scarcely ever looks up where heaven is said to be. Farmers go out to work the land, villagers enter and leave their homes, go out into the yard, to the fountain, or to squat behind a pine tree, only a woman who is lying on her back in a clearing with a man on top of her pays any attention to this strange apparition moving across the sky overhead, but she treats it as if it were a vision provoked by the ecstasies she is enjoying. Only the birds are curious as they circle avidly around the machine and ask themselves, Whatever can this be, Whatever can this be, perhaps it is the Messiah of birds, for the eagle by comparison is just any old St John the Baptist, After me comes He who is more powerful than I, and the history of flying does not end here. For some time they flew accompanied by a hawk that frightened off all the other birds, so that there were only two left, the hawk, beating and flapping its wings so that it is seen to be flying, and the Passarola whose wings do not stir, and if we did not know that it is made of sun, amber, dark clouds, magnets, and metal plates, we should find it difficult to believe our own eyes, nor could we offer the excuse of the woman lying in the clearing, who is no longer there now that she has taken her pleasure, and from here the spot cannot even be seen.

The wind is now southeasterly and blowing fiercely, the earth below sweeps past like the mobile surface of a river that carries with it fields, woodlands, villages, a medley of green, yellow, ochre, and brown, and white walls, the sails of windmills, and threads of water over water, what forces would be capable of separating these waters, this great river that passes and carries everything in its wake, the tiny currents that seek a path therein, unaware that they are water within water.

The three fliers are at the bow of the machine, which is heading west, and once more Padre Bartolomeu Lourenço is gripped by mounting disquiet, close to panic, he cannot suppress a cry of despair, when the sun sets, the machine will irremediably descend, perhaps crash, perhaps shatter into pieces, and they will all be killed, That is Mafra yonder, Baltasar calls out in excitement like the lookout shouting from the crow's nest, Land, never was there a more apt comparison, for this is Baltasar's land, he recognises it without ever having seen it from the sky, perhaps this is because we each possess our own innate perception of mountains, which instinctively leads us back to the place where we were born, my concave in your convex, my convex in your concave, like man and woman, woman and man, we are each on earth, hence Baltasar's cry, That's my land, he recognises it as if it were a body. They pass rapidly over the site where the convent is being built, but this time they are seen from below, people flee in terror, some fall to their knees and raise their hands in a plea for mercy, others throw stones, and thousands of people are caught up in the tumult, he who did not see, doubts, he who saw, swears it is true and asks his neighbour to testify on his behalf, no one can really prove anything, because the machine has already flown away, heading towards the sun, and is now invisible against that glowing disk, perhaps it was nothing but a hallucination, the sceptics are already gloating over the bewilderment of those who believed.

Within a few minutes, the machine reaches the seashore, the sun appears to be drawing it to the other side of the world. Padre Bartolomeu Lourenço realises that they are about to drop into the ocean, so he gives the cord a sharp tug, the sail moves to one side and suddenly folds up, their ascent is now so rapid that the earth below retreats once more and the sun emerges far above the horizon. But it is too late. In the east, shadows are already encroaching, inevitable night descends. The machine gradually begins to drift in a northeasterly direction and pursues a straight line, slanting towards the earth, subject to the twin attraction of the light, which is fast waning but still has sufficient strength to support the machine in mid-air, and of nocturnal darkness, which already enshrouds the remote valleys. The very wind is swallowed up in the powerful current of air produced by their descent, by the shrill hissing that pervades the entire machine as it suddenly begins to lurch. Over the distant sea, the sun rests like an orange in the palm of one's hand, it is a metallic disk drawn from the forge and left to cool, its fiery glare no longer wounds the eyes, white, then cerise, red, then crimson, it continues to glow but is now subdued, it is about to take its leave, farewell until tomorrow, if there should be a tomorrow for these flying seafarers who topple like a bird struck by death, awkwardly balanced on stunted wings, wearing its diadem of amber and spiralling down in concentric circles, in a fall that seems infinite yet will soon reach its end. A shadowy form looms up before them, the Adamastor, perhaps, of their voyage, and mountainous curves rise from the ground crested with streaks of crimson light. Padre Bartolomeu Lourenço has the appearance of someone who is indifferent to all around him and is removed from this world, resigned, he awaits the end that is fast approaching. Suddenly Blimunda detaches herself from Baltasar, whom she frantically embraced when the machine began its precipitous descent, and puts her arm around one of the globes containing the dark clouds, there are two thousand wills inside, but they are not enough, she covers them with her body as if trying to absorb them or merge with them. The machine gives a sudden jolt, it rears its head, a horse checked by the bridle, it remains suspended there for an instant, vacillates, then starts to come down again, but less rapidly this time. Blimunda calls out, Baltasar, Baltasar, there was no need to call a third time, for he had already embraced the other globe, holding it close to his body, Sete-Luas and Sete-Sóis supporting the machine with their enclosed clouds as it slowly descended, so slowly that the willow canes barely creaked as it touched the ground and swayed to one side, there were no supports there to ensure a comfortable landing, but one cannot have everything. Feeling limp and weary, the three voyagers staggered out, losing their grip on the rail, they rolled over and found themselves stretched out on the ground, without so much as a scratch, miracles were clearly still being worked, and this was one of the better ones, they did not even have to invoke St Christopher, he was there directing the traffic and realising that the airship was out of control, he put out his mighty hand, and averted a disaster, and considering that this was his first miracle in the matter of flying, it was not so bad.

The light of day has almost disappeared and night is fast approaching, the first stars twinkle in the sky, and even though they had been so close, they had not succeeded in touching them, after all, this was a mere flea-hop, we rose into the sky above Lisbon, we flew over the town of Mafra and the site where the convent was being built, and we almost crashed into the sea, And now where are we, asked Blimunda, as she let out a groan because of the terrible pain in the pit of her stomach, there was no strength left in her arms, and Baltasar felt just as bad as he struggled to his feet and tried to straighten up, tottering like a bull before collapsing in a heap with its skull pierced by a stake, but lucky Baltasar, unlike the ox, is passing from near-death to life, the shake-up will do him no real harm and will help to make him realise just how satisfying it is to put his feet firmly on the ground, I've no idea where we are, the place is unfamiliar but looks like some kind of sierra, perhaps Padre Bartolomeu Lourenço can tell us. The priest was getting to his feet, neither his limbs nor his stomach were giving him any pain, only his head, which felt as if a dagger had perforated his temples, We're in as much danger now as we were before leaving the estate, if the Inquisition didn't find us yesterday, they will certainly capture us tomorrow, But where are we, what is this place called, Every place on earth is the antechamber of hell, sometimes you arrive there dead, sometimes you arrive alive only to die soon after, For the moment, we are still alive, Tomorrow we shall be dead.

Blimunda went to the priest and tried to comfort him, We were in serious danger when our machine came down, if we have managed to survive that, we shall survive the rest, tell us where we should go, I don't know where we are, In the daylight we shall see better, we'll climb one of these mountains, and from there, by following the sun, find our way, and Baltasar added, We shall get the machine back into the air, we already know how to manoeuvre it, and unless the wind fails us, we should be able to travel a fair distance and escape the clutches of the Holy Office of the Inquisition. Padre Bartolomeu Lourenço did not reply. He buried his head in his hands and gesticulated as if he were having a conversation with some invisible presence, and his face became ever more indistinct in the darkness. The machine had landed on a patch of scrub, but some thirty paces away, on either side, high thickets stood outlined against the sky. There appeared to be no sign of life in the immediate vicinity. The night was chilly, and little wonder, for September was almost over and the days were no longer warm. Sheltered by the machine, Baltasar lit a small fire, more for its comforting glow than in the hope of getting warm, for they were careful to avoid a great bonfire, which might be spotted at a distance. He and Blimunda settled down to eat the food they had brought in their knapsacks, they invited the priest to join them, but he neither responded nor drew near, they could see him standing there in silence, perhaps watching the stars, the deep valley, or those extended plains where not a single light flickered, it was as if the world had suddenly been abandoned by its inhabitants, perhaps here, there was no lack of flying machines capable of travelling in any weather, even at night, everyone had left, leaving our trio with this stupid bird that loses its way once it is deprived of sunlight.

When they finished eating, Baltasar and Blimunda lay down under the machine, covered with Baltasar's cloak and a canvas cloth that they removed from the chest, and Blimunda whispered, Padre Bartolomeu Lourenço is ill, he no longer seems to be the same man, He hasn't been the same man for a long time, but what can we do, How can we help him, I don't know, perhaps tomorrow he will reach some decision. They heard the priest move away, dragging his feet through the undergrowth, muttering to himself, and they felt more relieved, the most trying thing of all was the silence, and despite the cold and discomfort, they dozed off. They both dreamt that they were flying through the air, Blimunda in a carriage drawn by winged horses, Baltasar riding a bull that wore a mantle of fire, suddenly the horses lost their wings and the fuse ignited, causing fireworks to explode, and in the midst of these nightmares they woke up, having slept very little, the sky lit up as if the world were on fire and they saw the priest with a flaming branch in one hand setting the machine alight, and the cane framework was crackling as it caught fire, Baltasar jumped to his feet, ran to the priest, grabbed him by the waist, and pulled him away, but the priest put up a struggle, forcing Baltasar to tighten his grip and throw him to the ground before stamping out the firebrand, while Blimunda used the canvas cover to beat out the flames, which had started to spread from shrub to shrub, and gradually the fire was extinguished. Overwhelmed and resigned, the priest rose to his feet. Baltasar covered the embers with soil. They could scarcely see each other amid the shadows. Blimunda asked him in a low, neutral voice, as if anticipating his reply, Why should you want to destroy our machine, and Padre Bartolomeu Lourenço replied in the same indifferent tone, as if he had been expecting the question, If I have to be burnt in a fire, let it at least be this one. He withdrew into the shrubbery on the side of the slope, they saw him descend rapidly, and when they looked a second time, he had disappeared, some urgent call of nature, perhaps, if a man who has tried to set fire to his dream still experiences such things. Time passed and the priest did not reappear. Baltasar went to look for him. He was nowhere to be seen. He called out his name, but there was no reply. The moon appeared and masked everything with hallucinations and shadows, Baltasar felt the hairs on his head and body stand on end. He thought of werewolves and ghosts, of phantoms in every guise and form, of wandering souls, he was convinced that the priest had been carried off by Satan himself, and before Satan could carry him off, too, to writhe in hell, he said a paternoster to St Giles, the saintly auxiliary and advocate in moments and situations inducing panic, epilepsy, madness, and nightmares. Could the saint have heard his plea, for so far, the devil had not come to fetch Baltasar, but his fears did not subside, and suddenly the whole earth began to murmur, or so it seemed, unless it was the influence of the moon, Seven-Moons is the best saint for me, he thought to himself as he turned to her, still trembling with fright, The priest has disappeared he told her, and Blimunda said, He has gone away and we shall see him no more.

That night they slept badly. Padre Bartolomeu Lourenço did not return. When day breaks, the sun will rise yonder, Blimunda warned Baltasar, If you don't extend the sail, and firmly stopper the amber balls, the machine will travel on its own, without any manual assistance, perhaps it would be best to release it, so that it might find itself reunited with Padre Bartolomeu Lourenço somewhere on earth or in the sky, and Baltasar added vehemently, Or in hell, the machine stays right here, and he set about extending the tarred sail and shading the amber globes, but he was not satisfied, fearing that the sail might get torn or be blown away by the wind. Using his knife, he lopped off branches from some of the taller shrubs and arranged them over the machine and, after an hour, in the clear light of day anyone looking from afar in that direction would have seen nothing other than a mound of greenery in the centre of that patch of scrub, not that this is anything unusual and it will look much worse when everything starts to wither. Baltasar ate some of the leftovers from their meal of the previous evening, after Blimunda had eaten something, for, as you will recall, she is always the first to eat, with her eyes closed, today she even buried her head under Baltasar's cloak. There's nothing more to be done here. What do we do now, one of them asked, and the other replied, We can do nothing more here, Let's go, then, We can go down past the place where Padre Bartolomeu Lourenço disappeared, and perhaps we can still find some trace of him. Throughout the morning they searched that side of the mountain, as they made their descent, they wondered what these great, round, silent mountains were called, and they found no trace of the priest, not even so much as a footprint or a shred of his black cassock that might have been caught on some thorn, the priest appeared to have vanished into thin air, Where could he be, What now, it was Blimunda who posed the question. We travel on, the sun is over there, the sea lies on our right, and when we reach some inhabited place, we shall find out where we are and what this sierra is called, so that later we can retrace our steps, this is the Serra do Barregudo, a shepherd told him a league ahead, and that high mountain is Monte Junto.

It took them two days to reach Mafra, after a lengthy detour in order to give the impression that they had come from Lisbon. On the road, they met a procession, everyone giving thanks to heaven for the miracle ordained by God, when the Holy Ghost flew over the site of the future basilica.

WE ARE LIVING in an age where a nun, as if it were the most natural thing in the world, is likely to encounter the Child Jesus in the cloister, or an angel playing the harp in the choir, and should she be locked away in her cell, where, in private, the manifestations are of a more corporeal nature, she is tormented by demons who shake her bed and wriggle her body, first the upper part, so that her breasts quiver, then the lower part, where her orifice trembles and perspires, that vista of hell or gate to heaven, the latter when enjoying an orgasm, the former when the orgasm has passed, and one believes in all of this, therefore, Baltasar Mateus, alias Sete-Sóis, cannot go around saying, I've flown from Lisbon to Monte Junto, or he will be taken for a madman, which might be just as well, if he wants to avoid the attention of the Holy Office of the Inquisition, for there are plenty of raving lunatics in this land beset by madness. So far, Baltasar and Blimunda have managed to survive with the money Padre Bartolomeu Lourenço had given them, and on a modest diet of cabbage and beans gathered from the kitchen garden, the odd piece of meat, and some salted sardines when there were no fresh ones, and whatever they spent or ate was not so much in order to nourish their own bodies as to ensure the well-being of the flying machine, if they cherished any hope of seeing it fly again.

The machine, if that is what one believes it to be, has flown, and its body demands nourishment, that explains why their dreams soar to such heights, Sete-Sóis cannot even ply his trade as a drover, the oxen have been sold, the cart is broken, and if God were not so inconsiderate, the chattels of the poor would be eternal. If he had his own yoke of oxen and cart, Baltasar would be able to offer his services to the Inspectorate General, and despite his disability they would employ him. But with only one hand, they would seriously question his ability to handle animals for the King, the nobles, or any other wealthy land-owners who had lent them to ingratiate themselves with the crown. So, what work can I hope to find, Baltasar asked his brother-in-law, Álvaro Diogo, after supper that same night, for they were all now living in the paternal home, but first Baltasar and Blimunda were given a detailed account by Inês Antónia of the Holy Ghost's remarkable flight over Mafra, With these very eyes, which the earth will consume one day, I saw the Holy Ghost, my dear Blimunda, and Álvaro Diogo saw the apparition, too, as he was working on the site, Is that not true, husband, whereupon Álvaro Diogo, blowing on a live ember, confirmed that something had passed over the site where they were building the convent, It was the Holy Ghost, Inês Antónia insisted, The friars said as much to all those who cared to listen, and people were so confident that it was the Holy Ghost that they organised a proces-sion of thanksgiving, So it was the Holy Ghost, then, her husband conceded, and Baltasar, looking at a smiling Blimunda, said, There are things in the heavens that we cannot explain, and Blimunda fell in with those sentiments by adding, If we were able to explain them, things in the heavens would be known by other names. In the corner by the hearth, old João Francisco drowsed quietly, bereft of cart, yoke of oxen, land, and Marta Maria, he seemed estranged from their conver-sation, but muttered before dozing off once more, In this world there is only life and death, they waited for him to finish, and it is strange how the elderly fall silent when they ought to go on speaking, oblig-ing the young to learn everything from scratch. There is someone else here who is asleep and therefore silent, but even if he were awake, it is doubtful whether he would be allowed to say anything, for he is only twelve years old, truth may come out of the mouths of babes, but they have to grow up before they are allowed to speak, and by then they have usually started telling lies, this is the boy who has survived, and he arrives home at night worn out from his labours as a builder's apprentice and all that climbing up and down scaffolding all day long, and no sooner does he eat his supper than he is fast asleep, There is work for any man who wants it, Álvaro Diogo assured Baltasar, you can run errands or work as a porter with a handcart, your hook is all you need for holding the shaft, these are the misfortunes of life, a man goes to war, he comes back wounded, flies through the air by some mysterious power, and then, when he tries to earn a modest living, this is what he is offered, and he is fortunate, for in all probability there were not even hooks a thousand years ago to substitute for a missing hand, and who knows what will have been invented a thousand years from now.

Early next morning, Baltasar and Álvaro Diogo, accompanied by the latter's son, left for work, the Sete-Sóis house, as has already been mentioned, is by the Church of St Andrew and the Viscounts' Palace, here in the oldest part of the town where the ruins of the castle built by the Moors are still standing, they left early, meeting up with other men along the route, whom Baltasar recognised as neighbours also helping to build the convent, which might explain why the surrounding fields have been abandoned, the old folks and the women cannot cultivate the land on their own, and since Mafra lies at the bottom of the valley, the men have to climb improvised paths, for those of former times have been covered over with the rubble cleared from the Alto da Vela. Seen from below, the walls of the future convent scarcely suggest another Tower of Babel, and as one reaches the bottom of the slope, the walls completely disappear, the work has now been in progress for some seven years, and at this rate it will not be ready before the Day of Judgment and will therefore turn out to be futile, It's a big job, Álvaro assures Baltasar, as you will see for yourself when we get nearer, and Baltasar, who feels a certain contempt for stone-masons and brick-layers, is astounded, not so much by the work that has been completed as by the hordes of workers swarming the place, an ant-hill of men rushing about in all directions, If all these people have come here to work, then I must eat my words. The boy has left them and gone off to start his day's work carrying hods of lime, while the two men cross the site to the left on their way to the Inspectorate General's office, Álvaro Diogo will explain, This is my brother-in-law, who lives in Mafra, and although he has spent many years in Lisbon, has now returned to his father's house and needs a job, not that personal recommendations necessarily do much good, but Álvaro Diogo has been here from the outset and is known to be a reliable worker and a word in the right ear always helps. Baltasar gapes in astonishment, he has come from a village and is now entering a city, and Lisbon, of course, is an impressive sight, as the capital of a great kingdom that incorporates the Algarve, which is small and nearby, but also other territories, such as Brazil, Africa, and India, not to mention the Portuguese domains scattered throughout the world, it is only natural, I say, that Lisbon should be so overwhelming and chaotic, but who would expect to find this vast conglomeration of rooftops of every conceivable shape and size so close to Mafra, it has to be seen to be believed, when Sete-Sóis flew over this place three days ago, he was in such an anxious state that he thought his eyes were deceiving him as he looked down on this conglomeration of houses and streets and thought the future basilica was no bigger than a chapel. If God Himself has the same difficulty in seeing things from up above, then He might do well to tread the earth on His own divine feet, and dispense with interme- diaries and envoys who are never trustworthy, and He might start by correcting the optical illusion whereby what looks small from a distance turns out to be large when seen up close, unless God uses a spyglass, like Padre Bartolomeu Lourenço and is looking at me this very minute as I wait to see whether they will offer me a job or turn me away.

Álvaro Diogo has already gone off to start laying stones, one on top of another, had he delayed any longer, it would have meant forfeiting a quarter of the day's wage, which would have been a serious loss, now Baltasar has to convince the recruiting officer that an iron hook is as good as a hand made of flesh and blood. The clerk seems doubtful about his chances and, rather than accept the responsibility, goes inside to make some inquiries, a pity that Baltasar cannot produce any docu- ments certifying that he is a builder of airships, or at least that he has fought in the war, if this were to do him some good, for the nation has been at peace for the last fourteen years, and who wants to know about wars, once wars are over, it is as if they had never taken place. The clerk returns looking cheerful, What's your name, and he takes up his duck quill and dips it into the brown ink, so Álvaro Diogo's recommendation has helped after all, or the fact that he has some claim on this land, or that he is still in his prime, thirty-nine years of age despite those first grey hairs, or simply that God might be offended if a man in need of work should be turned away when He has favoured Mafra by allowing the Holy Ghost to fly over the town three days before, What's your name, Baltasar Mateus, nicknamed Sete-Sóis, You can start work next Monday as a porter. Baltasar dutifully thanks the recruiting clerk and leaves the Inspectorate General feeling neither happy nor sad, a man must earn his daily bread by some means somewhere, and if that bread fails to nourish his soul, at least his body will be nourished while his soul suffers.

Baltasar knew that this place was known as the Ilha da Madeira, the Island of Wood, and it was well named, because, apart from a few houses built in stone and mortar, all the others were timber constructions, but built to last. There were also blacksmiths working on the site, and Baltasar could have mentioned his experience at the forge, although he had already forgotten much of what he had learned, not to mention the other skills about which he knew nothing, subsequently there would be coopers, glaziers, painters, and many other craftsmen on the site. Many of the timber houses had upper storeys, on the ground floor were housed the livestock and oxen, and above lodged the personnel of greater and lesser rank, the masters of works, the clerks and other officers of the Inspectorate General, as well as the military officers in charge of the troops. At this hour of the morning, oxen and mules were being led out of the stables, others had been led out even earlier, and the ground was soaked with urine and littered with manure, and as in Lisbon during the Corpus Christi procession, street urchins were running wild amid the crowds and cattle jostling and chasing one another, and one lad who was trying to escape from another slipped and fell under a yoke of oxen but escaped being trampled, because his guardian angel was watching over him, and he escaped without injury, apart from being covered with foul-smelling dung. Baltasar laughed along with the others and there was no doubt that the job had its moments of fun. It also had its own guard. Even now, some twenty foot soldiers were marching past as if on their way to war, they could be on manoeuvres or heading for Ericeira to resist a landing of French pirates, who will make so many attempts to land that they will finally succeed, and one day long after this Babel is over, Junot duc d'Abrantès will enter Mafra, where only some twenty aged friars will be left in the convent to fall off their stools with the shock, and Colonel or Captain Delagarde, his rank is of no importance, heading the vanguard, will try to enter the Palace and find the doors locked, whereupon the custodian, Friar Félix de Santa Maria da Arrábida, will be summoned, but the poor fellow will not have the keys, because they will be with the Royal Family, which has fled, and then perfidious Delagarde, as one historian will dub him, will deal the poor custodian a mighty blow, who with evangelical humility and divine example will proffer the other cheek, but if Baltasar, when he lost his left hand in Jerez de los Caballeros, had offered his right hand as well, he would now find it impossible to hold the shaft of the hand-cart. And speaking of *caballeros,* some horsemen have also passed, armed just like the foot soldiers who are even now entering the square. It soon becomes clear that they are arriving for guard duty and there is nothing quite like working with guards standing over you.

The men sleep in large wooden dormitories, each accommodating no fewer than two hundred, and from where he is standing, Baltasar finds it impossible to count all the huts, but he gets up to fifty-seven before losing count, not to mention that his arithmetic has not improved over the years, the best thing would be to take a bucket of limewash and a brush and to paint a sign here and a sign there to avoid repeating the count, as if he were nailing crosses of St Lazarus to the doors to ward off some skin disease. Baltasar would find himself sleep-ing on a mat or bunk like these men were it not for his father's house in Mafra, and he has a wife to keep him company at night, while most of these poor wretches have come from afar and left their wives behind, they say a man is not made of wood, it is much worse and more diffi-cult to bear when a man's penis is as hard as wood, for the widows of Mafra are certainly not going to satisfy all their demands. Baltasar left the sleeping quarters and went off to look at the military camp, there he felt a lump in his throat, all those pitched tents, it was as if he were stepping back in time for, however unlikely it may seem, there are moments when a former soldier feels nostalgia for war, and it is not the first time this has happened to Baltasar. Álvaro Diogo had already told him that there were many soldiers in Mafra, some having been drafted to help with the excavations and blasting operations, others to supervise the workers and deal with any disturbances and judging from the number of tents, the many soldiers to which Álvaro had referred ran into thousands. Sete-Sóis is dumbfounded, what new Mafra is this, there are some fifty houses down in the village itself, and some five hundred up here on the site, not to mention other notable differences, such as this row of communal refectories, sheds almost as large as the dormitories, with extended tables and benches fixed to the floor and long trestles for serving the food, there is no one around at present, but by mid-morning cauldrons are suspended over the fires for the main meal, and when the mess bugle is sounded, there will be one great stampede to see who can get there first, the men come off the site dirty from work, and the uproar is deafening, friends call to friends, Sit here, Keep my place for me, but carpenters sit with carpenters, builders with builders, and the hordes of unskilled labourers sit at the bottom, each man with his own kind, thank goodness Baltasar can go home to eat, otherwise he would be at a loss for company, for he knows nothing about handcarts, just as he is the only person there who knows anything about flying machines.

Álvaro Diogo can say what he likes in his own defence and that of his fellow workers, but the project is clearly making little progress. Baltasar has examined everything with the scrupulous eye of someone inspecting a house he hopes to occupy, there go the men with handcarts, whilst others mount the scaffolding, some carrying the lime and sand, others in pairs, easing the stone slabs up gentle ramps with poles and ropes, and the master-masons supervise operations with truncheon in hand, while the overseers check the diligence of each labourer and the standard of his work. The height of the walls is no more than three times that of Baltasar, and they do not embrace the entire perimeter of the basilica, but they are as thick as those of any fortress, and thicker than those of the surviving walls of the castle at Mafra, but those were of another age, before artillery came into use, only the width of the stone walls of the future convent can justify the slowness with which they are being raised. Baltasar comes across a handcart lying on its side and decides to have a go at holding the shaft, it is not too difficult, and once he has cut out a semicircle in the lower part of the left-hand shaft, he is ready to compete with any pair of hands.

He then descends by the same path he came up. The building site and Ilha da Madeira are hidden behind the slope and were it not for the stones and gravel that are continually being tipped down the slope, one would not suspect there will ever be a basilica, convent, or royal palace on that site, simply Mafra as before, the same small place that has existed for centuries and has scarcely altered from the time of the Romans, who made decrees, and of the Moors, who came after them and planted vegetable gardens and orchards that have virtually disappeared, up to the present, when we became Christians by the will of whosoever ruled us, for if Christ walked on earth, He never visited these parts, otherwise the Alto da Vela would have been His Calvary, now they are building a convent there, which probably amounts to the same thing. Pondering these holy matters more deeply, if they really are Baltasar's thoughts, but what would be the point in asking him, he remembers Padre Bartolomeu Lourenço, but not for the first time, because when he is alone with Blimunda, he scarcely speaks of anything else, he remembers him and is suddenly filled with remorse, he regrets having treated him so harshly and with such brutality in the sierra on that dreadful night, it was as if he had mistreated his own brother when the fellow was ailing, I know very well that he is a priest and I am no longer even a soldier, nevertheless, we are both the same age, and we worked together on the same invention. Baltasar repeats to himself that one day he will return to the Serra do Barregudo and to Monte Junto, to find out if the machine is still there, the priest might have secretly made his way back to the spot, flown off on his own to lands more favourably disposed to inventions, to Holland, for example, a country much devoted to the wonders of flying, as would be confirmed by a certain Hans Pfaall, who, because he was not pardoned for a number of petty crimes, continues to live on the moon to this day. The last thing Baltasar needed to know were these future events and even more impressive ones such as that of two men ascending to the moon and being seen there by everyone, and if they found no trace of

Hans Pfaall, that was probably because they did not look hard enough. For those paths are difficult to find.

Down here, they are much easier. From dawn until dusk, Baltasar, along with some seven hundred, one thousand, twelve hundred others, load their carts with earth and stones, in Baltasar's case, the hook secures the handle of the shovel, for during the last fifteen years, his right hand has trebled in strength and dexterity, and then an interminable procession of Corpus Homini in single file wends its way to dump the rubble down the embankment, covering not only the shrubs but also cultivated land. A kitchen garden from Moorish times is about to be wiped out after centuries of yielding cabbages, plump, tender lettuces bursting with freshness, oregano, parsley, mint, vegetables, and fruit in prime condition, and now farewell, water will no longer stream along these paths, the gardener will no longer turn over the soil to water this parched flower-bed while the adjacent one rejoices in the thirst that killed its neighbour. And just as the world goes around and around, the men who inhabit it revolve even more, perhaps that fellow up there who has just emptied a cartload of rubble, bringing down a torrent of stones and soil, with the heaviest of the stones descending first, was the man in charge of the vegetable garden, but it seems unlikely, for he does not even shed a tear.

The days pass, and the walls do not appear to be getting much higher. Cannon-fire blasts the solid rock that the soldiers are just about to storm, their efforts would be better rewarded if this type of rock could be used like other stones to fill in the walls, but, deeply embedded in the hillside, it can be quarried only with considerable difficulty, and once exposed to the atmosphere, it soon disintegrates and turns to dust unless loaded into the handcarts and dumped. Also used for transport are larger carts with wooden wheels and drawn by mules, some of them overloaded, and because of the heavy rain in recent days, the animals got trapped in the mud and had to be whipped to get them out, the poor beasts were given strokes of the lash on their rumps and, when God was not looking, on their heads, although all this labour is meant to serve and glorify the same God, and so one cannot be sure that He is not deliberately averting His gaze. The men pushing the handcarts have a lighter load to carry, and are in less danger of getting stuck, they can improvise cat-walks from wooden planks that were left scattered around when the scaffolding went up, but since there are never enough planks to go round, there is a constant battle of hide-and-seek to see who can get there first and, should they arrive simultaneously, to see who can push the hardest, and you can be sure that punching and kicking soon follow and missiles fly through the air, until a military patrol arrives, a manoeuvre which is usually sufficient to cool tempers, otherwise they receive a couple of blows with the flat edge of a sword, two strokes of the lash on their rumps like the mules.

It starts raining, but not heavily enough to bring the work to a halt, except in the case of the stone-masons for the rain loosens the mortar and seeps into the broad surfaces on top of the walls, so the workers take refuge in the sheds until the weather clears up, while the stone-cutters, whose task is somewhat more refined, work at their marble under cover, no matter whether they are cutting or sculpting it, but no doubt they, too, would rather take a rest. For the latter it is all the same whether the walls go up quickly or slowly, their work goes on regardless, tracing out the grain of the marble and carving out flutes, acanthus leaves, festoons, pedestals, and garlands and the minute the job is finished, the porters transport the stone with poles and ropes to the shed where it is stored along with the rest, when the time comes they will fetch the various pieces in the same manner, unless they are so heavy that tackle and ramps are required. The stone-cutters are fortunate in having their work guaranteed, whatever the weather, constantly under shelter and covered in white marble dust, they look like gentlemen in powdered wigs as they tap-tap, tap-tap, with their chisels and hammers, a job that needs two hands. Today the rain has not been heavy enough to force the overseers to suspend operations, and even the men pushing the handcarts are allowed to go on working, less fortunate than the ants, which at the first sign of rain raise their heads to pick up the scent of the stars and then scurry to their ant-hills, unlike men, who go on working in the rain. Coming in from the sea, a dark sheet of rain soon spreads over the countryside, the men abandon their handcarts at random and, without waiting for orders, make for the sheds or huddle behind the walls, if they think it will do any good, for they could not be more soaked. The harnessed mules stand placidly under the downpour, accustomed to being covered with perspiration, they are now soaked by rain, the yoked oxen chew their cud with apparent indifference, when the rain is at its fiercest, the animals shake their heads, who can tell what they are feeling, what nerves are twitching in their bodies, or whether those shiny horns touch, as if to say, So you're there. When the rain goes away or has become bearable, the men return to the site and the work starts up again as they load and unload, heave and push, drag and lift, there is no blasting today because of the general humidity, and so much the better for the soldiers, who can relax in the sheds in the company of the sentries, who are also sheltering from the rain, this is the happiness of peace. And since the rain is back again, pouring down from a glowering sky, and it looks as if it will continue for some time, orders are given for the men to put down their tools, only the stone-cutters go on chiselling at the stone, tap-tap, tap-tap, the sheds are spacious, nor will the spatterings of rain blown in by the wind mark the grain of the marble.

Baltasar went down into the town by a slippery path, a man going down ahead of him fell in the mud and everyone laughed whilst another fell down laughing, these are welcome distractions, for in Mafra there are no outdoor theatres, no singers or actors, opera is performed only in Lisbon, nor will there be any cinemas for another two hundred years, and by then flying machines will have engines, time is slow in passing until one finds happiness at last, Hello there. His brother-in-law and nephew must have arrived home already, lucky for them, for there is nothing like a good fire when a man is chilled to the marrow, to be able to warm your hands before those tall flames and toast the hard skin on the soles of your feet right up against the hot embers, the chill slowly thawing out your bones like dew melting in the sun. Better still if you find a woman in your bed, and if she is the woman you love, you need only catch sight of her, as we now see Blimunda, she has come to share the same cold and rain, and she is bringing one of her skirts to cover Baltasar's head, and the very scent of this woman brings tears to his eyes, Are you tired, she asks him, and these words are all he needs to make existence tolerable, the hem of her skirt is drawn over their two heads, and heaven could never match such bliss, if only God were to enjoy such harmony with our angels.

News reached Mafra sporadically that Lisbon was suffering the tremors of an earthquake, there is no real damage apart from the odd roof and chimney collapsing and cracks appearing in the walls of old buildings, but since somebody always benefits from misfortune, the chandlers did a roaring trade, the churches were crammed with lighted candles, especially before the altar of St Christopher, a saint noted for warding off plague and epidemics, lightning and fire, tempest and flood, as well as shipwreck and earthquake, in competition with St Barbara and St Eustace, who are also extremely reliable in providing such forms of protection. But the saints are like these workers building the convent, and when we refer to these workers, we mean all those others, too, who are employed elsewhere on buildings and demolitions, saints tire easily and value their rest, for they alone know how difficult it is to control the forces of nature, if they were the forces of God, things would be much easier, it would suffice to ask God, Look here, call off that tempest, earthquake, fire, flood, don't unleash that plague or allow that villain on to the highway, and only if He were an evil God would He ignore their pleas, but because these are the forces of nature and the saints get distracted, no sooner do we sigh with relief that we have escaped the worst than suddenly a storm breaks out, the likes of which has never been experienced in living memory, without rain or hail, but these might have been preferable and helped to break the strong wind, which tosses the anchored ships as if they were empty nutshells and goes tugging, stretching, and breaking the chains and yanking up the anchors from the depths of the sea, and once the ships are dragged from their moorings, they collide with one another and their sides are cracked open, causing them to sink as the sailors cry out, they alone know whom to ask for help, or they run aground where the relentless waves finally smash them to pieces. All the quays upriver collapse, the wind and waves dislodge the stones from their foundations and hurl them to the ground, doors and windows are shattered as if struck by cannon, what enemy can this be that wreaks havoc without sword or fire. Convinced that this upheaval must be the work of the devil, every woman and nursemaid, servant, and female slave, is on her knees praying, Most Holy Mary, Virgin and Mother of God, the men, meanwhile, looking deathly pale, and with neither Moor nor Indian on whom to inflict revenge, recite the rosary aloud, Pater Noster, Ave Maria, that we should invoke them with such insistence suggests that what we really need is a father and a mother. The waves break with such force on the shore of Boavista that the spray inundates the walls of the Convent of the Cistercian Nuns and the Monastery of St Benedict, which lies even farther inland. If the world were a boat and sailing a mighty ocean, it would sink this time, gathering waters upon waters in a flood that would be universal and save neither Noah nor the dove. From Fundição to Belém, which is almost a league and a half away, there was nothing but debris littered along the shores, splintered timber and cargo that had not been sufficiently heavy to sink and was swept ashore, which meant serious losses for the vessels' owners as well as for the King. The masts on some of the ships were sawn off to prevent them from capsizing, yet even with this precaution three men-of-war were driven ashore and would certainly have perished if they had not been rescued immediately. Countless skiffs, fishing boats, and barges finished up in fragments along the beaches, some one hundred and twenty large vessels used for cargo were grounded or lost at sea, and it would be futile to try to calculate the numbers of those drowned or killed, for many of the corpses were swept out beyond the straits or dragged to the bottom of the sea, but on the beaches alone, one hundred and sixty corpses were accounted for, the scattered beads of a rosary over which the widows and orphans weep, Ah, my beloved father, few women were drowned, some man will sigh, Ah, my beloved wife, for we are all beloved once we are dead. There were so many corpses that they had to be buried in haste, some could not be identified, nor their relatives located, and many who came to mourn the dead failed to arrive in time, but serious misfortunes call for serious measures, had the previous earthquake been more severe and the number of dead greater, the same measures would have been taken to bury the dead, and take care of the living, a sound piece of advice should any such calamity ever happen again, but spare us, oh Lord.

More than two months have gone by since Baltasar and Blimunda came to live in Mafra. A public holiday to mark a feast day meant that the work was suspended on the site, so Baltasar decided to make the trip to Monte Junto to see the flying machine. He found it in the same place, in exactly the same position, tilted to one side and resting on one wing beneath its camouflage of withered foliage. The mainsail, which had been left tarred and fully extended, cast shadows over the amber balls, and because of the angle of the hull, rainwater had not collected inside the sail, thus averting any danger of rot. Tall weeds sprouted everywhere from the stony ground, even brambles in certain places, and this was a curious phenomenon because neither the time nor the place was propitious, the Passarola seemed to be defending itself with its own mysterious powers, but, then, one can expect anything from such a machine. Somewhat hesitant, Baltasar added to the camouflage by cutting branches from the nearby bushes, as he had done before, but with less effort this time, because he had brought a pruning hook, and once the work was finished, he walked all around this other basilica and was pleased with the result. Then he clambered into the machine and, with the tip of his spike, which he had not had occasion to use recently, he scratched out a sun and a moon on one of the planks of the deck, so that if Padre Bartolomeu Lourenço should ever return here, he would see this sign and know at once that it was a message from his friends. Baltasar set out on the road, he had left Mafra at dawn, and it was already night when he returned after a ten leagues walk there and back, and although people say that those who walk for pleasure do not feel tired, Baltasar was exhausted by the time he reached home, yet no one had obliged him to go, so he must have captured the nymph mentioned by Camoens, and had a good time.

One day in mid-September, Baltasar was walking home from work when he saw Blimunda waiting for him on the road as she so often did, but somehow this time she looked anxious and distressed, which was most unlike her, for anyone who knew Blimunda could see that she went through the world as if she had gathered knowledge and experience from previous lives, and on reaching her, he asked, Is Father worse, No, she replied, and then in whispered tones confided, Signor Scarlet is with the Viscount, what can he be doing here, Are you sure, have you seen him, With these very eyes, It could be someone who looks like him, It's him, all right, I only have to see a person once to remember him, and I've seen Signor Scarlet lots of times. They went into the house and joined the others for supper, then everyone settled down for the night, each couple on their own pallet, and old João Francisco with his grandson, the boy is a restless sleeper and tosses and turns all night, but his grandfather does not mind, it is always company for the old man, who finds it difficult to sleep. This explains why he was the only person to hear, very late that same night, that is to say, late for someone who goes to bed early, gentle strains of music penetrating the cracks in the door and the roof of the house, there must have been a deep silence in Mafra that night, if music played on the harpsichord in the Viscounts' palace when the doors and windows were shuttered on account of the cold, and even when it was not cold, for the sake of decorum, was heard by an old man growing deaf with age, had Blimunda and Baltasar heard it, one might well have expected them to comment, It's Signor Scarlet who is playing, for it is quite true to say that the giant is recognised by his finger, this we would not argue with, since the proverb exists and is altogether apt. Next morning, as dawn broke, the old man sat down by the hearth and told them, I heard music last night, neither Inês Antónia nor Álvaro Diogo nor his grand-son paid any heed, for old people are always hearing something or other, but Baltasar and Blimunda felt envious to the point of sadness, if anyone there had the right to hear that music, it was them, no one else. When Baltasar went off to work, Blimunda spent the morning prowling around the palace.

Domenico Scarlatti had requested the King's permission to go and inspect the future convent. He was offered hospitality by the Viscount, not because the latter was particularly fond of music, but, since the Italian was music-master of the Royal Chapel and tutor to the Infanta Dona Maria Bárbara, he was regarded by the Viscount as a corporeal emanation from the palace itself. One can never tell when hospitality might be generously rewarded, the residence of the Viscount is no lodging-house, so just as well to choose one's guests with care. Domenico Scarlatti played the Vicount's harpsichord, which was sadly out of tune, the Viscountess listened to him playing in the evening with her three-year-old daughter, Manuela Xavier, on her lap and of all those present in the room, the child was the most attentive, she kept moving her little fingers in imitation of Scarlatti until she exhausted her mother's patience and was entrusted to her governess. There would not be much music in the child's life, tonight she would be asleep while Scarlatti played, and ten years from now she would die and be buried in the Church of St Andrew, where she still lies, if there is any place for such wonders on this earth, perhaps she will hear the music played by the water on the harpsichord that was thrown into the well of São Sebastião da Pedreira, if the well is still there, for sources of water are destined to become exhausted and filled in.

The musician made his way to the site of the convent and caught sight of Blimunda but they pretended not to know each other, for it would have aroused surprise and suspicion in Mafra if the wife of Sete-Sóis were to be seen socialising with the musician who is staying as a guest at the Viscount's residence, What can he be doing here, perhaps he's come to inspect the building, but why, if he is neither a mason nor an architect, and there is no organ as yet for any organist to play, no, there must be some other reason. I've come to tell you and Baltasar that Padre Bartolomeu de Gusmão has died in Toledo which is in Spain, to where he had escaped, and according to some, he was mad, and since no one mentioned you or Baltasar, I decided to come to Mafra to find out if you were still alive. Blimunda joined her hands, not as if she were praying, but like someone about to strangle her own fingers, Padre Bartolomeu Lourenço is dead, This is the news that reached Lisbon, On the night when the machine crashed into the sierra, Padre Bartolomeu Lourenço ran off and left us and returned no more, And the machine, It's still there, what shall we do with it, Guard and protect it, perhaps one day it will fly again, When did Padre Bartolomeu Lourenço die, They say it was on the nineteenth of November, and his death was marked in Lisbon that day by a great tempest, if Padre Bartolomeu de Gusmão were a saint, it could be a sign from heaven, What is it to be a saint, Signor Scarlet, You tell me, Blimunda.

The next day, Domenico Scarlatti departed for Lisbon. At a bend in the road outside town, Blimunda and Baltasar were waiting for him, the latter had forfeited a quarter of his daily wage to be able to bid the musician farewell. They went up to his carriage like beggars about to ask for alms, Scarlatti ordered the driver to stop and stretched out his hands to them, Farewell, farewell. In the distance, cannon fire could be heard, as if some feast were being celebrated, the Italian looks sad, and that is not surprising if he is coming away from the feast, but the others, too, look sad, and why should this be since they are going back to the feast.

SITTING ON HIS throne amid the radiance of the stars, with his mantle of night and solitude, and with the new sea and dead eras at his feet, is the only emperor who truly holds the globe of the universe in his hand, these are the words with which the Infante Dom Henrique will be acclaimed one day by a poet who is not yet born, everyone has his own preferences, but if we are speaking of the globe of the universe and of the empire and of the riches that empires yield, then Dom Henrique is a feeble monarch when compared with Dom João, the fifth sovereign with that name on the roster of kings, sitting in a chair with arms made from lignum vitae, where he can rest with greater comfort and pay closer attention to the accountant who is drawing up an inventory of the realm's possessions and riches, silks, fabrics, porcelain, lacquered goods, tea, pepper, copper, ambergris, and gold from Macao, unpolished diamonds, rubies, pearls, cinnamon, bales of cotton, and saltpetre from Goa, rugs, furniture upholstered in damask, and embroidered bedspreads from Diu, ivory from Melinde, slaves and gold from Mozambique, from Angola more black slaves but not so sturdy as those from Mozambique, and the best ivory to be found in Western Africa, timber, manioc flour, bananas, yams, poultry, sheep, goats, indigo, and sugar from São Tomé, some black slaves, wax, hides, ivory, for not all ivory comes from elephant tusks, from Cabo Verde, woven materials, wheat, liqueurs, dry wines, spirits, crystallised lemon peel, and fruits from the Azores and Madeira, and, from the various regions of Brazil, sugar, tobacco, copal, indigo, wood, cotton, cacao, diamonds, emeralds, silver, and gold, which alone gives the realm twelve to fifteen million cruzados annually in the form of gold dust or minted coins, not to mention the bullion lost at sea or stolen by pirates, and though it is true that not all of this represents income for the crown, which is rich but not all that rich, more than sixteen million cruzados all told go into the royal coffers, the tax alone, which is levied for navigating the rivers that lead to Minas Gerais, yields thirty thousand cruzados, the Good Lord worked so hard to open up channels where waters might flow, and along comes a Portuguese king to impose a profitable toll.

Dom João V ponders how he will spend these enormous sums of money and such excessive wealth, he ponders the matter today just as he pondered it yesterday, only to come to the same conclusion, that the soul must be his primary consideration, we must preserve our soul by all possible means, especially when it can also be consoled by material comforts on this earth. Let the friar and nun have what is necessary, even what is superfluous, because the friar remembers to put me first when he prays, and the nun arranges the folds of my sheet and provides other little comforts, and if we pay Rome handsomely for the upkeep of the Holy Office of the Inquisition, she is paid even more for less cruel services, in exchange for ambassadorships and gifts, and if from this impoverished land of illiterates, rustics, and unskilled craftsmen one cannot expect refined arts and crafts, let them be brought from Europe for my convent at Mafra, and let all the other necessary adornments and embellishments be bought with the gold from my mines and revenues from my estates, whereby, as one friar will record for posterity, artisans abroad will get rich while we shall be admired for the splendours of our realm. From Portugal all that is required are the stone, tiles, and wood for burning, and men of brute force and empty hands. If the architect is German, the master-carpenters, master-builders, and master-masons are all Italian, and if the traders and other rogues from whom we buy everything are English, French, and Dutch, then you can be quite certain that they import from Rome, Venice, Milan, Genoa, Liège, France, and Holland the bells and carillons, the oil lamps and chandeliers, the candlesticks, the bronze torch-holders, the chalices and the silver-gilt monstrances, the tabernacles and statues of saints to whom the King is particularly devoted, the adornments for the altars, the altar fronts, the dalmatics, the chasubles, the copes, the cords and tassels, the canopies, the baldachins, the albs, the lace cloths, and three thousand walnut panels for the sacristy cupboards and choir stalls, a wood much esteemed by St Charles Borromeo for this purpose, and from the countries of Northern Europe come whole shiploads of timber for the scaffolding, sheds, and lodging huts, and ropes and hawsers for the winches and pulleys, from Brazil, innumerable planks of angelin wood for the doors and windows of the convent, for the flooring of the cells, dormitories, refectory, and other outbuildings, including the steps of the delousing booths, because it is a wood that does not perish, unlike this splintering Portuguese pine, which is only good for heating saucepans and for people to sit on who do not weigh much and have nothing in their pockets. Eight years have now gone by since the first stone was laid for the basilica in the town of Mafra, this one, thank God, came from Pêro Pinheiro, the rest of Europe should remember us with gratitude for the large sums of money they received in advance, not to mention what they charged in instalments as the work progressed and what they received when the project was finally completed, for they provided the silversmiths and gold-smiths, the bell founders, the sculptors responsible for the statues and bas-reliefs, the weavers, lace-makers, and needlewomen, the clock-makers, the engravers and painters, the rope-makers, the sawyers and carpenters, the embroiderers, the tanners, the carpet-weavers, the bell-makers, and the ship-riggers, if the cow that so placidly allows itself to be milked dry cannot be ours, or as long as it cannot be ours, at least let it remain with the Portuguese, for soon they will be buying a pint of milk from us on credit to make milk puddings and meringue desserts, If Your Majesty would care for another helping, Mother Paula solicitously reminds him, you need only ask.

The ants swarm around the honey, around the sugar spilled on the floor and the manna that has fallen from heaven, all of them moving in the same direction, like certain maritime birds that gather in their hundreds on the shores to worship the sun, no matter if the wind is behind them, ruffling their feathers, their concern is to follow the trav-elling eye of the sky, and with short runs they pass in front of one another, until the beach abruptly terminates or the sun disappears, tomorrow we shall come back to this same spot, and if we do not come our children will. The twenty thousand people gathered on the site are nearly all men, the few women who are present remain on the periphery, not so much because of the custom of segregating the sexes at Mass, but because of the risks they might run in the thick of that gathering, for though they might emerge alive, they would in all probability be violated, to adopt a modern expression, Do not tempt the Lord thy God, and if you do, then don't go complaining that you've become pregnant.

As we have explained, Mass is being celebrated. Between the site and the Ilha da Madeira there is a vast space trampled by the comings and goings of the workers and furrowed by the wheels of the carts that travel back and forth, fortunately, the ground is quite dry at present, this is the virtue of spring just as she is about to fall into the arms of summer, soon the men will be able to kneel on the ground without worrying about getting their trousers wet, although these people are not greatly bothered about cleanliness and they wash in their own sweat. On an elevation at the far end a wooden chapel has been erected, and if those who have come to attend Mass imagine that they will all fit in by some miraculous means, then they are greatly mistaken, it would be easier to multiply the loaves and the fishes, or to put two thousand wills into a glass phial, this is no miracle, but the most natural thing in the world when one so desires it. The winches creak and the noise is enough to open the gates of heaven and hell, each with its own distinctive appearance, those of the House of God are made of crystal, while those of Satan are made of bronze, and even the resounding echoes are different, here, however, the din is coming from the friction of the wood, the front of the chapel is lifted slowly, until the wall is transformed into a porch and at the same time the sides are drawn back, it is as if invisible hands were opening up a tabernacle, and the first time this happened, there were not all that many workers on the site, but one could always be sure of a congregation of some five thousand faithful who would gasp in admiration, Ah, in every age there is always some new wonder to astound mankind until they grow accustomed to it and lose interest, the chapel is finally opened wide, to reveal the celebrant and the altar within, can this be a Mass like any other, it seems impossible that this is an ordinary Mass, but all these people have already forgotten that the Holy Ghost once flew over Mafra, Masses preceding military campaigns are different, who knows, when the dead are counted and buried, whether I shall not be among them, so let us profit from the Holy Sacrifice, unless the enemy attack first, either because they have been to an earlier Mass or because they adhere to a religion that dispenses with any such observance.

From his wooden cage, the celebrant preached to the sea of faces, and had it been a sea of fishes, what a lovely sermon he might have repeated here, with its clear, wholesome doctrine, but in the absence of any fishes his sermon was that deserved by men and heard only by those who were standing near the altar, however, if it is true that the habit does not make the monk, faith undoubtedly does, anyone in that congregation, upon hearing the word heathen, knows that it was heaven, that eternal was infernal, that Zeus was Deus, and when he hears no other word or echo, it is because the sermon has ended and we can now disperse. It is frightening to think that Mass is over and that they have not ended up dead on the ground or been struck down when the sun shone straight on to the monstrance, causing it to sparkle, times are much changed, for once when the Bethshemeshites were cutting their wheat in the fields, they happened to lift their eyes to heaven and saw the Ark of the Covenant from the land of the Philistines, which sufficed to make fifty thousand and seventy of them fall flat on their faces, now there were twenty thousand watching, Were you there, I didn't see you. This is a religion that can grow very lax, especially when the congregation is so large that it becomes impossible to hear confessions and give holy communion to everyone, so they will remain here, come what may, if anything comes at all, staring, quarrelling, having their way with women up against fences and in more secluded places, until tomorrow, when they go back to work.

Baltasar crosses the square, some men are playing innocent games of quoits, others are playing games the King has prohibited, such as heads or tails, if the magistrate should come on his rounds, they will be put into the stocks. Blimunda and Inês Antónia are waiting for Baltasar at the agreed place, and there they will be joined shortly, if they have not already been, by Álvaro Diogo and his son. They all go down into the valley together, waiting for them to arrive home is old João Francisco, who can scarcely move his legs, he has to be content with the simple Mass celebrated by the parish priest in the church of St Andrew which is attended by all the members of the Viscount's household, and perhaps this explains why his sermons are less intimidating, with the one disadvantage, however, that they have to listen to the entire sermon, and João Francisco's attention wanders, which is only natural, for he is old and weary. They have had their dinner, Álvaro Diogo takes his siesta, the boy goes off to chase sparrows with his playmates, the women knit and darn on the sly, for this is a day of holy observance, when God does not wish the faithful to work, but unless this rip is patched today, the hole will be much bigger tomorrow, and if it is true that God punishes without stick or stone, it is no less true that one should darn only with a needle and thread, although I am not much good at mending, nor is this surprising, for when Adam and Eve were created, the one knew as much as the other, and when they were expelled from paradise, there is no evidence that the Archangel gave them separate lists of jobs suitable for men and women, Eve was simply told, You will suffer pain when giving birth, but even that will no longer be necessary one day. Baltasar leaves his spike and hook at home, he goes with his stump exposed, anxious to see if he can revive those consoling pains in his hand, which are now ever less frequent, that itch on the inside of his thumb and that sensual feeling as he scratches it with the nail of his index finger, no point in telling him that he is imagining it, he will retort that there are no fingers inside his head, others may say, But, Baltasar, you've lost your left hand, Who can be so sure, but there is no point in arguing with people who are even capable of denying their own existence.

It is a well-known fact that Baltasar likes a drink, though without getting drunk. He has been drinking since he first heard the sad news of the death of Padre Bartolomeu Lourenço, it came as a terrible blow, as if he had been struck by one of those deep earth tremors that touch the very roots while on the surface the walls remain standing upright. Baltasar drinks because he cannot shut out the memory of the Passarola, there in the Serra do Barregudo on the slopes of Monte Junto, perhaps its presence has already been discovered by smugglers or shepherds, and just to think about such things causes him to suffer as if the rack were being tightened. But when he drinks there always comes a point when he feels Blimunda's hand rest on his shoulder, and that is all he needs, Blimunda's tranquil presence in the house is enough to restrain him, Baltasar reaches out for the tankard filled with wine, which he intends to drink as he also drank all the others, but a hand touches his shoulder, a voice says, Baltasar, and the tankard is returned to the table untouched and his friends know that he will drink no more that day. Baltasar will remain silent, doing nothing except listen, until the torpor induced by the wine passes and the words of the others begin to make sense even as they exchange the same old stories, My name is Francisco Marques, I was born in Cheleiros, which is close to Mafra, some two leagues away, and I have a wife and three small children, all my life I've worked for a daily wage, and since there seemed to be no escape from poverty, I decided to come help build the convent, even the friar who secured the King's pledge was born in my home town, according to what I've been told, for I was only a child then, about the same age as your nephew, but I really mustn't complain, for Cheleiros is not all that far away, from time to time I stretch my legs on the road, the two legs that walk and the one in the middle that means my wife is pregnant once again, whatever money I save I leave there, but poor people like ourselves have to pay for everything we receive, there are no profits for us from trade with India or Brazil, nor do we enjoy appointments or benefices from the Palace, what can I do with a daily wage of two hundred réis when I have to pay for my ration of food and wine, the only people who make any money here are those who provide us with our daily needs, and if it is true that many of them were forced to come here from Lisbon, I live here out of need, and needy I remain, My name is José Pequeno, I have neither father nor mother, nor woman to call my own, I do not even know whether this is really my name or if I had some other name in the past, what is certain is that I was born in a village at the foot of Torres Vedras, and the parish priest baptized me, José is the name I was given at my christening, and Pequeno, which of course means small, was added later because I suddenly stopped growing, with this hump on my back, no woman was keen to marry me, but they all ask for more once I get the chance to mount them, that's my only consolation in life, Come over here, now off with you, and once I grow old, I won't even be fit for that, I came to Mafra because I like working with oxen, oxen are for hire in this world, just like me, My name is Joaquim da Rocha, I was born in the region of Pombal, and there I've left a wife, I had four children, but all of them died before they were ten years old, two of the black plague, the others from malnutrition and anaemia, I rented a plot of land but it did not yield enough to provide us with food, so I told my wife, I'm off to Mafra, there work is guaranteed and for many years to come, and so far so good, six months have passed since I last went home and I shall probably never go back, there's no lack of women here, and anyhow mine must have been of dubious stock to have given birth to four children and allowed all of them to die, My name is Manuel Milho, I come from the countryside near Santarem, one day the magistrate's men arrived to announce that a good wage and good food could be earned on the building site at Mafra, I was hired with a few others, but the two men who came with me were killed in a landslide last year, I don't care for these parts, not because two of my countrymen perished here, after all, no one can decide where he will die unless he arranges his own death, but because I miss the river of my native land, I know there is plenty of water in the sea, as one can tell even from here, but what does a man want with all that water, with all those waves that beat incessantly against the rocks and sands, the river back home flows between two banks like a procession of penitents, it slowly wends its way as we stand there watching like the ash trees and poplars, and when a man wants to examine his face and to see how much he has aged, the water becomes his mirror, passing, yet at a standstill, and we who appear to be at a standstill are the ones who are really passing, what I cannot explain is why such things come into my head, My name is João Anes, I come from Oporto and I am a cooper, and coopers are also needed when a convent is being built, for who else could be relied upon to mend the vats, the pipes, and the buckets, if a bricklayer is on the scaffolding and they pass him a hod of mortar, he has to wet the stones with a brush so that they make firm contact as he lays one on top of another, that explains why he carries a bucket, and what do animals drink from, they drink from a trough, and who made the troughs, why, the cooper, of course, without wishing to brag, there's no better trade than mine, even God was a cooper, just look at that great vat known as the sea, if the work were not perfect and the staves not so well adjusted, its waters would cover the earth and there would be a second great flood, I have little to say about myself, I left my family behind in Oporto, they know how to look after themselves, I haven't seen my wife for two years, sometimes I dream that I'm lying by her side, but if it's me lying there, I don't see my face, next day my work always turns out badly, I would rather see all of myself in my dream, instead of that face without mouth, eyes or nose, I cannot imagine what face my wife sees there at such moments, but I hope it is mine, My name is Julião Mau-Tempo, I'm a native of Alentejo, and I came to work here in Mafra because of the famine that scourges my province, I don't know how anyone has survived there, for if we hadn't grown accustomed to eating grass and acorns, I'll bet everyone would be dead by now, it's distressing to travel over that vast territory, as anyone will tell you who has been there, only to find that there is nothing but barren land, there are few signs of habitation or growth, and the rest is wilderness and solitude, it's a region blighted by warfare, with Spaniards invading and departing as if they were on their own soil, at the moment there is peace, but who knows for how long, when they're not making us run and exposing us to the risk of being killed, our monarchs and nobles themselves do the running and killing as they go hunting, yet God help the wretched fellow who's caught with a rabbit in his knapsack, even though he might have found it already dead from some disease or old age, the least he can expect is a dozen lashes on his back to teach him that when God made rabbits it was for the pleasure and stewpot of gentlemen, but those whippings would be worthwhile if we were allowed to keep the animals we poached, I came to Mafra because my parish priest assured us from the pulpit that anyone who came here would soon be a servant of the King, not exactly his servant, but something like that, he also assured us that no one in the King's service goes hungry, that they are given more meat than one sees in paradise and are well dressed, for if it is true that Adam, having no one to squabble with over food, ate to his heart's content, he did not have much in the way of clothing, well, I soon discovered that I had been misinformed, I can't vouch for paradise, because I wasn't around at the time of Adam, but I can speak for Mafra, and if I haven't died from hunger, it's because I spend everything I earn on food, I'm as shabbily dressed as I ever was, as for becoming one of the King's servants, I live in hope of seeing my sovereign's face before I finally pine away after all these years of separation from my family, when a man has children, he is often nourished just by looking at their faces, how reassuring it would be if our children could be nourished just by looking at our faces, we're fated to consume our lives looking at one another, Who are you, What are you doing here, Who I am and what I am doing here is a question I've often asked myself without receiving any answer, no, none of my children has blue eyes, yet I'm certain that they're all my children, this matter of blue eyes is something that appears from time to time in families, my mother's mother had eyes this colour, My name is Baltasar Mateus, but everyone calls me Sete-Sóis, José Pequeno knows why he got his name, but I cannot say when and why they put seven suns in our house as if we were seven times more ancient than the only sun that shines on us, so we should be the kings of the world, this is the wild conversation of someone who has been too close to the sun and has had too much to drink, if you hear me talk nonsense, it's either because of the sun I caught or because of the wine that caught me, what is certain is that I was born here forty years ago, if I have added them up correctly, my mother, who is now dead and buried, was named Marta Maria, my old father can scarcely walk, I'm convinced that roots are growing from his feet, or that his heart is searching out the earth in order to rest, we once had a plot of ground like Joaquim da Rocha, but with all this disturbance of the soil we lost our land, I've even transported some of the soil from that plot in my handcart, who's going to tell my grandfather that a grandson of his has dumped earth that was once tilled and sown, now they're building a turret on top, These are the changes in life's fortunes, and my life has seen many changes, in my youth I dug the soil and sowed the fields for the farmers, our family plot was so small that my father worked it all the year round and still had time to cultivate other smallholdings here and there that he rented, real hunger we never experienced, but we were never well off and had barely enough to live on, then I joined the King's army and lost my left hand, it was only much later that I discovered that with one hand missing I had become God's equal, and since I could no longer fight in the war, I returned to Mafra, then I spent some years in Lisbon, and that's my life in a nutshell, What did you do in Lisbon, João Anes asked him as the only man in the group who could claim to be a skilled worker, I worked in the slaughterhouse in the Palace Square, but only as a porter, And when was it that you got close to the sun. Manuel Milho was anxious to know, since he was probably the only one there who was accustomed to watching the river flow past, That was when I once climbed a very high sierra, so high that by stretching out my hand I could touch the sun, What sierra could that be, for there are no sierras in Mafra high enough to reach the sun, just as there are no sierras in Alentejo, which is a region well known to me, Julião Mau-Tempo asked him, Perhaps it was a sierra that was high on that particular day and is now low, If it takes so much gunpowder to blast a hill like this, surely it would take all the gunpowder in the world to raze a sierra, observed Francisco Marques, who had been the first to comment, but Manuel Milho insisted, You could only have got close to the sun by flying like the birds, there in the marshes you often see hawks soaring up and up in circles until they finally disappear and they become so tiny that they can no longer be seen as they head for the sun, but we humans don't know the path or doorway that leads there, and you are a man and have no wings, Unless you're a sorcerer, José Pequeno suggested, like a woman from the region where I was found, who rubbed herself with ointments, straddled a broom, and flew by night from one place to another, at least that's what people said although I never saw her with my own eyes, I'm not a sorcerer, and if you start to spread such rumours the Holy Office of the Inquisition will arrest me, nor did I say to anyone here that I have ever flown, But you did say that you had been close to the sun, and you also said that you had become God's equal when you lost your left hand, if such heresies reach the ears of the Holy Office of the Inquisition, nothing will save you, We should all be saved if we were to become God's equals, said João Anes, If we were to become God's equals, we should be able to rebuke Him for not having granted us equality from the outset, said Manuel Milho, and Baltasar, who was feeling relieved that they had got off the subject of flying, explained, God has no left hand because the chosen sit at His right and, once the damned are sentenced to hell, no souls remain at His left, now, if no one sits there, why should God need a left hand, and if He doesn't need a left hand, that means it doesn't exist, my left hand is no use because it doesn't exist, and that's the only difference, Perhaps on God's left there is another God, perhaps God has been elected by another God, perhaps we are all enthroned Gods, I can't imagine how these things come into my head, Manuel Milho quipped, and Baltasar rejoined, Then I must be the last one in the row, because no one can sit at my left, and with me the world comes to an end, Who knows why such thoughts should occur to these simpletons, for they are all illiterate except João Anes, who has had some education.

The bells of the Church of St Andrew down in the valley rang out the Angelus. Above the Ilha da Madeira, in the streets and squares, in the taverns and hostels, there is a continuous drone of conversation, like the sound of the sea in the distance. It could be the sound of twenty thousand men reciting the Angelus or telling one another the story of their lives, Go and see for yourselves.

LOOSE SOIL, GRAVEL, and pebbles that the gunpowder or the pick had prised from the stony ground were loaded on to the hand-carts and dumped in the valley, which is rapidly being filled with the rubble blasted from the mountain and dug up from the new excavations. Heavier loads are transported on the larger carts, which are reinforced with iron plates and drawn by mules and oxen that pause only to load and unload. By means of firmly braced wooden ramps, men mount the scaffolding with the stone slabs suspended from yokes that rest on their necks and shoulders, forever be praised whoever invented the pad that lessens the pain. These labours, as we have already said, can be described more easily because they require brute force, however, by constantly coming back to them we are less likely to forget things that are so common, and call for so little skill, that they tend to be overlooked, it is rather like distractedly watching our own fingers write, so that in one sense or another the agent of the doing remains concealed beneath the thing which is being done. We would see much more, and much farther, if we were to look from above, for example, and hover in the flying machine over this place called Mafra, the much-trodden mountain, the familiar valley, the Ilha da Madeira, which the seasons have darkened with rain and sunshine, and where some of the planking is already rotting, on the felling of trees in the pine forest of Leiria, and on the boundaries of Torres Vedras and Lisbon, on the smoke fumes that rise day and night from the hundreds of furnaces of bricks and lime between Mafra and Cascais, the ships that carry different bricks from the Algarve and from Entre-Douro-e-Minho to be unloaded in the Tagus, through a branching canal at the docks of Santo António do Tojal, on the carts that transport these and other materials through Monte Achique and Pinheiro de Loures to His Majesty's convent, and on those other carts, which carry the stones from Pêro Pinheiro, there is no finer lookout than the one where we are now standing, and we should have had no idea of the magnitude of the project at Mafra if Padre Bartolomeu Lourenço had not invented his Passarola, what supports us in mid-air are the wills that Blimunda gathered into the metal globes, down below, other wills move around, stuck to the globe of the earth by the laws of gravity and necessity, if we were able to count the carts that travel back and forth along these routes, from near and afar we would count up to twenty-five hundred, seen from up here, they appear to be motionless, such is the weight of their load. But the men would have to be much closer before we could see them.

For many months Baltasar pulled and pushed hand-carts, until one day he decided that he was tired of being a beast of burden, of constantly being sent back and forth, and having given ample evidence of his diligence in the presence of his masters, he was allowed to handle one of the many yokes of oxen the King had purchased. José Pequeno was a great help in securing this promotion, for the estate manager found the little hunchback's appearance so amusing that he could not resist observing that the drover's face only came up to the muzzles of his oxen, and this was almost true, but if he thought the remark would offend José Pequeno he was much mistaken, for the little hunchback suddenly became aware of the pleasure it gave him to look with his human eyes straight into those large gentle eyes of the oxen, where he saw his own head and torso reflected, until his legs disappeared on the lower fringe of the immense eyelids, when a man can fit his entire being into the eyes of an ox, he is finally convinced that the world is well made. José Pequeno was a great help, because he remonstrated with the estate manager that Baltasar Sete-Sóis should be promoted to drover, and if there was already one disabled man in charge of the oxen, there might as well be two, and they could keep each other company, and if the fellow doesn't know anything about the job, no harm will be done, for he can always go back to pushing a cart, after all, it only takes one day to judge a man's capabilities. Baltasar knew a great deal about oxen, even though he had not handled them for many years, and it needed only two trips to prove that his hook was no real drawback and that his right hand had not forgotten any of the know-how of goading oxen. When he arrived home that night, he was as happy as the day he discovered an egg in a bird's nest for the first time, when he possessed a woman for the first time, and when he first heard a bugle call as a young recruit, and as dawn broke, he dreamed about his oxen and his left hand, he wanted for nothing, even Blimunda was mounted on one of the animals, and anyone who knows anything about dreams will understand.

Baltasar had not been long in his new job when he was told that he was being sent to Pêro Pinheiro to collect an enormous stone that was intended for the portico of the church, the stone was so huge that it was estimated to require some two hundred yoke of oxen to transport it, as well as hordes of men to assist with the job. In Pêro Pinheiro a special cart had been constructed to carry the stone, a kind of man-of-war on wheels, as described by someone who had seen it nearing completion, and who had presumably also set eyes on the vessel with which he was drawing comparison. Obviously he was exaggerating, much better that we should judge it with our own eyes, along with all the men who get up in the middle of the night and set off for Pêro Pinheiro, accompanying the four hundred oxen and more than twenty carts with the necessary equipment to transport the stone, namely, ropes and hawsers, wedges, brakes, spare wheels made to the same measurement as the existing ones, spare axles in case some should crack under the weight, braces of various sizes, hammers, pincers, metal plates, scythes for cutting hay to feed the animals, and provisions for the men, to be supplemented with fresh produce en route, so many things weigh down the carts that any man who imagined he would be riding down to Pêro Pinheiro in comfort soon finds he has to walk, but it is not any great distance, three leagues there and three leagues back, although, admittedly, the roads are not good, but the oxen and men have made this journey so many times with other transports that they only have to put down their hooves or the soles of their feet to know that they are treading familiar territory, however difficult it might be to climb, or dangerous to descend. From the men we got to know the other day, José Pequeno and Baltasar have been chosen for the trip, and each leads his own yoke of oxen, and among the labourers who have been hired for their strength is the fellow who has left a wife and children back in Cheleiros and whose name is Francisco Marques, as well as Manuel Milho, who gets the strangest ideas and cannot imagine where they come from. There are other fellows, too, named José, Francisco, and Manuel, very few named Baltasar, but many named João, Álvaro, António, and Joaquim, and perhaps even the odd Bartolomeu though never the one who disappeared, as well as Pedro, Vicente, Bento, Bernardo, and Caetano, every possible name for a man is to be found here and every possible kind of existence, too, especially if marked by tribulation and, above all, by poverty, we cannot go into the details of the lives of all of them, they are too numerous, but at least we can leave their names on record, that is our obligation and our only reason for writing them down, so that they may become immortal and endure if it should depend on us, names such as Alcino, Brás, Cristóvão, Daniel, Egas, Firmino, Geraldo, Horácio, Isidoro, Juvino, Luís, Marcolino, Nicanor, Onofre, Paulo, Quitério, Rufino, Sebastião, Tadeu, Ubaldo, Valério, Xavier, Zacarias, each representing a letter of our alphabet, perhaps not all of these names are fitting for the time and place, much less for the men concerned, but as long as there are those who labour there will be no end to labours, and some of these labours will in the future belong to those who are waiting for someone to come along and assume their name and trade. From among the men who are represented in this sample alphabet and are going to Pêro Pinheiro, we should have liked to say more about Brás, who is red-haired and has no sight in his right eye, it will not be long before people start getting the impression that this is a land of disabled men, some with a hump, some with only one hand or one eye, and to accuse us of exaggerating, when all believe that heroes should be handsome and dashing, lithe and sound of limb, that is certainly how we should have preferred them, but there is no avoiding the truth, and the reader should be grateful that we have not wasted any time counting up all those who are blubber-lipped stutterers, lame, heavy-jowled, bow-legged, epileptic, big-eared, half-witted, albinos, and dolts, or suffering from scabies, sores, ringworm, and scurvy, then you would certainly see a long procession of hunchbacks and lepers wending its way out of Mafra in the early hours of the morning, just as well that by night every cat looks black and every man a shadow, if Blimunda had seen those men off while still fasting, what would she have seen in each of them, other than the will to be someone else.

The sun had no sooner risen than the day became hot, as one might well expect, since it is the month of July. Three leagues is no great distance for this race of wanderers, especially since most of them adjust their gait to that of the oxen, and the oxen can find no good reason for hurrying. Detached from the carts and simply yoked in pairs, the animals are suspicious of such largesse, and almost feel envious of their fellow oxen who are drawing carts with all the equipment, and they feel like the fattened calf before the slaughter. The men, as we already mentioned, proceed slowly, some in silence, others conversing, each man seeking out his own kind, but one of them has been feeling positively lustful since the convoy left Mafra, he breaks into a brisk trot as if he were racing to Cheleiros to save his father from the gallows, it is Francisco Marques, who is taking this opportunity of going to push himself between his wife's legs, which are waiting to receive him, or perhaps this is not what he has in mind, perhaps he simply wishes to be with his children and pay his respects to his wife without fornicating, for any sexual intercourse would have to be hasty, because his workmates are catching up with him, and he must reach Pêro Pinheiro at the same time as they do, they're already passing our door, After all, we've always slept together, the baby is asleep and won't hear a thing, we can send the others out to see if it is raining, and they'll understand their father wishes to be with their mother, just think what would become of us if the King had ordered the convent to be built in the Algarve, and when she asks, Are you leaving so soon, he replies, I've got to go now, but on the way back, if we set up camp nearby, I'll come and spend the whole night with you.

When Francisco Marques arrived at Pêro Pinheiro, worn out and weak on his legs, the camp had already been set up, there were no huts or tents and the only soldiers to be seen were on guard, it looked more like a country fair, with more than four hundred head of cattle and the men dispersed among the cattle, shooing them to one side, some of the animals took fright and began to toss their heads wildly, though without malice, before settling down to eat the hay as it was unloaded from the carts, they had a long wait ahead, the men who wielded the spades and hoes were eating quickly, for they were needed up front. It was already mid-morning and the sun beat fiercely on the hard, parched ground covered with marble chips and splinters, on both sides of the deep quarry, massive blocks of stone were waiting to be transported to Mafra. Their departure was assured, but not today.

Some men had gathered in the middle of the road, while those behind them tried to look over their heads or force their way through, when Francisco Marques arrived and compensated for his lateness by eagerly inquiring, What's going on, it might have been the red-haired fellow who replied, It's the stone, and another added, I've never seen anything like it in my whole life, shaking his head in amazement. At this point the soldiers approached and broke up the gathering with force and shouted, Get back there, men are as inquisitive as street urchins, and the officer from the Inspectorate who was in charge of the expedition came in person to warn them, Break it up, clear the way, whereupon the men withdrew, tripping over one another, and then it appeared, The stone, just as the red-haired, one-eyed Brás had described it.

The slab was enormous and rectangular in shape, a massive block of unpolished marble set on two trunks of pine, drawing closer we would undoubtedly hear the sap groaning, just as we hear, at this very moment, the groan of fear escaping from the men's lips, as the colossal dimensions of the stone came into full view. The officer from the Inspectorate General comes up and places his hand on it, as if he were taking possession of the stone in His Majesty's name, but if all these men and oxen are unable to provide the necessary strength, all the King's power will be as wind, dust, and little else. However, they will do their best. This is why they have come, this is why they have abandoned their fields and labours, labours that also called for strength on lands that drained their energy, and the inspector may rest assured that no one here will let him down.

The men from the quarry come forward, they are about to finish cutting the small elevation to which the stone was towed, in order to form a vertical wall on the narrower side of the slab. This is where the man-of-war will rest, but first the men who have come from Mafra will open a broad track for the cart to go down, a ramp with a gentle incline sloping down on to the road, and only then can the journey get under way. Armed with picks and shovels, the men from Mafra advanced, the officer had already traced out a diagram of the excavation, and Manuel Milho, who was standing beside the fellow from Cheleiros, measured himself up against the stone, which was now within reach, and said, It's the mother of all stones, he did not say the father, but the mother of all stones, perhaps because it had come from the bowels of the earth still covered in primeval mud, a gigantic mother capable of supporting or crushing countless men, for the slab is thirty-five spans long, fifteen spans wide, and four spans deep, and to complete our report, once it has been carved and polished in Mafra, it will be only fractionally smaller, thirty-two by fourteen by three in the same order of dimensions, and one day, when measurements will no longer be taken in spans but in metres, others will describe the stone as being seven metres long, three metres wide, and sixty-four centimetres high, take note, and since the old system of weights has disappeared in much the same ways as the old system of measurements, instead of two thousand, one hundred and twelve arrobas, we shall give the weight of the stone forming the balcony of the house that will be known as Benedictione as thirty-one thousand and twenty-one kilos, or as thirty-one tons in round figures, ladies and gentlemen, and now let us pass to the next room, for we still have some way to go.

Meanwhile, the men spent the entire day digging. The drovers came to give a hand, and Baltasar Sete-Sóis returned to his hand-cart without dishonour, for no one should forget what it means to do hard labour, no man knows when he might have to go back to it, and if one day we were suddenly to lose the notion of leverage there would be no other solution except to use our arms and shoulders, until such time as Archimedes could be resuscitated and say, Give me a fulcrum so that you may move the world. When the sun set, the track had been opened to an expanse of one hundred paces right up to the paved road, which they had travelled at a much more leisurely pace that morning. The men ate their supper and went off to get some sleep, they scattered throughout the nearby fields, sheltering under trees or blocks of stone that were white as could be and glistened when the moon appeared. The night was warm. If bonfires could be seen burning, they were simply for gathering around, for the sake of company. The oxen chewed their cud, saliva trickling down and replenishing with its own juices that earth to which everything returns, even the stones that are being hoisted with such difficulty, the men who hoist them, the levers that prise them up, the wedges that support them, you have no idea just how much work there is involved in building this convent.

It was still dark when the bugle sounded. The men got to their feet and rolled up their cloaks, the drovers went off to yoke the oxen, the inspector came down to the quarry from the house where he had lodged for the night, accompanied by his aides and foremen so that the latter could be told what orders they were to give and for what purpose. The ropes and hawsers were unloaded from the carts and the yokes of oxen were lined up along the road in two rows. But the man-of-war still had to arrive. Consisting of a platform made from sturdy wooden planks resting on six massive wheels with rigid axles, it was marginally bigger than the slab itself. The platform had to be pushed manually amid the din and confusion as men struggled to move it and others shouted commands, one man, in a moment of distraction, lost his foot under one of the wheels, he let out a yell, the scream of someone in terrible pain, a bad start to the journey. Baltasar, standing nearby with his oxen, saw the blood spurt from the man's foot and suddenly imagined himself back in Jerez de los Caballeros, some fifteen years before, how time flies. With time, pain passes, but it will take some considerable time for a pain like this to pass, the man's agonised cries can still be heard as he is carried off on an improvised stretcher to Morelana where there is an infirmary, perhaps he will escape with a minor amputation to his leg, damn it. Baltasar also spent the night in Morelana, where he slept with Blimunda, and so the world unites, in one and the same place, the greatest joy and the greatest affliction, the consoling smell of wholesome humours and the foul stench of a gangrenous wound, in order to invent heaven and hell, a man would need to know nothing except the human body. There are no longer any signs of blood on the ground, the wheels of the cart have passed over the spot, the men have trampled the ground without forgetting the broad hooves of the oxen, and the earth has sucked in and absorbed the rest, only a pebble tossed to one side still bears the stains of the man's blood.

The platform was lowered very slowly, held on the slope by men who cautiously loosened the ropes in easy stages, until it finally made contact with the wall of earth that the masons had smoothed out. Now knowledge and skill would be put to the test. All the wheels of the cart were wedged with great boulders so that it would not move from the wall when the slab was heaved from the pine trunks and gently lowered and eased on to the platform. Its entire surface had been covered with mud to reduce the friction of the stone against the wood, and then the ropes were passed along and tied around the slab lengthwise, one on each side and clear of the trunks, while another was tied around the width of the slab, thus forming six ends, which were joined at the front of the cart and tied to a solid beam reinforced with iron plates, from these emerged two thicker hawsers, which acted as the main straps of the harness, to which thinner ropes were successively added for the oxen to pull. This operation took considerably longer to achieve than to explain, and the sun had already risen way above those mountains we can see over there, as the last knots were being tied, water was sprinkled on to the mud that had dried in the meantime, but the first priority was to spread out the yokes of oxen along the road and make certain that all the ropes were sufficiently taut, so that their drawing power would not be lost through any discordance, I pull, you pull, so much so that in the end there was not enough room for the two hundred yokes of oxen, and the traction had to be exerted to the right, the front, and above, It's a hellish job, said José Pequeno, who was the first man on the hawser to the left, if Baltasar expressed any opinion, it could not be heard, because he was too far away. Up there on the top, the master of works was about to raise his voice, his shout began in a drawl and ended hoarsely, like a blast of gunpowder, without echoes, Heave, if the oxen pull too much in one direction, we are in serious trouble, Heave, the order rang out clearly this time, and two hundred oxen jostled, first they pulled with one great tug, then with continued force, then stopped because some of the animals slipped while others turned inward or outward, everything depended upon the drovers' skill, the ropes chafed the animals' rumps until, amid shouts, insults, and incitements, the traction was just right for a few seconds and the slab moved forward one span, crushing the pine trunks underneath. The first pull was perfect, the second misfired, the third had to balance out the other two, now only these men were pulling, while the others took the strain, at last the slab began to move forward on the platform, still resting on the pine trunks, until it slipped and landed brusquely on the cart, a tombstone, its rough edge cutting into the wood, and there it lay motionless, to have covered or not covered the cart with mud would have come to the same thing if other solutions to the problem had not been devised. Men clambered on to the platform and with long, powerful levers began to lift the stone, which was still quite unstable, while others inserted wedges underneath with a metal base that slid easily over the mud, now it will be much easier, Heave, Heave, Heave, everybody pushed with enthusiasm, men and oxen alike, and what a pity Dom João V was not standing up there on the mountain, for no nation toils as willingly as this one. The hawsers on each side had already been removed and all the traction was now concentrated on the rope tied lengthwise around the slab, that is all it required, and the slab looks almost lightweight as it slides readily over the platform, only when it finally comes down can one hear the resounding thud of its weight, and the whole cart creaks, had it not been for the natural paving on that road, with stones upon stones, the wheels would have sunk right up to their hubs. The great blocks of marble that served as wedges were removed, since there was no further danger of the cart escaping. Now the carpenters came forward with their mallets, boring tools, and chisels, and at regular intervals cut rectangular holes in the thick platform on a level with the slab, into which they hammered quoins, which were then secured with thick nails, the job took considerable time. Meanwhile, the other workers rested in the shade of the trees nearby, the oxen chewed their cud and shook off the gadflies, and the heat was oppressive. The mess bugle summoned the men to dinner just as the carpenters were finishing the job, and the inspector gave instructions that the slab should be tied to the cart, an operation entrusted to the soldiers, perhaps because of the discipline and responsibility involved, perhaps because they were accustomed to handling artillery, within half an hour, the slab was securely tied with ropes and yet more ropes, as if it were part of the platform, so that wherever the one might go the other would have to follow. There were no further adjustments to be made, and the job was finished. Viewed sideways, the cart becomes an animal with a carapace, a squat turtle on short legs, and because it is covered with mud, it looks as if it has just come out of the soil, as if it formed part of the earth itself and were extending the elevation against which it is propped. The men and oxen are eating their dinner, and afterwards they will have their siesta, if life did not offer certain pleasures such as eating and resting, there would be little joy in building a convent.

The saying goes that no misfortune lasts forever, although judging by the weariness misfortune brings in its train, one is sometimes tempted to believe otherwise, what is certain is that good fortune does not last forever. A man is enjoying the most delightful slumber as he listens to the cicadas, and if the meal was not exactly lavish, a stomach accustomed to hunger is satisfied with very little, besides, the sunshine is also nourishing, when his peace is rudely interrupted by the blare of a trumpet, were we in the Valley of Jehoshaphat we should awaken the dead, but here there is no alternative other than for the living to rouse themselves. The various tools are checked and loaded onto the carts, for everything has to be accounted for in the inventory, the knots are checked, the cables are attached to the cart, and with another cry of Heave, the restless oxen start to pull unevenly, their hooves getting stuck on the irregular surface of the quarry, the ox-goads sting their necks, and the cart moves forward slowly, as if it were being drawn from the furnace of the earth, its wheels grind the marble splinters scattered on the ground, no stone as large as the one we are transporting today has ever been excavated from this quarry. The inspector and some of his qualified assistants have already mounted the mules, while others will make the journey on foot, in keeping with their rank as subalterns, although all of them can boast of some expertise and authority, the expertise because of their authority, the authority because of their expertise, but the same cannot be said of this encampment of men and oxen, who are simply under orders, the former as much as the latter, and any status they enjoy depends on the strength they can muster. Some additional skills, however, are expected of these men, for example, not to pull in the wrong direction, to put the wedge under the wheel in good time, to master the expressions that help encourage the animals, to know how to join strength to strength and multiply both, which, after all, is no mean feat. The cart has already progressed halfway up the track, some fifty paces at most, and it continues to sway awkwardly on the stones, for this is no royal coach or episcopal litter that is sprung as God intended. Here the axles are rigid, the wheels like weights, there are no brightly polished harnesses to admire on the backs of the oxen, or smart uniforms worn by the men as they go about their duties, this is a rabble, which one would never associate with a triumphal march or be likely to find taking part in the Corpus Christi procession. It is one thing to transport the stone for the balcony from where the Patriarch will give all of us his blessing in a few years' time, but it would be something else, and infinitely preferable, if we were both the blessing and the giver of that blessing, like sowing bread and eating it.

It is going to be a fine journey. From here to Mafra, even though the King has ordered the pavements to be repaired, the road is awkward, an endless climbing and descending, a constant skirting of valleys, scaling of heights, and plunging into depths, if there was any error in the counting of those four hundred oxen and six hundred men, it was to have underestimated their numbers, not that they are in any way superfluous. The inhabitants of Pêro Pinheiro went down to the road to admire the procession, they had never seen so many oxen assembled since the work first started, or heard such a commotion, some, however, felt a tinge of sadness as they watched the departure of that magnificent stone, which had been extracted from the earth here in Pêro Pinheiro, may it reach its destination in one piece, otherwise it would have been preferable to leave it undisturbed beneath the soil. The inspector was already heading the convoy like a general marching into battle with his captains, adjutants, and orderlies, they are about to reconnoitre the terrain, to measure the curve in the road, assess the slope, and choose a site for the encampment. Then they go back to meet the cart, to establish how far it has progressed, if it has left Pêro

Pinheiro or is still there. By the end of the first day, it had only advanced some five hundred paces. The road was narrow, the yokes of oxen kept jostling each other, with a rope on each side, little room for manoeuvre, and half of the force of traction was lost because they were pulling in disarray and orders could scarcely be heard. And there was the incredible weight of the stone. Whenever the cart had to pause, either because a wheel got stuck in a hole in the road, or because the oxen were straining as they tried to tackle some slope, it looked as if the stone would move no further. When it did finally advance, all the planking creaked as if it were about to free itself from the iron plates and clamps. But there would be even greater difficulties ahead.

That night the oxen were unyoked and left to rove freely, without being confined to a pen. When the moon finally appeared, many of the men were already asleep, their heads resting on their boots, if they were fortunate enough to possess boots. Some were drawn by that ghostly phosphorescence and saw the figure, clearly reflected in the moon, of the man who had gathered brambles on a Sunday and whom the Lord had punished by sentencing him to carry that bundle for all eternity, so that, condemned to lunar exile, his image became a visible symbol of divine justice and a warning to those guilty of irreverence. Baltasar went in search of José Pequeno, and they both came across Francisco Marques and several others who were gathered around a bonfire, for the night had become cool. They were later joined by Manuel Milho, who began to tell them a story. There was once a queen who lived with her royal consort in a palace along with their children, an infante and an infanta who stood this high, and the King is said to have enjoyed being king, but the Queen could not make up her mind whether or not she was satisfied with being queen, since she had never been prepared for any other role, therefore she found it difficult to decide whether she could honestly say, I prefer to be queen, even though her situation was no different from that of the King, who enjoyed being what he was, since he, too, had been prepared for nothing else, but the Queen felt differently, had she felt the same as the King, there would be no story to tell, now, it so happened that in their kingdom there was a hermit who had lived an adventurous life, and after many, many years spent in pursuit of adventures, he had withdrawn into a cave on the mountainside, if I haven't already mentioned that, but he was not one of those hermits devoted to prayers and penance, he was known as a hermit simply because he lived in isolation, he ate whatever food he managed to find, and though he never refused anything he was offered, he never begged for alms, now one day the Queen passed nearby with her retinue, and she confided in the oldest of her ladies-in-waiting that she wished to speak to the hermit and ask him a question, and the lady-in-waiting warned her, Your Majesty should know that this hermit is not a holy man, but a man just like any other, the only difference being that he lives alone in a cave, this is what the lady-in-waiting told her, as we already know, and the Queen replied, The question I wish to ask him has nothing to do with religion, and so they walked on, and when they reached the entrance to the cave, a page called inside and the hermit appeared, he was a man already advanced in years but strongly built, like some sacred tree at the crossroads, and as he appeared he asked, Who is calling me, and the page said, Her Majesty, your Queen, and that's enough for today, so let's try to get some sleep. The others protested, because they wanted to know the rest of the story about the Queen and the hermit, but Manuel Milho could not be persuaded, tomorrow was another day, so they had to resign themselves, each man went off to find himself a place to sleep, and each man's thoughts about the story reflected his own inclinations, José Pequeno mused that the King probably no longer made love to the Queen, and if the hermit was an old man, how could he, Baltasar imagined that the Queen was Blimunda and he himself the hermit, and why not, if this was a story about a man and a woman, despite some notable differences, Francisco Marques decided, I know how this story is going to end, and when I get to Cheleiros I'll explain everything. The moon is already travelling over there, not that a bundle of brambles weighs much, worst of all are the thorns, and Christ seems determined to avenge the crown of thorns that was placed on His head.

The following day was one of much anxiety. The road widened a little, allowing the yokes of oxen to manoeuvre more freely without serious collisions, but the cart took the bends with the utmost difficulty because of the rigidity of its axles and the enormous weight it was supporting, this meant it had to be dragged sideways, first in front, then from the back, the wheels resisted and got stuck on stones, which had to be broken up with a pick, but even so the men voiced no complaints as long as there was enough space to uncouple, and then couple once more, sufficient oxen to dislodge the cart in order to get it back on the road. Provided there were no curves, the slopes could be overcome with brute force, with one great heave as the oxen strained their necks forward till their snouts almost touched the buttocks of the oxen in front, occasionally to find themselves slipping in the excrement and urine that formed puddles along the furrows being gradually opened up by the treading of hooves and the pressure of the wheels. One man was in charge of each two yokes of oxen, and their heads and ox-goads could be seen from afar, rising amid the horns of the animals and above their tawny backs, only José Pequeno was hidden from view, and little wonder, for he was probably conversing with his oxen, which were as tall as he was, Heave, little oxen, heave.

But the anxiety soon turned to torment whenever there was a downward slope on the road. At any moment the cart could slip away and wedges had to be applied immediately, and nearly all the yokes of oxen had to be unleashed, three or four pairs were put on each side to move the stone, but then the men had to grab the ropes at the back of the platform, hundreds of men, like ants, their feet planted firmly on the ground, their bodies leaning backward, their muscles strained, as they sustained the weight of the cart, which threatened to drag them towards the valley and to propel them beyond the curve as if on the end of a whiplash. The oxen farther up and farther down the road chewed their cud placidly, watching the commotion, the men running back and forth giving orders, the inspector sitting astride the mule, the faces of the men flushed and bathed in perspiration, while the oxen stood there quietly awaiting their turn, so tranquil that not even the ox-goads resting against the yokes would stir. Someone suggested harnessing the oxen to the rear of the platform, but the idea had to be abandoned, because the ox does not comprehend the sum of exertion that results from two paces forward and three back. The ox either conquers the ramp and carries up what should go down, or is dragged without resistance and finishes up crushed to death where it should have been able to rest.

From dawn until dusk that day, they advanced fifteen hundred paces, less than half the league we use to measure nowadays, or, if we wish to draw an apt comparison, the equivalent of two hundred times the length of the slab. So many hours of effort for so little progress, so much sweat, so much fear, and that monster of a stone, slipping when it should be at a standstill, stationary when it ought to be moving, damn you, and damn whoever ordered that you be extracted from the earth and dragged through this wilderness. The men stretch out on the ground, drained of energy, they lie on their backs panting and looking up at the sky as it gradually darkens, initially as if day were about to break rather than draw to a close, then becoming transparent as the light begins to fade, until suddenly the translucence of crystal is obscured by shadows of dense velvet, it is night. The moon will be already waning when it makes its late appearance, and the entire encampment will be asleep, the light from the bonfires is fast disappearing and the earth is competing with the sky, for where there are stars above, here below there are fires, like those of yore where the men who hauled the stones to form the celestial dome probably gathered, perhaps they, too, had the same weary expressions, the same unshaven faces, the same thick-callused hands, the same nails black as mourning, to coin a phrase, and sweating just as profusely. Then Baltasar asked, Tell us, Manuel Milho, what did the Queen ask the hermit when he appeared at the entrance to the cave, and José Pequeno voiced his suspicions, She probably dismissed her ladies-in-waiting and pages, this José Pequeno is a malicious fellow, so let us leave him to the penance his father confessor will exact, should he ever confess his sins, which seems unlikely, and listen to what Manuel Milho has to say, When the hermit appeared at the entrance to the cave, the Queen advanced three paces and asked, If a woman is queen and a man is king, what must they do in order to feel like a woman and a man and not just like a queen and a king, this is what she asked him, and the hermit replied with another question, If a man is a hermit, what must he do to feel like a man and not simply like a hermit, and the Queen thought for a moment and said, The Queen will stop being queen, the King will cease to be king, and the hermit will abandon his cave, that is what they must do, but now I shall ask another question, What women and men can these be who are neither queen nor hermit but only women and men, and what does it mean to be man and woman if they are not hermit and queen, which is to be without being what one is, and the hermit replied, No one can be without being, men and women do not exist, all that exists is what they are and their rebellion against what they are, whereupon the Queen retorted, I rebel against what I am, now tell me if you rebel against what you are, and he replied, To be a hermit is the opposite of being, according to those who live in the world, but it is still to be something, and she rejoined, So what is the solution, and he told her, If you want to be a woman, stop being a queen, and the rest you will discover later, and she asked him, If you wish to be a man, why do you go on being a hermit, and he answered, Because what one fears most is to be a man, and she said, Do you know what it is to be a man and a woman, to which he replied, No one knows that, and with this reply the Queen withdrew, followed by her whispering retinue, tomorrow I will tell you the rest. Manuel Milho did well in interrupting his story, because two of his listeners, José Pequeno and Francisco Marques, were already snoring as they lay rolled up in their cloaks. The bonfires were almost extinguished. Baltasar stared at Manuel Milho for some time, This story of yours has neither a beginning nor an end and bears no comparison to the stories one is accustomed to hearing, such as the tale about the Princess who kept ducks, the little girl who had a star on her forehead, the wood-cutter who found a damsel in the forest, the story about the blue bull, or the devil from Alfusqueiro, or the animal with seven heads, where-upon Manuel Milho replied, If there were a giant in the world so big that he could reach to the sky, you would say that his feet were moun-tains and his head the morning star, for a man who claims to have flown and be equal to God, you are very sceptical. Thus rebuked, Baltasar had no more to say except good night, he turned his back on the fire and was soon fast asleep. Manuel Milho remained awake, thinking about the best way to finish the story he had started, whether the hermit should become king or the Queen become a hermitess, and one wonders why stories must always have such endings.

This had been such a long and trying day that they all agreed that tomorrow could not be worse, but they knew in their hearts that it would be a thousand times worse. They remembered the road that descended to the valley of Cheleiros, those narrow curves, those dreadful slopes, those steep cuttings that fell almost sheer to the road, How shall we ever get through, they murmured to themselves. It was the hottest day of the summer, the earth was like a furnace, the sun like a spur embedded in one's ribs. The water carriers ran the length of the convoy carrying pitchers of water on their shoulders, fetching the water from wells in the lower lying land, some nearby, others at a distance and they had to climb uphill by beaten paths to fill the casks, the galleys could not be worse than this. When it was almost time for supper, they reached an elevation from which they could see Cheleiros lying at the bottom of the valley. This is precisely what Francisco Marques had been hoping for, and whether they made it to the bottom or not, he was determined to spend the night with his wife. Accompanied by his aides, the inspector went down to the stream below, pointing out the most dangerous places as he went, points along the route where the cart would have to be propped up to give some respite to the men and animals and ensure greater safety in transporting the stone, and he finally decided that they should unharness the oxen and lead them to a clearing beyond the third curve, so that they would be far enough away not to impede the operation, yet sufficiently close to be brought back without delay should they be needed. The idea was to send the platform down the slope by its own force. There was no other way. While the animals were being led away, the men dispersed around the top of the mountain in the fierce glare of the sun and looked down at the tranquil valley, with its vegetable gardens, those refreshing shadows, houses that looked almost unreal, so powerful was the sense of calm. Difficult to say what the men were thinking, perhaps they simply mused, If we ever get down there, it will seem untrue.

Let others testify who may know more than we do. Six hundred men desperately clinging to the twelve cables that had been fixed to the back of the platform, six hundred men who felt that with time and continuous effort they were gradually losing the stiffness in their limbs, six hundred men who were six hundred creatures terrified of being there, and now more than ever, for, compared with this, yesterday was child's play and Manuel Milho's story a fantasy, for that is all man really is, when he is only the strength he possesses, when he is nothing other than the fear that he might not be able to summon the strength to detain this monster that implacably drags him on, and all because of a stone that never had to be so huge, with some three or ten smaller stones the balcony could have been built just as easily, even though we would no longer have been able to tell His Majesty with pride, It is made from a single stone, or to tell visitors before they pass into the next room, It is made from a single stone, and by means of these and other foolish vanities, absurdities become rife, with all their national and individual characteristics, such as the following statement one reads in manuals and history books, The Convent of Mafra was built by Dom João V in fulfilment of a vow he made should God grant him an heir, here go six hundred men who did not make the Queen pregnant yet they are the ones who pay for that vow and carry the can, if you will pardon that old-fashioned expression.

Were the road to descend straight, everything would be reduced to a game of alternation, one could even say an amusing game of release and restraint, as the ropes are slackened to give this stone kite its freedom and then tightened once more, as it is allowed to slide freely as long as the acceleration does not get out of control before being secured again so that it does not plunge into the valley, crushing as it goes those men who do not get out of the way quickly enough, the men themselves being like kites that are held by these and other cords. But there is the nightmare of the bends in the road. As long as the road was flat, the oxen were utilised, as we explained, by being positioned some on each side in front of the cart, where they could pull it into line with the curve itself, however short or extended. It was simply a matter of patience and had to be carried out so often that it soon became routine, unharnessing and harnessing, the oxen suffered most of all, for the men did not have to exert themselves apart from shouting. Now they were shouting in desperation when confronted with the diabolical combination of curve and slope that they would be obliged to manoeuvre time and time again, but to shout in this situation is to lose one's breath, and they do not have much breath to spare. Better to decide how the job should be tackled first and to leave the shouting for later, when it will bring some relief. The cart starts moving towards the opening of the curve, keeping as close to the inside as possible, and the front wheel on that same side is wedged, it is vital that the wedge should not be so firm as to secure the entire load on its own, nor so fragile that it is crushed by the weight of the cart, and anyone who imagines that this is easy should have carried that stone from Pêro Pinheiro to Mafra instead of simply watching the operation from a distance or viewing it in retrospect by reading this page. Wedged in this precarious fashion, the cart can sometimes come to a dead halt and capriciously refuse to move, as if its wheels were embedded in the ground. That is the most common setback. Only on those rare occasions when the circumstances are favourable and all the factors are taken into account, such as the incline of the curve towards the outside, the reduced friction on the ground, and the right gradient on the slope, will the platform yield without difficulty to lateral pressure applied from the rear, or, more miraculous still, turn independently on its own point of support up there in front. But the rule is that enormous pressure must be applied at focal points at the proper time, so that the momentum will not prove excessive and therefore fatal, or, thanks be to God for the lesser evil, insufficient, which calls for renewed pressure in the opposite direction. Crowbars are applied to the four wheels at the back, and an attempt is made to dislodge the cart, even though it may be only half a span towards the outer side of the curve, the men on the ropes lend a hand by pulling in the same direction, the scene is one of utter confusion, with those on the crowbars on the outside working amid a maze of hawsers, stretched and taut like metal wires, while the men on the ropes, who are working from various positions down the slope, find themselves slipping and rolling over from time to time, with no serious consequences for the present. The cart finally yields to pressure and is dislodged by several spans, but during this operation the outside wheel in front is successively blocked and released to prevent the platform from capsizing halfway through one of these manoeuvres at a point when the cart is poised to go forward and there are not enough men to secure it, for there is so much chaos that most of them have far too little space to work efficiently. Looking down on this activity, the devil marvels at his own innocence and compassion, for he could never have conceived such punishment to crown all those other punishments he metes out in hell.

One of the men working on the wedges is Francisco Marques. His expertise has already been put to the test, one bad curve, two very bad, three worse than the others, four only if we are mad, and for each of these curves some twenty manoeuvres are required, aware that he is doing a good job, perhaps he is no longer even thinking about his wife, everything in its own good time, besides, he must keep an attentive eye on that wheel, which is about to turn and has to be blocked, but not too quickly, in case he undoes the work carried out by his team-mates in the rear, and not too slowly, in case the cart starts to gather speed and break free from the wedge. And this is precisely what happened. Perhaps Francisco Marques was distracted or raised his arm to wipe the sweat from his forehead, or looked down on his native town of Cheleiros as he suddenly remembered his wife, but the wedge slipped from his hand at the same moment that the platform broke free, no one knew how but within seconds he was trapped under the cart and crushed to death, the first wheel passed over him, the stone alone, in case you have forgotten, weighs more than two thousand arrobas. They say that one calamity soon brings others in its wake, and that is nearly always true, as any man here can testify, but this time, whoever dispatches these calamities must have felt that it was enough that one man should lose his life. The cart, which could easily have gone tumbling down the slope, came to a standstill a little way ahead, its wheels caught in a pothole on the road, salvation does not always come where it should.

They pulled Francisco Marques out from under the cart. The wheel had gone over his stomach, which had been pounded into a paste of entrails and bones, his legs had almost been severed from the trunk of his body, we are referring to his left leg and his right leg, for that other leg of his, the one in the middle, the lustful one, which had taken Francisco Marques on so many journeys, was nowhere to be seen, it has disappeared without sign or trace. The men brought a stretcher, on which they laid his corpse wrapped in a blanket that was almost immediately soaked in blood, two men grabbed the shafts, and another two went along to share the burden, and all four would tell his widow,

We've brought your husband, they will announce his death to this woman, who is even now peeping out of her front door and gazing up at the mountain where her husband is working and saying to her children, Your father will be sleeping at home tonight.

When the stone arrived at the bottom of the valley, the yokes of oxen were harnessed once more. Perhaps whoever sends calamities was regretting his earlier restraint, for now the platform went over an outcrop of rock and trapped two animals against the sheer mountainside, breaking their legs. It was necessary to put them out of their misery with an axe, and when the news reached the inhabitants of Cheleiros, they came rushing to enjoy the spoils, the oxen were skinned and dismembered there and then, blood trickled down the road in rivulets, and the blows dealt by the soldiers trying to disperse the crowd were to no avail so long as there was flesh stuck to those bones, the cart was kept at a standstill. Meanwhile, night had fallen. The men set up camp, some still above the road, others scattered themselves along the banks of the stream. The inspector and some of his aides slept under shelter, but most of the men, as was their custom, huddled under their cloaks, worn out by this great descent to the centre of the earth, astonished to find themselves still alive, and all of them resisting sleep for fear that this might be death itself. Those who had been close friends of Francisco Marques went to pay their last respects, Baltasar, José Pequeno, Manuel Milho, and several of the others we spoke of, including Brás, Firmino, Isidro, Onofre, Sebastião, Tadeu, and another fellow, whom we have not mentioned so far, called Damião. They entered the house, looked at the corpse, and asked themselves how a man could die such a violent death and yet look so peaceful, more peaceful than if he were asleep, and released from all nightmares and worries, they murmured a prayer, that woman over there is a widow, whose name we do not know, nor would it add anything to our story if we were to ask her, just as nothing has been added by mentioning Damião and simply writing down his name. Tomorrow, before sunrise, the stone will recommence its journey, one man has been left behind in Cheleiros for burial, and the carcasses of two oxen for eating.

They are not missed. The cart travels as slowly up the slope as it came down, and if God had any feeling for mankind, He would have made the world as flat as the palm of one's hand, so that stones could be transported more rapidly. This operation is now entering its fifth day, and although the road is better now that the slope has been overcome, the men are ill at ease, every muscle in their bodies aches, but who is complaining, since this is why they have been given muscles. The herd of cattle does not argue or protest, it simply resists, by pretending to pull without pulling, the remedy is to leave them to rest a while and feed them a handful of straw, soon they will start behaving as if they had been resting since yesterday, their buttocks swaying as they move up the road, and it is a pleasure to watch them. Until they arrive at another descent or upward slope. Then the forces gather and distribute their efforts, so many here, so many there, Pull there, heave, a voice cries out, Taratata ta, blares a trumpet, this is a veritable battlefield with its dead and wounded.

In the afternoon, there was a welcome downpour of rain. It rained again during the night, but no one cursed. It is wisest not to pay too much attention to what heaven sends, whether it be sunshine or rain, unless it becomes unbearable, and even then the Great Flood did not suffice to drown the whole of mankind, and drought is never so great that a blade of grass does not survive, or at least the hope of finding one. It rained like this for an hour or so, then the clouds lifted, for even clouds get peevish if they are ignored. The bonfires became bigger, and some of the men stripped to dry their clothes, so that it began to look like a pagan festival, although we know that this was the most Catholic of enterprises, to carry that stone to Mafra, to struggle forth and bring the faith to all who deserved it, a matter we might well have discussed forever if Manuel Milho had not been there to tell his story, there is one listener missing, only I, and you, and you, notice his absence, the others do not even know who Francisco Marques was, some may have seen his corpse, most of them not even that, and who could believe that six hundred men filed past that corpse in a final moving tribute, these are scenes one associates only with epics, so let us get back to our story, One day the Queen vanished from the palace where she lived with her husband the King and their children the infantes, and since there had been rumours that the words exchanged in the cave had been no more like the conversation one might expect between a queen and a hermit than a dance step or a peacock's tail, the King went into a jealous fury and set off for the cave, quite convinced that his honour had been offended, for kings are like that, they are endowed with a sense of honour that is superior to that of other men, as one can see immediately from the crowns on their heads, and when he arrived there, he saw neither hermit nor Queen, but this made him all the more furious, because he saw it as an unmistakable sign that they had fled together, so he sent his army to pursue the fugitives the length and breadth of the realm, and while the search is under way, let us try to get some sleep, for it is late. José Pequeno protested, No one has ever heard such a tale narrated bit by bit, and Manuel Milho reminded him, Each day is a little bit of history, and no one can narrate everything, and Baltasar thought to himself, Padre Bartolomeu Lourenço would surely have approved of this Manuel Milho.

The next day was Sunday, and there was Mass and a sermon. In order to be heard to great advantage, the friar preached from the top of the cart, as dignified as if he were in the pulpit, and the saucy fellow was not aware that he was committing the greatest blasphemy of all by planting his sandals on that altar stone where innocent blood had been sacrificed, the blood of the man from Cheleiros who had a wife and children, and of the man who lost his foot in Pêro Pinheiro before the convoy had even set off, and that of the oxen, let us not forget the oxen, because the local inhabitants who slaughtered them will not readily forget and on this very same Sunday they are having a somewhat better meal. The friar preached and said, as is the wont of all preachers, Beloved children, from heaven above Our Lady and her divine Son look down upon us, from heaven above our father St Antony also watches over us, he for whose love we are carrying this stone to the town of Mafra, it is certainly heavy, but your sins are heavier still, yet you walk with them in your hearts as if you felt no burden, so you must accept this hard labour as penance and also as a devout offering, a singular form of penance and a strange offering, for not only are you being paid a daily wage but you are also being recompensed with an indulgence from heaven, in truth, I say to you, this stone of Mafra is as holy a mission as those ancient crusades that set out for the Holy Places, and know that all who perished there have been rewarded with eternal life, and united with them in the contemplation of the Lord is that companion of yours who was killed the day before yesterday, it was most fortunate that he should have died on a Friday, and no doubt he died unconfessed, for there was no time to summon a confessor, but he was saved because he was struck down in this crusade, just as those who died in the infirmaries of Mafra were saved, or those who fell from the ramparts, except those sinners who were beyond redemption and were carried off by shameful diseases, and such is the mercy of heaven that the gates of paradise are opened even to those who have died from stab wounds in those brawls you all indulge in, never has there been a nation so staunch in its faith yet so disorderly, but never mind, the work goes on, God grant us patience, give you strength, and the King enough money to complete the enterprise, for this convent is much needed in order to strengthen the Franciscan Order and propagate the faith, Amen. The sermon ended, the friar got down from the cart, and since it was Sunday, a holy day of rest, there was nothing more to do, some went to confession, others to communion, but not everyone, and just as well, for there were not enough consecrated hosts to go around, unless some miracle should multiply them, and no such miracle has been witnessed. As the evening drew to a close, a commotion arose between five crusaders on this holy crusade, but we shall spare you the details because it came to nothing more serious than an exchange of punches and one or two bloody noses. Had they lost their lives they would have gone straight to heaven.

That night Manuel Milho concluded his story. Sete-Sóis asked him if the King's soldiers succeeded in capturing the Queen and the hermit, and he replied, No, they did not capture them, they scoured the kingdom from end to end and carried out a house-to-house search without finding any trace of their whereabouts, and with these words he fell silent. José Pequeno asked him, So this is the story it has taken you almost a week to narrate, and Manuel Milho replied, The hermit ceased to be a hermit and the Queen stopped being a queen, but it was never discovered whether the hermit succeeded in becoming a man or the Queen succeeded in becoming a woman, in my opinion, had any such changes occurred, the effects would not have gone unobserved, and should anything like this ever come to pass, it will not happen without a clear sign, but there was no sign, and it all happened so many years ago that they must be long since dead, for all stories end in death. Baltasar tapped with his hook on a loose stone. José Pequeno rubbed his stubbly chin and asked, How does a drover become a man, whereupon Manuel Milho replied, I don't know. Sete-Sóis threw a pebble on the bonfire and said, Perhaps by flying.

They spent yet another night on the road. The journey from Pêro Pinheiro to Mafra took eight whole days. When they arrived on the site, they looked like the survivors from some disastrous battle, dirty, ragged, and bereft of spoils. Everyone was astounded at the dimensions of the stone, It's so huge. But looking up at the basilica, Baltasar murmured, It's so small.

SINCE THE FLYING machine landed on Monte Junto, Baltasar Sete-Sóis has gone there some six, or was it seven, times to examine and repair as best he can the ravages caused by time and the elements despite the machine's protective covering of foliage and brambles. When he discovered that the iron plates had become rusty, he took along a pot of tallow and greased them thoroughly, repeating the process each time he went back. He had also got into the habit of carrying on his back a bundle of reeds that he collected on marshland he encountered along his route, and these he used to repair such cracks and rents in the cane framework as had been made by natural causes, such as when he found a lair with six fox cubs inside the shell of the Passarola. He killed them as if they were rabbits by striking them on the crown of the head with his hook, then tossed their lifeless bodies here and there in the vicinity. The parent foxes would discover their dead cubs, smell the blood, and almost certainly return there no more. During the night the foxes could be heard yelping. They had scented out the trail. When they found their dead cubs, the poor creatures made a great din, and since they did not know how to count, and were uncertain whether all the cubs were dead, they approached the hostile machine that had been their downfall, a machine capable of flying, although now grounded and motionless, they drew near cautiously, worried by the scent of a human presence, and sniffed once more the spilled blood of their offspring, then retreated, snarling and bristling as they went. They were never to return to that spot. But the story might have ended differently if, instead of being a tale about foxes, it had been a tale about wolves. This also crossed Baltasar's mind, so, from that day on, he carried his sword with him, the tip of the blade somewhat eroded by rust but still perfectly capable of beheading a wolf and its mate.

He always went alone, and he was planning to go back on his own, when Blimunda said to him for the first time in three years, I'm going too, and this caused him some surprise, and he warned her, It's a long journey and will tire you out, but she had made up her mind, I want to know the route in case I should ever have to go without you. This made good sense, although Baltasar had not forgotten the danger of encountering wolves in that wilderness, Come what may, you mustn't go there alone, the roads are bad, the place is deserted, as you may remember, and you could be attacked by wild beasts, whereupon Blimunda replied, You should never say, Come what may, for something unexpected might happen if you use that expression, Very well, but you sound just like Manuel Milho, Who is Manuel Milho, He worked with me on the building site, but he decided to go back home, he said that he would rather die in a flood, should the Tagus burst its banks, than be crushed to death under a stone at Mafra for, contrary to what people say, all deaths are not the same, what is the same is to be dead, and so he went back to his native province, where the stones are small and few and the water is soft.

Baltasar was reluctant to see Blimunda make the long journey on foot, so he hired a donkey, and after making their farewells, they set off, they had not answered when Inês Antónia and their brotherin-law inquired, Where are you going, and warned them, This journey will cost you two days' wages, and if any crisis should occur we won't know where to find you, the crisis to which Inês Antónia referred was probably the death of João Francisco, for death was already prowling around the old man's door, it took one step forward as if about to enter, then relented, perhaps inhibited by João Francisco's silence, for how can anyone say to an old man, Come with me, if he neither speaks nor responds but only sits there staring, confronted with such a stare, even death loses its nerve. Inês Antónia does not know, Álvaro Diogo does not know, their son, who is at an age where he is interested only in himself, does not know that Baltasar has already confided in João Francisco, Father, I'm going with Blimunda to the Serra do Barregudo, to Monte Junto, to see how the machine is faring in which we flew from Lisbon that time when, you may remember, people claimed that the Holy Ghost had flown over the building site at Mafra, it wasn't the Holy Ghost, but us, together with Padre Bartolomeu Lourenço, you remember the priest who came here to the house when Mother was still alive, and she wanted to kill a cockerel, but he wouldn't hear of it, saying that it was preferable to hear a cockerel crowing than to eat it for supper, besides, it would be unkind to hens to deprive them of their cockerel. João Francisco listened to these reminiscences, and the old man, who rarely spoke, assured him, Yes, I remember it well, now go in peace, for I'm not ready to die yet, and when the moment comes I shall be with you wherever you may be, But Father, do you believe me when I tell you that I have flown, When we get old, things that are destined to come about start to happen, and at last we're capable of believing those things we once doubted, and even when we find it difficult to believe that such things can happen, we believe that they will happen, I have flown, Father. My son, I believe you.

Giddy-up, giddy-up, giddy-up, pretty little donkey, no one could say that of this little donkey, which, unlike the donkey in the refrain, has sores underneath its saddle, but it trots along merrily, the load is light and is carried with ease wherever the ethereal, slender Blimunda goes, sixteen years have passed since first we set eyes on her, but an admirable vigour stems from this maturity, for there is nothing like a secret for preserving youth. No sooner did they reach the marshland than Baltasar set about gathering reeds, while Blimunda collected waterlilies, which she fashioned into a garland and arranged over the donkey's ears, it made a charming picture, and never had such a fuss been made of a humble donkey, it was like a pastoral scene from Arcadia, although this shepherd was disabled and his shepherdess the custodian of wills, donkeys rarely appear in such a setting, but this one had been specially hired by the shepherd, who did not wish his shepherdess to get tired, and anyone who imagines that this is any common hiring is clearly unaware just how often donkeys get irritated when some heavy load is dumped on their back to aggravate their sores and cause the tufts of hair to chafe. Once the willow canes had been bundled and tied, the load became heavier, but any load that is carried willingly is never tiring, and matters improved when Blimunda decided to dismount from the donkey and proceed on foot, they were like a trio out for a stroll, one bearing flowers, the other two providing companionship.

Spring is here and the countryside is covered with white daisies and mallows, where they cover the path the travellers cut through them, and the firm heads of the flowers are crushed beneath the bare feet of Baltasar and Blimunda, who both have shoes or boots but prefer to carry them in their knapsacks until the road becomes stony, and a pungent odour rises from the ground, it is the sap of the daisies, the perfume of the world on the day of its inception, before God invented the rose. It is a perfect day for their trip to inspect the flying machine, great white clouds pass overhead, and they muse how pleasant it would be to fly just once more in the Passarola, to soar into the sky and circle those castles suspended in mid-air, to venture where birds do not venture, by jubilantly penetrating those clouds trembling with fear and cold, before emerging once more into the blue and heading towards the sun, to contemplate the earth in all its beauty and exclaim, Earth, how beautiful Blimunda looks. But this route is dull, Blimunda looks less beautiful, and even the donkey has shed the lilies, which have become parched and withered, let us sit down here to eat the world's stale bread, let us eat and then travel on without delay, for there is still a long way to go. Blimunda commits the itinerary to memory as they go along, carefully noting that mountain, that thicket, four boulders standing in a row, six hills forming a semicircle, and the villages, now then, what are they called, Ah yes, Codeçal and Gradil, Cadriceira and Furadouro, Merceana and Pena Firme, and on and on we go until we reach Monte Junto and the Passarola.

As in tales of yore, a secret word was uttered and before a magic grotto there suddenly arose a forest of oak trees that could be penetrated only by those who knew the other magic word, the one that would replace the forest with a river and set thereon a barge with oars. Here, too, words were uttered, If I must die on a bonfire, let it at least be this one, the demented Padre Bartolomeu Lourenço had once exclaimed, perhaps these bramble thickets are the forest of oak trees, this woodland in flower the oars and the river, and the distressed bird the barge, what word will be spoken that will give meaning to all of this. The donkey was relieved of its saddle and hobbled to prevent it from straying too far, and it began to eat whatever it could reach and fancied, if one may speak of choice within the simple confines of the possible, and meanwhile, Baltasar went off to clear a path through the brambles that would lead them to the machine, which was carefully hidden from sight, this is a task that, no matter how many times Baltasar does it, no sooner does he turn his back than the shoots sprout up again, a maze of entangled foliage that makes it almost impossible to clear a passage, to burrow through the brambles, but unless a path is cleared, there will be no hope of restoring the entwined canes, of protecting the wings that time has eroded, of raising the Passarola's drooping head, of supporting her tail, and of getting the rudders back into working order, it is true that we and the machine are grounded, but we are prepared. Baltasar worked for hours, hurting his hands on the thorns, and once he had cleared a path he called Blimunda, who found that she still had to crawl on all fours until she finally arrived, they were immersed in a green shadow that looked translucent, perhaps because of the fresh shoots that criss-crossed the blackened sail without entirely concealing it, because of the tender leaves that allowed the light to filter through, and above this cupola there was another one of silence, and above the silence, a vault of blue light, glimpsed in fragments, patches, and secret revelations. Climbing up the wing that was resting on the ground, they arrived on the deck of the machine. There, carved on a plank, were the sun and the moon, no other sign united them, and it was as if no other human being existed in this world. In certain places the floor had rotted, once again Baltasar would have to bring some planking from the building site, battens that were rejected when the scaffolding went up, for it would be futile to repair the metal plates and external casing if the timber itself was crumbling away. The amber balls glimmered dimly under the shadow cast by the sail, like eyes refusing to close or resisting sleep in order not to miss the hour of departure. But the entire scene has an air of desolation, withered leaves darkening in a puddle of water which continues to resist the first days of hot weather and were it not for Baltasar's perseverance, this would be a derelict ruin, the decomposed skeleton of a dead bird.

Only the globes, with their mysterious amalgam, continue to shine as on the first day, opaque but luminous, their ribbing clearly defined, their grooves precisely outlined, and who would believe they have been here for four long years. Blimunda touched one of the globes and discovered that it was neither hot nor cold, it was just as if she had clasped her hands to find them neither hot nor cold but simply alive, The wills inside here are still alive, they certainly haven't escaped, I can see the globes have suffered no damage and the metal is well preserved, poor wills, imprisoned all this time and waiting for what. Baltasar, who was working below deck, heard part of Blimunda's question or divined it, If the wills escape from the globes, the machine will be useless, and it will have been a waste of time returning here, but Blimunda reassured him, Tomorrow I'll be able to tell you.

They both toiled until sunset. Blimunda made a broom with some branches from the nearby hedges and swept up the leaves and the debris, then helped Baltasar replace the broken canes and smear the metal plates with grease. She sewed the sail, which had become torn in two places, like any dutiful wife, just as Baltasar, like any good soldier, had gone about his duties on numerous occasions and even now was engaged in finishing the task of covering the restored surface with tar. Dusk fell. Baltasar went off to unshackle the donkey, so that the poor creature would be more comfortable, he tied it to the machine, where it would warn them if any animal should approach. He had inspected the interior of the Passarola beforehand, by descending through a hatch in the deck, the hatch of this aerial barge or airship, a term that will easily be coined one day when it becomes necessary. There were no signs of life, not so much as a snake, not so much as a simple lizard that tends to dart wherever there is darkness and concealment, not even a spider's web, or there would be flies around. The cavity below deck was like the inside of an egg, the same inner shell and silence. They lay there on a bed of foliage and used the clothes they had taken off as a pallet and covering. Fumbling in total darkness, they reached out to each other, naked, he penetrated her with desire and she received him eagerly, and they exchanged eagerness and desire until their bodies were locked in embrace, their movements in harmony, her voice rising from the depth of her being, his totally submerged, the cry that is born, prolonged, truncated, that muffled sob, that unexpected tear, and the machine trembles and shudders, probably no longer even on the ground but, having rent the screen of brambles and undergrowth, is now hovering at dead of night amid the clouds, Blimunda, Baltasar, his body weighing on hers, and both weighing on the earth, for at last they are here, having gone and returned.

When the first light of day began to filter through the reeds, Blimunda, avoiding Baltasar's eyes, slipped quietly out of bed and, without attempting to dress, went up through the hatch. She shivered in the chilly morning air, she was probably chilled even more by the now almost forgotten vision of a world created from successive transparencies behind the bulwark of the machine, the net of brambles and creepers, the unreal presence of the donkey, by thickets and trees that appeared to float, and, beyond, the dense solidity of the nearby mountain, which made it impossible to perceive the creatures in the distant sea. Blimunda went up to one of the globes and peered in. A shadow moved inside like a whirlwind seen from afar. In the other globe was a similar shadow. Blimunda climbed down through the hatch once more. She plunged into the penumbra of that egg and searched among the clothes for her piece of bread, Baltasar had not awakened, his left arm was half-hidden by the foliage, so that no one would have suspected that his hand was missing. Blimunda went back to sleep. It was already day when she felt herself awakened by the instant contact of Baltasar's body. Before opening her eyes she said, You may come to me, for I have already eaten my bread. Whereupon Baltasar penetrated her without fear, for she had promised that she would never penetrate him. When they finally emerged fully dressed from the machine, Baltasar asked her, Have you been to see the wills, I've been, she replied, and they are still there, They are, Sometimes I feel that we should open the globes and set them free, If we set them free, it will be as if nothing had happened, as if we had never been born, neither you nor I, nor Padre Bartolomeu Lourenço, They still look like dark clouds, They are dark clouds.

Halfway through the morning, they finished the work. The fact that a man and a woman had taken care of its restoration was more significant than the fact that there were two of them, the machine looked as good as new and as spick and span as the day it made its maiden flight. Plucking and entwining branches of bramble, Baltasar closed off the entrance. After all, this is a fairy tale. Before the grotto there stands a forest of oak trees, unless what we are seeing is a river without barge or oars. Only from on high could one discern the singular black roof of the grotto, only a large bird passing overhead, but the only large bird that exists in this world lies here grounded, while ordinary birds, those made or ordained by God, pass and pass once more, look and look once more, and fail to understand. Even the donkey does not know why it has been led here. A beast on hire, it goes where it is taken and carries whatever is loaded on its back, one journey is much the same as any other for the poor donkey, but if only they could all be journeys like this one, the donkey has been free of baggage for most of the way and has worn a garland of lilies around his ears, so perhaps the springtime of donkeys will soon be here.

They went down into the sierra and cautiously decided to return by a different route, through Lapaduços and Vale Benfeito, which wended in continuous descent, and because they felt they would be less conspicuous if they kept close to inhabited areas, they skirted Torres Vedras, then headed south along the Ribeira de Pedrulhos, and if only there were no gloom or misery, if streams flowed over pebbles everywhere, and birds were singing, then life would be simply to sit on the grass, holding a daisy without stripping off the petals, either because one already knew the answers or because they were so unimportant that to discover them would not be worth a flower's life. There are other simple, rustic pleasures, such as when Baltasar and Blimunda bathe their feet in the stream, she hoisting up her skirts above her knees, and better that she should lower them, because for every nymph who bathes there is a faun spying nearby, and this one is dangerously close and about to pounce. Blimunda escapes from the stream laughing merrily, Baltasar grabs her by the waist and they both fall, one on top of the other, and they no longer appear to belong to this century. The donkey raises its head, pricking up its large ears, but it does not see what we are seeing, only a stirring of shadows, ash-coloured trees, for every creature's world is perceived through its own eyes. Baltasar lifts Blimunda into his arms and seats her on the saddle, Come on, little donkey, giddy-up, giddy-up. It is late afternoon, there is neither wind nor breeze nor whiff of air, you can feel the air on your skin as if it were another skin, there is no perceptible difference between Baltasar and the world, and between the world and Blimunda what difference could there be. It is already night by the time they reach Mafra. Bonfires are burning on the Alto da Vela. Where the flames fan out in all directions, you can see the irregular walls of the basilica, the empty niches, the scaffolding, the black apertures of the windows, more like a ruin than a new building, but that is always the impression when workers have left a building site.

Days of endless fatigue and sleepless nights. The men rest in these great sheds, more than twenty thousand of them accommodated on rough beds, yet for many of them the bunks are better than what they would have had at home, where they slept on a mat on the floor with only the clothes they wore and their cloak for protection, at least when it is cold here the men can keep one another warm as they huddle together, things get worse in the heat of the summer, when they are tormented by fleas and mosquitoes that suck their blood, their hair and bodies are covered with lice and they itch all over. They feel lustful and crave sex, some discharge semen in their sleep, and the fellow on the next bunk lies panting with desire, but if there are no women what can we do. Or, rather, there are some women, but not for everyone. The most fortunate are the men who have been on the site from the beginning, they have found themselves women who were either widowed or abandoned, but Mafra is a small town, and very soon there were no unattached women left and the main concern for the men was to defend their garden from would-be intruders and assailants, however few or non-existent its charms. This has led to a number of stabbing incidents. When someone is killed, the criminal magistrate arrives with his constables and, if it is considered necessary, the soldiers are asked to intervene, the culprit is sent to prison, so that one of two things ensues, if the criminal was the woman's husband he will soon have a successor, and if the dead man was the woman's husband he will have a successor in even less time.

And what about the other men. They roam the streets, covered with mud because of the constant rain, and visit certain alleyways where the houses are made of timber, perhaps because they were built by the provident Inspectorate General, which is fully aware of the men's needs, or for the benefit of some contractor of brothels, whoever built the house sold it, whoever bought it rented it, and whoever rented it also rented themselves, the donkey hired by Baltasar and Blimunda was much more fortunate, for they decked it out with waterlilies, but no one has offered any flowers to these women lingering in the doorways, all they receive is a rampant penis that enters and withdraws by stealth, often bringing syphilis with it, and the wretched fellows groan in their misery like the wretched women who infected them, as the pus trickles down their legs in an interminable flow, this is not an illness physicians admit to their infirmaries, the remedy, if such a thing exists, is to treat the infected parts with the juice of the miraculous plant already mentioned, which is good for everything and cures nothing. Strapping youths came here and now, after three or four years, they are disease-ridden from head to foot. Healthy women came here, then went to an early grave and had to be buried deep because their corpses decomposed quickly and poisoned the air. Next day the house has another tenant. The pallet is the same, the filthy bedclothes have not been washed, a man knocks at the door and enters, no questions are asked or answered, the price is known, he unbuttons his trousers, she hoists up her skirts, he moans with pleasure, and she is not required to put up any pretence, for we are among serious people.

The friars from the hospice keep their distance when they pass, for the sake of appearing virtuous, we feel no pity for them, for there has never been such a wily congregation when it comes to alternating and compensating sacrifices with consolations. They walk with lowered eyes, rattling their beads, those of the rosary they wear around their waist as well as those of their thingamajig, which they secretly give to their penitents to pray with, and if some shirt made of horsehair girds their loins, perhaps even equipped with prongs in certain extravagant cases, you can be sure that they are not worn for punishment, and read this carefully, so that you get my meaning. When the friars are not engaged in other charitable tasks and duties, they visit the sick in the hospital, cooling and holding out bowls of broth for the patients and assisting the dying, some days they die in twos and threes despite all those prayers to the saints who protect the sick, to St Cosmas and St Damian, the patron saints of doctors, to St Antony, who is capable of mending bones as well as mending jugs, to St Francis, who knows all about stigmata, to St Joseph, who can mend crutches, to St Sebastian, who can resist death, to St Francis Xavier, who is well versed in the medicines of the Far East, and to Jesus, Mary, and Joseph, the Holy Family, the rabble, however, are carefully segregated from patients of rank and military status, who have their own separate infirmary, and because of this discrimination the friars, who know perfectly well who will help them to secure their convent, administer treatment and the last rites accordingly. Let any man who has not committed similar transgressions cast the second stone, Christ Himself was guilty of favouring Peter and of spoiling John, although there were twelve apostles. One day it will be revealed that Judas betrayed Jesus because he felt jealous and unwanted.

It was about this time that João Francisco Sete-Sóis died. He waited until his son returned home from work, Álvaro Diogo was the first to arrive, eager to eat quickly and get back to the mason's workshop, he was just breaking bread into his soup when Baltasar entered, Good evening, your blessing, Father, it was an evening like any other, only the boy, who was always the last to arrive, was missing, perhaps he is already lurking in the street where the prostitutes ply their trade, but Álvaro Diogo asks himself where he would find the money to pay them, since he hands over his entire daily wage to his father without spending anything on himself, Gabriel has still not arrived, just imagine, after all these years we have known the boy, it is only now that he has grown up that we learn his name, and Inês Antónia tries to make excuses for his lateness, He'll be here any minute, it is an evening like any other, they make the same conversation, and no one notices the look of terror that has come into João Francisco's face as he sits by the hearth despite the heat, not even Blimunda, who became distracted when Baltasar entered, said good evening to his father, and asked for his blessing without waiting to see if the old man would grant it, when someone has been a son for many years, he tends to fall into these careless ways, he simply said, Your blessing, Father, and the old man responded by raising his hand with the slowness of someone who has barely the strength to do it, this was his final gesture, and before he could finish, his hand fell beside his other hand, resting on the folds of his cloak, and when Baltasar finally turned to his father to receive his blessing, he saw him leaning back against the wall with open hands, his head slumped on his chest, Are you ill, a futile question, and they would have been terrified if João Francisco had answered, I am dead, and that would have been the greatest of spoken truths. They wept natural tears, Álvaro Diogo did not return to work that day, and when Gabriel came in he felt obliged to express sorrow, even though he was still savouring the fruits of paradise, let us hope that hell has not scorched him between his legs.

João Francisco left an orchard and an old house. He had owned a plot of land on the Alto da Vela. He had spent years clearing away the stones, until he was finally able to dig into the soft earth. He laboured in vain, the stones are back now, and one might well ask why a man is born into this world.

THE BASILICA OF Saint Peter in Rome has rarely been taken out of the chests in recent years. Contrary to what the ignorant populace believes, kings are just like ordinary men, they grow up, become more mature, and their tastes change as they become older, when their inclinations are not deliberately concealed in order to curry public favour, they are sometimes feigned out of political expediency. Besides, the wisdom of nations and the experience of individuals have shown that repetition makes for boredom. The Basilica of Saint Peter holds no further secrets for Dom João V. He could assemble and dismantle the entire model with his eyes shut, alone or assisted, starting from north to south, with the colonnade or the apse, piece by piece or section by section but the final result would always be the same, a wooden construction, a child's set of blocks, a place of pretence where real Masses will never be said, even though God is omnipresent.

What matters, however, is that a man should prolong himself in his offspring, and if it is true that in his anguish at the thought of old age or its imminent approach, man does not always relish seeing certain of his own actions repeated that were once a cause for public scandal or discord, it is no less true that a man is delighted when he can persuade his children to repeat some of his own gestures, his own attitudes, even his own words, thus appearing to recover some justification for what he himself has been and accomplished. His children, needless to say, keep up the pretence. By means of other signs, which were, it is hoped, clearer, Dom João V, having lost any desire to assemble the Basilica of Saint Peter, still found a way of reviving his interest indirectly and demonstrating in a single gesture his paternal and royal affection, by summoning his children, Dom José and Dona Maria Bárbara, to help him. Both have already been mentioned, and both will be further discussed anon, for the moment all that need be said about Dona Maria Bárbara is that the poor girl was badly disfigured by small-pox, but princesses are so greatly favoured that they always find someone to marry them, even when they are disfigured and extremely ugly, if such a marriage should prove to be in the best interests of the crown and of His Majesty. It goes without saying that the Infantes do not waste much energy in building the model of the Basilica of Saint Peter in Rome. If Dom João V had his footmen to fetch and carry the pieces when he set up the dome of Michelangelo, which opportunely reminds us how the vast architecture prophetically reverberated the night the King went to the Queen's private apartments, then these delicate adolescents need even more assistance, the Infanta a mere seventeen years of age, the Infante barely fourteen. The important thing here is the spectacle itself, at least half of the entire court has gathered to watch the Infantes at play, their Majesties sit under a canopy, the friars exchange conventional pleasantries in whispers, the nobles wear expressions that simultaneously convey the respect due to princes, the tenderness one extends to youth, and devotion toward the holy shrine that is at present being constructed, all these emotions embodied in one and the same expression, so it is small wonder that they look as if they are suppressing some secret and perhaps even illicit sorrow. When Dona Maria Bárbara carries in her own hands one of the miniature statues that adorn the coping, the court breaks into applause. When Dom José places the cross on the crest of the dome with his own hands, all those present fall to their knees, for this Infante is the heir to the crown. Their Majesties smile, then Dom João V summons his children, praises their accomplishments, and gives them his bless-ing, which they receive on bended knees. There is such harmony here on earth, or so it would appear from the scene we have just described, that the universe clearly mirrors the perfection of heaven. Every gesture witnessed here is noble, even divine, in its studied solemnity, words are uttered like the fragments of a phrase that is neither inclined nor meant to reach any conclusion. This is surely how those who inhabit the celestial dwellings speak when they walk adamantine roads, when they are received in audience by the Father of all universes in His golden palace, when reunited at court they watch His Son and Heir at play as He assembles, dismantles, and reassembles a wooden cross.

Dom João V gave orders that the basilica not be dismantled or disturbed. The court dispersed, the Queen withdrew, and the Infantes departed, the friars in the background go on intoning their litanies while the King gravely examines every detail of the construction and the nobles in attendance try to emulate his expression, ever on their guard at such moments. The King and his retinue remained in this state of contemplation for at least half an hour. We shall make no attempt to probe the thoughts of the footmen, who knows what thoughts were passing through their heads, perhaps they were bothered by the twinges of cramp in one leg, or thinking about a pet dog, due to give birth tomorrow, the unloading at the custom-house of bales of cloth that have just arrived from Goa, a sudden urge to eat toffee, the memory of that soft little hand of the nun at the convent grille, the itchy feeling under their wig, anything and everything except the sublime inspiration that gripped His Majesty as he thought to himself, I want a basilica exactly like this one for my court, this was something we did not expect.

The following day, Dom João V summoned the architect from Mafra, a certain João Frederico Ludovice, a German name translated here into Portuguese, and the King bluntly informed him, It is my will that a church be built for my court like that of the Basilica of Saint Peter in Rome, and as he uttered these words, he looked at the architect with the utmost severity. A king must always be obeyed, and this Ludovice, who was known as Ludovisi in Italy, thus having twice renounced the name Ludwig, knows that if an artist is to pursue a successful career, he must be ever accommodating, especially if he depends on the patronage of altar and throne. However, there are limits, this King has no idea what such a demand involves, and he is a fool if he imagines that simply by willing it, one conjures up an artist like Bramante, Raphael, Sangallo, Peruzzi, Buonarroti, Fontana, Della Porta, or Maderno, if he believes that he needs only to come and command me, Ludwig, or Ludovisi, or Ludovice if intended for Portuguese ears, I want the Basilica of Saint Peter, and the basilica will appear in every detail, when the only churches I am capable of building are those on a scale suitable for places like Mafra, I may be an architect of renown, and as presumptuous as the next man, but I know my own limitations and the ways of Portugal, where I have lived for the last twenty-eight years amongst a race known for its pride and lack of perseverance, the essential thing here is to reply with tact, to phrase a refusal that will sound more flattering than any words of acceptance, which would be even more laborious, and may God defend me from such speeches, Your Majesty's command is worthy of the great King who ordered that Mafra should be built, however, life is short, Your Majesty, and the Basilica of Saint Peter in Rome, from the moment the foundation stone was blessed until its consecration, swallowed up one hundred and twenty years of labour and expense, Your Majesty, who, if I am not mistaken, has never been to Rome, may judge from the replica you have there before you that perhaps not even the next two hundred and forty years would suffice to build such a basilica, and by then Your Majesty will be dead, as well as your son, grandson, great-grandson, great-great-grandson, and great-great-great-grandson, therefore I must respectfully urge you to consider whether it is worth building a basilica that will not be completed until the year two thousand, assuming that by that time there will still be a world, nevertheless, it is for Your Majesty to decide, Whether there will still be a world, No, Your Majesty, whether a second Basilica of Saint Peter in Rome should be erected in Lisbon, although it strikes me that it would be much easier for the world to come to an end than to achieve a full-scale copy of the Basilica of Saint Peter, So you think I should forget this whim, Your Majesty will live eternally in the memory of your subjects, as well as in the glory of heaven, but the memory is a poor terrain when it comes to establishing foundations, the walls would soon start to crumble, and the heavens are one united church, where the Basilica of Saint Peter in Rome would make as much impact as a grain of sand, If that's the case, then why do we build churches and convents on earth, Because we've failed to recognise that the universe has always been both church and convent, a place of faith and obligation, a place of refuge and freedom, I don't quite grasp your meaning. Just as I don't quite understand what I am saying, but, to return to the question, if Your Majesty wishes to see the walls of the basilica raised even as much as one span before your death, you must issue the necessary orders without a moment's delay, otherwise the building will make no progress beyond the foundations, Is my life likely to be so short, Art is long, life is short.

They might well have remained there conversing for the rest of the day, but Dom João V, who as a rule tolerates no opposition once he has made up his mind, suddenly became melancholy as he visualised the funeral cortège of his descendants, of his son, grandson, great-grandson, great-great-grandson, great-great-great-grandson, each of them dying off without ever having seen the basilica completed, and it was clearly pointless even to start on the project if this was to be the outcome. João Frederico Ludovice tries to conceal his satisfaction, he has already understood that there will be no Basilica of Saint Peter in Lisbon, he has quite enough work in hand with the main chapel of the Cathedral at Évora and the buildings of São Vicente de Fora, which are on a scale suited to Portugal, because it is desirable that everything should be measured appropriately. There is a sudden lapse in the conversation, the King does not speak and the architect remains silent, and so ambitious dreams vanish into thin air, and we should never have known that Dom João V once dreamed of building a replica of the Basilica of St Peter in the Parque Eduardo VII had Ludovice not betrayed the King's secret to his son, who confided in a nun with whom he was intimate, who told her confessor, who told the Superior General of his order, who told the Patriarch, who asked if it was true of the King, who retorted that anyone who dared raise the subject again would incur his wrath, so everyone held his tongue, and the King's plan has now been revealed because the truth always comes out in the end, it is simply a question of time until the truth unexpectedly comes to the surface and announces, I've arrived, and we are forced to believe, the truth emerges naked from the depth of the well like the music of Domenico Scarlatti, who continues to reside in Lisbon.

Then suddenly the King taps his forehead, and his entire head glows, encircled by a halo of inspiration, And suppose we were to increase the number of friars at the convent of Mafra to two hundred, let's say, even five hundred, or one thousand, for I'm convinced this would make the same overwhelming impact as the basilica we're not going to have.

The architect reflected, One thousand friars, even five hundred friars, would constitute a vast community, Your Majesty, and we should need a church as huge as that of St Peter in Rome in order to accommodate them, How many would you say, then, Let's say three hundred, for even then the basilica I have designed and am about to build with the utmost care is going to be much too small for that number, if you will pardon my saying so, Let's settle for three hundred, then, without any further discussion, for I have made my decision, Whatever is decided will be done as soon as Your Majesty gives the necessary instructions.

They were given. But not before the King arranged a meeting with the Provincial Superior of the Franciscans from Arrábida, the treasurer of the royal household, and the architect once again. Ludovice brought along his designs, spread them out on the table, and explained the layout in detail, Here is the church, to the north and south are the galleries and towers belonging to the Royal Palace, and behind are the outbuildings of the convent, which must now be extended even farther back in order to comply with Your Majesty's instructions, here there is a mountain of solid rock, which will be the last major operation in terms of mining and blasting, and much work has already gone into excavating the base of the mountain and levelling the terrain. Upon learning that the King wanted to increase the number of friars in the convent from eighty to three hundred, you can imagine the reaction of the Provincial Superior, who had gone to the Palace without any forewarning of this latest development, he threw himself to the ground in histrionic fashion and kissed His Majesty's hands profusely, before declaring in a voice that quivered with emotion, Your Royal Highness may rest assured that God is this very instant preparing new and even more luxurious apartments in paradise to reward those who exalt and praise His name on earth with living stones, rest assured that for every brick that is laid in the convent of Mafra, a prayer will be offered up for Your Majesty's intentions, not for the salvation of your soul, which is abundantly assured because of your good works, but to embellish with flowers the crown you will wear when you appear before the Supreme Judge, may God grant that you will remain with us for many years to come, so that the happiness of your subjects will not be diminished and the gratitude of the Church and order I serve and represent may endure. Dom João V rose from his throne and kissed the Provincial Superior's hand, thus subordinating temporal power to that of heaven, and when he sat back down a halo of light once more encircled his head, unless this King exercises caution, he will find himself being sanctified. The royal treasurer wipes a tear from his eye as he watches this moving scene, Ludovice stands there with the index finger of his right hand pointing out on the plan the aforesaid mountain that will be so difficult to raze, and the Provincial lifts his eyes to the ceiling, which here symbolises heaven, while the King looks at all three in turn, mighty, pious, and most faithful, as papal authority has testified, this is what one sees reflected on that magnanimous countenance, for it is not every day that orders are given for a convent to be enlarged from eighty to three hundred friars, good and evil will out, as the popular saying goes, and what we have just witnessed is the greatest good.

Bowing and scraping, João Frederico Ludovice took his leave of the King and went off to modify his designs, the Provincial returned to his diocese to organise the appropriate manifestations of thanksgiving and to spread the glad tidings, only the King stayed behind, and is waiting even now in his Palace for the treasurer of the royal household to return with the accounts, and when he finally appears and places the enormous ledgers on the table, the King inquires, Tell me, what is the balance between our debit and credit. The treasurer strokes his chin with one hand, absorbed in some profound meditation, he opens one of the ledgers as if about to make a definitive statement, but amends the gesture and simply says, Your Majesty should know that as our funds dwindle our debts increase, Last month you gave me much the same report, And in the month before that and in the year before that, and at this rate, Your Majesty, we shall soon empty our coffers, We have a long way to go before we empty our coffers, with one in Brazil and one in India, and when they are exhausted, the news will take so long to reach us that we shall find ourselves saying, so, we were poor, after all, without even having realised it. If Your Majesty will permit me to speak frankly, I am of the opinion that we are facing bankruptcy and must be fully aware of our difficult situation. But, thanks be to God, there has never been any lack of money, That is true, but my experience as treasurer has taught me that the most persistent beggar is the one who has money to squander, just like Portugal, which is a bottomless coffer, the money goes in its mouth and comes out of its arse, if Your Majesty will pardon the expression. Ha ha ha, the King laughed, that's very funny, are you trying to tell me that shit is money, No, Your Majesty, that money is shit, and I'm in a position to know, squatting down here like everyone else who finds himself looking after someone else's money. This dialogue is fictitious, apocryphal, and libellous, and also deeply immoral, it respects neither throne nor altar, It makes a king and his treasurer speak as if they were drovers conversing in a tavern, and all we need are a few comely wenches to provoke the most awful outbursts of foul language, what you have just read, however, is simply an updated rendering of colloquial Portuguese, since what the King really said was, As from today, your stipend is doubled so that you will be under less pressure, whereupon the treasurer replied, I kiss Your Majesty's hand in gratitude.

Even before João Frederico Ludovice had time to finish his designs for the enlarged convent, a royal courier was dispatched in haste to Mafra with strict orders from His Royal Majesty that the mountain be razed without delay. The courier accompanied by his escort dismounted at the door of the Inspectorate General, he shook the dust from his clothes, mounted the stairs, and entered the reception hall, Are you Dr Leandro de Melo, for that was the inspector's name, That's me, the man told him, I have brought you these urgent dispatches on behalf of the King, I am delivering them safely into your hands, and in return I would ask Your Honour to give me a receipt and quittance, for I must return to court and report to His Majesty without delay. This was granted, and the courier and his escort took their leave while the inspector opened the dispatches, after having kissed the seal with reverence, but when he finished reading them, he turned so pale that his deputy was convinced that the inspector had received notice of dismissal, which might augur well for his own promotion, but he was soon to be disappointed, Dr Leandro de Melo rose to his feet and summoned his staff, Let us get down to business, within minutes he was joined by the treasurer, the master carpenter, the master builder, the master mason, the chief steward, the chief engineer in charge of mining operations, the captain of the troops, and everyone else from the site who held a position of any authority, and once they were gathered together, the Inspector General addressed them, Gentlemen, guided by piety and infinite wisdom, His Majesty has decided that the convent should be enlarged to accommodate three hundred friars and that the task of razing the mountain that lies to the east should begin immediately, for that is where the new part of the building is to be erected, in accordance with the specifications roughly outlined in these dispatches, and since His Majesty's orders must be obeyed, I suggest that we proceed to the site at once to see how the job should be carried out. The treasurer pointed out that in order to pay any subsequent costs it was not necessary to measure and weigh up the mountain, the master carpenter insisted that he was only concerned with timber, the plane, and the saw, the master builder suggested that when they were ready to build walls and lay floors they should send for him, the master mason pointed out that he only worked with stones that had already been hewn, the chief steward said that he would be ready to supply oxen and horses as soon as they were required, and if these replies smack of insubordination they are also full of common sense, for what was to be gained from having all these people inspect a mountain when they knew perfectly well just how much it would cost to raze it to the ground. The Inspector General accepted their excuses and finally left, accompanied by the engineers who would supervise the operation and the captain of the troops, who would carry out the blasting.

On a small plot of land situated behind the convent walls lying to the east, the friar in charge of the kitchen-garden attached to the hospice had planted fruit trees and laid out beds with a variety of produce and borders of flowers, the mere beginnings of a fully established orchard and kitchen-garden. All of this would be destroyed. The workers watched the Inspector General go past and the Spaniard in charge of the mines, then they looked at the mountain looming up before them like some apparition, for the news had spread at once that the convent was to be enlarged on that location, it is incredible how rapidly news is leaked about royal decrees that are supposed to be confidential, at least until such time as a formal statement is issued by the Inspectorate General. One might be tempted to believe that even before writing to

Dr Leandro de Melo, Dom João V had forewarned Sete-Sóis or José Pequeno, telling them, Be patient, for I have just decided to provide accommodation for three hundred friars instead of eighty, as agreed previously, good news for all those who work on the site, since their jobs will be guaranteed for an even longer period of time, for there is no lack of funds, according to the report submitted by my reliable treasurer several days ago, and bear in mind that we are the wealthiest nation in Europe, we are indebted to no one and pay everyone what we owe, and we have no financial worries, give my regards to the thirty thousand Portuguese who are trying to make a living and who are making strenuous efforts to give their King the supreme satisfaction of seeing built, for all posterity, the greatest and most beautiful sacred monument in history, which will make the Basilica of St Peter in Rome look like a tiny chapel, farewell, until we meet again, convey my best wishes to Blimunda, of Padre Bartolomeu Lourenço's flying machine I have heard nothing, and to think how I encouraged the venture and provided so much money to ensure its completion. The world is full of ungrateful people, that's for certain, farewell.

Dr Leandro de Melo feels somewhat overwhelmed as he stands at the foot of the mountain, the monstrous projection that will tower over the convent walls that are under construction, and since he is merely the magistrate of Torres Vedras, Dr Leandro de Melo relies on the expertise of the engineer in charge of the mining, who, being Andalusian and somewhat given to exaggeration, declares boastfully, Even if it were the Serra Morena, I would pull it down with my own bare hands and throw it into the sea, words that should be translated thus, Leave it to me and soon you will see a square laid out on this location that will make even Lisbon sit up with envy. For some eleven years now the slopes of Mafra have shuddered to the reverberations of continuous blasting, although these have been less frequent of late, and occurred only when the obstinate projection of some spur or other has impeded progress. A man can never tell when the battle will finally be over. He says to himself, It's all over, and suddenly it's not all over and fresh hostilities break out, for if yesterday it was the brandishing of swords, today it is the thundering of cannon balls, if yesterday it was the demolition of ramparts, today it is the destruction of cities, if yesterday it was the extermination of countries, today worlds are shattered, yesterday it was thought to be a tragedy if a man lost his life, while today no one gives a damn if a million men go up in smoke, this is not exactly the situation in Mafra, where we shall never see quite so many people gathered together, numerous as they are, but for anyone who had become accustomed to hearing some fifty or a hundred blasts every day, it now sounded like the end of the world, with this thundering explosion of a thousand discharges lasting from dawn until dusk, occurring in sequences of twenty, and with such violence that the air was rent with soil and stones, so that the workers on the site had to take shelter behind walls or underneath the scaffolding, and, even so, some of the men were seriously injured, not to mention the five charges that exploded unexpectedly and blew three men to pieces.

Sete-Sóis has still not replied to the King, and he continues to postpone doing so, he feels much too shy to ask anyone to write a letter on his behalf, but should he succeed one day in overcoming his embarrassment, this is the reply he will dictate, Dear King, I've received your letter and taken careful note of everything you have told me, there has been no shortage of work here, we only stop working when it rains so heavily that even the ducks complain, or when the stone was delayed along the way, or when the bricks turned out to be of poor quality and we had to wait for replacements to arrive, now there is a great stir here with the news that the convent is to be enlarged, for, dear King, you cannot imagine how big the mountain is that we have to raze, or the number of men it will take to do the job, they have had to abandon work on the church and the palace, and nothing will be finished on time, even the masons and carpenters are helping to load the stone, and I myself transport it, sometimes with the oxen, sometimes with a hand-cart, I felt very sorry for the lemon and peach trees that were uprooted, and for those pretty little pansies that were destroyed, there wasn't really any point in planting flowers only to see them treated with such cruelty, but, then, as you yourself have said, dear King, we don't owe anyone anything, and that's always reassuring, for, as my old mother used to say, Pay your debts no matter who you owe them to, poor woman, she's now dead, and will never see the greatest and most beautiful sacred monument in history, as you said in your letter, although, to be frank, in the legends I'm familiar with, no one ever speaks about sacred monuments, only about bewitched Moorish women, and hidden treasure, Blimunda is well, thank you, she's not so pretty as she was when I first met her, but there's many a young girl not half as pretty as she is, José Pequeno has asked me to inquire when the marriage of the Infante Dom José will be, for he wants to send him a present, probably because they have the same name, and thirty thousand Portuguese send you their greetings and thanks, their health is so-so, the other day there were so many men with the runs that Mafra stank to high heaven for three leagues on all sides, we must have eaten something that didn't agree with us, weevils rather than flour, botflies rather than meat, but it was funny to watch all those chaps with their bottoms up in the air to catch the fresh breeze coming in from the sea, and no sooner had one bunch relieved themselves than another took their place, and sometimes they were so desperate that they squatted down on the spot, ah, it's true, I almost forgot to mention that I've heard nothing more about the flying machine, it's just possible that Padre Bartolomeu Lourenço took the machine with him to Spain and perhaps the King over there now has it, for rumour has it that he'll soon be a relation of yours, be careful, I'll say no more and leave you in peace, give my regards to the Queen, farewell, dear King, farewell.

This letter was never written, but the paths of communication between souls are as manifold as they are mysterious, and of the many words that Sete-Sóis never got around to dictating, some affected the King deeply, such as that fatal judgment that, as a warning to Baltasar, appeared engraved in fire on the wall, weighed, counted, and divided, this Baltasar is not the Mateus we know, but that other Baltasar or Belshazzar the King of Babylon who, having desecrated the sacred vessels during a feast at the Temple in Jerusalem, was punished and put to death at the hands of Cyrus, who was destined to execute this divine sentence. The transgressions of Dom João V are of another order, any sacred vessels he desecrates are likely to be the brides of the Lord, but they enjoy the experience and the Lord turns a blind eye, so let us proceed. What struck a deep chord like the stroke of a bell for Dom João V was that phrase when Baltasar, speaking of his mother, expresses his regret that she will never see that greatest and most beautiful of sacred monuments. The King suddenly realises that his own life will be of short duration, that many people have died and will continue to die before the convent of Mafra is finally built, and that he himself might close his eyes tomorrow forevermore. You will recall that he abandoned the idea of building St Peter of Rome precisely because Ludovice convinced him that life is short, and that the same St Peter, as has been recorded, from the time the foundation stone was blessed until the Basilica's consecration, swallowed up one hundred and twenty years of labour and expense. So far, Mafra has already taken eleven years of labour and who knows how much expense, Who can guarantee that I shall still be alive when the consecration finally takes place, when not so many years ago I was not expected to survive, stricken as I was by a melancholia that threatened to carry me off before my time, the simple truth is that Sete-Sóis's mother, poor woman, saw the beginning but will not see the end, and a king is not exempt from a similiar fate.

Dom João V is in a room in the tower that overlooks the river. He orders the footmen, secretaries, friars, and a singer from the Teatro da Comédia to withdraw, for he wishes to be alone. Written on his face is fear of death, the greatest humiliation of all for so mighty a monarch. But this horror of dying is not such as to reduce him in body and spirit, but enough to ensure that his eyes will no longer be open and shining when the consecrated towers and dome of Mafra are finally erected, that his hearing will no longer be sensitive to the sonorous chimes that will triumphantly ring out, his hands no longer be able to touch the sumptuous vestments and hangings of the religious solemnities, his nostrils no longer able to inhale the incense spiralling from those silver thuribles, that he will simply be the monarch who gave the orders that the sanctuary be built, not the monarch who saw it completed. Yonder sails a ship, and who can tell if it will arrive safely in port, A cloud passes overhead, and perhaps it will be obliterated by a rainstorm, Beneath those waters, a shoal of fishes swims toward the fisherman's net, Vanity of vanities, Solomon once declared, and Dom João V repeats these words, All is vanity, to desire is vanity, to possess is vanity.

To overcome vanity, however, does not mean to have achieved modesty, much less humility, it is, rather, an excess of vanity. Upon rousing himself from this anguished meditation, the King did not don the sackcloth of penance and renunciation but summoned back the footmen, secretaries, and friars, the singer from the Teatro da Comédia would arrive later, and asked them if it was really true, as he had always been led to believe, that basilicas should be consecrated on a Sunday, and they assured him that it was so according to the Holy Liturgy, so the King asked them to check in which year his birthday, the twenty-second of October, would fall on a Sunday, and after consulting the calendar, the secretaries verified that such a coincidence would occur twenty years hence, in the year seventeen hundred and thirty, Then on that day the basilica of Mafra will be consecrated, that is what I wish, ordain, and decree, and when they heard these words, the footmen kissed the hand of their sovereign, you will tell me which is the more excellent thing, to be king of the world or of these people.

João Frederico Ludovice and Dr Leandro de Melo dampened the King's ardour when they were urgently recalled from Mafra, where the former had been sent and the latter offered his assistance, with the place they had come from fresh in their memory, they warned the King that the slow progress of the work at Mafra did not justify any such optimism, the walls of the enlarged section of the convent were going up very slowly, and the church, because of its delicate stone structure and intricate design, could not be built in haste, as Your Majesty knows better than anyone else, from your long experience of reconciling and balancing the different forces that constitute a nation. Dom João V glowered, because this importunate flattery did nothing to console him, he suppressed the temptation to reply with some chilling words of rebuke and instead recalled his secretaries, whom he ordered to verify when his birthday would next fall on a Sunday after the year seventeen thirty, which was obviously too soon. They struggled with their arithmetic and replied with some uncertainty that the coincidence would recur ten years later, in the year seventeen forty.

There were some eight to ten people present, including the King, Ludovice, Leandro, the secretaries, and the nobles in attendance that week, and they all nodded their heads gravely as if Halley himself had just expounded the frequency of the comets, the things that men are capable of discovering. Dom João V, however, was suddenly assailed by a sombre thought, it was reflected in the expression on his face as he rapidly made a mental note with the help of his fingers, In the year seventeen forty I shall be fifty-one years of age, and added mournfully, If I'm still alive. For a few dreadful moments, this King once more ascended the Mount of Olives and there he agonised over his fear of death, terrified at the thought of all that would be taken from him, and envious of the son who would succeed him, along with his young Queen, who would shortly arrive from Spain, together they would share the joy of seeing Mafra inaugurated and consecrated, while he rotted in the Tomb at São Vicente de Fora, alongside the tiny Infante Dom Pedro, who had died in infancy from the shock of being weaned. Those who were present watched the King, Ludovice with scientific curiosity, Leandro de Melo indignant at the intransigent laws of time, which do not even respect the sovereignty of kings, the secretaries wondering whether they had calculated the leap year correctly, the footmen pondering their own chances of survival. Everyone waited. Then João V announced, The consecration of the basilica of Mafra will take place on the twenty-second of October in the year seventeen thirty, whether the building is finished or otherwise, whether there be rain or shine, snow or wind, flood or bedlam.

If you eliminate the emphatic expressions, you will observe that these words have been used before, this would appear to be nothing other than one of those declarations intended for posterity, like that well-known phrase, Father, into Your hands I commend my spirit, so take it, which just goes to prove that God is not one-handed after all, and Padre Bartolomeu Lourenço committed a minor sacrilege when he led Baltasar Sete-Sóis astray, when all he had to do was go and ask God the Son, who ought to know how many hands God the Father possesses, but in addition to what João V has already said, we should add what we ourselves have discovered about the number of hands his subjects have and to what uses they might be put, for the King went on to say, I hereby command that all the magistrates of the realm should be told to round up and dispatch to Mafra as many skilled workers as they can find in their regions, whether they be carpenters, bricklayers, or manual labourers, even if they should have to be removed by force from their place of work, and they should not be exempt on any pretext whatsoever, no exceptions are to be made for domestic reasons or because of any other commitments or obligations, for nothing surpasses the royal will, and the latter will be appealed to in vain, because it is precisely to serve the divine will that these provisions have been made, I have spoken. Ludovice nodded gravely, as if he had just verified the constancy of a chemical reaction, the secretaries made rapid notes, the footmen exchanged glances and smiled, this was truly a king, Dr Leandro de Melo was safe from this latest decree, because in his region there were no skilled labourers left who were not already engaged, directly or indirectly, in building the convent.

The King's orders were proclaimed and the men arrived. Some went willingly, enticed by the promise of good earnings, or because they craved adventure or experienced some sense of mission, but nearly all of them under duress. The decree was posted in the public squares, and since there were few volunteers, the local magistrate went from street to street, accompanied by his henchmen, forced entry into homes and private property, and scoured the surrounding countryside in search of recalcitrants, by the end of the day, he had rounded up some ten, twenty, thirty men, and when they outnumbered their jailers, they bound them with ropes, adopting various methods, sometimes the men were tied to one another at the waist, sometimes with an impro- vised halter, and sometimes fettered at the ankles like galley slaves or serfs. Much the same scene was to be witnessed everywhere. By order of His Majesty, you will help to build the convent of Mafra and if the magistrate was particularly zealous, it mattered not whether the prisoner was a man in his prime, on his last legs, or a mere stripling. The men would start off by refusing to go or threatening to escape, then they would make excuses, one had a wife about to give birth any day now, another had to look after his old mother, or there was a brood of children to be provided for, a wall to be finished, a chest to be mended, land to be worked, but if they started to make excuses, they were not allowed to finish, the henchmen would set upon them if they showed any signs of resistance, and many of the men set out on the journey covered with blood.

The women ran behind them weeping, and the screams of the children added to the uproar, one would have thought that the magistrates were recruiting the men by force for the army or for an expedition to India. Rounded up in the main square of Celorico da Beira, Tomar, Leiria, Vila Pouca, Vila Muita, or in some town known only to those who live there, on distant frontiers or along the coast, around the pillories, in the church squares, at Santarém and Beja, at Faro and Portimão, Portalegre and Setúbal, Évora and Montemor, in the mountains and plains, at Viseu and Guarda, Bragança and Vila Real, Miranda, Chaves, and Amarante, Vianas and Póvoas, and in all those places where His Majesty's jurisdiction extends, the men were tied like sheep, the ropes loosened just enough to prevent them from tripping over one another, while their wives and children looked on and pleaded with the magistrate, or tried to bribe the henchmen with some eggs or a chicken, pathetic expedients that proved to be useless, for the King of Portugal prefers to collect any tribute due to him in gold, emeralds, diamonds, pepper, cinnamon, ivory, tobacco, sugar, and precious wood, tears achieve nothing in the custom-house. When there was time, some of the henchmen took the opportunity to rape the wives of their prisoners, the wretched women submitted in the hope of saving their husbands, only to see them dragged off while they looked on in despair and their seducers mocked their gullibility, May you be damned unto five generations, may you be stricken from head to foot with leprosy, may your mother, wife, and daughter be forced into prostitution, may you be impaled from arse to mouth, thrice-cursed villain. The band of men rounded up are already on their way to Arganil, and the disconsolate women accompany them until they are outside the town, weeping as they go, heads uncovered, Oh, sweet and beloved husband, while another wails, Ah, my beloved boy, who gave me comfort and protection in my weary old age, the lamentations went on and on until the nearby mountains echoed those cries, moved by pity for these poor creatures, the men are already at some distance and finally disappear from sight where the road curves, their eyes filled with tears, large teardrops in the case of the more sensitive among them, and then a voice rends the air, it is that of a farmer so advanced in years that the magistrate's men were reluctant to take him, and mounting an embankment, a natural pulpit for countryfolk, he calls out, Ah, empty ambition, senseless cupidity, infamous King, nation without justice, but no sooner has he uttered these words than one of the henchmen deals him a blow on the head and leaves him for dead on the ground.

The might of kings. There he is, seated on his throne, he relieves himself as and when necessary by defecating, or ejaculating inside the womb of some woman or other, and here, there, or yonder, if so required by the interests of the state, namely himself, he issues orders that men should be brought from Penamacor, able-bodied or otherwise, to build this convent of mine at Mafra, built because petitioned by the Franciscan friars since the year sixteen twenty-four, and because the queen was delivered of a daughter who will not even become the Queen of Portugal but of Spain, because of dynastic and private intrigues. Meanwhile, the men who have never even set eyes on the King arrive against their will, guarded by soldiers and henchmen, unfettered if they are of a peaceful disposition or have already resigned themselves to their fate, or tied with ropes, as we explained, if rebellious, and permanently shackled if they perversely gave the impression of going along willingly and then tried to escape, and all the worse for him who succeeds in escaping. They make their way cross-country from one region to another, along the few royal routes in existence, sometimes along the roads built by the Romans, and most frequently of all along narrow footpaths, and the weather is unpredictable, scorching sunshine, torrential rain, and freezing cold, while in Lisbon the King expects every man to do his duty.

From time to time they meet up with fellow victims. Some more men were drafted from the northern and eastern regions of Portugal joining up with those from Penela and Proença-a-Nova in Porto de Mós, none of them knowing where these places are located on the map, or about the form of Portugal itself, whether it is square or round or pointed, if it is a bridge for crossing or a rope used for hanging, if it cries out when they beat it or hides in some corner. Both contingents are merged into one, and since the art of detention is not without its refinements, the men are paired up in some mystical way, one from Proença with another from Penela, as a precaution against subversive plotting and with the additional advantage of providing an opportunity for the Portuguese to get to know Portugal, Tell me something about your region, they inquire of one another, and while they are engaged in such exchanges they have no time to think about anything else. Unless one of them should die during the journey. A man might collapse foaming at the mouth after a sudden attack, or perhaps simply topple over, dragging with him to the ground the man in front and the one behind, who panic when they find themselves shackled to a dead man, a man might become ill without any warning in some remote place and be carried on a litter, his arms and legs dangling over the sides, only to die farther ahead and be hastily buried at the roadside, with a wooden cross stuck into the ground near his head, or if he is more fortunate, he might receive the last rites in some village while the men sit around waiting for the priest to finish, *Hoc est enim corpus meum,* this body worn out by fatigue after marching all those leagues, this body tormented by the chafing of ropes, this body deprived of even the most frugal diet. Their nights are spent on haystacks, in convent doorways, in empty granaries, and, when God and the elements permit, out in the open air, thus combining the freedom of nature with human bondage, and there would be much food for thought here if we had time to pause. In the early hours, long before sunrise, and perhaps it is just as well, for these are the coldest hours of all, His Majesty's labourers get to their feet, frostbitten and weak from hunger, fortunately, the henchmen have untied them, since they expect to reach Mafra today and it would give the worst possible impression if the inhabitants were to see a procession of tramps fettered like slaves from Brazil or a drove of pack horses. When the men glimpse the white walls of the basilica in the distance, they do not cry out, Jerusalem, Jerusalem, therefore that friar was lying who preached, when the stone was being transported from Pêro Pinheiro to Mafra, that all these men were the crusaders of a new crusade, for what crusaders are these, who scarcely know why they are crusading, the henchmen call a halt so that the men may survey from this elevation the sweeping panorama encircling the site where they are about to settle, to the right lies the sea, which is navigated by our ships, sovereign and invincible as they ply those waters, and straight ahead, to the south, lies the justly renowned Serra de Sintra, the pride of the nation and the envy of foreigners, for Sintra would make an admirable paradise if God were to decide to have another go, and that town down there in the valley is Mafra, which scholars tell us is aptly named, but one day the meanings will be modified to read letter by letter, dead, burned, drowned, robbed, dragged off, and it is not I, simple henchman carrying out my orders, who will be so bold as to give such a reading, but a Benedictine abbot in his own time, when he gives his reasons for not attending the consecration of this monstrous edifice, however, let us not anticipate events, for there is still a great deal of work to be done, which explains why you have been brought all this way from your native regions, pay no attention to the lack of concordance, for no one has taught us how to speak properly, we learn from the mistakes of our parents, and, besides, we are a nation in a period of transition, and now that you have seen what awaits you, move on, once we have delivered you, we must go in search of more men.

To arrive at the site from this direction, the men are obliged to go through the town and pass under the shadows of the Viscounts' Palace and alongside the threshold of the house where Sete-Sóis lives, and they know as little about the one as about the other, despite the existing genealogies and annals, Tomas da Silva Teles, Visconde de Vila Nova da Cerveira, and Baltasar Mateus, builder of airships, in the fulness of time we shall see who will win this war. The palace windows are not opened to witness this procession of miserable wretches, the stench they give off, your Ladyship, is quite bad enough. But the front door of the house of Sete-Sóis was opened, and Blimunda peeped out, the scene is familiar, so many detachments have passed this way, but whenever she is at home, Blimunda always watches them go by, it is one way of welcoming whosoever may arrive and when Baltasar returns that evening she tells him, More than a hundred men passed by today, forgive this vagueness on the part of someone who has never learnt how to count properly, however great or small the number involved, just as when she refers to her age by saying, I have passed the age of thirty, and Baltasar retorts, They tell me that five hundred men have arrived in town, So many, Blimunda exclaims in astonishment, and neither he nor she knows exactly how many five hundred make, not to mention that there is nothing in the world so imprecise as numbers, one says five hundred bricks just as one says five hundred men, and the difference between a brick and a man is the difference that one believes to exist between five hundred and five hundred, and anyone who fails to grasp my meaning the first time around does not deserve to have it explained a second time.

The men who entered Mafra today are herded together and settle down to sleep wherever possible, tomorrow they will be sorted out. Just like bricks. If a load of bricks is judged to be no good, it is dumped on the spot, and the bricks will end up being used for jobs of lesser importance, someone will make use of those bricks, but when they are men, they are dismissed without further ado, You're no good to us, go back to where you came from, and off they go along unfamiliar routes, they get lost on the way, become vagrants, die on the road, sometimes they steal or murder, sometimes they actually reach their homes.

YET CONTENTED FAMILIES are still to be found. The Royal Family of Spain is one of them. That of Portugal is another. The offspring of the one marry the offspring of the other, from the Spanish dynasty comes Mariana Vitória, from that of Portugal, Maria Bárbara, their bridegrooms José from Portugal and Fernando from Spain respectively, as one would say. These unions are the fruit of careful planning, and negotiations have been under way since the year seventeen hundred and twenty-five. Innumerable discussions have taken place, there has been much shuttling of ambassadors, much haggling, much coming and going of plenipotentiaries, many arguments about the various clauses in the wedding contracts, about their respective prerogatives and the dowries of the Princesses, for these royal marriages cannot be entered into lightly or quickly settled at the butcher's shop, as the lower orders quip when referring to some illicit affair, only now after almost five years of protracted negotiations has an agreement been reached about a formal exchange of Princesses, one for you and one for me.

Maria Bárbara has just turned seventeen, her face is as round as a full moon, pockmarked, as we already mentioned, but she has a sweet nature and as good an ear for music as anyone has a right to expect of a royal princess, the lessons she received from Maestro Domenico Scarlatti have borne fruit, and soon he will follow her to Madrid, whence he will not return. The bridegroom who awaits her is two years younger, the said Fernando, who will be the sixth descendant of the Spanish dynasty to bear that name, but he will merely be king in name, a detail we mention in passing lest we are accused of interfering

[283]

in the internal affairs of a neighbouring country. A country from which, once historical links have been established with Portugal, Mariana Vitória will come, an eleven-year-old girl who, despite her tender years, has already experienced great sorrow, suffice it to say that she was about to marry Louis XV of France when he repudiated her, a word that may seem excessive and lacking in diplomacy, but how else can one describe it if a child at the age of four is sent to reside at the French court in order to be prepared for the aforesaid marriage, only to be sent back home two years later because her betrothed suddenly decided he wanted an heir to the crown, or it suited the interests of whoever was advising him, a demand that would have been physiologically impossible for another eight years. So the poor child, delicate and undernourished, was sent back to Spain on the feeble pretext that she was visiting her parents, King Felipe and Queen Isabel, and there she remained in Madrid, waiting for a bridegroom to be found who would be in less of a hurry to beget heirs, perhaps even our own Infante José, who will soon be fifteen. There is not much to say about the things that afford pleasure to Mariana Vitória, she is fond of dolls and adores sweetmeats, which is not surprising since she is still a mere child, she already shows considerable aptitude for hunting, and as she grows older she will develop a taste for music and literature. When all is said and done, there are those who govern with fewer accomplishments.

Stories about nuptials often relate how some people are treated as outsiders, therefore, to avoid any disappointment, never go to a wedding or a baptism without being invited. Someone who most certainly was not invited was João Elvas, who had befriended Sete-Sóis during the years he spent in Lisbon before he met Blimunda and came to live with her, João Elvas had offered him shelter in the hut where he slept along with other tramps and vagabonds close to the Convent of Hope, as you will remember. Even then João Elvas was getting on in years, and he is now in his sixties, weary and filled with nostalgia for the land of his birth, from which he took his name, certain longings take possession of the elderly, while there are other things they no longer crave. He hesitated about starting out on the journey, not because of his weak legs, which were still remarkably strong for a man of his age, but because of those vast barren plains of the Alentejo, no one is safe from some evil encounter, such as that experienced by Baltasar Sete-Sóis in the pine forests of Pegões, although on that occasion it was the brigand killed by Baltasar who encountered evil, and his corpse would have lain there exposed to vultures and stray dogs if his companion had not returned to the spot in order to bury him. For a man never really knows what fate awaits him, what good or evil is likely to befall him. Who could ever have told João Elvas when he was still a soldier, or even now that he has become a harmless vagabond, that the day would come when he would accompany the King of Portugal on his journey up the river Caia to deliver one royal princess and bring back another, who would have believed it. No one ever told him, no one ever predicted such a thing, fate alone knew that this would happen, as it began to select and weave the threads of destiny, diplomatic and dynastic intrigues in both courts and a lasting sense of nostalgia and destitution for the veteran soldier. If we ever succeed in unravelling those threads, we shall finally solve the mystery of existence and attain supreme wisdom, if such a thing exists.

Needless to say, João Elvas does not travel by coach or mounted on a horse. We have already mentioned those sturdy legs of his, and he puts them to good use. But, whether farther ahead or farther behind in the procession, Dom João V will continue to keep him company, as will the Queen and the Infantes, the Prince and the Princess and all the powerful nobles who are making the journey. It will never occur to these mighty lords that they are escorting a vagabond, and that their supreme authority is protecting his life and worldly possessions, which will soon be at an end. But lest they should come to an end too quickly, especially his life, which João Elvas cherishes, he carefully avoids getting too close to the main procession, for everyone knows how readily soldiers, God bless them, may strike and with what dire consequences, if they should suspect that the safety of their precious sovereign is at risk.

Ever cautious, João Elvas left Lisbon and made for Aldegalega at the beginning of January in the year seventeen hundred and twenty-nine, and there he lingered, watching coaches and horses disembark that would be used for the journey. Anxious to know what was happening, he began to make inquiries, What is that, where did it come from, who made it, who will use it, these may sound like foolish indiscretions, but, confronted by this venerable old man, however unwashed and dishevelled, any stable hand felt obliged to offer some reply, which encouraged João Elvas to pluck up enough courage to start questioning the head steward himself, he only needs to put on that pious air to achieve what he wants, for if he knows little about prayers, he knows more than enough about the art of deception. And even when his questions are answered with some rebuff, abuse, or cuff on the ear, that in itself allows him to guess what information has been withheld, for one day, the errors on which history is based will finally be clarified. And so, when Dom João V crossed the river on the eighth of January to embark on his great journey, there awaited him in Aldegalega more than two hundred carriages, including coaches, barouches, chaises, wagons, trailers, and litters, some had been brought from Paris, others had been specially made in Lisbon for the journey, not to mention the royal coaches, with their fresh gilding and refurbished velvet upholstery, their tassels and hand-painted drapes. The household cavalry boasted almost two thousand horses, without counting those of the mounted soldiers who accompanied the royal progress. Aldegalega, because of its strategic location for traffic en route to Alentejo, has seen many expeditions in its time, but never on such a scale, one need only consider the small roster of domestic staff, two hundred and twenty-two cooks, two hundred halberdiers, seventy porters, one hundred and three valets to look after the silver, over a thousand men to attend to the horses, and innumerable other servants and dusky slaves in every shade and hue. Aldegalega is aswarm with people, and the crowds would be even greater if the nobles and other dignitaries had not travelled on ahead in the direction of Elvas and the river Caia, nor was there any other solution, for if they had all set out at the same time, the royal princes would have married before the last of the invited guests entered Vendas Novas.

The King sailed past in his brigantine, having first worshipped at the shrine of Our Lady, Mother of God, and he disembarked accompanied by Prince Dom José and the Infante Dom António and their respective attendants, namely, the Duke of Cadaval, the Marquis of Marialva, and the Marquis of Alegrete, who acted as equerry to the Infante along with other members of the nobility, that they should have fulfilled such a role need cause no surprise, for it is ever an honour to serve the Royal Family. João Elvas was among the crowd that broke ranks and shouted, Long live the King, as Dom João V, sovereign of all Portugal, went past, and if that was not what they were shouting, it sounded very much like it, for one can always tell the difference between acclaim and derision, besides, who would dare to voice resentment in public by shouting insults, it is unthinkable that anyone should show lack of respect for the King, even if he does happen to be the King of Portugal. Dom João V took up residence in the apartments of the Clerk of Council, João Elvas suffered his first disappointment when he discovered there was a horde of beggars and tramps accompanying the procession, on the lookout for scraps of food and alms. Wherever they found something to eat, he would find something, too, but whatever their reasons for making the journey, his were the most worthy of all.

It was about five-thirty and still dark when the King set out for Vendas Novas, but João Elvas had left before him, because he was determined to see the procession pass in full array, in preference to seeing the chaotic preparations for departure while the various carriages took up their positions as dictated by the master of ceremonies amid the cries of outriders and coachmen, who are notorious for their loud behaviour. João Elvas was unaware that the King still had to attend Holy Mass at the Church of Our Lady of Atalaia, so when dawn broke and there was still no sign of the procession, he slackened his pace and finally came to a halt, where the devil could they be, he thought to himself as he sat by a ditch, sheltered from the morning breeze by a row of aloes. The sky was overcast with clouds that promised rain, and the cold was biting. João Elvas drew his cloak tightly around his body, pulled the brim of his hat down over his ears, and settled down to wait. He waited for an hour, perhaps even more, he saw scarcely anyone go past, and there was nothing to suggest that this was a feast day.

But the feast is on its way. In the distance a fanfare of trumpets and banging of kettledrums can already be heard, those military sounds cause the blood to course through the old man's veins, forgotten emotions are suddenly revived, it is just like watching a woman go by when there is nothing left except the memory of desire, trifling details like a sudden peal of laughter, the swaying of her skirt, or a fetching way of arranging her hair are enough to melt a fellow's heart, take me, do with me what you will, just as if one were being summoned to battle. And behold the triumphal march as it passes. João Elvas sees nothing but horses, people, and coaches, he has no idea who is participating and who is simply looking on, but it costs us nothing to imagine that some kind nobleman sat down beside him, one of those charitable souls whom one sometimes encounters, and since this nobleman is knowledgeable about royalty and court protocol, we listen attentively to what he has to say, Look, João Elvas, behind the lieutenant and the trumpeters and drummers who have just passed by, as you know from your time as a soldier, comes the quartermaster general in charge of billeting the soldiers accompanied by his subalterns, those six horsemen are the royal couriers who carry the dispatches and orders, in the berlin carriage now passing sit the confessors of the King, the Prince, and the Infante, you cannot imagine the burden of sin being transported in that carriage, the penances weigh infinitely less, then comes the carriage with the grooms in charge of the royal wardrobes, why look so startled, His Majesty is not a pauper like yourself, whose only clothes are the ones you're wearing, how curious to possess nothing other than the clothes on your back, and don't be alarmed at the sight of those two carriages packed with clergymen and priests from the Society of Jesus, not always fish or fowl, at some times the Society of Jesus, at others the Society of João, both of whom are kings, but these companions are always agreeable, and while we're on the subject, here comes the carriage of the assistant steward, and the three carriages behind are those of the judicial magistrate and the nobles assigned to the royal household, then comes the coach of the chief steward, then the carriages of the footmen who serve the Infantes, and now watch carefully, for this is where the procession becomes exciting, those empty coaches and carriages now going past are the ceremonial coaches and carriages of the Royal Family, and immediately behind follows the deputy steward on horseback, the great moment has arrived at last, get down on your knees, João Elvas, for His Majesty the King along with the Prince Dom José and the Infante Dom António are passing, did you ever see such splendour, such dignity, such a noble and imperious monarch, this is how God Himself will appear when we reach heaven, João Elvas, and however long you may live, you will never forget this moment of perfect bliss, when you saw Dom João V go past in the royal coach while you knelt respectfully at the foot of those aloes, be sure to cherish these images in your mind, for you have been truly privileged, and now you may get up, since the royal party has passed and is well on its way, six grooms have also ridden past, then came four carriages carrying members of His Majesty's council, then the chaise carrying the royal surgeon, for if there are so many in the party who take care of the King's soul, it's only fitting that someone should look after his body, from this point on, there is little of interest, six carriages in reserve, seven unmounted horses led by their reins, the cavalry guard led by their captain, and another twenty-five carriages reserved for the King's barber, valets, footmen, architects, chaplains, physicians, apothecaries, secretaries, porters, tailors, laundry-maids, head cook and his assistant, and so on and so forth, two wagons containing the wardrobes of the King and the Prince, and, closing the procession, twenty-six horses in reserve, have you ever seen such an entourage, João Elvas, now join that horde of beggars and tramps trailing behind, for that is where you belong, and don't bother to thank me for having taken the trouble to explain everything to you, for we are all children of the same God.

João Elvas caught up with the throng of vagrants, but though he was more informed about court etiquette than any of them, he was not made welcome because alms distributed to a hundred beggars are not the same as alms distributed to a hundred and one, but the thick cudgel he carried over one shoulder like a lance, and his military bearing and gait, helped to intimidate the hostile rabble. By the time they had marched half a league, they were all like brothers. When they finally reached Pegões, the King was already at supper, a light repast eaten on foot, consisting of water fowl stewed with quinces, pastries filled with marrow, and a traditional Moorish stew, a mere morsel sufficient to fill the cavity of a tooth. Meanwhile, the horses were changed. The horde of beggars swarmed around kitchen doors and intoned a chorus of paternosters and salve reginas, until they were finally served a bowl of broth from a large cauldron. Some, once they had eaten, decided to linger and digest their food without giving any thought to where the next meal might come from. Others, although they had satisfied their hunger, knew from experience that today's bread does not eliminate yesterday's hunger, much less that of tomorrow, and they were determined to keep up with the procession in the hope of scraps. João Elvas, motivated by personal reasons both worthy and unworthy, decided to tag along.

It was about four in the afternoon when the King arrived at Vendas Novas, and João Elvas got there about an hour later. Darkness fell quickly, and the clouds hovered so low that one felt they might be touched simply by stretching out a hand, I think we said this once before, and when left-overs were distributed among the beggars and tramps that evening, the veteran soldier opted for solid food, which he could carry off and eat in peace in some sheltered place, even under a wagon, remote from the conversation of the beggars, who caused him annoyance. The threat of rain appears to have nothing to do with João Elvas's desire to be alone, and one must not forget that, strange as it may seem, some men can spend their entire life alone and enjoy solitude, especially if it is raining and their crust of bread is hard.

Later that night, João Elvas could not tell if he was awake or dreaming, he heard a crackling sound as if hay were being trampled, someone was approaching and carrying an oil lamp in one hand. From the appearance and quality of the stranger's hose and breeches, from the rich material of his cloak and the lacing of his shoes, João Elvas could see that the newcomer was an aristocrat, and soon recognised him as the nobleman who had given him such a detailed description of the King's entourage when they conversed together by the roadside. Breathless and irritated, the nobleman sat down and complained, I've worn myself out chasing after you. I've been all over Vendas Novas asking, Where is João Elvas, where can I find him, no one could give me an answer, why is it that the poor never tell one another of their whereabouts, now I've found you, at long last, I have come to tell you about the palace the King has ordered to be built for this expedition, the work has been carried out day and night for almost ten months, more than ten thousand torches were needed for the night shift alone, and more than two thousand men were engaged, between painters, blacksmiths, masons, cabinetmakers, apprentices, foot soldiers, and cavalry troops, and I must tell you that the stone was transported for more than three leagues, it took over five hundred wagons and smaller carts to carry all the necessary materials, lime, joists, timber, stone slabs, bricks, tiles, pegs, and metal fittings, more than two hundred yokes of oxen were used to draw the carts, a number exceeded only for the convent at Mafra, I don't know if you have seen it, but it was worth all the labour and expense, I can tell you in confidence, but don't repeat this to anyone, a million cruzados has been spent on the palace and on the house you saw in Pegões, yes, sir, one million cruzados, obviously, you can't imagine what a million cruzados means, João Elvas, but don't be miserly, for though you wouldn't know what to do with all that money, the King has no such difficulty for he has known all his life what it means to be wealthy, the poor may not know how to spend money, but the rich certainly do, just think of all those expensive paintings and sumptuous decorations, and those lavish apartments for the Cardinal and Patriarch, the audience chamber, study, and stateroom for Dom José, and the equally luxurious apartments for Dona Maria Bárbara when she makes her journey here, as well as the private suites for the King and Queen so that they may enjoy some privacy and be spared the discomfort of sleeping in cramped conditions, for, let's be frank, the spacious bed you occupy is a rare privilege indeed, you have the entire universe at your disposal, as you lie there snoring like a pig, if you'll pardon the expression, sprawled out on the hay and wrapped up in your cloak, and you smell terrible, João Elvas, but never mind, for if we should meet up again, I'll bring you a bottle of lavender water, and this is all the news I have to give you, don't forget that His Majesty will leave for Montemor at three o'clock in the morning, so if you want to travel with the King, don't oversleep.

But João Elvas did oversleep and when he awoke it was already after five and raining cats and dogs. The daylight was such that he realised that, if the King had set out on time, he should already be well on his way. João Elvas wrapped his cloak tightly around him, tucked up his legs as if he were still in his mother's womb, and snoozed in the warmth of the hay, which gave off a pleasant odour generated by the heat of his body. There are refined men and women, and sometimes not all that refined, who cannot bear such odours and who take great pains to cover any traces of their natural smell, and the day will come when artificial roses will be sprayed with the artificial scent of roses, and these refined souls will exclaim, How lovely they smell. João Elvas was at a loss as to why such thoughts came into his head, and he feared that he might be dreaming or suffering from hallucinations. He finally opened his eyes and emerged from his slumber. The rain was falling heavily, vertical and sonorous, pity Their Royal Majesties being forced to travel in such foul weather, their children will never be able to thank them enough for the sacrifices they are making on their behalf. Dom João V was on his way to Montemor, and God alone knows with what courage, as he coped with so many obstacles, with floods, swamps, and rivers that overflowed their banks, it grieves one to think of the fear that gripped those nobles, chamberlains, confessors, chaplains, and aristocrats, I bet the trumpeters put their instruments away in their sacks, and that no drumsticks were needed to hear the ruffling of the drums, as the rain beat down on them. And what about the Queen, whatever became of Her Majesty, she has already made her departure from Aldegalega, accompanied by the Infanta Dona Maria Bárbara and the Infante Dom Pedro, who bears the same name as the child who died, a delicate woman and a delicate child, exposed to the horrors of this inclement weather, yet people continue to insist that heaven is on the side of the rich and mighty, yet it is clear for all to see that when there is a heavy downpour of rain, it falls on everyone alike.

João Elvas spent the entire day in the warmth of the taverns, where he seasoned the scraps of food generously provided by His Majesty's pantry with a bowl of wine. Most of the beggars had decided to remain in the town until the rain stopped before joining the tail of the procession. But the rain did not stop. It was already growing dark when the first coaches of Dona Maria Ana's entourage arrived at Vendas Novas, looking more like an army in retreat than a royal procession. The horses were so tired that they could scarcely pull the coaches and carriages, some even collapsed and died on the spot, still strapped in the harnesses. The grooms and stable hands waved their torches frantically and created the most deafening uproar, and there was such a commotion that it proved impossible to direct all the members of the Queen's party to their respective lodgings, so that many were obliged to return to Pegões, where they somehow managed to secure accommodation in the most wretched conditions. It was a disastrous night. Next day the damage was assessed and it became clear that scores of beasts had perished, without counting those that had been abandoned on the road with severe injuries and broken limbs. The ladies had the vapours or swooned, the gentlemen shrugged off their exhaustion as they swirled their cloaks and preened themselves at social gatherings, while the rain continued to inundate everything, as if God, because of some deep resentment concealed from mankind, had perversely decided to unleash another great deluge, which this time would be conclusive.

The Queen would have preferred to travel on to Évora that same morning, but she was dissuaded from making such a risky journey, besides, many of the coaches had been delayed along the route, which would seriously undermine the prestige of her retinue, and they warned her, Your Majesty should know that the roads are impassable, when the King travelled through he faced terrible problems, so things are now likely to be much worse after all this perpetual rain, day and night, night and day, but orders have already been dispatched to the acting magistrate of Montemor to enlist men to repair the roads, drain the swamps, and level out the ravines, Your Majesty would be wise to rest on this eleventh day in Vendas Novas, in the magnificent palace the King has commissioned, it has every conceivable amenity, amuse yourself in the company of the Princess, and take advantage of these few days together to impart some final words of maternal advice, Remember, my child, that all men are brutes, not only on the first night but on all the other nights, too, although the first night is always the worst, they promise to be extremely gentle, that it will not hurt in the slightest, and then, good gracious, I don't know what gets into them, but without any warning they start to snarl and howl like wild beasts, if you will pardon the expression, and we poor women have no choice save to put up with their vicious assault, either until they have had their way with us, or, as sometimes happens, till they go limp and when this occurs, we must never laugh, for nothing could offend them more, better to pretend that we do not mind, for if he does not succeed on the first night, he will certainly make it on the second or third night, and no one can save us from this torture, and now I'm going to send for Signor Scarlatti so that he may take our minds off these painful facts of life, music is wonderfully consoling, my child, prayer, too, indeed, I find that everything is music, even though prayer is not quite everything.

While these words of advice were being given and the keyboard of the harpsichord was being fingered, João Elvas was busily engaged in repairing the roads, these are adversities from which one cannot always escape, a man runs from one shelter to another to escape the rain, and suddenly he hears a voice crying, Halt, it is one of the magistrate's henchmen, the tone of that voice was unmistakable, and the challenge so sudden that João Elvas did not even have time to pretend that he was a frail old man on his last legs, the henchman hesitated when he saw more white hairs than he had expected, but what proved decisive in the end was the agility with which the old man fled, anyone capable of running as fast as that was obviously quite capable of wielding a pick and shovel. When João Elvas, along with the others who had been rounded up, arrived at the wilderness where the road disappeared amid bogs and swamps, they found that there were large numbers of men already there, carrying earth and stones from the low hills nearby, which had been less affected by the rain, it was a chore that meant transporting earth and stones from over there and dumping them here, and sometimes canals had to be dug to drain away the water, each man resembled a spectre cast in clay, a puppet or a scarecrow, and it was not long before João Elvas took on much the same appearance, he would have fared better had he chosen to stay in Lisbon, for no matter how hard a man may try, he cannot recapture his youth. The men toiled relentlessly throughout the day, and the rain eased up, which was a great blessing, because the holes they were filling in now had a better chance of gaining some consistency, unless another storm were to break out and ruin everything. Dona Maria Ana slept soundly under her luxurious feather quilt, which she takes with her everywhere, lulled into peaceful slumber by the sound of falling rain, but because the same causes do not always produce the same effects, much depends on the individuals, the circumstances and the cares they take to bed, it came about that Her Royal Highness Dona Maria Bárbara continued to hear the echoes of those heavy raindrops well into the night, or perhaps they were the distressing words spoken by her mother. Among the men who had marched along that road, some slept well and others badly, much depended on how tired they were, as for shelter and food, they could not complain, for His Majesty did not stint on lodgings and hot food if the workers earned his approval.

Before dawn the Queen's party finally left Vendas Novas, now with all the carriages that had been delayed, although some were lost forever and others needed extensive repairs, the entourage presented a sorry sight, the draperies and hangings saturated, the gilding and paintwork discoloured, and unless a little sunshine should filter through, these are likely to be the most dismal nuptials ever witnessed. The rain has stopped at long last, but the biting cold scorches the skin, and covers one's hands with chilblains despite the use of muffs and cloaks, we are referring to the ladies, of course, who look so cold and feverish that they arouse pity. The procession is headed by a gang of road repairers who travel in ox-drawn carts, and where they come across a hole or a ditch that has been flooded or has caved in, they jump down and set to work, meanwhile, the convoy is delayed in this desolate landscape. Yokes of oxen have been brought from Vendas Novas and other towns in the vicinity, scores of them, to help rescue the chaises, berlins, wagons, and other carriages, which keep getting trapped in the mud, this operation took considerable time as they unharnessed the horses and mules, then harnessed the oxen, then heaved, only to reverse the process by unharnessing the oxen and harnessing the horses and mules once more, amid much shouting and lashing of whips, and when the Queen's coach sank right up to the hubs of the wheels, and it took six yokes of oxen to drag it out of the mud, one of the men there, who had left his home under orders from the district magistrate, observed, as if speaking to himself, One would think we were here to heave that enormous stone destined for Mafra. This being the moment when the oxen were being put to work and the men were allowed to relax, João Elvas asked, What stone was that, my friend, and the other replied,

A stone as large as a house that was brought from Pêro Pinheiro for the construction of the convent at Mafra, I only saw it when it arrived, but I also lent a hand, for it was at a time when I used to frequent the place, And was it big, it was the mother of all stones, in the words of a friend of mine who helped transport it from the quarry and then went back to his province, I myself left shortly after that, for I had had enough. The oxen, submerged to their bellies, pulled without any apparent effort, as if they were trying to coax the mud to release them. The wheels of the coach finally settled on firm ground and the enormous vehicle was pulled from the swamp to the sound of applause, while the Queen smiled graciously, the Princesses nodded, and the young Infante Dom Pedro concealed his annoyance at being denied the pleasure of splashing about in the mud.

It was like this all the way to Montemor, a journey of less than five leagues took almost eight hours of continuous effort and strain by men and beasts as they plied their respective skills. The Princess Dona Maria Bárbara tried to sleep, anxious to overcome her persistent insomnia, but the jostling of the coach, the shouting of those burly road repairers, and the stamping of the horses as they went back and forth obeying orders made her poor little head feel quite dizzy and caused her unspeakable torment, so much effort, dear God, so much disturbance to marry off a young woman, but, then, she is a princess. The Queen goes on muttering her prayers, not so much to ward off any unlikely perils as to while away the hours, for the Queen has lived long enough in this world to have come to terms with life, now and then she dozes off, only to wake up again and continue her prayers as if they had never been interrupted. About the Infante Dom Pedro, for the time being, there is nothing more to be said.

The conversation, however, between João Elvas and the man who had mentioned the stone was resumed as the journey got under way, the old man told him, A fellow I befriended many years ago hailed from Mafra, I never found out what happened to him, he lived in Lisbon, and one day he suddenly disappeared, these things happen, perhaps he went back to his native parts, If he went back to Mafra, it's possible that I might have met him, what was his name, His name was Baltasar Sete-Sóis, and he lost his left hand in the war, Sete-Sóis,

Baltasar Sete-Sóis that's the one person I got to know, for we worked together, Well, I never, what a small world this is when all is said and done, we two meet each other by chance only to discover that we have a mutual friend, Sete-Sóis was a fine fellow, Do you think he may be dead, I cannot say, but I doubt it, with a wife such as his, a certain Blimunda, whose eyes were a colour that defied description, when a man has a wife like that, he clings to life and does not let go even if he does only possess his right hand, I never met his wife, sometimes Sete-Sóis would come out with the most incredible statements, one day he even claimed to have been within reach of the sun, It must have been the effect of the wine, We had all been drinking when he said it, yet none of us was drunk, as far as I can remember, what he was trying to say in his own odd way was that he had flown, Flown, Sete-Sóis, I've never heard of such a thing.

Their conversation was interrupted when they reached the bank of the river Canha, which was swollen and turbulent, on the other side, the population of Montemor had assembled outside the gates to await the Queen's arrival, and with the combined efforts of everyone and the assistance of some barrels, which made it possible to float the carriages across the river, within the hour they were sitting down to supper in the town, the nobility seated at specially reserved tables in accordance with their rank, and their aides and servants wherever they could find a place, some eating in silence while others conversed, such as João Elvas who said, in the tone of someone holding two conversations simultaneously, one with his interlocutor, the other with himself, It now comes back to me that when Sete-Sóis lived in Lisbon he was on friendly terms with the Flying Man, and it was I myself who pointed him out to Sete-Sóis one day when we were together in the Palace Square, I can remember it as clearly as if it were yesterday, who was this Flying Man, The Flying Man was a priest, a certain Padre Bartolomeu Lourenço, who ended his days in Spain, where he died four years ago, the case caused quite a stir, and it was investigated by the Holy Office of the Inquisition, it's possible that even Sete-Sóis was involved in this strange affair, But did the Flying Man actually fly, Some said that he did, while others said that he did not, there's no way now of ever knowing the truth, What is certain is that Sete-Sóis claimed that he had been within reach of the sun, for I myself heard him say so, There must be some mystery here, Of course there is, and with this reply, which begged the question, the man who had reminisced about the stone at Mafra fell silent and they finished their meal.

The clouds lifted, hovered high overhead, and it looked as if the rain might be over. The men who had come from the towns and villages between Vendas Novas and Montemor proceeded no farther. They were paid for their labours, and because of the Queen's kind intervention the day's wages were doubled, there is always some recompense for carrying the burden of the rich and mighty. João Elvas continued his journey, perhaps now with greater ease since he had become friendly with outriders and coachmen who might offer him a lift on one of the wagons, where he could ride with his legs dangling clear of the mud and dung. The man who spoke about the stone stood at the edge of the road, watching with his blue eyes the old man who settled down between two large trunks. They will never see each other again, at least that is what one assumes, for God Himself does not know what the future holds, and as the wagon set off, João Elvas said, If you should ever meet Sete-Sóis again, tell him that you were speaking to João Elvas, for he is sure to remember me, and remember to give him my regards, I shall pass on your message, but I doubt whether I shall ever see him again, By the way, what's your name, I'm called Julião Mau-Tempo, Farewell, then, Julião Mau-Tempo, Farewell, João Elvas.

From Montemor to Évora there would be no lack of work. The rain started up again, and more puddles began to form, axles cracked, and the spokes of the wheels split like kindling wood. The evening drew in quickly, the air grew cold, and the Princess Dona Maria Bárbara, who had fallen asleep at long last, assisted by a consoling languor induced by sweetmeats to settle her stomach and by a stretch of five hundred paces along the road free of any potholes, woke up with a great shudder, as if an icy finger had stroked her forehead, and turning her somnolent gaze to the fields enshrouded in twilight, she saw shadowy human forms lining up along the roadside and tied to one another by ropes, some fifteen men in all.

The Princess took a closer look. She was neither dreaming nor delirious, the sad spectacle of fettered slaves troubled her on the eve of her nuptials, which should have been an occasion for universal gaiety and rejoicing, as if the awful weather, the rain and clouds were not enough to lower one's spirits, it would have been so much better to have been married in the spring. Dona Maria Bárbara ordered the equerry who was riding beside the carriage to investigate who these men might be, to find out what crimes they had committed, and if they were heading for Limoeiro or for Africa. The officer went in person, probably because he worshipped the Infanta, ugly and pockmarked as she was, and now she was being taken to Spain, far from his pure and despairing love, that a commoner should love a princess is sheer madness, he went and returned, Your Highness, these men are on their way to Mafra to help build the Royal Convent, they are skilled labourers from the region of Évora, But why are they tied with ropes, Because they are being taken there against their will, and if the ropes were untied they would almost certainly escape, Ah. The Princess reclined against her cushions, looking thoughtful, while the officer repeated and engraved in his heart those sweet words they had exchanged, even as an old man, long since retired from military service, he would remember every word of their delightful conversation, and what would she be like after all those years.

The Princess is no longer thinking about the men she saw on the road. It has just occurred to her that she has never been to Mafra, how strange that a convent should be built because Maria Bárbara was born, that a pledge should be honoured because Maria Bárbara was born, yet Maria Bárbara has never seen, known, or touched with her plump little finger either the first or the second stone of its foundations, she has never served broth with her own hands to the workers, never soothed with balm the pain Sete-Sóis feels in his stump when he detaches the hook from his arm, she has never wiped away the tears of the woman whose husband was crushed to death, and now Maria Bárbara is leaving for Spain, for her the convent is like some vision in a dream, an impalpable haze, something beyond the powers of imagination but for this encounter that assists her memory. Ah, the grievous sins of Maria Bárbara, the evil she has already committed simply by being born, the proof is at hand, one need only look at those fifteen men who walk bound to one another, while carriages go past carrying friars, berlin coaches with nobles, wagons with the royal wardrobes, chaises carrying the ladies with their caskets of jewellery and all their other finery, embroidered slippers, flasks of cologne, golden rosary beads, scarves embellished with gold and silver, bracelets, opulent muffs, lace trimmings, and ermine stoles, women are so delightfully sinful, and beautiful to behold even when they are as pockmarked and ugly as this infanta we are accompanying, that seductive melancholy and thoughtful expression are all the wickedness she needs as she confides, Dearest Mother and Queen, here I am on my way to Spain, whence I shall never return, I know that a convent is being built in Mafra because of a vow that partly concerned me, yet no one has ever taken me to see it, there is so much about this affair that leaves me perplexed, My daughter and future Queen, do not waste precious time that should be devoted to prayer on such idle thoughts, the royal will of your father and our sovereign lord decreed that the convent be built, the same royal will has decreed that you go to Spain without seeing the convent, that the King's will should prevail is all that matters, and everything else is futile, So the fact that I am an Infanta means nothing, nor do those men led like captives, nor this coach in which we travel, nor that officer who walks in the rain while gazing into my eyes, That is correct, my child, and the longer you live the more you will realise that the world is like a great shadow pervading our hearts, that is why the world seems so empty and eventually becomes unbearable, Oh, Mother, what does it mean to be born, To be born is to die, Maria Bárbara.

The best thing about these long journeys is the philosophical discussions. The Infante Dom Pedro is tired and falls asleep, leaning his head against his mother's shoulder, it makes a pretty picture of domestic intimacy, and shows how the Infante is no different from any other child, as he sleeps, his little chin sags in confident abandon and a thread of saliva trickles down the ruffles of his wide embroidered collar. The Princess brushes away a tear. Torches light up the entire length of the procession like a rosary of stars that might have slipped from the Virgin's hand and which, by chance or by some special grace, have landed on Portuguese soil. We shall make our entry into Évora after dark.

The King awaits our arrival with the Infantes Dom Francisco and Dom António, the people of Évora cheer wildly as the light from the torches becomes radiant, the soldiers fire the customary salvos, and when the Queen and the Princess transfer to the King's coach, the enthusiasm of the crowds knows no bounds, one has never seen such rejoicing and happiness. João Elvas has already jumped down from the wagon on which he arrived, he has a cramp in both legs, and he decides that in future he will put them to the use for which they were intended instead of letting them dangle idly while he sits back, there is nothing healthier for a man than to walk on his own two legs. That night, the nobleman did not appear and if he had, what would he have described on this occasion, royal banquets and ceremonies, perhaps, or visits to convents, the conferment of titles, the distribution of alms and the kissing of hands. The only thing here of any interest to João Elvas would have been a few alms, but no doubt these, too, will eventually come his way. The following day, João Elvas could not decide whether he should accompany the King or the Queen, but in the end he chose to travel with Dom João V, he made the right decision, because poor Dona Maria Ana, who set out one day later, got caught in such a snowstorm that for a moment she thought she was back in her native Austria instead of heading for Vila Viçosa, a place noted for its hot climate in another season, like all those other places we have passed through. Finally, on the morning of the sixteenth, eight days after the King set out from Lisbon, the entire procession left for Elvas, monarch, soldier, beggarman, thief, mocked the street urchins who had never seen such pomp and splendour, just imagine, there were one hundred and seventy carriages just for the royal household, to which one must add those of countless nobles and dignitaries, as well as those of the guilds of Évora, and of private individuals who did not wish to lose this opportunity of enhancing their family history, their descendants would be able to boast that their great-great-grandfather had accompanied the Royal Family to Elvas where an exchange of princesses took place, Something you must never forget, is that clear.

Wherever they passed, the local inhabitants flocked to the roadside and fell to their knees, beseeching their sovereign's blessing, as if the poor wretches had guessed that Dom João V was travelling with a chest of copper coins at his feet which he tossed in handfuls into the crowds on either side with the broad gestures of someone scattering seed, this provoked an uproar and cries of gratitude, the crowds spilled onto the road, where they fought over the money, and it was amazing to watch young and old alike rolling in the mud where some of the coins became embedded, to see blind men groping in the puddles to retrieve a coin that had fallen into the water, while the royal party drove past looking solemn, grave, and imperious without so much as a smile, for God Himself never smiles, and He must have His reasons, who knows, perhaps He has ended up feeling ashamed of this world He has created. João Elvas is also there, when he extended his hat to the King, which he felt to be his obligation as one of His Majesty's loyal subjects, he collected a few coins, what a lucky fellow this old man is, he does not even need to get to his knees, happiness comes knocking at his door, and money falls into his hand.

It was after five that evening when the procession reached the city. The artillery gave a salvo, and things appeared to have been so well timed that a gun salute came resounding back from the other side of the frontier as the Kings of Spain made their entry into Badajoz, anyone arriving here unexpectedly would have thought that a great battle was about to take place, but contrary to custom, monarch and beggarman joined in the hostilities alongside the more familiar soldier and captain. These, however, are salvos of peace, fireworks in the style of those illuminations and pyrotechnics one associates with feast days, the King and Queen have now alighted from their coach, the King wishes to proceed on foot from the city gates to the cathedral, but the bitter cold rasps both hands and face so much that Dom João V resigns himself to losing this first skirmish and climbs back into his coach, that night he may well say a few sharp words to the Queen, for it was she who refused to go any farther, complaining of the chilly air, when it would have given the King pleasure and satisfaction to stroll through the streets of Elvas on foot behind the cathedral chapter who awaited him with raised cross and the Holy Wood, which was kissed but not accompanied, João V did not walk that *via crucis*.

God has given every proof that He loves His creatures dearly. After testing their patience and constancy for many days and many kilometres by exposing them to unbearable cold and torrential rain, as we have narrated in detail, He decided to reward their faith and resignation.

And since with God all things are possible, He only had to raise the atmospheric pressure and, little by little, the clouds lifted and the sun appeared, and all this took place while the ambassadors were drawing up the terms of the treaty between the two realms, a thorny business that took three days of discussion before an agreement was finally reached, and every move, gesture, and word had been carefully calculated, stage by stage, so that neither crown should be tarnished or diminished when compared with its partner. When the King set out from Elvas on the nineteenth and made his way to the River Caia, which lay immediately ahead, accompanied by the Queen and the Crown Princes and all the Infantes, the weather was perfect, with blue skies and the most agreeable sunshine. As you can imagine, everybody was there to see the pomp and splendour of this never-ending procession, the glossy curls of the braided manes of the horses pulling the coaches, the scintillating gold and silver, the alternating sounds of trumpets and kettledrums, the velvet trappings, halberdiers, cavalry troops, the religious insignia and sparkling gems, we have already admired all these sights under the rain, now we shall be able to affirm that there is nothing like sunshine to gladden the hearts of men and enhance festivities.

The people of Elvas and from all the districts for leagues around gathered by the roadside, having raced across fields to find a vantage point overlooking the river, crowds swarm the banks on either side, the Portuguese over here, the Spaniards over there, as one listens to their cheers and vivas, it is difficult to believe that we have been killing one another for centuries, so perhaps the solution would be to wed the people across the frontier to those who live here, so that any wars in future will be purely domestic since the latter are unavoidable. João Elvas has been here for three days and has found himself a good position, a view from the gallery, as it were, if such a thing existed here. Moved by some curious whim, he decided to avoid entering his native city, notwithstanding his deep longing to return. He will go when all the others have departed and he is able to wander undisturbed through the silent streets, with no rejoicing other than his own, unless it should turn to painful bitterness once he tries to retrace the paths of his youth. Thanks to this decision he was able to lend a hand with the movement of baggage and enter the house where the royal parties would meet which was built on a stone bridge that crosses the river. The house has three rooms, one on either side for the sovereigns of each nation, a third in the middle where the exchange will be made, I hereby deliver Bárbara, now hand over Mariana. No one has any idea of the problems that had to be dealt with at the last minute, it fell to João Elvas to carry the heaviest load, but just at this moment there emerged the kind nobleman whose presence had been so providential during the journey, he told João Elvas, If you could see how that house has been transformed beyond recognition, the room allotted to the Portuguese is decked out in tapestries and draperies in crimson damask with valances of gold brocade, and the same is true of our half of the room in the middle, while the other side, allotted to Castile, is adorned with strands of green-and-white brocade suspended from an ornamental branch made of solid gold, and standing in the centre of the room where the Princesses are being presented is an enormous table with seven chairs on our side of the room and seven on the Spanish side, our chairs are upholstered in gold tissue and theirs in silver, this is all I can tell you, for I saw nothing more, and now I am off, but don't be envious, for even I may not enter there, so imagine if you can, if we should meet again one day, I will tell you what it was like, if anyone tells me first, for if we wish to find out, we must confide in one another.

It was extremely moving to watch the mothers and daughters weep, the fathers put on a severe expression to disguise their true feelings, while the betrothed couples looked out of the corner of one eye to see whether they approved or disapproved of their partners but kept their thoughts to themselves. Gathered along the river-banks, the crowds saw nothing of the proceedings, but they relied on their own experiences and memories of their own wedding days to visualise the scene, in their mind's eye, they could see the respective parents embrace one another, the sly exchanges between the bridegrooms, and the affected blushes of the brides, now, now then, whether a man be king or commoner, there is nothing more enjoyable than a good fuck, ours is truly a nation of vulgarians.

The ceremony lasted a considerable time. The crowds gradually fell silent, as if by some miracle, the banners and standards scarcely moved in the breeze and all the soldiers turned their gaze towards the house on the bridge. The gentle strains of the sweetest music filled the air, a tinkling of tiny glass and silver bells, an arpeggio, which occasionally sounded hoarse, as if emotion was constricting the throat of harmony, What is that, a woman standing beside João Elvas inquired, and the old man replied, I'm not sure, but it could be someone playing for the pleasure of Their Sovereign Majesties and families, if my nobleman were here I should ask him, because he knows everything, after all, he is one of them. The music ends, everyone goes back where they belong, the River Caia flows quietly past, no shred of bunting remains, nor the tiniest echo of ruffling drums, and João Elvas will never know that he heard Domenico Scarlatti playing his harpsichord.

HEADING THE PROCESSION because of their enormous size, which makes it seem natural that they should have pride of place, are the statues of St Vincent and St Sebastian, both martyrs, although of the former's martyrdom there is no sign other than the symbolic palm, the rest being simply the emblems of his diaconate and the heraldic raven, whereas the other saint is characteristically represented in the nude, lashed to a tree, and with the perforations of those ghastly wounds from which the arrows have been prudently removed in case they should get broken during the journey. Immediately behind come the ladies, three virtuous beauties, and most beautiful of all St Isabel, the Queen of Hungary, then St Clare, and finally St Teresa, who was an extremely passionate woman consumed by spiritual ardour, at least that is what one assumes from her actions and words, and we could assume much more if we understood the souls of the saints. The saint right next to St Clare is St Francis, and this preference comes as no surprise, for they have known each other from their days in Assisi and now they have met up with each other again on the road to Pintéus, their friendship, or whatever it was that brought them together, would count for little if they were not to resume their dialogue at the point where they left off, as we were saying. If this is the most fitting place for St Francis, since of all the saints who are represented in this parade he has the most feminine of virtues, with that soft heart and cheerful disposition, equally well placed are St Dominic and St Ignatius, both Iberian and austere, subsequently demonic, if that does not offend the Demon, if it would not be just, in the end, to say that only a saint could have invented the Inquisition and another saint the spiritual formation of souls. It is evident to anyone familiar with these subtleties, that St Francis is under suspicion.

When it comes to sanctity, however, there is something for everyone. For those who prefer a saint who devotes his time to working the land and cultivating the written word, there is St Benedict. For those who prefer their saint to lead a life of austerity, wisdom, and mortification, bring forth St Bruno. For those who admire a saint of crusading zeal capable of reviving the missionary spirit, there is none to surpass St Bernard. The three saints are placed together, perhaps because they bear a striking resemblance to one another, perhaps because their combined virtues would make an honest man, or perhaps because the names of all three saints begin with the same letter of the alphabet, it is not uncommon for people to come together because of such coincidences, this could also explain why some people known to us, like Blimunda and Baltasar, should come together, and speaking of Baltasar, he is in charge of the yoke of oxen that is carrying the statue of St John of God, the only Portuguese saint among the confraternity that disembarked from Italy at Santo António do Tojal, and is heading for Mafra, like almost everyone else we have mentioned so far in this story.

Behind St John of God, whose house in Montemor was visited more than eighteen months ago by Dom João V when he accompanied the Princess to the frontier, although we omitted to say so earlier, which shows our lack of respect for national shrines, and may the saint forgive this omission, behind St John of God, as we were saying, come half a dozen more saints of lesser glory whose many laudable attributes and virtues we do not wish to disdain, but daily experience teaches us that unless assisted by fame in this world, one cannot achieve glory in heaven, a flagrant disparity to which all of these saints are subjected and who, because of their inferior status, have to be content with names like John of Matha, Francis of Paola, Cajetan, Felix of Valois, Peter Nolasco, Philip Neri, names that sound like those of ordinary men, but they cannot complain, for each saint has his own cart and is carefully transported horizontally, like the others with five stars on a soft bed of flock, wool, and sackfuls of husks, this prevents the folds in their robes from becoming creased or their ears from getting bent, for these marble statues are fragile, despite their solid appearance, and it takes only two knocks for Venus to lose her arms. We begin to lose our memory as we confuse Bruno, Benedict, and Bernard with Baltasar and Blimunda, and we forget Bartolomeu de Gusmão or Lourenço, whichever form you prefer, but who is never to be readily dismissed. For, as the saying truly goes, Woe to the man who dies, twice woe, unless there be some true or false sanctity to save him.

We have already passed Pintéus, and we are on our way to Fanhões with eighteen statues loaded on eighteen carts and the appropriate number of oxen, and a vast number of men handling the ropes, as already mentioned, but this expedition cannot be compared to the one that transported the Benediction stone, the stone for the balcony from where the Patriarch will give his blessing, these things can happen only once in a lifetime, and if human ingenuity did not invent means of rendering difficult things easy, it would have been preferable to leave the world in its primitive state. The people line the route to greet the procession as it passes, they are all surprised to see the saints lying down, and with good reason, for surely it would have been much nicer and more edifying to see the holy statues standing upright on the carts, as if they were on litters, then even the smallest of the statues, which are under three metres high, our own height, in fact, would have been seen from a distance, and you can imagine the impact of the two statues in front, St Vincent and St Sebastian, which are almost five metres high, two mighty giants, two Christian Hercules and champions of the faith, looking down from their great height over the terraces and crests of the olive groves at the vast world, for them this would truly be a religion comparable with those of ancient Rome and Greece. The procession came to a halt in Fanhões because the local inhabitants insisted upon knowing, name by name, who the various saints were, for it was not every day that they received, even if only in transit, visitors of such corporeal and spiritual stature, the daily transport of building materials is one thing, but quite another was the sight witnessed several weeks ago, when an interminable convoy of bells went past, over a hundred of which will ring out from the bell towers of Mafra, the imperishable memory of these events, and yet another is this sacred pantheon. The local parish priest was summoned to identify the saints, but his answers were not entirely satisfactory, because not all of the statues had the saint's name clearly inscribed on the pedestal, and in many instances the name was all the parish priest could provide, it is one thing to recognise immediately that this is St Sebastian and quite another to recite from memory, Beloved brethren, the saint you see here is St Felix of Valois, who was a disciple of St Bernard, who is up there in front, and who established, together with St John of Matha who is at the back there, the Order of Trinitarians, which was founded to rescue slaves from the clutches of the infidels, just think of the edifying tales that help strengthen our holy faith, Ha ha ha, laugh the inhabitants of Fanhões, And when will orders be given to rescue slaves from the clutches of the faithful, Reverend Prior.

Anxious to extricate himself, the priest went to the governor in charge of the expedition and asked to be allowed to consult the documents of exportation that had come from Italy, a cunning move that helped him recover his shaken confidence, and soon the inhabitants of Fanhões were watching their ignorant pastor mounted on the churchyard wall and heard him read aloud the blessed names of the saints in the order they went past on the carts, right down to the very last saint, who chanced to be St Cajetan, on a cart drawn by José Pequeno, who smiled as much at the applause as at those who were applauding. But, then, José Pequeno is a mischievous fellow who has been justly punished, by God or the devil, with that hump he carries on his back, but it must have been God who punished him, because there is no proof that the devil has any such powers over the human body in this life. The spectacle is over and the procession of saints is now on its way to Cabeço de Monte Achique, Have a good journey.

Less good is the journey made by the novices from the Convent of St Joseph of Ribamar, over there toward Algés and Carnaxide, who are even now trudging along the road to Mafra on account of the pride or transposed mortification of their Provincial Superior. It happened that, as the day approached for the consecration of the convent, trunks were carefully packed and dispatched from Lisbon with the vestments and linen required for the religious ceremonies, along with all the essential supplies for the community of friars assigned to the aforesaid convent. These orders were given by the Provincial, who at the appropriate hour gave fresh orders, namely, that the novices should proceed to their new quarters, and when the King was informed, this compassionate sovereign was so deeply concerned that he invited them to use his own merchant vessels as far as the port of Santo António do Tojal, thus lessening the burden and fatigue of their journey. The waves, however, were so high and turbulent because of the fierce wind that it would have been suicidal madness to attempt any such sea voyage, so the King suggested that the novices might travel in his carriages, whereupon the Provincial Superior, aflame with holy scruple, protested, Surely Your Majesty is not providing comforts for those who should be wearing hairshirts, encouraging leisure for those who should be constantly on their guard, feathering cushions for those preparing for a bed of thorns, I would prefer to give up being provincial superior, Your Majesty, rather than condone such laxity, let them travel on foot so they can give a good example to the people, for they are no better than Our Lord Jesus Christ, who rode on a donkey only once.

Persuaded by these sound arguments, Dom João V withdrew his offer of carriages, just as he had withdrawn his offer of merchant vessels, and the novices, carrying nothing except their breviaries, set out from the Convent of St Joseph of Ribamar in the morning, thirty apprehensive and dispirited adolescents with their novice master, Friar Joseph of St Teresa. Poor boys, poor little fledglings, as if it were not enough that novice masters should, by some infallible rule, be the most awful tyrants, with a mania for daily floggings of six, seven, eight strokes of the lash until the wretched creatures had their backs covered in raw flesh, as if all this and worse were not enough, the novices also had to carry on their festering and lacerated backs the heaviest loads imaginable, so that their wounds refused to heal, and now they were being ordered to walk barefoot for six leagues across hill and dale, over stone and mud, along roads so bad that the path trodden by the ass that carried the Virgin when she made her flight into Egypt was a pleasant meadow by comparison, as for St Joseph, we have deliberately avoided saying anything about him, for he is a model of patience.

Half a league on, because of some injury to a big toe, some treacherous stone, or the continuous rubbing of their soles on the rough ground, the more delicate novices had bleeding feet, leaving a trail of pious crimson flowers, it would make a lovely religious picture were it not so cold, were the little snouts of the novices not quite so frost-bitten, and their eyes not smarting so badly, it costs dearly to gain heaven. They recited their breviaries, a palliative recommended for all spiritual torments, but these are physical torments and a pair of sandals would be a welcome substitute for any form of prayer, however efficacious, Dear God, if You really insist upon this penance, lead me not into temptation, but first of all remove this stone from my path, since You are the Father of stones and friars, and not their Father and my Stepfather. There is nothing worse than the life of a novice, save perhaps that of a shop assistant in years to come, we were about to say that the novice is the shop assistant of God, as a certain Friar John of Our Lady can testify, a former novice of this very same Franciscan Order, who will go as preacher to Mafra on the third day of the religious solemnities to mark the consecration of the convent but will not be given an opportunity to preach, for he is merely a substitute, as can also be attested by Friar John the Paunch, who was given this name because of his corpulence once he became a friar, although as a scrawny, underfed novice he had tramped throughout the Algarve collecting lambs for the convent, for three whole months, dressed in tatters, barefoot, and starving, just imagine what he suffered collecting those animals, which he had to herd from one village to another as he begged for one more newborn lamb to increase his flock, taking them out to pasture, and carrying out his various religious duties which had to be observed, suffering the pangs of hunger, nothing but bread and water, and with that tempting vision of lamb stew before his eyes. A life of sacrifice always comes to the same thing, whether it be that of a novice, a shop assistant, or a conscript.

There are many roads but sometimes they repeat themselves. Departing from St Joseph of Ribamar, the novices travelled in the direction of Queluz, then to Belas and Sabugo, stopped to rest for a while in Morelena, where they patched up the sores on their aching feet in the local infirmary, and then, suffering twice as much pain as they resumed their journey, they gradually got used to this new torment as they headed for Pêro Pinheiro, the worst stretch of all, because the road was strewn with marble chips. Farther ahead, as they made their descent to Cheleiros, they saw a wooden cross at the roadside, a clear sign that someone had died there, probably the victim of a crime and whether this was the case or not, one should always say a paternoster for the repose of the dead person's soul, the friars and novices knelt down and prayed together, God bless them, for it is a supreme act of charity to pray for a person one does not even know, and as they knelt there, you could see the soles of their feet, which were in such a pitiful state, covered in blood and grime, clearly the most vulnerable part of the human body, and turned toward a heaven they would never tread. Having finished their paternoster, the novices descended into the valley and crossed the bridge, once more absorbed in reading their breviaries, they had no eyes for the woman at her front door, nor did they hear her mutter, Cursed be all friars.

Fate, that agent of good and evil, ordained that the statues should come face to face with the novices where the road from Cheleiros joins up with the one from Alcainça Pequena, and this fortuitous omen was seen as an occasion for much rejoicing on the part of the congregation. The friars moved up to the front of the convoy of carts and acted as scouts and exorcists, intoning sonorous litanies as they went but raising no cross, for they had none, even though the liturgy required that it be held aloft. And so they entered Mafra to a triumphant welcome, tortured by the pain in their feet and transported by a faith that makes them look delirious, or could it be hunger, for since leaving St Joseph of Ribamar, they have had nothing to eat except stale bread softened in water from some well or other, but they are hoping for some respite at the hospice where they will spend the day, they can hardly take another step, like bonfires whose flames are reduced to ashes, their elation has given way to melancholy. They even missed seeing the statues being unloaded. The engineers and manual labourers arrived armed with windlasses, pulleys, hoists, cables, pads, wedges, and chocks, treacherous implements that easily slip and cause serious accidents, which explains why the woman from Cheleiros muttered, Cursed be all friars, and with much sweating and gnashing of teeth, the statues were eventually unloaded and set upright in the form of a circle, facing inwards, they look as if they are taking part in some reunion or game, between St Vincent and St Sebastian stand St Isabel, St Clare, and

St Teresa, the latter look like midgets by comparison, but women should not be measured in spans, even when they are not saints.

Baltasar goes down into the valley and makes for home, it is true there is still work to be done before the convent is finished, but since he has had such a long and arduous journey, having come all the way from Santo António do Tojal, remember, in a single day, he is entitled to stop earlier, once the oxen have been unyoked and fed. There are moments when time appears to be slow in passing, like a swallow building its nest in the eaves, it enters and leaves, comes and goes, but always within sight, and both we and the swallow might think that we are bound to go on like this for all eternity, or at least half of it, which would be no bad thing. But suddenly the swallow is there, then gone, it is no longer there, yet I saw it a moment ago, so where can it have disappeared to, as when we look into the mirror and think, Dear God, how time has passed, how I have aged, only yesterday I was the darling of the neighbourhood, and now both darling and neighbourhood are in decline. Baltasar possesses no mirrors, save for these eyes of ours, which watch him descend that mud track leading to the town, and it is they that tell him, Your beard is full of white hairs, Baltasar, your forehead is covered with wrinkles, Baltasar, your neck has become scraggy, Baltasar, your shoulders are beginning to droop, Baltasar, you are a shadow of your former self, Baltasar, but surely this is a question of our failing eyesight, because it is a woman, in fact, who is coming towards us, and where we saw an old man, she sees a young man, who is none other than the soldier whom she once asked, What is your name, perhaps it is not even him she sees but simply this dirty, white-haired, one-handed man, nicknamed Sete-Sóis, coming down the mud track, who, despite his haggard look, is a constant sun in this woman's life, not because he always shines, but because he is so forcefully alive, hidden by clouds and screened by eclipses, but alive, dear God, as arms are outstretched, Whose arms, you may ask, Why, his to her and hers to him, this ageing couple are the scandal of the town of Mafra as they hug each other in the public square, but perhaps because they have never had any children they still think of themselves as being younger than they are, poor deluded creatures, or perhaps they are the only two human beings who see themselves as they really are, which is the most difficult thing of all, and now watching them together, even we can perceive that they have suddenly become physically transformed.

During supper, Álvaro Diogo reveals that the statues must remain where they have been unloaded, for there is no time to set them in their respective niches, the consecration is due to take place on Sunday, and, however carefully they plan or hard they work, there is simply not enough time to put the finishing touches to the basilica, the sacristy has been completed, but the vaults still have to be plastered, and since they look bare it has been decided that they should be covered with hessian dipped in gesso to create the illusion that they have already been plastered and whitewashed, in this way the overall effect will be much more impressive, and even the absence of the dome will scarcely be noticed. Álvaro Diogo knows a great deal about these details, having been promoted from mason to stonecutter, then from stonecutter to carver, and he is held in esteem by his masters and foremen, for he is invariably punctual, hardworking, and reliable, and as capable with his hands as he is willing to please, in no sense can he be compared to the rabble of drovers who disobey orders on the slightest pretext, smell of dung and sweat, while he is covered in marble dust which whitens one's hands and beard and sticks to a man's clothing for the rest of his life. As in the case of Álvaro Diogo, and precisely for the rest of his brief life, because shortly he will fall from a wall that he need never have climbed, since it was not part of his job, to straighten a stone which he himself had dressed and therefore must surely have been cut properly. He will fall to his death from a height of almost thirty metres, and Inês Antónia, who at this moment is so proud of the favourable position her husband holds, will soon turn into a sorrowing widow who will live in fear lest her son meet a similar fate, the afflictions of the poor are never-ending. Álvaro Diogo also informs them that, prior to the consecration of the convent, the novices will be moved to two wings that have already been built over the kitchens, and this piece of news led Baltasar to point out that, since the plaster was still damp and the weather so cold, there was every likelihood of illness among the friars, whereupon Álvaro Diogo replied that there were braziers already burning night and day in the cells that had been completed, but even so, water was running down the walls, And what about the statues of

[314]

the saints, Baltasar, were they difficult to transport, Not really, the greatest problem was actually loading them, but, with know-how and brute force as well as the patience of the oxen, we finally made it. Their conversation waned as the fire turned to embers in the hearth, Álvaro Diogo and Inês Antónia retired to bed, and we shall say nothing of Gabriel, who was already dozing off as he chewed his last mouthful of food, then Baltasar asked, Would you like to go to see the statues, Blimunda, the sky ought to be clear, and the moon will be up soon, Let's go, she replied.

The night was clear and cold. While they were climbing the slope to the Alto da Vela the moon appeared, enormous and blood-red, outlining first the bell towers, then the irregular projections of the upper walls, and in the distance the crest of the mountain that had been the cause of so much labour and cost so much gunpowder. Baltasar told Blimunda, Tomorrow I'm off to Monte Junto to see how the machine is faring, six months have passed since I was last there, and who knows what I shall find, I'll go with you, It's scarcely worth it, I'm leaving early, and if there's not much to repair, I shall be back before nightfall, I'd better go now, for later there will be festivities to mark the consecration, and if the rain persists the roads will be much worse, Be careful, Don't worry, I shall not be attacked by thieves or savaged by wolves, I'm not speaking about thieves or wolves, About what, then, I'm speaking about the machine, Stop fussing, woman, I shall go and come straight back, you can't ask more than that, Promise me you'll be careful, Don't fret, woman, my time has not yet come, I cannot help fretting, husband, for our time comes sooner or later.

They had walked up to the large square in front of the church, a massive structure that appeared to burgeon from the earth and rise into mid-air as if quite separate from the other buildings. Of the future palace there was nothing but the ground floor, and on either side stood wooden constructions where the religious ceremonies were to be held. It seems incredible that thirteen years of constant toil should have produced so little, the church unfinished, the convent rising to the second floor on two wings of the projected building, but the rest barely to the height of the doorways, and only forty cells ready for occupation whereas three hundred are needed. So little appears to have been achieved, yet it is a great deal, perhaps even too much. An ant advances across the threshing floor and seizes a beard of corn. From there to the ant-hill is a distance of ten metres, less than twenty paces if covered by a man. However, it is not a man making this journey but an ant. Now, the unfortunate thing about this construction at Mafra is that the work is being done by men rather than by giants, and if with this and similar projects, both in the past and the future, the idea is to prove that men are capable of doing the work of giants, then one must accept that it will take them as long as it takes the ant to cross the threshing floor, everything must be seen in its proper perspective, whether it be ant-hills or convents, a foundation stone or a beard of corn.

Baltasar and Blimunda enter the circle of the statues. The moon shines directly on the two large effigies of St Sebastian and St Vincent and the three saints set between them, then the forms and faces ranged on either side are cast in encroaching shadows until total darkness conceals the statues of St Dominic and St Ignatius, a grave injustice since St Francis of Assisi has already been cast into total darkness, when he deserves to be illumined at the feet of his St Clare, not that any hint of carnal union is intended here, and even if it were, what harm would be done, this does not prevent people from becoming saints, and it does help make saints more human. Blimunda inspects the statues at length and tries to establish the identity of each saint, some she recognises at a glance, others she identifies after much thought, while still others baffle her completely. She is aware that those letters and markings on the base of the statue of St Vincent clearly indicate the saint's name for anyone who is capable of reading them. With her finger she traces out the curves and the straight lines like a blind man who is still trying to cope with Braille, Blimunda cannot ask the statue, Who are you, the blind man cannot ask the page in front of him, What are you saying, only Baltasar was able to answer, I am called Baltasar Mateus, alias Sete-Sóis, on the fateful day when Blimunda had asked him, What is your name. Everything in this world can volunteer some reply, what takes up time is posing the questions. A solitary cloud wafted in from the sea, alone in that vast expanse of clear sky, and for one long minute it covered the moon. The statues were transformed into amorphous spectres, without form or feature, like blocks of marble before they take shape under the sculptor's chisel. They are no longer saints but simply primitive relics without voice or design, as diffuse in their solidity as that of the man and woman in their midst who dissolve in the shadows, for the latter are not made of marble but merely living matter, and, as we know, nothing merges more readily with its shadow on the ground than human flesh. Beneath the enormous cloud that was slowly drifting past one could distinguish more clearly the glow of the bonfires that accompanied the vigil of the soldiers. In the distance, the Ilha da Madeira was a blurred mass, a huge dragon in repose, snorting through forty thousand nostrils, so many men sleeping there as well as the paupers from the hospices where there is not a bed to spare unless the nurses shift some of the corpses, the one whose internal ulcers burst, the one who bled from the mouth, and this one who was left paralysed after an apoplectic stroke and died when it recurred. The cloud retreated inland, which is another way of saying away from the sea, towards the interior of the country, although we can never be sure what a cloud is doing once we take our eyes away or it hides behind that mountain, it might have gone underground or settled on the surface of the earth in order to fertilise who knows what strange existences and rare powers, Baltasar said, Let's go home, Blimunda.

They left the circle of statues, which were once more bathed in light, and just as they were about to descend into the valley, Blimunda looked back. The statues glistened like crystallised salt. By listening attentively one could hear the sound of conversation from that direction, some council perhaps, or debate or tribunal, probably their first since they had been shipped from Italy, travelling in damp, rat-infested holds or brutally tied down on the decks, and probably the last conversation they would ever enjoy like this under the moonlight, for soon the statues will be placed inside their niches, where some of them will no longer be able to face one another but will only be able to look sideways, while others will go on looking up at the sky, as if they were being punished. Blimunda said, The saints must be unhappy, as they were made, so they remain, and if this is sanctity, what must damnation be like, They're only statues, I'd like them to come down from those plinths and be human like us, for you can't hold a conversation with a statue, Perhaps they speak to one another when they're alone,

That's something we don't know, but if they speak only to each other, and without witnesses, I can't help asking myself why we need them, I've always heard it said that the saints are necessary for our salvation, They didn't save themselves, Who told you that, That's what I feel deep inside me, What do you feel deep inside you, That no one is saved, and no one is lost, It's sinful to think such things, Sin doesn't exist, there is only death and life, Life comes before death, You're deceiving yourself, Baltasar, for death comes before life, who we were has died, who we are is being born, and that's why we do not die all at once, And when we go under the earth, and when Francisco Marques is crushed beneath the cart carrying the stone, is that not death without recourse, If we're talking about Francisco Marques, he is born, But he doesn't know it, Just as we don't really know who we are, yet we are alive, Blimunda, where did you learn these things, My eyes were open when I was still inside my mother's womb, and from there I saw everything.

They entered the yard. The moon was already the colour of milk. More clearly defined than if they had been outlined by the sun, the shadows were black and impenetrable. There was an old hut covered in withered bulrushes where in happier times a donkey could rest from the chore of fetching and carrying. It was known as the donkey's hut, although its occupant had died many years ago, so many that even Baltasar could no longer remember, I used to ride that donkey, no, I didn't, and whenever he vacillated in this way or said, I'll store my rake in the donkey's hut, he was agreeing with Blimunda, it was as if he were seeing the beast standing there before him with its baskets and pack saddle, and were hearing his mother call out from the kitchen, Go help your father unload, he could not offer much help, for he was still a little boy, but as he grew up he gradually got used to heavy work, and since every endeavour brings its rewards, his father would lift him on to the donkey, which was damp with sweat, and take him for a little ride around the yard, and in the end I looked upon that donkey as if it were mine. Blimunda led him inside the hut, it was not the first time that they had gone in there at night, sometimes to please him, sometimes to please her, they went there when they could no longer repress their urgent need, when they could no longer resist giving way to passion with moans and cries likely to provoke a scandal when compared with the discreet embraces of Álvaro Diogo and Inês Antónia and the anguished restlessness of their nephew, Gabriel, who was driven to relieve himself by sinful means. The huge, old-fashioned manger, which had once been attached to supports at a convenient height from the ground, was now lying on the floor, badly cracked but as comfortable as a royal couch once furnished with straw and two old blankets. Álvaro Diogo and Inês Antónia knew what took place there but said nothing. They themselves felt no desire to experience such novelties, being tranquil creatures whose sexual needs were modest, only Gabriel will come here for amorous encounters after their fortunes have altered, which will be sooner than anyone imagines. Save perhaps someone like Blimunda, not because she pulled Baltasar towards the hut for, after all, she was always the sort of woman who made the first move, uttered the first word, and made the first gesture but because of a sudden anxiety that catches at the throat, because of the violence with which she embraces Baltasar, because of her eagerness to kiss him, poor mouths, their bloom gone, with some teeth missing and others broken, but in the end it is love that prevails.

Contrary to their custom, they spent the night there. When dawn broke, Baltasar announced, I am going to Monte Junto, and Blimunda got up and went into the house, the kitchen was plunged in semi-darkness as she rummaged and eventually found some food, her in-laws and nephew were still asleep when she left, closing the door behind her, she also brought Baltasar's knapsack, into which she packed the food and his tools, taking care not to forget the spike, for no one can be certain of avoiding some evil encounter. They left together, and Blimunda accompanied him until they were outside the town, in the distance, the white towers of the church were visible against the clouds in the sky, quite unexpected after such a clear night. They embraced each other sheltered by the branches of a tree and the burnished leaves of autumn, while treading those that had fallen until they merged with the soil, thus providing nourishment for another verdant spring. This is not Oriana in courtly dress bidding Amadis farewell, or Romeo gathering Juliet's kiss as he descends from her balcony, it is only Baltasar on his way to Monte Junto to repair the ravages of time, it is only

Blimunda trying in vain to arrest the fleeting hours. In their dark clothing they look like two restless shadows, no sooner do they part than they come together, who can tell what these two perceive, or what new intrigues they are preparing, perhaps it will all turn out to be illusory, the fruit of a certain time and a certain place, for we know that happiness is short-lived, that we fail to cherish it when it is within our grasp and value it only when it has vanished forever, Don't stay away too long, Baltasar, You must sleep in the hut, it will probably be dusk by the time I get back, but if there are many repairs to be done, don't expect me before tomorrow, Of course, Farewell, Blimunda, Farewell, Baltasar.

There is little point in narrating journeys that have already been described. Enough has been said about the considerable changes in those who made those journeys, and as for the locations and settings, one need only observe that men and seasons pass, the former in gradual stages, as that house, roof, plot of land, wall, palace, bridge, convent, carriage, street, and mill, the latter more abruptly, as if never to return, spring, summer, autumn as at present, then winter, which is fast approaching. Baltasar knows these roads like the palm of his right hand. He rests on the riverbank at Pedrulhos, where he once relaxed with Blimunda in a season of flowers, of marigolds in the woodlands, of poppies in the cornfields and muted colours in the copses. Along the route he meets people making their way down to Mafra, throngs of men and women who roll drums both large and small and play the bagpipes, sometimes accompanied by a priest or a friar and often by a cripple on crutches, could this be the day of consecration, marked by one or more miracles, one can never tell when God may decide to apply His remedies, which helps explain why the blind, the lame, and the paralytic walk in perpetual pilgrimage, Will Our Lord appear today, perhaps I have deceived myself with this false hope, probably I shall make the journey to Mafra only to discover that it is the Lord's day for resting, or that He has sent His Mother to Our Lady of the Cape, it is impossible to fathom this distribution of powers, but in the end our faith will save us, Save us from what, Blimunda would inquire.

Early that afternoon, Baltasar reached the foothills of the Serra do Barregudo. In the background towered Monte Junto, bright in the sunlight, which had just emerged from clouds. Shadows flitted over the sierra like great nocturnal beasts roving the hills and creasing them as they went, until the sun brought warmth to the trees and was reflected in the puddles. The wind beat against the stationary vanes of the windmills and whistled in the clay pots, these are details observed by those who stroll without care in the world, who are content just to stroll and contemplate that cloud in the sky, the sun as it begins to set, the wind that blows up here only to die down over there, the leaf shaken from its branch or dropping to the ground when it withers, that an old and cruel soldier has eyes for such details, a soldier who has a man's death on his conscience, a crime perhaps redeemed by other episodes in his life, such as to have been marked with a cross signed in blood over his heart, and has perceived how huge the world is and how small all that inhabits it, and speaks to his oxen in a low and gentle voice, this may seem little, but someone will know if it is enough.

Baltasar was already tackling the rugged slopes of Monte Junto and searching out amid the undergrowth the almost invisible path that would lead him to the flying machine, he invariably feels tense as he approaches the spot, afraid that someone might have discovered its presence, that it might have been damaged or even been stolen, and with every visit he is surprised to find it sitting there as if it had just landed, still vibrating after its rapid descent as it nestles in shrubs and wondrous creepers, truly wondrous, because this is not their natural habitat. The flying machine has not been stolen or damaged, it stands in the very same spot, its wings sagging, its birdlike neck entangled with the tallest branches, its dark head like a nest suspended in mid-air. Baltasar drew near, threw his knapsack to the ground, and sat down to rest a while before setting to work. He ate two fried sardines on a slice of bread, using the tip and the blade of the knife with the dexterity of someone carving ivory miniatures, when he had finished, he cleaned the blade on the grass, wiped his hand on his breeches, and went up to the machine. The sun was fierce, the heat stifling. Climbing on to the wing and treading carefully so as not to disturb the camouflage of willow canes, Baltasar entered the Passarola. Some of the timber planks on deck had rotted. He would have to fetch the necessary materials and stay here several days to replace them, or, and only now did he think of this, he would have to dismantle the machine section by section, take the pieces back to Mafra, and conceal them under some haystack or in an underground passage of the convent, provided he could enlist the help of a few close friends by confiding part of his secret, he was amazed that he had not thought of this solution before, when he got back home, he would talk to Blimunda. Lost in thought, he scarcely noticed where he was putting his feet, suddenly two planks gave way and caved in. He made a desperate attempt to break his fall, causing the hook attached to his arm to get caught in the metal ring used to tie back the sails, hanging there in mid-air, Baltasar watched the sails slip away to one side with a resounding thud, Sunlight flooded into the machine, the amber balls and globes started to gleam. The machine turned on itself twice, broke free of the surrounding shrubs, and rose into the air. There was not a cloud to be seen in the sky.

BLIMUNDA DID NOT sleep that night. She settled down to wait for Baltasar's return at dusk, as on other occasions, fully expecting to see him at any moment, she set out to meet him and walked almost half a league along the road that he would travel, and for some considerable time, until the twilight closed in, she sat by the side of the road watching the pilgrims pass on their way to the consecration ceremonies at Mafra, for this was an event not to be missed, there would certainly be food and alms for everyone who turned up, or at least there would be plenty for those who were most alert and insistent, for if the soul needs to be satisfied, the same is true of the body. Seeing that woman seated by the roadside, some ruffians who had come from distant parts thought that this must be how the town of Mafra welcomed male visitors, with all comforts provided, and they began making lewd remarks which they soon swallowed when confronted by that forbidding stare. One fellow who was bold enough to attempt further advances withdrew in terror when Blimunda warned him in a low voice, I spit upon the toad in your heart, upon you, and your children. When dusk had finally settled, there were no more pilgrims, Baltasar is unlikely to turn up at this late hour, or he will arrive so late that he will find me in bed, or, if he has found there are many repairs needing to be done, he might postpone his departure until tomorrow after all. Blimunda went back to the house and sat down to supper with her in-laws and nephew, So Baltasar hasn't turned up, one of them commented, I'll never understand these trips of his, the other rejoined, Gabriel remained silent, for he is still far too young to speak up in the presence of his elders, but he was thinking to himself that his parents had no right to meddle in the affairs of his uncle and aunt, one half of the human race is obsessively curious about the other half, while the latter are just as curious about them, and for a child of his age, this boy is already quite shrewd. After supper, Blimunda waited until everyone had retired to bed before going out into the yard. The night was peaceful, the sky clear, the coolness of the night air barely perceptible. Perhaps at that very moment Baltasar was walking along the river at Pedrulhos, with the spike attached to his left arm instead of the hook, for no one can avoid evil encounters, as we have already had occasion to observe and verify. The moon is shining, which will help Baltasar see the road more clearly, soon we shall almost certainly hear his footsteps, in the cautioning silence of night, he will push open the yard gate, and Blimunda will be waiting there to greet him, the rest we shall not see, because discretion forbids it, and all we need to know is that this woman is haunted by a sense of foreboding.

She has not slept all night. Lying in the manger and wrapped in blankets, which smell of human sweat and sheep's dung, she opened her eyes and looked toward the chinks in the thatching, where the moonlight came filtering through, the moon began to wane, dawn was about to break, and the night had scarcely had time to settle. Blimunda got up with the first glimpse of light and went into the kitchen to find some food, she feels so uneasy, despite Baltasar's warning that he might be delayed, perhaps he will get back around midday, there were lots of repairs on the machine, so old, and exposed to all that wind and rain. Blimunda cannot hear us, for she has already left the house and is walking the familiar route that Baltasar must follow, there is no risk of their missing each other. One person, however, whom they will both miss meeting will be the King when he enters the town of Mafra that same afternoon, accompanied by the Prince Dom José and the Infante Dom António, as well as by all the servants of the royal household, with all due pomp and ceremony, opulent coaches drawn by prancing horses, everything in perfect array as the procession comes into sight, wheels turning, hooves stamping, an amazing sight such as has never been seen before. Royal pomp and ceremony we have experienced elsewhere, and we are aware of the distinctions, a little more brocade here, a little less brocade there, a little more gold here, a little less gold there, but our concern is to follow that woman who asks everyone she meets whether they have seen a man with such-and-such characteristics, the most handsome man in the world, and from this false description it is clear that one cannot always express one's true feelings, who would ever recognise the swarthy, grizzled, one-handed Baltasar from such a description, No, good woman, they tell her, we have not seen him, and Blimunda walks on, now remote from the main roads and taking short cuts, as when they made the journey together, she passes that same mountain, that same wood, those four boulders in a row, those six hills forming a circle, it is getting late and there still is no sign of Baltasar. Blimunda did not pause to eat but chewed some food as she continued walking, but after a sleepless night, she felt exhausted, anxiety is sapping her energies as the food churns in her mouth, and Monte Junto, which can already be seen in the distance, gives the impression of receding, what phenomenon is this. There is no mystery, it is simply the slowness of her progress as she struggles to go on, thinking to herself, At this pace I shall never arrive. There are certain places Blimunda cannot remember having passed, others she suddenly recognises upon seeing a bridge, a merging of slopes, or a meadow set in some valley. She realised that she had already passed this way because at that same door sits that same old woman sewing that same skirt, everything remains unchanged, except Blimunda, who now travels alone.

She recalls that they met a shepherd in these parts who told them that they were in the Serra do Barregudo, beyond stands Monte Junto, which looks just like any other hill, but this was not how she remembered it, perhaps because of its bulge, which makes it look like a miniature of this side of the planet so that one is convinced that the earth is truly round. Now there is neither shepherd nor flock but only a deep silence as Blimunda comes to a halt, only a deep solitude as she looks around her. Monte Junto is so close she has the impression that she need only stretch a hand to touch those foothills, like a woman on her knees who is stretching out an arm to touch her lover's hips. Blimunda was clearly incapable of such subtle thoughts, therefore, we are perhaps not inside these people and cannot tell what they are thinking, all we are doing is putting our own thoughts into the heads of others and then saying, Blimunda thinks, or Baltasar thought, and perhaps we have also imagined them with our own sensations, just as when Blimunda touches her lover's hips and imagines that he has touched hers. She stopped to rest because her legs were trembling, weary after such a long walk and weakened by that imaginary physical contact, but suddenly she felt certain in her heart that she would find Baltasar up there toiling and sweating, perhaps tying the final knots, perhaps slinging his knapsack over one shoulder, perhaps already making his way down into the valley, and this caused her to cry out, Baltasar.

There was no reply, nor could there be, a cry means nothing, it reaches that escarpment and reverberates, a feeble echo that no longer sounds like a human voice. Blimunda began to clamber up rapidly, her strength comes rushing back, she even starts running where the slope diminishes before becoming steep once more, and farther ahead, between two dwarf holm oaks, she can barely perceive the track opened up by Baltasar on the successive journeys, that will lead her to the Passarola. She calls out once more, Baltasar, now he must hear her, for there are no mountains in between, only several hillocks, if she had time to stop, she would surely hear him cry out, Blimunda, she feels so certain that she has heard him call that she smiles and uses her hand to wipe the sweat or tears from her face, or perhaps she is arranging her hair or cleaning her dirty face, that gesture could be interpreted in so many different ways.

There is the place, like the nest of a huge bird that has taken flight. Blimunda's cry, her third, and invoking the same name, was not nearly so loud, a strangled utterance as if the entrails were being ripped from her body by some monstrous claw, Baltasar, and even as she called out his name, she realised that she had known from the start that she would find this place abandoned. Her tears dried at once, as if some scorching wind had blown from the bowels of the earth. She approached by fits and starts, saw the uprooted shrubs and the depression caused by the weight of the flying machine, and on the other side, at a distance of six paces, Baltasar's knapsack lay on the ground. There were no other signs of what might have happened there. Blimunda raised her eyes to the sky, which was now less clear, clouds drifted serenely as the light of day faded, and for the first time she felt the emptiness of space, as if musing, There is nothing beyond, but this was precisely what she refused to believe, Baltasar had to be flying somewhere in that sky and struggling with the sails to make the machine come down. Blimunda looked at the knapsack again and went to retrieve it, she felt the weight of the spike inside and then remembered that if the machine had gone up the previous day, it would have come down at night, so that was why Baltasar was not to be seen in the sky, he must be somewhere on earth, perhaps dead, perhaps alive, but almost certainly injured, for she still remembered how violent their descent had been, although on that occasion the machine had had a heavier load.

She slung the knapsack over her shoulder, there was nothing more to be done there, so she began searching in the vicinity, going up and down the slopes, which were covered with scrub, looking out for vantage points and wishing that her powers of vision were sharper, not the powers she enjoyed when she fasted, but those of the falcon and lynx, which were capable of sighting everything that moved on the surface of the earth. With bleeding feet and her skirt torn by briers and thorns, she went around the northern side of the mountain and then returned to her point of departure in search of a higher level, and it now occurred to her that neither she nor Baltasar had ever reached the summit of Monte Junto, now she must try to get up there before dark, from the top she would have a much wider view, it is true that from a distance the machine would not be all that conspicuous, but sometimes fortune steps in, and perhaps once she was up there she would see Baltasar waving to her with one arm, from beside a fountain where they could both quench their thirst.

Blimunda began to clamber up farther, reproaching herself for not having thought of this sooner, before the evening light began to dim. Unexpectedly, she found a path that went winding up the slope and, higher up, a road wide enough for carts to pass, she was surprised at this discovery, what could there be on the summit of the mountain to have justified opening up this road, it showed every sign of being in use and of having been there for a considerable time, and who knows, perhaps Baltasar had also come across it. Upon turning a bend, Blimunda halted in her tracks. Directly ahead she saw a friar on foot, a Dominican, to judge from his habit, which scarcely disguised his thickset body and bull neck. In her panic, Blimunda hesitated before running or calling out, the friar appeared to have sensed her presence. He halted, looked to one side and the other, and then turned around. He made a gesture as if blessing himself, and waited. Blimunda approached, *Deo gratias,* said the Dominican, and what brings you here, I'm looking for my husband, she replied, without knowing what more she should say, for the friar might think she was demented if she started to talk about a flying machine, to explain about the Passarola and about those dark clouds. She retreated several paces, We hail from Mafra, and my husband came here to Monte Junto because of a huge bird we were told inhabited these parts, I'm afraid the bird may have carried him off, I have never heard anyone, not even the other friars, speak of such a bird, Is there a convent up here on the mountain, Yes, there is, I didn't know. The friar, as if distracted, descended a few paces down the slope. The sun was rapidly setting, clouds had gathered seawards, and the evening sky was turning grey. You haven't by any chance seen a man around here with a hook strapped to the stump of his left arm, Blimunda asked him, Is he your husband, Yes, No, I haven't seen him, And you haven't seen a large bird flying over in that direction, either yesterday or today, No, I haven't seen any large bird, Well, I'd better be off, then, give me your blessing, Father, It's almost dark, you might lose your way if you set out at this hour, or be attacked by the wolves that prowl this region, If I leave at once, I should be able to reach the valley before dark, It's much farther away than it looks from here, listen, near the convent stand the ruins of another convent, which was never finished, you can spend the night there and continue the search for your husband tomorrow, No, I must go, As you wish, but don't forget that I warned you of the dangers, and with these words the friar started to climb back up the wide track.

Blimunda remained standing there, unable to decide what she should do. Up here there was still some light, although the countryside was enveloped in darkness. The clouds dispersed throughout the sky, and a hot, clammy wind began to blow, perhaps there was rain on the way. Blimunda felt so weary that she believed herself capable of dying from sheer exhaustion. She had hardly thought about Baltasar. In her muddled state of mind she was somehow convinced that she would find him next day and that there was little point in searching any further that night. She sat down on a boulder at the side of the road, slipped her hand into the knapsack, and found the remains of Baltasar's provisions, a sardine as dry as a bone and a stale crust of bread. If anyone were to pass at this moment, they would get the shock of their life upon finding seated there a woman who betrayed no fear, almost certainly a witch lying in wait to suck the blood of some traveller or waiting for her cronies, whom she will accompany to a witches' sabbath. In fact, she is simply an unfortunate woman who lost her husband when he vanished into thin air, and though she would cast every conceivable spell in order to get him back, she does not know, alas, any such spell, so she has achieved nothing by seeing what others cannot see, just as she has achieved nothing by gathering wills, for it was those very wills that carried him off.

Night fell. Blimunda rose to her feet. The wind became more chilly and fierce. There was an overpowering sense of helplessness on those slopes, which made her weep, and it was timely that she should unburden herself in that way. The night was full of alarming noises, the screeching of an owl, the rustling of holm oaks, and unless her ears deceived her, a wolf howling in the distance. Blimunda still had enough courage to descend a further hundred paces in the direction of the valley, but it was like slowly lowering herself to the bottom of a well without knowing what gaping jaws might be waiting to swallow her up. Later there would be a moon to show her the way, provided the sky cleared, which would also make her visible to any living creature who might be roving in the mountains, she might frighten some of them off, but others would make her freeze in terror. She came to a sudden halt, covered in goose-pimples. A short distance away, something crept off in haste. She could bear it no longer. She darted up the road as if she were being pursued by all the demons in hell and all the monsters who inhabit the earth, whether real or imagined. As she came round the last bend, she saw the convent, a low, squat building. Pale light filtered through the church windows. There was a deep silence beneath the starry sky, beneath the murmuring clouds, which were so close that Monte Junto might well have been mistaken for the highest mountain in the world. Blimunda approached, she thought she heard prayers being intoned in a low voice, almost certainly those of compline, and as she drew closer the chanting became louder, the voices more sonorous, as the friars prayed to heaven, prayed so humbly that Blimunda began to weep once more, perhaps those friars were unwittingly rescuing Baltasar from the skies or from the perils of the forest, perhaps the magical Latin words were healing the wounds he must surely have sustained, so Blimunda joined in the prayers by mentally reciting the ones she knew that serve for everything, a personal loss, an attack of malaria, some private anxiety, somebody up there must be responsible for sorting out our needs.

On the other side of the convent, in a hollow facing the slope, stood the ruins. There were high walls, vaulted roofs, and recesses that one could visualise as cells, the perfect shelter, where she could spend the night and ward off the cold and wild beasts. Blimunda, still apprehensive, penetrated the dark interior of those ruins, fumbling with her hands and feet as she tried to find her way without falling into a hole. Gradually her eyes grew accustomed to the dark, then the diffused light in this space outlined the openings of the windows and defined the walls. The ground was covered with grass but reasonably tidy. There was an upper floor without any visible access, at least for the present. Blimunda stretched out her cloak in one corner, improvised a pillow with her knapsack, and lay down. The tears came back. Still weeping, she fell asleep, she passed from wakefulness to sleep between two tears, and continued to weep as she slept. This did not last very long. Pushing aside the clouds, the moon appeared. The moonlight penetrated the ruins like a mysterious presence, and Blimunda woke up. She could have sworn that the light of the moon had shaken her gently, had stroked her face or her hand resting on the cloak, but the grating noise she now heard was the same sound she imagined she had heard earlier in her sleep. The noise seemed to draw closer, then recede, as if someone were searching in vain yet reluctant to abandon the search as he retraced his steps, like an animal taking refuge after momentarily losing the scent. Blimunda sat up, rested on her elbows, and listened attentively. She heard wary footsteps, almost inaudible yet alarmingly close. A form passed in front of one of the windows, and the light of the moon outlined a profile that became distorted on the rough surface of the stone wall. Blimunda knew at once that it was the friar she had met on the road. He had told her where she could find shelter and he had come to see whether she had followed his advice, but not out of Christian charity. Blimunda lay back quietly and remained quite still, perhaps he had not seen her, or perhaps he had seen her and said, Rest, poor weary soul, if this were so, it would have been truly miraculous and spiritually uplifting, but it was not so, the friar had come to satisfy his lust, and who could blame him, lost in this desert here on the summit of the world, human existence is so miserable. The form shuts out the moonlight streaming through the window, it is that of a tall burly man, and she can hear him breathing heavily. Blimunda had pushed her knapsack to one side, and when the man knelt down beside her she quickly slipped her hand into the bag and grasped the spike firmly, as if it were a dagger. We already know what is about to happen, it has been decreed ever since that farrier in Évora made the spike and hook, the spike is here in Blimunda's hand, and who can tell where the hook might be. The friar stroked Blimunda's feet and slowly eased her legs apart, her motionless body excited him beyond endurance, perhaps she is awake and welcomes his advances, her skirts have already been pulled back, the friar's habit is already turned up under his belt, his hand reaches out to explore her sex, the woman trembles but makes no other movement, in triumph, the friar thrusts his penis toward that invisible orifice, feels the woman's arms clasp him by the waist, there are great consolations in the life of a Dominican friar. Driven by two hands, the spike embeds itself between his ribs, grazing his heart for a second before plunging deeper, for twenty years the spike has pursued this second death. The cry that had begun to form in the friar's throat became a hoarse death-rattle of short duration. Blimunda writhed in terror, not because she had killed him, but because of that inert body that threatened to crush her beneath its weight. Using her elbows, she pushed his body away with all the strength she could muster, and finally managed to crawl out. The moon lit up a fragment of his white habit and the dark stain, which was rapidly spreading. Blimunda struggled to her feet and listened carefully. All was silent in the ruins, she could hear nothing except her own heart beating. She fumbled on the ground, retrieved her knapsack and the cloak, which had become entangled around one of the friar's legs, and set them down in a spot where there was light. She then returned to the corpse, seized the groove of the spike, and tugged once, then a second time. With the contortion of the body, the spike must have got trapped between two ribs. In despair, Blimunda placed one foot on the man's back and with a sharp pull released the spike. There was a deep gurgle, and the black stain spread like an inundation. Blimunda wiped the spike on the friar's habit and put it in the knapsack, which she threw over one shoulder along with her cloak. Just as she was about to leave, she looked back and noticed that the friar was wearing sandals, so she went back to remove them, a dead man travels barefoot wherever he may go, be it heaven or hell.

In the shadows projected by the walls of the ruins, Blimunda paused to decide which route she should take. She could not risk crossing the square in front of the convent. Someone might see her, perhaps another friar, who had shared the dead man's secret and was waiting for him to return, while no doubt thinking to himself that he must be taking so long because he was thoroughly enjoying himself, Cursed be all friars, muttered Blimunda. Now she had to overcome all those fears, the wolf, which could be sheer fantasy, the mysterious noise of someone prowling in the dark, which she had not imagined after all, the thought of losing herself in the woods before she found the path where she could no longer be seen. She removed her shabby clogs and slipped into the dead man's sandals, which were much too big and flat, although sturdy, she tied the leather thongs around her ankles and set off, making certain that she was screened from the convent by the ruins until she found herself protected by the undergrowth or some hillock or other. She was bathed in the moon's silvery light, then clouds enshrouded her in darkness, but realising that she was no longer afraid, she descended into the valley without further hesitation, and should she encounter ghosts or werewolves, wandering souls or flashes of lightning, she would ward them off with her spike, a much more powerful weapon than any witchcraft or physical onslaught, May the lamp I carry before me illuminate my path.

Blimunda walked all night. She was anxious to be as far away as possible from Monte Junto before dawn, when the community would assemble for matins. Once they discovered that one of the friars was missing they would examine his cell and search the entire convent, the refectory, the chapter house, the library, and the kitchen garden, the abbot would come to the conclusion that he had fled, and there would be endless gossiping in corners, but if one of the friars had been taken into the missing friar's confidence, he would be anxious, perhaps envying the other's good fortune, for she must have been quite a wench to drive him to abandon his habit among the nettles, then the search would be extended beyond the convent walls, and it would probably be broad daylight before they found the corpse, I've had a narrow escape, the friar would think to himself, no longer feeling envious, for after all he is still in the grace of God.

When Blimunda arrived mid-morning at the river-bank at Pedrulhos, she decided to rest a while after her reckless journey. She had thrown away the friar's sandals lest the devil use them to have her exposed, and she had got rid of the clogs because they were beyond repair, now she plunged her legs into the cold water, taking care to examine her clothing for any bloodstains, such as this mark on her torn skirt. She ripped off any tatters and threw them away. Watching the water flow, she asked herself, What now. She had already washed the iron spike, and it was as if she were washing the missing hand of Baltasar, who was also missing, and wandering who knows where. She stepped out of the water, And now what, she asked herself once more. Then suddenly it dawned on her that Baltasar must be waiting for her in Mafra, and she felt certain that she would find him there, they had simply missed each other on the road, the machine had probably flown off on its own, whereupon Baltasar had come away, he must have forgotten to collect his knapsack and cloak before leaving, or perhaps he had panicked and fled, for every man is entitled to his own fears, and now he was probably wondering what he should do next, whether he should wait or set out at once, for that woman was capable of doing something foolish, ah, Blimunda.

Along the road approaching Mafra, Blimunda ran like one possessed, outwardly exhausted after two sleepless nights, inwardly glowing after two nights of battle, she catches up with and overtakes, the pilgrims who are on their way to attend the consecration, and they are coming so thick and fast that Mafra will soon be overcrowded. As far as the eye can reach there are flags and banners and milling crowds, until Sunday the work on the convent will be suspended, all that remains to be done is to put the finishing touches on the decorations. Blimunda heads for home, there stands the Viscounts' Palace, with soldiers from the royal guard on duty at the gates, and carriages and coaches lined up along the road, this is where the King has been lodged. She pushed the yard gate open and called out, Baltasar, but no one appeared. She sat down on the stone step, dejected and close to tears when it suddenly occurred to her that she would be unable to explain how Baltasar's cloak and knapsack came to be in her possession if she were to confess that she had gone to look for Baltasar without finding any trace of him. Barely able to stand up, she struggled as far as the hut and concealed them under a bundle of reeds. Now she could not muster enough strength to go back. She lay down in the manger, and since the body sometimes takes pity on the soul, she was soon fast asleep. Therefore she missed the arrival of the Patriarch from Lisbon, who rode in a truly magnificent coach, with four more coaches in the rear carrying his private retinue, and preceded by a mounted cross-bearer holding the patriarchal crucifix aloft, accompanied by the apparitor of the clergy, followed by the officers of the municipal council, who had set out to receive the King some considerable distance from the town, words cannot describe the splendour of this procession, which gladdened the hearts of the crowds who came to watch, Inês Antónia's eyes almost popped out of her head, Álvaro Diogo looked on gravely, as befitted a stonemason, as for Gabriel, the scoundrel was nowhere to be seen. Blimunda even missed the arrival of more than three hundred Franciscans from various provinces who had come out of obedience to attend the solemn act of consecration and to grace the proceedings, as it were, with their presence, had it been a congregation of Dominicans, one would have been missing. Blimunda was not there to see this parade of the triumphant militia as they marched past four-deep, they had come to make certain that the religious garrison was ready, the artillery range aimed at souls, the arsenal of altar breads, the storehouse of sacraments, the embroidered lettering of the banner, *In hoc signo vinces,* and should that motto fail to secure victory, they would resort to more aggressive tactics.

At this hour Blimunda is asleep, like a stone resting on the ground, and unless someone disturbs her with a foot, she will settle there, and the grass will grow all around her, as tends to happen whenever there is a long vigil.

Late that same afternoon, once the festivities had ended, Álvaro Diogo and his wife returned home, they did not go in through the yard and therefore did not discover Blimunda immediately, but when Inês António went to gather in the hens that were still running loose, she found her sister-in-law, fast asleep but making wild gestures, which was not so surprising since she was murdering a Dominican in her sleep, although Inês António could not be expected to know this. She went into the hut and shook Blimunda by the arm, but did not touch her with her foot, for Blimunda was not a stone to be kicked around, and Blimunda opened her eyes in terror and was baffled by her surroundings, for whereas there was nothing but darkness in her dream, here there was still twilight, and instead of the friar there was this woman, Who can she be, ah, it is Baltasar's sister, And where is Baltasar, asks Inês António, the very same words Blimunda was asking to herself, what reply could she give, she struggled to her feet, aching in every limb, a friar had died one hundred times, only to resuscitate one hundred times, Baltasar cannot come just yet, and to say this is to say nothing, the question is not whether he can or cannot come, the question is that he is not coming because he is thinking of staying on as a farm steward in Turcifal, every explanation is valid as long as it is accepted, sometimes even indifference can be useful, as in the case of Inês António, who feels little affection for her brother and, when she inquires about him, it is merely out of curiosity and little else.

During supper, Álvaro Diogo, after having expressed his surprise that Baltasar had not yet returned after three days, gave them a full account of those who had arrived or were expected to arrive for the consecration, the Queen and the Princess Dona Mariana Vitória had remained in Belas, because there was no suitable accommodation in Mafra, and for the same reason the Infante Dom Francisco had gone to Ericeira, but what gives Álvaro Diogo the greatest satisfaction of all, in a manner of speaking, is that he should breathe the same air as the King, the Prince Dom José, and the Infante Dom António, who are lodged immediately opposite in the Viscounts' Palace, as we sit down to supper, they sit down to supper, each family on its own side of the road, Say, neighbour, can you spare me some parsley. The Cardinals Cunha and Mota had already arrived and the Bishops of Leiria and Portalegre, of Pará and Nanking, who are not there, but are here, and members of the court are arriving, and an endless train of nobles, God willing, Baltasar should be here on Sunday to attend the ceremony, Inês Antónia declared, as if she felt it was expected of her, He'll be here, murmured Blimunda.

That night she slept in the house. She forgot to eat her bread before getting up, and when she entered the kitchen she saw two diaphanous ghosts that were suddenly transformed into bundles of entrails and clusters of white bones, it was the nausea of life itself, and she felt like vomiting, she looked away in haste and began to chew her bread, whereupon Inês Antónia let out a roar of laughter, though without meaning to give offence, Don't tell me you're pregnant after all these years, innocent words that only intensified Blimunda's sorrow, Now not even if I wanted to be pregnant, she thought to herself, as she suppressed her inner cries of despair. This was the day on which they blessed the crosses, the paintings in the chapels, the vestments and other sacred objects pertaining to the sacraments, and then the convent and all the outbuildings. The crowds were kept at a distance, Blimunda did not even get around to leaving the house and had to be content with a glimpse of the King accompanied by the Prince and Infante getting into his coach, he was on the way to meet the Queen and the Princesses, and that night Álvaro Diogo described the spectacle as best he could.

At last the most glorious day of all arrived, the immortal date of the twenty-second of October in the year of grace seventeen hundred and thirty, when King Dom João V celebrates his forty-first birthday and attends the consecration of the most prodigious monument ever to have been built in Portugal, and only the short-sighted will argue that it is still unfinished. So many wonders defy description, Álvaro Diogo has not yet seen everything, and Inês Antónia became terribly confused, Blimunda accompanied them, because it would have looked bad to refuse, but she could not tell whether she was dreaming or awake. They set off at four o'clock in the morning to be sure of having a good view in the square, at five o'clock the troops assembled and torches were alight wherever one looked, then dawn began to break, a fine day, to be sure, for God looks after His estates, now the splendid patriarchal throne can be seen on the left-hand side of the portico, with matching chairs and canopy in crimson velvet trimmed with gold, and precious rugs on the floor, perfect in every detail and resting on a credence are the silver bowl and aspergillum along with all the other liturgical objects required for the service, the solemn procession has already formed and will circle the entire church, the King at its head, followed by the Infantes and nobility in order of rank and precedence, but the main protagonist is the Patriarch himself, who blesses the salt and the water, sprinkles holy water on the walls, though probably not enough, otherwise Álvaro Diogo would not fall from a height of thirty metres several months later, and then he taps three times with his crozier on the main door, which was closed, at the third stroke, God's sacred number, the door opened and the procession entered, and we regret that Álvaro Diogo and Inês Antónia were unable to get into the church, and Blimunda too, accompanying them with reluctance, where they could have witnessed the solemnities, some of which were truly sublime, others deeply moving, some compelled one to prostrate oneself, while others uplifted the soul, such as when the Patriarch used the tip of his crozier to write characters in Greek and Latin on piles of ashes set on the church floor, it sounds more like witchcraft, I inscribe and divide you, than a canonical rite, and the same is true of all that freemasonry that is standing over there, gold dust, incense, more ashes, salt, white wine in a silver carafe, lime and powdered stone on a tray, a silver spoon, a golden shell, and heaven knows what else. There is no lack of hieroglyphics, scribblings, toings, and froings, back and forth, holy oils, blessings, the relics of the twelve apostles, twelve of them, and this took up the entire morning and the greater part of the after-noon, and it was five o'clock when the Patriarch began to celebrate the pontifical High Mass, which, needless to say, took some considerable time, the service finally ended, and the Patriarch then came out on to the balcony for the Benediction, and blessed the people waiting outside, some seventy or eighty thousand people, who with a great flurry of gestures and rustling of garments fell to their knees, a moment I shall never forget as long as I live, Dom Tomás de Almeida, up there on the pulpit, recites the words of blessing, anyone with good eyesight can see those lips moving, but no one can possibly hear what he is saying, and if those ceremonies were being enacted today, electronic fanfares would resound throughout the world, the papal blessing *urbi et orbi,* the true voice of Jehovah, who would have to wait thousands of years to be heard, but the wise man contents himself with what he has, until such time as he invents something better, that is why there is such great rejoicing in the town of Mafra among the pilgrims who have gathered there, well satisfied with those measured gestures as the Patriarch moves his right hand up and down and from left to right, with that sparkling ring, that resplendent gilt and purple, the snow-white linen, the resounding thud of the crozier against the stone that came from Pêro Pinheiro, as you will recall, Behold the blood spurting from the stone, a miracle, a miracle, a miracle, as the wedge is finally removed and the pastor withdraws with his entourage and the flock rises to its feet, the festivities will go on, solemnities to mark the consecration for eight days, and this is only the first.

Blimunda told her in-laws, I'm coming straight back. She made her way down the slope to the deserted town. In their haste, some of the town's inhabitants had left their doors and shutters open. The fires were spent. Blimunda entered the shed to retrieve the cloak and the knapsack. Then she went into the house and collected some provisions, a wooden bowl, a spoon, some clothing for herself and for Baltasar. She packed everything into the knapsack and left. It was already growing dark, but she no longer feared the night, for there was no greater night than her inner darkness.

FOR NINE LONG years, Blimunda searched for Baltasar. She came to know every road and track from the dust and mud, the sandy soil and treacherous stones, experienced many severe frosts and two blizzards, which she survived only because she had no intention of dying just yet. In summer she was blackened by the sun like a log drawn from the fire before it turns to ashes, and her skin wrinkled like that of a parched fruit, she was a scarecrow amid cornfields, a ghostly presence amongst the villagers, an awesome vision in tiny hamlets and abandoned settlements. Wherever she arrived, she inquired if anyone had seen a man with his left hand missing, as tall as any soldier from the royal guard, with a full beard already turning grey but, should he have shaved it off in the meantime, a face not easily forgotten, At least I haven't forgotten it, and he could be travelling along the common highways or along paths crossing the countryside, just as he might have fallen from the sky in a bird made of iron and wicker with a black sail, balls of yellow amber, and two globes in base metal that contain the greatest secret in the world, even if nothing should be left of all this except the remains of the man and the bird, lead me to them, for I need only touch them in order to know who they are. People thought that she must be mad, but if she lingered there for any time they found her so rational in everything else she said and did that they began to doubt their initial impression that she was unsound of mind. She soon became known from one province to the next, so that her reputation often preceded her and they called her the Flying Woman on account of the strange tale she told. She would sit in doorways conversing with the women, who confided their grievances and woes, less frequently their joys, which were all too few, besides, joys are better kept to oneself, lest they be lost. Wherever she passed, there remained a ferment of disquiet, the men did not recognise their womenfolk, who suddenly began to stare at them, sorry that they, too, had not disappeared so that they, too, might go in search of them. But these same men asked, Has she already gone, with an inexplicable sorrow in their heart, and if the women replied, She is still wandering about, the men went out again in the hope of finding her in that wood, or in those ripe cornfields, bathing her feet in the river or stripping behind a canebrake, it did not matter which, because they could do no more than feast their eyes on her body, for between the hand and the fruit there was an iron spike, but fortunately, nobody else was to die. Blimunda never entered a church if there were people inside, otherwise she would rest a while, seated on the floor and leaning against a pillar say, I just came in for a moment, I'm off now, for this is not my house. Priests, upon hearing people speak of her, sent messages urging Blimunda to come and be confessed, anxious to probe the mysteries surrounding this wandering pilgrim, to know what secrets were lurking in that inscrutable face, in those expressionless eyes, which rarely closed and which at certain moments, under a certain light, gave the impression of lakes where the shadows cast by clouds hovered. She sent word back to the priests that she would accept their offer whenever she had some sin to confess, no reply could have provoked a greater scandal, since we are all sinners, but when she discussed this matter with other women, she often gave them food for thought, after all, what are these sins of ours, of yours, of mine, if we women are truly the lamb that will take away the sins of the world, the day when this message is understood, it will be necessary to start everything anew. But her experiences along the way were not always in this vein, sometimes she was stoned and mocked, and in one village where she was subjected to abuse, she worked such a miracle that they almost took her for a saint, for it so happened that there was a serious drought in this locality, because all the fountains were exhausted and the wells had dried up, and Blimunda, after having been driven out of the village, roved the outskirts using her fasting and powers of vision, and the following night, when the inhabitants were asleep, she stole back into the village and, standing in the middle of the public square, called out that in such-and-such a place, at such-and-such a depth, there flowed a rivulet of pure water which she herself had seen, and this explains why she was given the name Eyes of Water, the first eyes to bathe therein. She also encountered eyes capable of generating water, many such eyes, and when she said that she had come from Mafra, women asked her if she had known a man there with such-and-such a name with such-and-such physical characteristics, for he was my husband, my father, my brother, my son, my betrothed, and he was dragged off to work on the convent by order of the King, and I never saw him again for he never returned, he must have died there, or perhaps got lost on the way, for nobody has ever been able to give me any news of him, his family has lost its breadwinner and his land has been neglected, or he might have been carried off by the devil, but I already have another man, for that is one animal that never fails to appear if a woman allows him into her lair, if you get my meaning. Blimunda passed through Mafra and heard from Inês Antónia how Álvaro Diogo had met his death, but there was nothing to suggest that Baltasar had died, or, for that matter, that he was still alive.

Blimunda searched for nine long years. She started off counting the seasons, until they lost any meaning. At the outset, she also tried to calculate the number of leagues she walked each day, four, five, sometimes six, but she soon began to get muddled, and there came a point when space and time ceased to matter, she then began appraising everything in terms of morning, afternoon, night, rain, the midday sun, hail, fog, and mist, deciding whether the road was good or bad, whether the slope went up or down, whether this was plain, mountain, seashore, or river-bank, and then there were those faces, thousands upon thousands of faces, countless faces, which exceeded by far those that had gathered in Mafra, and among the faces those of the women, which invited questions, those of the men, which might provide the answers, and among the latter neither the very young nor the very old, but a man who was forty-five years old when we left him yonder in Monte Junto, that day he went up into the sky, and in order to work out how old he is now, we only need to add one year at a time, for every month add on so many wrinkles, for each day so many white hairs. How often Blimunda imagined herself seated in some village square begging alms, and a man coming up to her who, instead of offering alms, would extend his iron hook, whereupon she would put her hand into her knapsack and bring out a spike forged at the same anvil, the symbol of her constancy and vigil, And so I've found you, Blimunda, And I've found you, Baltasar, Where have you been all these years and what things and misfortunes have befallen you, First tell me about yourself, for it was you who was lost, Let me tell you what happened, and there they would remain, conversing until the end of time.

Blimunda walked thousands of leagues, nearly always barefoot. The soles of her feet became hard and scarred like the bark of a tree. Those feet walked the length and breadth of Portugal, on several occasions they even crossed the Spanish border, because Blimunda failed to notice any line on the ground dividing this territory here from that territory there, she simply heard a foreign language being spoken and turned back. In the space of two years she travelled from the beaches and rocks of the ocean to the frontier, then explored other places and different routes, and her travels and explorations made her realise just how small this country was where she was born. I've been here before, I remember passing through this place, and she came across faces she recognised, Don't you remember me, they used to call me the Flying Woman, Ah, of course I remember, so you found the man you were looking for, You mean my man, That's right, No, I didn't find him, Ah, poor woman, He didn't turn up here by any chance, after I went away, No, he hasn't been seen and I haven't heard anyone mention him in these parts, Well, then, I'm off, farewell, Have a good journey, If only I could find him.

She did find him. She had passed through Lisbon six times and this was the seventh. She had come from the south, from near Pegões. It was almost night when she crossed the river in the last boat to take advantage of the tide. She had not eaten for almost twenty-four hours. There was still some food in her knapsack, but every time Blimunda was about to put it into her mouth, it was as if another hand had been placed on hers and a voice warned her, Don't eat, for the hour has come. Beneath the dark waters of the river, she saw fish swimming past at a great depth, shoals of crystal and silver fish, their elongated backs covered in scales or quite smooth. The light inside each house filtered through its walls like a beacon in mist. She entered the Rua Nova dos Ferros and turned right at the Church of Our Lady of Oliveira towards the Rossio, the same journey she had made twenty-eight years ago. She walked amid phantoms, among mists that were human. Amid the thousand rancid smells of the city, the evening breeze brought to her nostrils that of charred flesh. Crowds were milling around the Church of St Dominic amid the torches, black smoke, and bonfires. Blimunda pushed her way through until she reached the front row, Who are they, she asked a woman holding a child in her arms, I only know three of them, that man there and the woman beside him are father and daughter who have been found guilty of Judaism and are to burn at the stake, and the one at the end is a fellow who wrote comedies for puppet shows named António José da Silva, but I know nothing about the others.

Eleven people have been sentenced. The stake is already ablaze and the faces of the victims are barely distinguishable. The last man to be burned has his left hand missing. Perhaps because of his blackened beard, a miraculous transformation caused by the soot, he looks much younger. And there is a dark cloud in the centre of his body. Then Blimunda said, Come. The will of Baltasar Sete-Sóis broke free from his body, but did not ascend to the stars, for it belonged to the earth and to Blimunda.

Translator's Note

Padre Bartolomeu Lourenço de Gusmão is a historical figure. He was born in Santos, Brazil (1685?) and studied for the priesthood at the Seminary of Belém in Bahia. In 1708 he travelled to Portugal, where he soon attracted attention because of his prodigious memory and his mechanical skills. The following year he sent a memorandum to João V, informing the King that he had invented an instrument "that could travel through the air over land and sea". Lourenço then published a treatise on the art of air navigation. His theories were ridiculed in satirical verses, and he was called "O Voador" (The Flying Man). He confounded his critics by inventing a rudimentary airship, which he launched August 8, 1709. A sketch of this strange invention circulated in Lisbon, and because of its resemblance to an enormous bird it was called "La Passarola".

From 1713 until 1716 Lourenço studied in Holland. Upon his return to Portugal, he completed a doctorate in canon law at Coimbra. Such was his prestige in academic circles that João V made him a member of the Academy of History and appointed him to a chaplaincy in the royal household. Lourenço went on to invent many other devices, including a machine for grinding sugar-cane.

It has not been established precisely when he converted to Judaism, but when he realised that the Inquisition had begun investigating him and was about to order his arrest, he fled from Lisbon in September 1724 and found sanctuary in Spain. He died several months later at the Hospital de la Caridad in Toledo, finally reconciled with the Roman Catholic Church.

Today, Lourenço is largely remembered as a pioneer of aviation.

Publishers' Note

The English text as originally published embodied a number of editorial amendments which the author requested be overruled; the labour of reinstating the text in accordance with the author's wishes was undertaken by Giovanni Pontiero. The text of the present edition is thus in conformity with the author's and the translator's wishes.

Please visit the Harvill Press website at

www.harvill.com